SCP Foundation
Secure, Contain, Protect

Foundation Handbook

Essential containment procedures
For emergency situations
Volume I

The following is an adaptation and a collection of tales from the collaborative fiction website SCP Foundation, which can be reached at http://www.scp-wiki.net/
All content contained in this book is either used with permission from the SCP Foundation wiki under the Creative Commons Attribution-ShareAlike 3.0 license or original and released under the same license. All derived content is to be attributed to their original authors.

WARNING: THE FOLLOWING BOOK IS

CLASSIFIED

ACCESS BY UNAUTHORIZED PERSONNEL IS STRICTLY PROHIBITED*
PERPETRATORS WILL BE TRACKED, LOCATED, AND DETAINED

*Exceptions in case of emergency apply, including but not limited to incidents related to XK-Class End-of-the-World Scenarios.

Foreword

The following book is meant as a short guide, providing the reader with basic information about the foundation and its various Secure Containment Procedures (From now on, they will be referred as "SCPs"). The guide has no pretension to be, by any means, a complete archive, but it contains sufficent reading material if The Database cannot be reached at the given time: A reliable source of information during events such as power outages, reality displacements and time displacements.

It should be also noted that the SCPs contained in this handbook have been ordered to maximize overall knowledge, rather than following the numerical order. If it appears you are having trouble with a specific entity, please refer to the table of contents and feel free to skip directly to the necessary procedure. Nevertheless, single entries can be read separately and out of order.

A quick informal note about object classes: Object classes do not define the danger of an anomaly, but rather it measures the difficulty to contain it. It's easier to approximate with the example of the "Box":

- If you leave your anomaly in a box, and nothing happens, it's probably Safe.
- If you leave your anomaly in a box, and you don't know what'll happen, it's probably Euclid.
- If you leave your anomaly in a box, and it breaks out of it, it's probably Keter.
- If your anomaly IS the box, it's probably Thaumiel.

There are of course precise and rigorous descriptions of these classes, but these get the point across and I've never approved of verbosity.

Dr. Peter James Defort

Contents

1. SCP-087 — 7
2. Document #087-I — 9
3. Document #087-II — 12
4. Document #087-III — 16
5. SCP-055 — 19
6. SCP-093 — 23
7. SCP-093 'Blue' Test — 27
8. SCP-093 'Green' Test — 31
9. SCP-093 'Violet' Test — 35
10. SCP-093 'Yellow' Test — 41
11. SCP-093 'Red' Test — 44
12. SCP-093-Recovered Materials — 46
13. SCP-148 — 60
14. SCP-173 — 63
15. SCP-239 — 65
16. SCP-500 — 68
17. SCP-038 — 71
18. SCP-1342 — 74
19. SCP-3008 — 78
20. SCP-624 — 89
21. Experiment Log 624 — 93
22. SCP-231 — 97
23. Fear Alone — 103
24. SCP-682 — 111
25. SCP-079 — 115
26. SCP-711-EX — 118
27. SCP-882 — 121
28. Interview 882-1 — 123
29. SCP-063 — 126
30. SCP-447 — 127
31. Experiment Log 447 A — 129

Contents

32.	SCP-914	143
33.	Experiment Log 914	146
34.	SCP-005	156
35.	SCP-2295	158
36.	SCP-426	162
37.	SCP-4999	165
38.	SCP-1313	168
39.	SCP-1322	171
40.	SCP-1012	180
41.	SCP-1733	183
42.	SCP-701	188
43.	Incident Report SCP-701-19█-1	192
44.	Document SCP-701-1640-B-1	196
45.	SCP-1000	200
46.	SCP-2000	207
47.	SCP-1025	217
48.	SCP-1101	221
49.	SCP-3043	226
50.	To Be Noir Not To Be	254
51.	SCP-3143	256
52.	SCP-423	272
53.	Experiment Log 423 A	274
54.	SCP-140	295
55.	SCP-067	300
56.	SCP-085	303
57.	SCP-826	307
58.	Experiment Log 826	309
59.	SCP-1472	317
60.	SCP-2432	323
61.	SCP-3521	331
62.	SCP-1981	335
63.	SCP-2966	341

SCP-087

Figure A: Still frame taken from video footage of Exploration I

Item #: SCP-087

Object Class: Euclid

Special Containment Procedures: SCP-087 is located on the campus of [REDACTED]. The doorway leading to SCP-087 is constructed of reinforced steel with an electro-release lock mechanism. It has been disguised to resemble a janitorial closet consistent with the design of the building. The lock mechanism on the doorknob will not release unless ▓▓ volts are applied in conjunction with counter-clockwise rotation of the key. The inside of the door is lined with 6 centimeters of industrial foam padding.

Due to the results of the final exploration (see Document 087-IV), no personnel are permitted access to SCP-087.

Description: SCP-087 is an unlit platform staircase. Stairs descend on a 38 degree angle for 13 steps before reaching a semicircular platform of approximately 3 meters in diameter. Descent direction rotates 180 degrees at each platform. The design of SCP-087 limits subjects to a visual range of approximately 1.5 flights. A light source is required for any subjects exploring SCP-087, as there are no lighting fixtures or windows present. Lighting sources brighter than 75 watts have shown to be ineffective, as SCP-087 seems to absorb excess light.

SCP-087

Subjects report and audio recordings confirm the distressed vocalizations from what is presumed to be a child between the ages of ▮ and ▮. The source of the distress calls is estimated to be located approximately 200 meters below the initial platform. However, any attempts to descend the staircase have failed to bring subjects closer to the source. The depth of descent calculated from Exploration IV, the longest exploration, is shown to be far beyond both the possible structure of both the building and geological surroundings. At this time, it is unknown if SCP-087 has an endpoint.

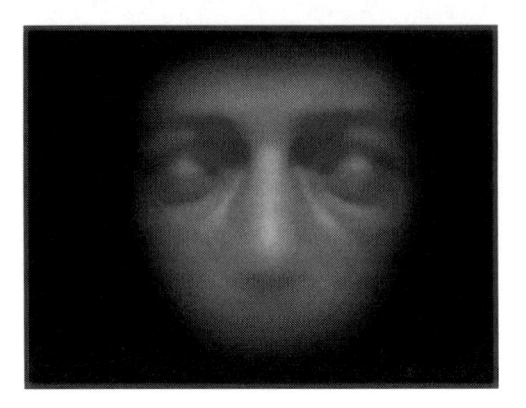

Figure B: SCP-087-1; Enhanced image from still taken from Exploration I.

SCP-087 has undergone four video recorded explorations by Class-D personnel. Each subject conducting an exploration has encountered SCP-087-1, which appears as a face with no visible pupils, nostrils, or mouth. The nature of SCP-087-1 is entirely unclear, but it has been determined that it is not the source of the pleading. Subjects exhibit feelings of intense paranoia and fear when faced with SCP-087-1, but it is undetermined whether said feelings are abnormal or simply natural reactions.

Addendum:
Over a period of 2 weeks following Exploration IV, several members of the staff and students from the [REDACTED] campus reported knocking at a variable rate of 1-2 seconds per knock coming from the interior of SCP-087. The door leading to SCP-087 has been fitted with 6 centimeter thick industrial padding. All reports of knocking have ceased.

Document #087-I

Document #087-I: Exploration I

D-8432 is a 43-year old Caucasian male of average build and appearance and unremarkable psychological background. Class-D designation is a result of demotion due to mishandling SCP-███. D-8432 is equipped with a 75 watt flood lamp with battery power capable of lasting 24 hours, a handheld camcorder fitted with a transmission stream, and an audio headset for communication with Dr. ███████ at Control.

D-8432 steps through doorway onto initial platform. Despite the wattage, the flood lamp only illuminates the first 9 steps. The second platform is not visible.

D-8432: It's fucking dark.
Dr. ███████: Is your flood lamp functioning properly?

D-8432 shines the light out the door and into the academic building's hallway. The light reaches significantly further.

D-8432: Yeah, it's working, it just won't light these stairs all the way down.
Dr. ███████: Thank you. Please continue.

D-8432 descends for 13 steps before reaching the second platform. The platform is in the shape of a semicircle with an apparently concrete surface and walls. There are no distinct markings, aside from nondescript patches of dust, dirt, or wear consistent with that which is found in a typical concrete stairwell. D-8432 rotates 180 degrees to begin descent down the second flight, then pauses.

Dr. ███████: Reason for stopping?
D-8432: You hear that? There's a fucking kid down there. Sounds like one.

None of the described audio is feeding through the camera or mic at this time.

Dr. ███████: Could you please describe the sound?
D-8432: It's young. Either female or a very young boy. It's crying and sobbing and saying *[pause]* please *[pause]* help *[pause]* please *[pause]* Yeah, it keeps repeating that and crying.
Dr. ███████: Can you estimate its distance from your current location?

Document #087-I

D-8432: Uh, fuck, I don't know, maybe 200 meters down?
Dr. ▮▮▮▮▮▮▮: Please continue down the next flight.

The subject descends another 13 steps. As he reaches the landing, audio of the child as described is picked up. The child alternates between sobbing, wailing, and the words "please," "help," and "down here." The level of audio is consistent with D-8432's report of it being approximately 200 meters below.

Dr. ▮▮▮▮▮▮▮: Can you still hear the crying?
D-8432: Yeah.
Dr. ▮▮▮▮▮▮▮: We're picking it up as well. Please continue down. Stop if you notice any changes in the audio or environment.

The subject descends another 3 flights of stairs before stopping.

D-8432: Keep going?
Dr. ▮▮▮▮▮▮▮: Please.

D-8432 continues another 17 flights (total of 22 flights) before stopping. There are no visual changes in the environment, and each flight has been a consistent 13 steps.

D-8432: I'm not getting any fucking closer to the kid.

Stereo audio confirms that the crying noise has not increased in volume and remains approximately 200 meters below the subject.

Dr. ▮▮▮▮▮▮▮: Noted. Please continue.

The subject continues another 28 flights before stopping. (50 flights total.) D-8432 is standing on the 51st landing, counting the initial ground level landing. D-8432 is estimated to be 200 meters below the initial platform. 34 minutes have elapsed. The volume of the crying has not increased.

D-8432: I feel a little uneasy.
Dr. ▮▮▮▮▮▮▮: You've spent a long time in a dark, unknown stairwell. It's natural. Please continue.

The subject hesitates before stepping down on the next stair. As the subject moves forward, the flood lamp illuminates a face located approximately at the bottom of the flight (SCP-087-1). It appears to be the same size and shape as a human head, except it is lacking a mouth, nostrils, and pupils. The face is completely motionless, but is making direct eye contact, indicating its awareness of D-8432.

Document #087-I

D-8432: [Yelling] Fuck! What the fuck is that? Shit! Holy fucking shit. What the fuck!

Dr. ▮▮▮▮▮: Can you please describe what you see?

D-8432: It's some sort of fucking person face thing and it's fucking looking right at me fuck fuck fuck it's looking right at me —

Dr. ▮▮▮▮▮: Is it moving?

D-8432: [pause, heavy breathing] No, it's just staring at me. Fuck fuck fuck it's creepy.

Dr. ▮▮▮▮▮: Please approach and further illuminate the entity.

D-8432: Fuck fuck fuck I don't want to fucking —

The face jerks forward about 50 centimeters directly toward D-8432.

D-8432: *[yelling]* Fuckfuckfuckfuckfuck [REDACTED]

D-8432 enters a panicked state and rapidly ascends SCP-087. D-8432 reaches the ground floor in 18 minutes, at which time he collapses and passes out. There is no sign of SCP-087-1. Review of the footage indicates an equal number of flights and steps ascending as descending. Audio of the crying and pleading remains at the same volume until the last flight, at which point it ceases. Medical reports indicate collapse was a result of the rapid ascension of the stairs, causing fatigue.

Document #087-II

Document #087-II: Exploration II

D-9035 is a 28-year old African-American male of strong build. Psychological background indicates no abnormalities except an extreme hatred for women. Subject has an extensive record of [DATA EXPUNGED]. D-9035 is equipped with a 100 watt flood lamp with battery power capable of lasting 24 hours, a handheld camcorder fitted with a transmission stream, and an audio headset for communication with Dr. ▓▓▓▓▓▓ at Control. D-9035 is also equipped with a backpack containing 100 small LED lights with adhesive backs and battery lives of approximately 3 weeks. Lights turn on and off by compressing them.

D-9035 shines the flood lamp down the first flight of stairs. Despite the extra wattage, the light does not illuminate beyond the 9th step.

D-9035: You wan' me to go down there, Doc?
Dr. ▓▓▓▓▓▓: Please shine your flood lamp outside of SCP-087 to verify it is functioning properly.

D-9035 shines the light into the hallway. Comparison with the footage from Exploration I confirms it is indeed brighter.

Dr. ▓▓▓▓▓▓: Thank you. Please continue to the first landing.
D-9035: Hey Doc, I know what you said an' all, but I don' think I wanna go there.
Dr. ▓▓▓▓▓▓: Please continue to the first landing.
D-9035: Doc, look, I-
Dr. ▓▓▓▓▓▓: *[interrupting]* As per our earlier conversation, please continue to the first landing.

D-9035 pauses for 18 seconds, then descends 13 steps to the first landing and stops.

D-9035: Is that a kid?
Dr. ▓▓▓▓▓▓: Please remove one of the adhesive lights and affix it to the wall on the landing.
D-9035: Doc, you hear that? Is that a kid down there?
Dr. ▓▓▓▓▓▓: That's unconfirmed. Please affix an adhesive light to the wall and verify it functions.

Document #087-II

D-9035 hesitates, then removes one of the lights from his backpack and adheres it to the wall. He presses on the light, and it turns on.

Dr. ▮▮▮▮: Please turn off your flood lamp.

D-9035 hesitates again before turning off the lamp. The LED light illuminates the landing, but does not extend beyond the first step either way.

Dr. ▮▮▮▮: Thank you. You may turn your flood lamp back on. Please continue to descend. At each landing, affix an LED light to the wall and turn it on. If you notice anything unusual, please report it.

D-9035 turns the flood lamp back on, then descends the next flight of stairs. As he sets foot on the landing, the audio picks up sounds of pleading and crying, consistent with those of the first exploration.

Dr. ▮▮▮▮: Can you still hear the previously reported audio?
D-9035: Uh, yeah. She sounds 'bout 150, maybe 200 meters down. Am I supposed to get her? Look, Doc. I don't do good with kids.
Dr. ▮▮▮▮: Please place the light and continue down until you notice anything unusual.

The subject adheres the light to the wall and turns it on, then continues to the next landing. He adheres the third LED light to the wall and turns it on. D-9035 continues in this manner for the next 25 flights before stopping.

D-9035: I don't think I'm getting any closer to the kid, doc.
Dr. ▮▮▮▮: How far below would you estimate the source of the sound to be?
D-9035: Same as before. 150 to 200 meters down.
Dr. ▮▮▮▮: Thank you. Please proceed.

D-9035 continues in the same fashion for the next 24 flights. At the 51st landing he stops. Footage shows an arced gouge in the concrete wall, estimated to be approximately 50 centimeters long and 10 centimeters wide. The first step down from the landing appears to be completely smashed into rubble.

D-9035: You see that?
Dr. ▮▮▮▮: Yes. Can you please describe what you see?
D-9035: Looks like something slashed at the wall, and the step over here's all crumbled up and stuff. The slash mark looks really smooth -

D-9035 touches the gouge mark.

Document #087-II

D-9035: Yeah, it's smooth. Feels like glass.
Dr. ▊▊▊▊▊: Thank you. Please continue down.
D-9035: Look, Doc. I think I've gone far enough.
Dr. ▊▊▊▊▊: Please continue, as per our agreement.
D-9035: I don't wanna be doing this, agreement or not.

[DATA EXPUNGED]

D-9035 steps over the destroyed step and continues down the staircase. Nothing is notable at the next landing. D-9035 adheres an LED light to the wall and continues in the same fashion for another 38 flights. The sound of the crying and pleading still has not gotten closer. D-9035 is on the 89th landing and 74 minutes have elapsed from the beginning of the exploration. Subject is estimated to be 350 meters below the initial platform.

D-9035: I feel like the kid's just trying to lure me down here, Doc. I think it's time for me to—

D-9035 stops talking and moving as the flood lamp illuminates SCP-087-1. The face is staring directly at D-9035, again indicating awareness of the subject's presence. Although SCP-087-1 appears to be unmoving, its location is 38 flights below the initial encounter in Exploration I, indicating it is mobile.

Dr. ▊▊▊▊▊: Is there a reason you stopped?
D-9035: *[unresponsive]*

D-9035's breathing grows labored. SCP-087-1 remains immobile for an additional 13 seconds. SCP-087-1 blinks.

D-9035: *[yelling, incomprehensible]*

SCP-087-1 jerks forward until it is approximately 90 centimeters from D-9035. Subject turns and flees up the stairs.

Dr. ▊▊▊▊▊: Please relax and calm down. Turn around. We need a closer look at the face.

D-9035 ignores Dr. ▊▊▊▊▊ and continues rapid ascent. He continues to scream incomprehensibly.

Dr. ▊▊▊▊▊: D-9035, can you hear me? Please slow down.

Document #087-II

D-9035 is unresponsive and continues rapidly climbing the stairs. His screaming diminishes to babbling. After ascending 72 flights, D-9035 collapses on the 17th landing.

Dr. ▮▮▮▮▮▮▮: D-9035, can you hear me?

D-9035 is unresponsive, but labored breathing can be heard through the audio feed. For the next 14 minutes, D-9035 is immobile. The visual feed is black, and audio picks up only the subject's breathing and the continuous pleading coming from below. After 14 minutes and 32 seconds of unchanging visual and audio feeds, the sound of a rapid heartbeat not consistent with a human heartbeat, and a low cracking noise is heard. 7 seconds later, D-9035 gasps and revives, continuing his ascent of the stairs rapidly and wordlessly. The heartbeat and cracking cease, and nothing abnormal is detected on the visual feed. He remains unresponsive. D-9035 exits SCP-087 and sits on the floor outside of the entrance.

D-9035 then enters a catatonic state from which he has not yet recovered.

Document #087-III

Document #087-III: Exploration III

D-9884 is a 23-year old female of average build and appearance. Psychological background indicates a history of depression. Subject has a minimal record of using excessive force to [DATA EXPUNGED]. D-9884 is equipped with a 75 watt flood lamp with battery power capable of lasting 24 hours, a handheld camcorder fitted with a transmission stream, and an audio headset for communication with Dr. ▓▓▓▓▓▓ at Control. D-9884 is also equipped with a backpack containing 3.75 litres of water, 15 nutrient bars, and 1 thermal blanket.

D-9884 stands on the ground level landing of SCP-087. The flood lamp illuminates only the first 9 steps. LED lights placed on the wall during the last exploration are not visible.

Dr. ▓▓▓▓▓▓: Please descend the first flight and examine the landing wall.

D-9884 descends 13 steps and stops at the landing. There is no trace of the LED light at the location footage from Exploration II indicates it was placed.

D-9884: Yeah, um, it's just a dirty, concrete wall. There's like nothing on it. No, wait. It's a little bit sticky right here.

D-9884 indicates the spot on the wall the LED light should have been located.

D-9884: There's a child crying down there! She's [pause] she's begging for help and crying.
Dr. ▓▓▓▓▓▓: Thank you. Please continue down the steps until you notice anything unusual.

D-9884 descends. Upon reaching the next landing, audio of the crying child consistent with the prior two explorations is picked up. No LED lights appear to be present on any of the landing walls. D-9884 continues with no incident until she reaches the 17th landing.

D-9884: Eww, there's something on the ground here and it smells really bad. It's all sticky and stuck on my shoe. Ugh, it's so gross.

Document #087-III

Video feed confirms presence of substance occupying a space approximately 50 centimeters in diameter.

Dr. ▮▮▮▮: Can you describe the scent?
D-9884: Uh... It kinda smells like old rusty metal and pee.
Dr. ▮▮▮▮: Thank you. Please continue until you notice anything else.

D-9884 continues to the 51st landing without incident. The 51st landing remains unchanged from the previous expedition, and similar observations are made. D-9884 is asked again to descend until anything unusual is noticed. Subject continues her descent until the 89th landing is reached. The video feed jerks and the subject yells.

D-9884: Ahh, fuck! There's a hole in the ground and I almost fell in.

Video feed confirms the presence of a hole approximately 1 meter in diameter. The subject shines the floodlight down, revealing only blackness. Approximately 4 seconds pass, and a light of an indeterminate distance down the hole flicks on for approximately 2 seconds and then back off.

D-9884: There was a light down there! It's gone now, but it was on for like a second! Did you see it?
Dr. ▮▮▮▮: Yes. Can you estimate the depth of this hole?
D-9884: No way. It's too deep. At least a kilometer. Like, way more than a kilometer.
Dr. ▮▮▮▮: Thank you. Can you still hear the sounds of the child?
D-9884: Uh huh. She still sounds far away. I don't feel like I'm getting any closer. It's like for every step I take, she takes one down.
Dr. ▮▮▮▮: Please continue down until you encounter anything unusual.

D-9884 continues to descend SCP-087 for approximately an hour, covering an additional 164 flights. She stops to rest on the 253rd landing, consuming 1 nutrient bar and several gulps of water. D-9884 is at an estimated 1.1 kilometers below the initial landing, yet the sound of the child has not changed in volume. After pausing for 4 minutes, D-9884 resumes her descent, making no stops for another 216 flights, 1.5 hours later. D-9884 is on the 469th landing, an approximate 1.8 km below the ground level.

D-9884: I'm not getting anywhere. I think it's time I went back. I mean, going down is one thing, but this is a long climb back.
Dr. ▮▮▮▮: You have been provided with food, water, and blankets to last you 24 hours. Please continue down.
D-9884: No, I think I'm gonna go back up.

Document #087-III

D-9884 turns toward the previous flight of stairs.

D-9884: I - [screams]

SCP-087-1, the face, is directly behind D-9884, blocking her ascent. The face appears approximately 30 centimeters from the lens of the camera; its eyes are fixed directly on the lens, this time looking not at the subject but the person viewing the video feed. The video feed glitches and freezes for 4 seconds, accompanied by a static-like screeching noise from the audio feed. It then cuts to bumpy visuals of D-9884 descending the stairs rapidly.

D-9884: [panicked and hysterical] It's been following me! This whole time it's been right behind me oh God it's right behind me it was looking right at me! Dr. ▮▮▮▮ please do something please help me oh God no please get it away please no please I knew it was following me help make it leave please no it was looking at me it was staring at me it knew I was here it's been watching me this whole time oh God please help me no please [this continues in a similar fashion until the end.]

D-9884 continues to scream and plead hysterically as she rapidly descends the staircase. The previously heard static-like screeching seems to overlay the audio feed, beneath which can still be heard the original sound of the crying child. Approximately 14 flights down, the video feed swings to show the area directly behind D-9884. The face is now approximately 20 centimeters from the camera lens. It is not staring at the subject; rather it is fixated on the camera lens, giving the illusion it is making eye contact with those viewing the footage. It is important to note that since the sighting of SCP-087-1, the sound of the girl crying and pleading has been increasing in volume, indicating D-9884 is nearing the source. After an approximate 150 panicked flights of descent with 3 visual confirmations of SCP-087-1 still in pursuit, D-9884 trips and appears to fall unconscious. Audio feed indicates strong proximity to the source of the crying. The static and screeching noise continue. Video feed shows yet another descending flight of stairs, indicating D-9884 still has not reached the base of the stairwell. 12 seconds of motionlessness pass before the face comes in full view of the camera, eye contact being made directly with the viewer.

Audio and video feeds cut out, and no connection is reestablished.

SCP-055

SCP-055

Item #: SCP-055

Object Class: Keter

Special Containment Procedures: Object is kept within a five (5) by five (5) by two point five (2.5) meter square room constructed of cement (fifty (50) centimeter thickness), with a Faraday cage surrounding the cement walls. Access is via a heavy containment door measuring two (2) by two point five (2.5) meters constructed on bearings to ensure door closes and locks automatically unless held open deliberately. Security guards are NOT to be posted outside SCP-055's room. It is further advised that all personnel maintaining or studying other SCP objects in the vicinity try to maintain a distance of at least fifty (50) meters from the geometric center of the room, as long as this is reasonably practical.

Description: SCP-055 is a "self-keeping secret" or "anti-meme". Information about SCP-055's physical appearance as well as its nature, behavior, and origins is self-classifying. To clarify:

- How Site 19 originally acquired SCP-055 is unknown.
- When SCP-055 was obtained, and by whom, is unknown.
- SCP-055's physical appearance is unknown. It is not indescribable, or invisible: individuals are perfectly capable of entering SCP-055's container and observing it, taking mental or written notes, making sketches, taking photographs, and even making audio/video recordings. An extensive log of such observations is on file. However, information about SCP-055's physical appearance "leaks" out of a human mind soon after such an observation. Individuals tasked with describing SCP-055 afterwards find their minds wandering and lose interest in the task; individuals tasked with sketching a copy of a photograph of SCP-055 are unable to remember what the photograph looks like, as are researchers overseeing these tests. Security personnel who have observed SCP-055 via closed-circuit television cameras emerge after a full shift exhausted and effectively amnesiac about the events of the previous hours.
- Who authorized the construction of SCP-055's containment room, why it was constructed in this way, or what the purpose of the described Containment Procedures may be, are all unknown.
- Despite SCP-055's container being easily accessible, all personnel at Site 19 claim no knowledge of SCP-055's existence when challenged.

SCP-055

All of these facts are periodically rediscovered, usually by chance readers of this file, causing a great deal of alarm. This state of concern lasts minutes at most, before the matter is simply forgotten about.

A great deal of scientific data has been recorded from SCP-055, but cannot be studied.

At least one attempt has been made to destroy SCP-055, or possibly move it from containment at Site 19 to another site, meeting failure for reasons unknown.

SCP-055 may present a major physical threat and indeed may have killed many hundreds of personnel, and we would not know it. Certainly it presents a gigantic memetic/mental threat, hence its Keter classification.

Document #055-1: An Analysis of SCP-055

The author puts forward the hypothesis that SCP-055 was never formally acquired by ███████ ███████ and is in fact an autonomous or remotely-controlled agent, inserted at Site 19 by an unidentified third party for one or all of the following purposes:

- to silently observe, or interfere with, activities at Site 19
- to silently observe, or interfere with, activities at other SCP locations
- to silently observe, or interfere with, activities of humanity worldwide
- to silently observe, or interfere with, other SCP objects
- to silently observe, or interfere with, ███████████

No action to counter any of these potential threats is suggested, or indeed theoretically possible.

Addendum A :

> Hey, if this thing really is an "anti-meme", why doesn't the fact that it's an "anti-meme" get wiped? We must be wrong about that somehow. Wait a minute, what if we were to keep notes about what it isn't? Would we remember those? *Bartholomew Hughes, NSA*

SCP-055

Document #055-2: Report of Dr. John Marachek

Survey team #19-055-127BXE was successfully able to enter SCP-055's container and ascertain the appearance and, to some degree, the nature of the object. Notes were taken according to the project methodology (see ███████████████), after which the container was sealed again.

Excerpt from a transcript of personnel debriefing follows:

> Dr. Hughes: Okay, I'm going to need to ask you some questions about number 55 now.
>
> ███████: Number what?
>
> Dr. Hughes: SCP object 55. The object you just examined.
>
> ███████: Um, I don't know what you're talking about. I don't think we *have* a 55.
>
> Dr. Hughes: Okay, then, ███████, I'd like you to tell me what you've been doing for the past two hours.
>
> ███████: What? I... <subject appears uncomfortable> ... I don't know.
>
> Dr. Hughes: Okay, then, do you remember that we all agreed that it wasn't spherical?
>
> ███████: That what wasn't... Oh! Right! It isn't round at all! Object 55 isn't round!
>
> Dr. Hughes: So you remember it now?
>
> ███████: Well, no. I mean, I don't know what it is, but I know there is one. It's something you can't remember. And it's not a sphere.
>
> Dr. Hughes: Wait a minute. What's not a sphere?
>
> ███████: Object 55.
>
> Dr. Hughes: Object what?
>
> ███████: Doc, do you remember agreeing that something wasn't shaped like a sphere?

SCP-055

> Dr. Hughes: Oh, right!

It appears to be possible to remember what SCP-055 is not (negations of fact), and to repeatedly deduce its existence from these memories.

Personnel involved in Survey #19-055-127BXE reported moderate levels of disorientation and psychological trauma associated with cycles of repeated memory and forgetfulness of SCP-055. However, no long-term behavioral or health problems were observed, and psych assessments of survey personnel showed consistent reports of this distress fading over time.

Recommendations: It may be worthwhile to post at least one staff member capable of remembering the existence of SCP-055 to each critical site.

SCP-093

Item #: SCP-093

Object Class: Euclid

Special Containment Procedures: See testing document SCP-093-T1 for outline of testing conditions. SCP-093 must remain on a mirror at all times and under video surveillance. Admittance into the area of SCP-093's containment must be authorized only with proper video recording and subject retrieval procedures in place. Any attempt to use SCP-093 outside of an approved test will be dealt with severely, up to and including termination.

Description: SCP-093 is a primarily red disc carved from a stone composite resembling cinnabar, with circular engravings and unknown symbols carved at 0.5 cm depth around the entire object. Deeper cuts are present on SCP-093 with a depth of 1 to 1.5 cm. SCP-093 is 7.62 cm in diameter and fits comfortably into most palms without abrasion. SCP-093 will change hue when held by a living individual. The colors taken by SCP-093 are still being researched to establish a link. Current belief holds that the changes depend upon regrets carried by the holder.

If SCP-093 is removed from a mirror and not held by a person, it will seek out the nearest mirror-like surface. SCP-093 has been observed to travel in the largest possible circle while rolling, building up phenomenal speed. The mechanism of this acceleration is currently unknown. If an obstacle is between SCP-093 and the nearest mirror-like surface, it will use this momentum to punch through the obstacle and continue on its course at this speed. It will only stop when a mirror-like surface is contacted. Despite tremendous impact velocities, no damage will be dealt to SCP-093 or the mirror.

Additional Notes: No records exist to clarify the nature of SCP-093's discovery or presence in the Foundation. See SCP-093-OD. Since no records exist explaining SCP-093's method of containment, a test procedure was initiated to establish why mirrors must be used to contain it. The results of SCP-093-T1 lead to the discovery of living beings holding SCP-093 being able to move through mirrors and the series of tests in SCP-093-T2 to ascertain the destination reached through this travel.

SCP-093

SCP-093 Original Documentation

Item #: SCP-093

Object Class: Euclid

Special Containment Procedures: Item SCP-093 is to be kept on a silver lined mirror on a 0.3x0.23m (1ftx9in) pedestal at least 1.22m (4ft) off the ground floor in containment cell block ▮▮▮. Object is not to be contained in areas exceeding 3.66x3.05m (12x10ft) nor placed on mahogany, pine, cherry or aluminum pedestals above or below level 1 of containment cell block ▮▮▮. Object can be handled safely, albeit gently, without consequences. Tests and consequences thereof involving containment conditions can be viewed in Section-B:35-1 of the attached report.

Description: Object was found on the shore of the Red Sea, 30 Jan 1968, emitting a low sigh and a dim blue gleam. Its color has since turned into an orange mix of red only emitting a hum of varying volume whilst in the presence of female examiners of ages between 34 and 41. SCP-093 resembled the documented blue for 54:34 at 1:23 on 26 April 1986 coincidentally when the body of 194-9834 was discovered in Research Facility ▮▮▮.

Ties between 194-9834 and SCP-093 remain inconclusive and effects of prolonged exposure to 093 remain unknown except for infrequent reports of periods of calmness and in the case of 242-0049 as periodic waves of depression, loss of balance and thoughts of suicide. These feelings have reportedly not exceeded eleven days in duration. Object seemed to react to the presence of 242-0056 by turning light violet for no more than 2:09, as documented on 12 March 1993. Effects of this reaction remain unknown.

Additional Notes: Origins of 093 remain unknown and documents of recovery of 093 have since been destroyed in a fire in Research Facility ▮▮▮, 09 December 1989. Reports on the feelings of researchers who handled 093 have remained inconsequential since 19 April 1995.

SCP-093

SCP-093-T1: Containment Test

Testing of SCP-093 against conditions set forth for existing containment procedures to assess viability of continuing such containment. Beginning with changing the type of mirror used as a position of rest:

Mirrored surface, brass frame, retail-grade mirror: SCP-093 rests without activity when placed on the mirror. This test alone removes the need for costly silver or wooden containment systems.

Standard-grade table: SCP-093 turns upright and begins to roll across the table surface in one direction, making a U-turn and rolling to the other, completing an oval shape and repeating this action until a mirror is brought into vicinity of it, at which time SCP-093 rolls toward the mirror and lays flatways against it, sliding toward the center. It is noted that despite the grainy feel of SCP-093, it does not mark the mirror in any fashion while moving across it.

Two mirrors at either end of a standard-grade table: SCP-093 gravitates toward the closer mirror regardless of orientation and makes no distinction between different types of mirrors, favoring a factor of distance above all else in choosing the mirror to move to.

A mirror held by a person and moved around: SCP-093 follows the mirror as it moves, gaining speed until a maximum velocity of ███████ is reached. At any velocity, the impact of SCP-093 against a mirrored surface results in no damage to either object.

A person holding SCP-093 placing it on a mirror: This test was accidental, the result of one of the staff tripping another after some debate about who would be covering the lunch tab. As a result of the behavior of the researchers, it was discovered that a person holding SCP-093 and placing it against a mirror will in fact move into the mirror.

Addendum: Containment testing discontinued after establishing that SCP-093 requires only a mirror to rest inert. Testing on human interaction with mirrors while holding SCP-093 authorized by Dr. ███████.

SCP-093

SCP-093-T2 : Mirror Test

Testing Protocols : Subjects testing SCP-093 must wear a Class 3 buckle harness strapped to the chest and attached to a tension pulley system allowing for 300 m (~1000 ft) of movement. Additional spools may be added to extend movement if necessary. The clasps connecting these spools must be high grade and capable of withstanding applied force of 0.2 tons.

A field kit containing the following should be standard issue for testing of SCP-093:

- One (1) wrist mounted light source with three (3) hours lifespan and additional power sources providing up to six (6) additional hours.

- Four (4) 0.5 L water bottles with water.

- Four (4) MREs of any type, plus two (2) plain granola bars (chocolate chips allowed).

- One (1) standard-issue Beretta 9mm firearm with twenty-four (24) rounds of ammunition, loaded. This is not to be issued until subject has passed into a mirror using SCP-093 and should be given under armed supervision ensuring that the subject passes through entirely. This item is to be requisitioned first upon subject's return and subject to be made aware of this before leaving line of sight within SCP-093's mirror.

- One (1) standard-issue field knife. The subject is not to be made aware of this item and must find it on his own within the kit.

The subject must also be attached to a video system, with a camera mounted on the subject's head or shoulders. The video device should be cable based and allow for the same length of travel as the return system. Wireless cameras have shown mixed results and should only be used in testing conditions where SCP-093 is a currently known color. New colors must be tested using wired feed.

During testing, the color of SCP-093 must be recorded, as well as history of the subject in terms of their incarceration to identify how SCP-093 determines the color to assume. A link appears to be connected to guilt or a lack thereof in the subject's psyche. The attached test results should be read in order.

SCP-093 'Blue' Test

SCP-093 'Blue' Test

Mirror Test 1: Color (Blue)

Subject is D-20384, male, 34 years of age, strong physique. Subject's background shows instance of murder/attempted suicide. Subject is co-operative in all steps of testing. Subject entered the provided mirror while holding SCP-093, which emitted a blue color. Outside technicians observed that the mirror retained a true reflection until subject had completely passed into it, at which time the view changed to an outdoor landscape, heavily tinged in blue. Video feed follows in attached media:

> Camera activates, flickers to view. Subject is looking out over the same field reported by technicians. Looks like typical lowland plains, everything has a heavy blue tinge overlapping the normal colors. No discernible landmarks visible as subject pans view left to right, only grass, weeds, and a breeze moving the taller grass. No trees. No living beings visible.
>
> Subject moves forward as instructed, traveling for approximately 500 steps before something becomes visible, a patch of the land up ahead is barren and grass can be seen dying as subject approaches it. Approximately 300 steps forward subject is standing before a hole in the ground. The hole has been dug using unknown tools of primitive origin.
>
> Pulley system engaged and the camera suffers a light shudder. Subject is instructed to enter the hole, and after mild protesting agrees to do so. There is no apparent method of descent such as ladder or rope, subject relies entirely on his own hands and the pulley system to slow the descent. Approximately 100 m of cable is used before a bottom is reached, light source provided in field kit activated 50 m down when outside sources become unreliable. Sweeping gestures of the light reveal nothing more than dirt even at the bottom of the hole.
>
> Subject moves forward with assistance of light source. Asked about the blue tinge subject expresses confusion and says there is no such tinge from his perspective, and never was. Light is visible down the passage and 150 m of cable has been used. Out of the camera's eye sound is recorded of the firearm being prepared. When questioned about these actions subject states justified precaution and moves forward.

SCP-093 'Blue' Test

The tunnel turns from bare dirt to a concrete enclosure, subject complains of a stench. The light source is revealed to be ceiling light fixtures, a series of which with less than a quarter broken while the others function. A series of six doors, three to a side, span before the camera view with a seventh door visible at the end of the corridor that has been blocked by what looks like generic metal shelving debris. Debris shows signs of rusting and is typical of retail store units suggesting other human presences.

Subject requested to try doors, in whatever order he chooses. Subject tries first door on right, door is locked, does not open. Second door tries to open but does not budge, unlocked but blocked. Closing second door, third door is tried, same results as first. Going up the other side the third door does open fully and light is bright in the room. Portable light switched off at this time as subject pans camera to inspect room.

Room is bare, no contents, but walls are filthy. Subject states material on walls isn't dirt, but he can't identify it, seems to resemble melted plastic but is brown in color rather than black. Door is closed. Second door on left side has no handle, does not move when pushed. The hole where the handle was is plugged by unknown material. All doors are shaped in such a way that nothing can visibly escape from the sides and space for movement is too thin to look through even at ground level. First door on left hand is locked, but part of key is present in lock from stem to the ridges, the back has been broken off.

With effort subject manipulates key to open door and immediately begins coughing, complaining of a stench. Walls of room are clean as is floor, ceiling is coated in the same strange brown material as the third room. In this room there is a makeshift cot made from aged blankets with a pillow, a wooden crate containing open boxes of what appears to have been food stuffs, language appears on video as squiggles however subject states they simply read 'Cereal'. A second crate in the room contains what appear to be empty water bottles that have dried out. A book lays next to the cot, closed, no title or identifying marks.

On the wall is what appears to be clipped articles but language cannot be read, subject asked to remove clippings for retrieval. All articles but one crumble at the touch due to age. The intact article is put in a field sample container and seems the most recent compared to the others. Asked to investigate the book, subject begins to move toward it.

SCP-093 'Blue' Test

Audio on the tape goes strange and a high pitched screeching noise like grinding metal dominates all communication for 3.5 seconds. Subject has not touched the book still, and when the noise stops, subject asks control to repeat request. Control made no requests during that time as headsets were removed. Subject advised to leave room and notes that the door has begun closing slowly on its own and if left alone, will close. Subject advised to leave door alone and to investigate door on right.

Careful review of the following ten seconds of tape shows that as the camera pans, a figure is visible at the end of the tunnel where the seventh door is. The door is open only enough for a face to be seen through a crack just before the door silently closes. No details can be seen.

Subject investigates the second door on the right with no mention of anything seen out of the ordinary. This door when pushed against moves, and after repeated bashings, moves enough to view inside at an angle. A cork board is visible with more articles attached to it, the top of a box of 'cereal' can be seen on the floor, and what appears to be a hand laying palm up. Subject closes door and pans camera past door seven which remains closed. Seeing nowhere else to explore, subject requested to return. Subject poses no protest and complains of ever increasing stench.

As subject returns back down tunnel his camera feed does not change or show anomaly but control reports a sudden surge in cable movement pulling an additional 100 m of cable through before going slack again and then tightening. Video feed shows subject ascending tunnel slowly while control attempts to verify integrity of the pulley system. Subject requested to stop ascent but states he is not climbing, the rope is pulling him up. Panic sets in on both sides and subject informed to ready firearm.

Upon reaching top of hole, nothing is visible on camera and subject reports nothing has changed in landscape, then begins a return trip following the path of the cable. Traveling for approximately 900 steps subject asks how much cable he has used. Control admits they are unsure due to complications but subject traveled in a straight line to reach the hole so it should be a straight line back. Subject becomes concerned when he states that more cable is visible now, moving in a 90 degree angle away from a point in the ground.

SCP-093 'Blue' Test

Subject pans camera around full circle slowly. On film, behind subject, a crowd of 37 countable figures stand silently, features are unidentifiable and they are lacking the blue tinge that dominates the landscape. Panic breaks in control again but subject notes only oddity as being the cable having an angled path. Subject tugs his end of the cable, it is taut and does not move. Control begins to reel in the pulley system and slack rapidly winds. Watching the angled cable movement can be seen as grass is disturbed further down the angled portion from the reeling in then the line vibrates as it meets resistance and emits a 'twang' from the recoil. Subject's camera pans back along length of cable which now appears to slowly be allowing more slack before suddenly all slack is returned and pulley system begins again.

Control requests subject return following cable path and screams are caught on the audio with panic from subject. Five shots fired as subject aims pistol at something not visible on camera. Control reports being able to see subject returning toward point of origin while camera shows wire disappearing into a point floating in the air. As subject passes this point all cable is now in the pulley system and camera films only the floor. Control reports that the mirror took approximately five seconds to return to a reflection and SCP-093 remained blue in color until one hour after being recovered from subject.

A vile smelling fluid was present on subject's clothes around his hands when firearm was recovered. This fluid dried quickly and was deemed insignificant of study due to lack of quality sample. Control personnel monitoring the mirror state having seen a massive human being, crawling on the ground, easily fifty times the size of a normal person with no facial features and a very short arm reach, pulling itself toward the mirror before it returned to a reflection. Due to proximity fine details could not be made out but at least one observer noted the being appeared to have been shot from the marks in the otherwise smooth featureless face.

Field Test Kit recovered from subject containing a news paper article that reads: [DATA EXPUNGED] and was filed as item [DATA EXPUNGED].

SCP-093 'Green' Test

SCP-093 'Green' Test

Mirror Test 2: Color (Green)

Subject is D-54493, female, 23 years of age, average physique. Subject's background shows instance of grand theft auto and second degree murder of two children during escape with vehicle. Subject is co-operative in all steps of testing. Subject entered the provided mirror while holding SCP-093 which emitted a green color. Outside technicians observed that the mirror retained a true reflection until subject had completely passed into it, at which time the view changed to a farming landscape, heavily tinged in green, similar to the first test. Video feed follows in attached media:

> Camera activates, flickers to view. Subject is looking out over the same farmland reported by technicians. All greens through video feed are deeper and green tinge overlays the normal colors of objects similar to the blue tinge in Test 1. No landmarks from Test 1 are discernable as subject pans camera over area.
>
> Present is a field, long abandoned, in the middle of which stands the remains of a scarecrow of unknown design, fragments left are rotted and torn. Nothing grows in the tilled land. A farm house is visible to the right of the field, large, two stories, a basement shelter entrance is visible at one end. Subject prepares her sidearm immediately and is asked by control to relax before proceeding, her heavy breathing dominating the audio feed.
>
> Subject takes a few minutes and announces that she's fine, then proceeds as directed to walk the perimeter of the farmhouse. Children's bicycles, two, a boy's and girl's, lay against the house near the shelter doors. One of the doors to the shelter lay in the grass, torn from the entrance as evidenced by splintering wood. On the stairs lay clothes arranged in a descending order, shoes to shirt going down them, belonging to a boy. Subject begins screaming at control asking if this is some sort of sick joke. Control assures her they have never seen this environment either and to please calm down. Subject takes several minutes to regain herself before continuing. It is unknown if SCP-093 is linking the subject's past with her landscape.
>
> After several minutes subject agrees to continue.

SCP-093 'Green' Test

Communication to subject is muted and conversation of control making commentary about subject's jittery attitude make up audio for one and a half minutes. Communication restored as subject reaches bottom of stairs. The cellar of the farmhouse is unremarkable and typical. Several wooden shelves line the far wall containing unidentified canned substances. Broken light fixtures sway gently from support beams. Camera is panned across the basement slowly, no evidence of footprints are visible and the basement can be assumed to have been abandoned for some time. Subject begins to comment about a stench.

As subject pans the area a metal hatch is visible in the ground, similar to a bulkhead on a submarine with a turn handle. Subject remarks that the smell is at its worst around the hatch and the dirt around the hatch is noted as being clumped and claylike. The handle of the hatch is old and the paint chipped. Subject coerced into turning the handle which, when fully turned, opens the hatch. Subject begins coughing at the release of assumed old, stale air. When camera is tilted to view down the hatch, it is a white concrete tunnel similar to the one found in the blue experiment but in much better condition. Subject asked to descend ladder and close hatch behind her.

After some convincing subject agrees to descend but does not close the hatch, overlooked concerns about severing the pulley return system in doing so are acknowledged. Descent down the ladder and trip to the farmhouse has consumed approximately 53 m of cable when bottom is reached. The inside of the hatch appears to be a bunker ill-suited to long term usage. It is spacious, about half the size of the actual cellar itself, containing three bunks, one for a couple and two for single use.

Several boxes of food similar to those found during Blue marked as 'Cereal' fill a waste container near the hatch bottom. On the beds are two skeletons and on the floor is a third, lying next to which is a simple six shooter revolver containing no ammunition. Three spent casings are across the floor near the gun. On the other side of this skeleton is a bound book in good condition, this is retrieved and placed into a Field Kit container upon request. The gun is left alone per request from control.

Subject examines more of the bunker, focusing on a desk where a newspaper has been cut and is in good condition. The clipped articles are recovered using a Field Kit container. Little else of interest to be brought back is in the bunker as the camera is panned around. Trash bags containing clothing, a few children's toys resembling popular 1950s era products are lined against the wall.

SCP-093 'Green' Test

Subject is requested to leave the bunker and then sharply asked to wait by a control technician who directs the camera view to an area near the exiting doorway to the hatch. Closer inspection as subject moves in finds that a small area has been fitted with what appears to be an Ethernet jack, the cover of which has been forced slightly away from the wall by a strange amber-like substance. Subject refuses to touch or collect a sample commenting that it stinks so bad that if they want it they can come get it themselves. Control declines and subject leaves bunker.

As subject grips ladder to leave the camera pans up for a moment and at the top of the tunnel a humanoid figure is seen peering down. Control asks subject to confirm figure, subject states nothing is up there and begins to climb. Figure draws out of camera view after first rung is touched by subject who ascends without incident. At the top of the tunnel, no other life is seen, nothing has been disturbed. Subject insists nothing was there and closes the hatch, then immediately vomits.

Subject coughs and uses a supplied water bottle to gargle then freezes and asks if control is hearing 'that'. Control reports no audio. Subject approaches cellar hatch cautiously with firearm drawn and lifts her head just enough so camera can view outside area. In the distance, approximately 700 m from the farm, two massive, humanoid beings are crawling across the landscape. The entities do not notice the subject who remains quiet but whose drawn sidearm is visibly trembling.

Subject requested to remain still and silent as beings move. They are featureless, facing at an angle moving across the field of vision so the faces are only visible for a few moments. During this time it is clear they have no facial features. The arms they use to drag themselves are short at times and long at others, stretching out to varying lengths each time they move. There is no rear area to the beings, all bodily design appears to end at the torso. The two creatures take approximately ten minutes to disappear into the distance before the subject begins to panic and begs to return. Request declined. Subject instructed to enter the home from the cellar, and not to leave the home under any circumstances.

The first floor is entered through a hatch in the ceiling/floor that opens with rusty creaks that cause subject to pause for 37 seconds before continuing upward and entering a kitchen. A heavy layer of dust coats all items in the kitchen. The refrigerator is left open, all food is spoiled. Adjacent the kitchen is a living area that subject enters slowly.

SCP-093 'Green' Test

There is a recliner, a couch, and a television all of 1950s style design. In the recliner is a laptop whose case also resembles 1950s decor and is coated in heavy dust. Opening the laptop reveals the last moments of its operating system, "Faithful OS" leaving a standby mode and immediately shutting off. Laptop has no external power source and will not power back on. When asked to recover laptop, it brings the cushion of the recliner with it, the two stuck together. Subject advised to leave laptop where it is.

The inside door leaving the home is nailed shut with thick wood planks, no attempt made to interact with these. Camera view pans to a staircase leading upstairs. Subject ascends the stairs without being asked and the stairs remain silent to control's surprise. When subject reaches top of stairs a hallway with two doors is viewed, one on each side, and at the end of the hall a dumbwaiter is inlaid into the wall.

Subject opens door on left on her own, which opens to a master bedroom. The bed is neatly made but the wardrobe next to it is thrown open and clothes are everywhere on the floor. Subject finds laid out on the bed several pieces of jewelry and is informed to leave them. Subject begins to protest, then comments they stink and leaves them alone, promptly leaving room. Subject asked to open second door.

The second door opens and gives a view of a shared children's bedroom, obviously boy and girl given the types of toys and clothes scattered on the floor. There is also a window which subject approaches and wipes with a curtain to clear dust. Subject requested to move camera to window and does so. The farmland is visible, and approximately 40 km from it at best guess, a city. As the camera starts to draw back it pans down and films the area around the house. Approximately 300 figures similar to those from the footage captured during Blue test are visible around the home, all staring up. Subject asked to confirm figures but states nothing is there. Subject requested to return and quickly agrees.

Egress from the house is uneventful, pulley system shows no erratic behavior. As subject returns to point of pulley wire's origin a loud groaning noise causes the picture to reverberate. Technicians at control report they were also able to hear the noise and experienced the vibration. Subject returns through point of origin without investigation and mirror returns to reflective surface. SCP-093 relinquished. Video ends.

Returned newspaper fragments filed as ▮▮▮▮▮.

SCP-093 'Violet' Test

SCP-093 'Violet' Test

Mirror Test 3: Color (Violet)

Subject is D-84930, male, 21 years of age, average physique. Subject's background shows instance of second degree murder of a police officer during a drug bust. Normally this crime, while severe, would not qualify a person for a sentence that would end up with us, but the murder of the officer was especially brutal and excessive violence was used. This subject was uncooperative and had to be reminded that his cooperation would only benefit him. Subject entered the provided mirror while holding SCP-093 which emitted a violet color. Outside technicians observed that the mirror retained a true reflection until subject had completely passed into it, at which time the view changed to a cityscape, urban, lightly tinged in purple, similar to the first test. Video feed follows in attached media:

> Camera flickers to life and pans around the area. Subject is in what appears to be a modern downtown district similar to a city like New York. The streets are mostly bare except for a few cars of unknown make or model. These cars look highly advanced and streamlined. Subject attempts to look into the car windows without being instructed to but backs away remarking there is a 'rank ass stank' coming from the areas around most of them.
>
> Subject is persuaded to move closer to one car and does so with coughing, wiping off a window which is covered in dirt. The inside of the car appears to be completely filled with a strange brown matter, there is nothing at all visible other than the brown matter. Two other cars produce the same results however a fourth vehicle seems more recent than the others and the insides are immaculate. The doors to this vehicle also are unlocked and subject quickly gets inside then shuts the doors. Subject is chastised for this behavior by control who reminds him his lifeline is nothing more than a cable, which is sturdy enough that closing the car door does not injure it, but they cannot recover a person in motion.
>
> Subject argues with control over this issue and pans the camera across the dashboard, pointing out he couldn't drive away even if he tried.

SCP-093 'Violet' Test

The dashboard is void of any recognizable controls, no ignition, no steering, it has several small blank screens that are theorized to be a GPS system. Subject remains in the car while control discusses how to proceed since the city landscape is far larger than the previous test destinations.

Control debates this issue while subject stares around the cityscape from the car. During one pan a face is clearly seen staring into the car, eyes watching the subject; however, this was not noticed until post-test footage review. Subject made no comment regarding this entity at any point. Control shortly after informs subject to remain where he is and an escort team is dispatched through the mirror to join him.

A team of four armed personnel is sent through the mirror and proceeds to subject's location. Subject is then instructed to remove his harness, which is recovered. This subject's video feed then ends and is replaced by a wireless unit used by the escort team. The video quality on this unit is subject to more interference but in order to mark the mirror exit a receiver system is placed through the mirror.

Subject leaves the car and now travels with the escort team. Given the myriad of possible options they are instructed to simply move to the closest building and attempt to enter it. This building has etched glass doors bearing the name 'X.E.A. Research Partners Inc.' and the doors are ajar; a magnetic lock system is present, but has lost power. Team enters the building and main lobby.

This area resembles a stereotypical corporate lobby. There is a C shaped receptionist desk with a chair pushed far from it as if it was left in a hurry. A PC terminal is at the desk as well. Team approaches the desk and the camera bearer is instructed to examine the PC. The unit does appear to have power and "Faithful OS" appears on the screen requesting a login and password. A keyboard is present but is remarkably slim with touch sensitive keys rather than press down keys. After one failed attempt the lock screen replies that maximum attempts have been exceeded and the PC turns off. No actual tower or power button can be located so team moves forward.

Behind the receptionist desk are two elevator doors, one to the left and one to the right, with similar touch-sense keys. The elevator on the left is broken, the door open and the shaft empty. The elevator on the right appears functional and has power.

SCP-093 'Violet' Test

Without a clear destination the team is instructed to proceed to the highest floor to get a lay of the city. All floors appear to be accessible with the highest being 114, in reality 112 as 13 and 113 are missing from the keypad. Journey up the elevator is uneventful during this time, the elevator does appear to take longer as it passes by 13 and then 113, suggesting that entire floor was built and nothing put on it. At 114 the doors open and team enters a large lounge type area. There are many couches with dust on them, a wide screen apparently LCD TV of approximately 60+ inches in size dominates the wall in front of them with no power. A series of windows are open, allowing in sunlight at the far end to which the team proceeds and angles the camera outside.

The view of the city is astonishing. This building is one of the tallest visible but certainly not alone in its stature. The city below is gray and silent, no evidence of life at this altitude. Some buildings in the city have a strange brown growth that appears to have been splashed against them as if a gelatinous mass was flung and then seeped down before hardening. Other buildings have floors where the glass has been shattered and the same brown substance is seeping out the edges. One member of the team calls the camera bearer to the windows on the other side.

From the other side of the building, the city edges can be seen. Attention is pointed toward an expressway that encircles the city upon which crawls another of the large half-body humanoids, dragging itself with its elastic arms as witnessed in previous tests. It travels the highway then moves out of sight. The team returns to the elevator and notes that a button has already been activated for floor 74. No one has approached the elevator so the team agrees to travel to this floor.

On the 74th floor the doors open and reveal a waiting area to what appears to be a doctor's office. At the reception desk there is a sign in sheet with a series of names and dates. The dates on the sign in sheet all carry the year 1953. A PC at the receptionist area is on and functioning at a user desktop. The background for the PC is a large set of praying hands with the word "Faithful OS" under them. On the desktop are a series of folders with years on them containing files that, when clicked using the center button of the mouse, open to a word viewer. All files appear to be appointment information.

SCP-093 'Violet' Test

On the desk is a notepad titled 'From the desk of Dr. Borisizki, Blessed Purificationist'. The door to the doctor's area is sketched with the same name and title as well as a crucifix. Opening this door leads to a white dust-free hallway that has two examination rooms and a key coded door at the end. The examination rooms are unremarkable and typical of any doctor's office. All medicine cabinets are empty. A small amount of C4 is placed at the lock to the key coded door at the request of control and then blown, forcing the door open.

The area it opens into is much larger than the reception area itself and seems to contain a series of large containment capsules. There are a total of six of these capsules, two are broken and a brownish amber material coats the floor coming from them. One is empty, the last three have nude humans floating in them with breathing masks. Attached to the front of these tubes are medical charts showing vital signs and conditions. For symptoms, the charts explain in somewhat awkward English ailments that seem more like flaws of personality or character, or just incidents that have occurred with the patient.

Control asks for a zoom of one of the patient pages on the chart. After focusing, it reads 'Citizen Jennifer McZirka did suffer a lapse of the heart that did lead her to lay with her neighbor twice upon nights of her husband's departure from their home. Patient did submit herself into the Lord's and our hands for cleansing of mind and body. Prayer administered by High Father Uwalakin and patient submitted to a three day period in the Lord's tears to cleanse her system then released in good spirits.'

The topmost page reads 'Citizen Alberious Farafan struck out at a High Father during a sermon, blaspheming that the Lord's tears did turn his daughter to be unright in mind and heart thusly laying blame for her whoreish activities at the feet of the High Father and his blessing. With no proof of these blasphemes the Forgiving Judge and the Punishing Judge did agree that Alberious Farafan should bathe in the Lord's tears himself for a week to be cleansed of mind and soul thus to prove his daughter's ways are fault of not The Fathers Hands and to give him peace of self.'

SCP-093 'Violet' Test

Subject who has been traveling quietly with the escort team now begins to panic. The camera pans to focus on him and he is surrounded by entities similar to those witnessed in the first two tests. Escort team reports in that subject is having a panic attack but control requests them to stand still and wait. Subject screams at the entities, which are denied to exist by team commander, stating Subject is alone in the corner. Control requests that one team member be dispatched to approach and recover the subject. The escort team member approaches the subject as ordered. On the video the figures part to make a pathway for the approaching member who lifts Subject to his feet and brings him out of the corner. Figures on video are then seen closing ranks to close the path. Subject is lifted to his feet by an arm and escorted through the figures that close their ranks when the subject is moved. They remain steadfastly staring at the subject no matter where he moves to. Control requests the team to return now. Team turns to leave. Before leaving a team member mentions something noticed at the reception desk, a binder labeled 'The Lord's Tears'. Control requests binder be returned as well, and it is stowed into Subject's field kit.

The team returns to the elevator and returns to the ground floor. Upon leaving the building, subject points down the street toward direction of entry point. The camera pans to a section of raised expressway across which one of the large torsos is crawling slowly. The entity turns its featureless head to look at the escort team, raises its head to the sky, and emits a bellowing sound. Team leader issues the order to move, heading for the spot marked by the wireless video receiver. The creature on the expressway extends an arm down that stretches to touch the ground, before the camera moves to the port. All team members save one move through entry point. Subject moves through entry point and mirror returns to reflective surface.

SCP-093 'Violet' Test

SCP-093 is dropped by subject who panics and tries to fight his way out of the room. Subject is terminated by team leader after he draws the field kit pistol. Team leader requests portal be reopened but it takes several minutes to find someone who can hold SCP-093 and generate a similar color. When a matching color is displayed and applied to the mirror the video receiver is visible and all individuals report a horrific smell. Team Leader moves through the entryway with control person ███. The uniform and possessions of the escort team member who was left behind are present and recovered, but the member himself is nowhere to be seen and does not respond to shouts. Member assumed K.I.A. and wireless receiver recovered, control and escort return through entry point and mirror returns to reflective surface.

Later review of the recovered camera shows escort member ███ grasping at the air where entry point should be and then turning to look up at the oversized torso. A brown gel seems to drip off the creature as it moves that disappears shortly after being dislodged as if evaporating. Several shots are fired at the creature's face with the automatic weapon carried by ███ that land in the 'face' of the creature, causing a spray of less viscous brown liquid to pour forth from the 'wounds'. ███ screams obscenities as the face of the creature descends upon him and the camera is pushed to the ground. Camera feed remains dark for approximately 65 seconds before light comes back and the camera films the creature crawling back to the expressway and pulling itself onto it, then crawling in the direction it was originally headed.

███ believed to have been 'absorbed' by the creature and perhaps digested. This may have been an example of how these unknown entities feed by direct contact with living material. Further study is recommended to be avoided on this issue. Returned ledger filed as ███.

SCP-093 'Yellow' Test

Mirror Test 4: Color (Yellow)

D-class subjects no longer authorized for testing. Testing focus has been shifted to data collection after analyzing the articles brought back from the previous three tests to better understand the fate of the world accessed by SCP-093 and determine if safeguards or practices are required for our own world. Analysis of the brown fluid on the clothing of the lost escort team member ▇▇▇ has been filed with other recovered articles.

Dr. ▇▇▇ has volunteered for this test as out of the possible candidates, he was able to cause SCP-093 to undergo a new color change. There is no evidence in Dr. ▇▇▇'s background of any illegal or criminal behavior, nor of any psychological problems. When presented to the mirror, the view changed to that of a cubicle office environment.

For this test Dr. ▇▇▇ opted to use the wireless video system and forgo the pulley return system, stating he was confident he would be safe as none of the torso-creatures have been witnessed within a building where the mirror's destination showed. Video feed commences after Dr. ▇▇▇ has crossed the mirror. As with prior tests, SCP-093's current color, yellow, tinges all video material.

> Camera flickers to life and pans across a series of plain white cubicle constructs. Approximately 30 are visible. At the far end from the point of entry is an office module built into the wall with frosted glass walls and a glass door. Dr. ▇▇▇ approaches this door and investigates the etched writing on it: 'Senior Manager - Stanlee Milamitz'. The door is unlocked.
>
> Dr. ▇▇▇ enters the office and examines the desk. A coffee cup is on the desk, a dark brown stain covering half of the inside as the liquid evaporated. There is a donut on a plate which Dr. ▇▇▇ picks up and lobs at a wall, on impact it thumps like a rock and falls. A file cabinet in the corner of the room draws Dr. ▇▇▇'s attention and he goes through each shelf one at a time, stopping in the second drawer and taking out a file, then going back to the first and taking out two others. Continuing to the third and fourth drawers he withdraws four additional files and spreads them all out on the desk.

SCP-093 'Yellow' Test

The files are blue filing folders and he points with his finger and camera at a symbol on each of praying hands, stating aloud for the camera that all other files are stored in yellow folders. The blue folders are placed in his field kit.

Camera attention is turned to the PC on the desk that is logged in and functional, Dr. ▮ comments aloud wondering where these devices are getting their power from as he has noticed no power outlets. This PC's desktop contains the logo of 'Faithful OS' and even has sounds, clicks of the mouse followed by soft hymn-like hums and opening of icons followed by angelic bells. The PC fails to yield any useful information to Dr. ▮ who abandons it and leaves the office.

Approaching the other end of the office floor Dr. ▮ presses a button on the wall for the elevator and enters, finding he is on the 34th floor of a building having an unusual number scheme. The keypad layout goes from -115 to 115, and includes all floors. Before pressing a floor button Dr. ▮ requests that the wireless video transponder be moved to the elevator, and replaced with a construction cone to mark the entry point. A second transponder unit is placed outside the elevator and Control is instructed to recover the second unit and seal the test chamber should something happen to him, then when all is arranged he presses the button for floor -115.

The descent down the elevator is long, consuming 15 minutes, during this time the camera experiences one malfunction where the image jerks and turns to snow, restoring to show 14 other figures in the elevator with Dr. ▮ as video pans around, all of whom move as he moves to allow him space. They remain for 35 seconds then the camera flickers to snow and returns, Dr. ▮ is now alone in the elevator dancing as is assumed by the ducks and sways of the video feed.

Dr. ▮ pauses to comment on a rising stench coming from below. At this point the elevator has reached floor -108. Dr. ▮ presses -110 to interrupt the descent down and exits when that floor is reached. The elevator doors open to an enclosed observation deck with several PCs and chairs. All PCs appear to have power. The ceiling to this deck is also glass and above it another deck is visible. Dr. ▮ approaches the monitoring stations and checks one of the PC screens.

SCP-093 'Yellow' Test

On the screen is the Faithful OS logo and a video feed toggling between four different views. The first view is a room of tubes similar to those found in test Violet which number in the thousands. The second view is a closer up view of these tubes as a camera glides in front of each to monitor the contents. All tubes the camera passes by are broken. The third view is facing the opposite direction as a camera glides vertically checking each observation station. A total of 10 can be counted and Dr. ▓▓▓ is visible as the camera passes by his own station. Looking up, a hovering camera unit with no visible means of propulsion glides up past him. The fourth view shows the ground floor below the observation deck where a single astonishingly large torso being is crawling in circles, bumping into walls and changing directions. From the camera feed the creature's estimated size is six stories.

Returning attention to the contents of the PC Dr. ▓▓▓ moves the video log aside to see a simple text editor that was hidden behind it. A printout of this text was recovered and filed in the Field Kit. The printout directed Dr. ▓▓▓ to a safe on floor 54 and provided a combination. Dr. ▓▓▓ leaves the observation deck and proceeds to 54 without event, arriving on a cubicled office floor. He proceeds to the desk mentioned in the document and found a safe hidden beneath a desk undisturbed. The combination provided opens the safe and reveals a notebook, filed in the Field Kit, and a peculiar revolver that has been returned as ▓▓-▓▓, in addition to the 24 rounds of ammo found with it.

Dr. ▓▓▓ proceeds back to the elevator without event and returns to 34. Given the sheer number of floors available to explore and the vital information obtained from the observation deck, the test is considered over and equipment is retrieved. Before returning through the entry point, Dr. ▓▓▓ investigates a terminal nearby that has power, and finds it shows the exact same screen the one on -110 shows. It is theorized that the author of the note installed a network virus to propagate it through the building so any PC on that network would be found and the information discovered.

Dr. ▓▓▓ returns through the entry point and the mirror returns to a reflective surface. All materials filed with other SCP-093 recovered materials. Analysis of ▓▓-▓▓ and the ammunition for it postponed for reason that it would require deconstruction of one of the rounds and they may be beneficial until testing of SCP-093 is resolved. Video ends.

SCP-093 'Red' Test

SCP-093 Mirror Test 5: Color (Red)

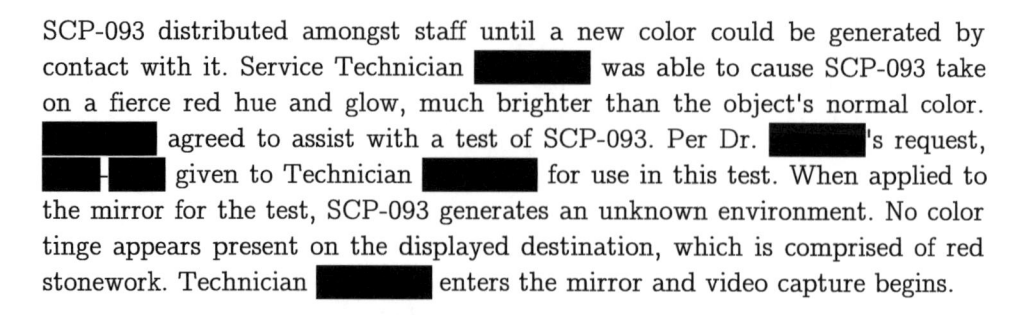

SCP-093 distributed amongst staff until a new color could be generated by contact with it. Service Technician ▮▮▮▮ was able to cause SCP-093 take on a fierce red hue and glow, much brighter than the object's normal color. ▮▮▮▮ agreed to assist with a test of SCP-093. Per Dr. ▮▮▮▮'s request, ▮▮▮▮ given to Technician ▮▮▮▮ for use in this test. When applied to the mirror for the test, SCP-093 generates an unknown environment. No color tinge appears present on the displayed destination, which is comprised of red stonework. Technician ▮▮▮▮ enters the mirror and video capture begins.

Video flickers to life and Technician ▮▮▮▮, known hereafter as Subject, is viewing a large cylindrical pillar that is rotating on its own. Object is of unknown height and appears to be 1.8 m (6 ft) in width. Holes are distributed throughout the object at seemingly random intervals. On occasion a beam of white light is emitted from these holes. Turning of the camera finds that the beams are connected to a multitude of objects similar to SCP-093 that are part of the room's wall. The room turns out to also be cylindrical in shape with countless copies of SCP-093.

Subject turns back to entry point and finds it is a section of the wall that is missing its copy of SCP-093, presumably the one carried with Subject. Other sections of the wall on inspection are also found to be missing their copies, leading to speculation that this may be some sort of central array. Subject finds a ladder in the floor while examining the room and proceeds down it at Control's request.

The ladder exits into a large clean room full of computer equipment that appears antiquated compared to previously encountered equipment. Large computers running on reel-to-reels are clicking and spinning at various locations, a light bulb of unknown meaning turns on for ten seconds then turns off. A large CRT monitor is displaying single words in 8 colors at roughly 5 second intervals. While observed the words 'Clean' 'Unclean' 'Clean' 'Clean' 'Lost' 'Unclean' flash on the screen.

Proceeding through the room it ends in a large glass window as another observation deck.

SCP-093 'Red' Test

> This deck looks out over another series of tubes as witnessed before but far fewer and filled with a blue liquid. What appears to be electrical current dances over many of the tubes at erratic intervals. At least five tubes at first glance are empty and broken. At the observation window a keyboard is present on a pedestal awaiting a selection to be made. The options available on the screen are 'Tube Status' which waits for a numerical input, 'Reports', 'Situation X-549', 'Situation X-550', 'Evacuation Log', 'Bullshit', 'Agent ▊▊▊ Report', and 'Facility Fire Plan'. <Video Expunged: All selections that generated text were transcribed by Subject and verified by a Control member who passed through the portal to recover them. This process took approximately two hours and video feed was deleted to condense this report. Recorded Documents are filed as ▊▊▊▊▊▊> Video Interrupted.

Control lost contact with Subject approximately 30 minutes after departure of Control tech. Subject was asked to remain in area and observe the machinery and the containment room to make observations for debriefing. The SCP-093 mirror portal returned to a reflective surface prematurely and all video contact with Subject was lost. Control was unable to re-establish due to SCP-093 being across the mirror. A time lapse of one minute and forty-eight seconds (1:48) was recorded before mirror portal re-established itself and Subject returned through portal. Subject appeared to be in good health and condition despite the time loss but spoke little.

During immediate debriefing Subject underwent sudden convulsions and medical staff was alerted. While attempting to subdue Subject he displayed enhanced strength and used ▊▊▊ to shoot one of the debriefing staff, killing them. Guards shot Subject once with a sidearm in the heart and once in the chest but Subject did not fall. All staff evacuated room and a second shot was fired by Subject which missed. A more heavily armed team entered debriefing room and used automatic weapons to dispatch Subject. Reports confirm that Subject did not bleed when shot but instead leaked a green/brown substance that seemed to be a mix of solution observed in some containment tubes and the material recovered during Test 3.

All further SCP-093 tests have been discontinued while review of materials recovered is in effect. A secondary tape recording device was found to have activated in the field kit after loss of video feed and its contents have been filed with other recovered materials.

All recovered materials from SCP-093 testing are Level 4 Classification. Release must be approved by no fewer than two Level 4 personnel.

SCP-093-Recovered Materials

Recovered Materials

All documents contained in this file are Class 4 Clearance requiring two signed approvals to access. Any employee reading past this point who does not have proper classification should consider themselves to be terminated from employment and now subject to disciplinary actions up to and including: Forced administration of Class A Amnesic, immediate transfer to Keter class security, and death.

Blue Test - Newspaper Article 1

Only one item could be recovered during our initial test and that was a newspaper clipping found attached to a cork board in an abandoned bunker. Most of the articles were in a state of decay but one was firm enough for recovery.

Most Holy Father Announces Progress, Unclean Being Cleansed!

A rare public address directly from the Most Holy Father of The United Lands of the Son has declared that the Blessed Militia has driven back many of the Unclean who are skulking our lands now. New Rome, our capital, has been purged of the Unclean and citizens are encouraged to come back to their homes. Citizens who live in the surrounding countryside should not return to their farms, as the Unclean still roam the fields and plains around our glorious city and continue to grow in size.

The Blessed Militia has developed new weapons which have proven capable of punishing the Unclean and driving them back into the Unfertile Lands. Construction has begun of a system to permanently close the Unfertile Lands off from our Blessed Lands in each affected area once all the Unclean have been driven away. The Most Holy requests that all citizens of our United Lands bow in prayer and offer tithe to recognize the sacrifices of our Blessed Militia in these troubled times. Reports have been coming in that falsely accuse the Blessed Militia of having committed sin against the citizens whose homes they are inhabiting as they travel bravely through Contaminated lands.

SCP-093-Recovered Materials

> The Most Holy would like to remind the people that blasphemy against any who wear His mark is the most grave of sin and unfounded accusations will be punished accordingly. We should work to support He and His Men however possible just as they lay down their lives for us.
>
> The Sinful Rebels who ——

Green Test - Newspaper Articles 2, 3, 4, Diary

Our second test recovered many materials that helped to establish a sequence of events for this alternate world. The diary recovered provided a glimpse into the last days of the owners of the home from which it was recovered and may represent activity in other areas of the world as well.

Newspaper Article 2

> Farms surrounding the city of Silver Feathers have reported being unable to contact neighbors across voice or video feeds in the last week. Until an approval is granted by the Regional High Father, an investigation cannot commence but he assures the people that these events have not escaped his attention.
>
> Residents are advised to notify their local Blessed Voice daily so any further disappearances can be addressed immediately. Residents are also advised to begin stocking their shelters to be ready for any situation.

Newspaper Article 3

> Following the disappearance of the Blessed Voices from several outlying regions around the city of Silver Feathers, the Regional High Father has declared a Concern for Safety and Livelihood. Under this declaration, all farmland residents must evacuate immediately to their shelters. Scattered reports of an Unclean have come in but have yet to be verified.

SCP-093-Recovered Materials

Newspaper Article 4

— the city of Glorious Song has stopped responding to any and all communications, the worst can only be assumed and our hearts go out to any who are in the region who are unable to hear our words. The city of Silver Feathers Blessed Militia has reported several incursions by the Unclean into the city and have exterminated four of the abominations before they could become a danger to any residents. The Regional High Father reminds the citizens to avoid direct confrontation with the Unclean, conventional arms do nothing to the Unclean, only the most holy of implements will penetrate their sin, so do not put yourself in danger.

Any citizens who suspect their neighbors indulging in heavy sin should immediately contact the Blessed Militia through designated check points —

Diary

███-█-████ I have the distinct feelin we're gonna die so I'm gonna write this all down now fer whoever comes along an finds our bones. My name is Herverf Jakulsiv and Im a farmer, I grows the rabsticks and the huskears. We raise the inks and the ooms. It's me, my wife, Opheri, and our two lil uns Treven and Lisstieria. I got this book en trade from the Blessed man who came by fer food and shelter, he told us to start gettin our shelter ready and not to let no other Blessed who comin by even know we're here, says the whole thing break down, nothing right no more. So I does as he said, got it all ready, we goin down there in the next day or so. In the morn, he was gone, which made the wife sad as he was polite to us unlike most of the others. Figure he didn wanna be no burder. Liss went out lookin fer him to be sure he weren't just round the house.

███-█-████ He didn't turn up nowheres so we guess he left. Strange nuff Liss found is clothes round a mile er so away, an all his gear, but no him. She lef it all there and tha's fer the best if what happen that I think. I'm clearly no educated man, don't claim to be, but I can put two and two together and tell you that things are bad out there. For everyone and especially for us cause it's comin way too close. Sometimes, you can smell it, that's when we hide.

SCP-093-Recovered Materials

Smells like a leg of meat that's been rotten for way too long and just won't go back into the dirt. Even the soil is rejectin em I guess, refusin to let them be buried to die

███-█-███ It came. Too fast, we weren't ready. The smell came in the night, maybe we woulda been fine but the lil uns were afraid so we went to the shelter. Trev was slow, he saw it, kept starin at it as it shambled by. It ignored us until he screamed when I was gettin Liss and the miss down in the shelter. I went to get him but... it was too fast. I saw him standin up there, screamin, and then its head came down on him, pressed over him. He tried to run for the stairs, tried to get to us, but then in a blink, he was gone and it pulled away. His clothes fell into the cellar like he vanished out of em. I got into the shelter, slammed the hatch and locked it. I think it knows we're here now, it'll try to get in, take us too.. no tellin how long we got, plenty of food tho..

I was wrong. The food was rotten, something got into it, or I just didn't notice. We're eatin what we can. There's food, but not enough, and that thing ain't leavin. It's tryin to find ways in, smelt the smell, comin from the lifeweb plug in the wall, something seeped through it and we kept away. It got all hard like a rock and don't smell no more. Maybe the power in the plug finally let it die.

I went up, to peek. Cellar is fine, Trev's clothes still on the stairs. Peeked outside. We're not gonna make it. There were ten..twenty..thirty.. couldn't count, so many, all goin in a circle around the house, lookin at it with those faceless faces, and the stink, oh the stink. Went back into the shelter and locked the door. I think, I don't want to see my family rot away. I think faster is better, the miss, she agrees, we won't tell Liss, she'll be first, then my wife, my love.. then me. I'm sorry, but I'm not sorry. I gave the best life to my family possible. It was them Holy ones what brought this.

I'm gonna pen this in memory to my great pap. He was old and knew stories older than himself. Says those Unclean they preach about, those Unfertile Zones they say stay out of. All cause of the Most Holy bringin the world together. Them things are the ultimate sin. Everything about us that was evil and impure, it's them. They don't know nothin but doin what they do, don't even know why they do it, they just do it, take us into them, then we're gone.

I asked pap what they were and he lit a stick, took a puff, an he said - Don't know. Nobody knows, nobody who'll admit it. But if you see this symbol, if you see it.. you run boy, you run fast, you run far, and

SCP-093-Recovered Materials

> you hide, and you never go back where you saw it. That's all I know. - I remember the symbol, was on the rock he kept on his neck under his shirt. Next day, pap was gone, nowhere to be found, dad weren't sad, said he knew it'd happen one day, pap went home. See you soon dad, pap..

[DATA EXPUNGED] Symbol matched symbol found on SCP-093's surface as one of the deeper engravings. Also matches symbols noticed on video feed of final test on SCP-093 duplicates.

Violet Test - Office Ledger

The third test with SCP-093 resulted in the unfortunate loss of a security member but also allowed us to recover a ledger with insight into the medical procedures carried out on the alternate Earth now termed E-093.

> Patient: Jennifer McZirka
> Recovery Tube: 001-1
> Mixture: 35% Tears, 30% Nutrient, 10% H.F.T., 25% Blessing
> Summary: Jennifer McZirka is 20 cycles of age and during her 18th cycle was the victim of a hov-ride accident that resulted in brain damage and misalignment of her moral processes. She is prone to violent outbursts and can only be calmed down by impure stimulation. Because of this she actively seeks out strangers to mingle with and her parents have requested of the High Father that she be set to the Tears to mend her mind and body. Patient accepted.
>
> During preparation for the Tears subject went into a rage and the attending Hand went to recover a sedative. Jennifer tore her clothes off and screamed impure words at me so I locked the door and instructed the Hand to wait outside. I am half shameful to admit I laid with Jennifer a total of seven times before putting her to the Tears. It has been very long for me and her parents have abandoned her to our care, so care for her I will. Before setting her to the Tears I authorized a Blessed Probe of her body functions and found she is settled now with young and tests confirm it shall be mine. I have mixed her bath to accommodate this and she will soak in the Tears until her body is ready to give life.
>
> Patient: None
> Recovery Tube: 001-2

SCP-093-Recovered Materials

Mixture: None
Summary: None

Patient: Alberious Farafan
Recovery Tube: 001-3
Mixture: 80% Tears, 20% Nutrient
Summary: Alberious Farafan is a farmer from outside the city of Silver Feathers who claims to have lost family to the Unclean. He confronted the High Fathers of the city and demanded compensation and retribution for the loss. The High Fathers deny the existence of Unclean beyond the Unfertile Lands and refuse compensation or retribution. Alberious struck a High Father and was arrested and sentenced to a cleansing of the soul.

His mixture is primarily Tears to seep into the soul and cleanse his heart and ease his pain. The Lawkeepers state his family is indeed missing so his sentence beyond the Tears has been dropped in sympathy for their loss. I used the last of the H.F.T. on Jennifer or I would have used less Tears in this bath, 80% is higher than I am comfortable with but the H.F.T. is becoming hard to obtain. I may have to go through the Dark.

Patient: <====>
Recovery Tube: 002-1
Mixture: 75% Nutrient, 25% Blessing
Summary: A Member of the Blessed Militia who was wounded in combat. Request is from the High Father, details withheld.

Patient: <====>
Recovery Tube: 002-2
Mixture: 75% Nutrient, 25% Blessing
Summary: A Member of the Blessed Militia who was wounded in combat. Request is from the High Father, details withheld.

Patient: <====>
Recovery Tube: 002-3
Mixture: 75% Nutrient, 25% Blessing
Summary: A Member of the Blessed Militia who was wounded in combat. Request is from the High Father, details withheld.

SCP-093-Recovered Materials

Yellow Test - PC Printout, Safe Diary, ▇-▇

The fourth test into E-093 provided us with documentation assumed to be written by a technician in either a medical or government facility. ▇-▇, found in the safe, is being considered for SCP classification primarily due to the composition of the ammunition found with it and the advanced firing mechanism attached to what should be a very base firearm.

PC Printout

> I did not trust the Overwatchers, I felt something was wrong years ago. Under my desk on floor 54 is a safe with a weapon in it, it is one of those used by the Blessed Militia, my brother has sent it to me. He says they are also not what they claim, they have done things to our fellows even more vile than what the Unclean would do. He tells me to be ready to fight. I cannot, it is not me, I do not know violence, I am too frail. You, use it, save yourself.

Safe Diary

> My name is Herval Toliwis, I am a hard systems watcher here. My job is to monitor the Sinful who bathe in the Lord's Tears and then make sure that they reach the prescribed dilution time. I have been doing this job for 23 years, and now things are falling apart. I can no longer abide by The Most Holy, I must speak the truth.
>
> We are being told to evacuate. The containment tubes have been breached. An Unclean has appeared in the Place of Rest and we are unable to destroy it. The livemotion footage shows how it came to be and this is what has unsealed my heart and mind and tongue. I must speak. Should the Overwatchers see this I will be silenced so I must hide it, thankfully they are ignorant with the hardware so I can hide this easily.
>
> The Overwatchers told us, we should leave last, to ensure the hardware contains the Unclean. What that means is we should distract it and die in case it breaches the watching decks. It has shattered nearly all the tubes and absorbed the people in them. I have dispatched the Eyes to the Unclean and they have touched it, bringing me back a sample of it. The Unclean are not sinners, they are not

SCP-093-Recovered Materials

products of our disobedience. I suspect they are us. The Eyes have dated the sample, it is older than myself, older than my elders. It is over 200 cycles in ages. 200!

The sirens are still sounding, but no signal has come for us to leave. I do not think this Unclean is alone. I have seen how they can get into places, between places. Between places! Is that where they have been, all this time? Between places? The makeup of the Unclean is unstable, molecules detach and reattach almost before my eyes, as if to move the entire thing reforms itself in space and time. Why does it not come up here? Too much effort? Or does it not sense me? They have no eyes, no mouth, no face, they cannot speak, cannot see, but they must be able to sense us.

The smell, it is so strong, it comes from all directions. It is not a smell of the dead, it is a smell that comes from something that should be dead but does not know how to die. The War of The Holy Union, I think that was where it may have started. We are united under the Most Holy but what does he owe us? Nothing. We merely keep society running while those on high benefit. Is this not how it has always been? But now we are told we are pleasing the will of those above us in the clouds, those great beings who gave us the power to live and prosper. Those who we have never laid eyes upon but are told we must revere. Lies, all of it, it must be.

I am using the Eyes to create a fluid to oppose the make up of the Unclean's sample. Perhaps they will cancel each other out. I will leave soon and store the rounds here, I cannot use the weapon, I am too weak a man for this. I will protect my family with my mind and not with my rage, we will be safe in the fields, I know where to go.

I will go above now, to my family. I will leave the hardware running, I was told to turn it off, but this is where I defy them, it will run, this will watch, the Eyes will see for however much time they have. Someone will read this, and someone will know. Take the gun, take the fluid, do not listen to the Most Holy, we did, and we are damned.

███████ is a revolver style weapon with two 12 bullet cylinders. The design of the gun has one cylinder on each side, raised slightly, so they may flip into the gun itself and then rotate, firing all rounds, before flipping back out and allowing it to be reloaded while the second is usable allowing a total of 24 shots before it runs empty. There is no firing pin on this gun, but instead there is a pull-back slide mechanism that must be used to prime the active

SCP-093-Recovered Materials

cylinder. At the time of recovering, all 24 slots contained a syringe style bullet with 32 needles on the end. On impact it is assumed the force of the shot will press the liquid inside into the target. None have been tested.

Of express interest is that these cylinders can hold standard .45 caliber ammunition which has been tested. The gun uses an ultra high power magnetic rail system to deliver the shot so the gunpowder in the bullet is never used. In consideration is a redesign of a round that would utilize the gunpowder midflight to add even higher velocity to the round or that would explode on impact for higher yield.

Red Test - PC Printouts

The final authorized test with SCP-093 resulted in the loss of a skilled service technician but allowed us to recover very revealing documents that can only be assumed to not have been intended for public knowledge in any world. Curious among these is 'Agent ▆▆▆ Report' which appears to have been written by a Foundation employee several decades ago.

While these paper printouts were the best material recovered it seems that the system used to create them allowed for multiple forms of input including typed and verbal speech-to-text. Some audio logs of the printouts below are available but must be requested in advance with fully written explanations as to why. This dual input system seems to explain the variances in the style between users as well with assumptions made on the part of the software while performing conversions.

Facility Fire Plan

> In the event of any Emergency requiring the Facility to be evacuated, all Clear-4 staff should report to Train Station 3 and use their Vial to call the Evacuation Train. Only one Vial is required to call the train and may contain any amount of Tears. An Empty Vial will not call the train. Clear 2 and 1 staff should remain at their posts until either 10 minutes after the departure of Clear-4 persons or until authorized by Clear-4 staff. Clear-3 staff should utilize the Protective Garments at their stations and weapon lockers before proceeding to designated Crisis Areas as dictated by Clear-4 staff.

SCP-093-Recovered Materials

Reports

Three Unfertile Zones have increased 25% in size in the last seven days. Containment Teams are not finding any presence of Unclean in these zones but they are visibly confirmed as expanding. Clear-5 level High Fathers have confirmed breaches in the Holy Chambers at each of these zones, all chambers found empty. It is believed that the Unclean have breached containment on the Holy Chambers. Dispatching additional guard to remaining Chambers.

Situation X-549

Expansion of Zone 6-4-TO has been confirmed. Unfertile Zone containment procedures in effect. Containment Staff dispatched to site. This is the tenth report in 30 days, upgrading to Situation Status. Reports from Clear-5 High Fathers have stopped at all affected. The City of His Word has been placed on full lockdown and all travel denied in or out. Other cities are now in Alert mode and combat teams are being dispatched to city perimeters.

Situation X-550

The Great Land of Hufussia has fallen per satellite images. Entire landmass considered tainted. Outbreak of Sin reported in Levina and that landmass has requested assistance from the Holy Union. Assistance denied due to our own outbreak and mass reportings of Unclean. Clear-10 staff have issued the order to evacuate via the Gateway and for all Holy Union authorized persons to proceed to the nearest Sky Platform for evacuation to Star Eye Eden to continue monitoring status. Gateway Keys are being ejected to prevent spread from this center to other space/time vectors. Resurrecting Staff are being awakened to monitor and continue reports here as we evacuate. May His Blessings Forgive Our Greatest Sin.

SCP-093-Recovered Materials

Evacuation Log

Evacuation in progress. Shuttle 1 away. Shuttle 2 away. Shuttttttttttttttttttttttle 3error error error error error release us release us release us why why why why Shuttle 3 error launch aborted proceed to Shuttle 4. Shuttle 4 reporting delayed launch, overloaded, triage protocols engaged. Shuttle 4 reports passenger limit obtained preparing to laaaaunnnnnn why why why why release us why us release why us what did we do why why system detecting electrostatic activity compensating compensating comp comp comp comp 10101101110110101010101110011 arrrrrrrrrrrrrrrrrrrrrrrrrrrrrr why were we hurt what did we do why were we hurt what did we do system shut down

system restore purge of contaminated data in progress WHY US WHY US WHY US WHY US WHY US WHY US WHYYYYYYYYYYYYYYYYYYYYYYYYYYY LISTEN

record 5432-104-392 paasssssworrrrdddd forrrgivveeeusss 5554444332 2 2 2 2 22222222 1 111111111

WHY WHY WHY WHY WHY WHY WHY WHY WHY

system purge

purge

pur

bullshit

wtf is this place lol ok so lyk there r ppl typin stuff here so im gonna type 2 lol. so lyk i found this rock in the pond by the house and it was all kinda glowy and stuff when i picked it up so im lyk o wow pretty and when i pick it up the pond u culdnt see the bottom it was this weird room with a glowy rock thing lol i dunno so i lyk i guess fell into it oops and now im here and not there and rly im kinda scurred but this place is like a movie set so it's cool lol theres some guy i can hear talking he keeps asking me to come downstairs but i dont see no door he keeps screaming for help too cause i told him to eat me laff and he

SCP-093-Recovered Materials

wont shut up i guess i could try goin back into that room but its so creepy in there im sorta scurred to laff

oh so hey i found a door its like in the floor instead of on a wall so lyk im gonna go tell that guy yellin 2 shut it up so i can go home bbl

Agent ▇▇▇ Report

My name is ▇▇▇▇▇▇▇ ▇▇▇▇▇▇▇▇▇▇ and I am an agent at The Foundation, the year in my world is 1972. I assume it is the same in this world, but from what I have seen due to SCP-093, life on this world ended in approximately 1954. I have used SCP-093 to visit a number of locales starting and ending here in this center. I have seen the landscapes where no grass will grow. I have run from the 'Unclean' as they pursue anything they sense. I have no understanding of how they hunt but I have learned what they are.

Approximately 350 years ago or so this world experienced a technological boom ours did not. The source of this seems to have been the arrival of He, a god-like being of unknown origin. He declared the world Unclean and full of Sin, and the only way to purge itself of this Sin was to purge the Sinners. A war, whoever was left alive, was Clean. Amazing advances in science were bestowed to all cultures for a period of ten years to prepare them for this war and during that time, He disappeared. The war happened anyway, the instigator, The Holy Union of Land, apparently the landmass that for us would become the United States.

Records are sketchy and books that detail anything about this time period are forbidden in the world. I located a cache of recorded history by following a series of corrupted computer communications. It seems the primary weapon used in this war for His Love was in fact, people. Exposed to something called His Holy Tears, a liquid compound I have seen in use even today in abandoned medical facilities. His Holy Tears purge the Sin from the Unclean and make them love Him; at least that's what the label states.

The records I recovered are very unclear about how this war was waged except to state 'His Holy Chosen walked the lands of the Sinful and took their sin unto themselves. Those who cried for His Salvation received it and are now our children. Those who denied His Love were purified in His Radiance.

SCP-093-Recovered Materials

But something apparently happened no one knew how to deal with. The Unclean, the large creatures that are half a man and devour whatever they touch that lives and breathes. I actually found a scientific report written by someone who stumbled here with a SCP-093 copy. These creatures are the result of exposure to a very pure form of His Tears resulting in a genetic apocalypse occurring within the exposed. There are terms in here, something about Quantum Restructuring, I don't understand any of this but it means they were once humans like everyone else, that couldn't be controlled. But they COULD be contained. They seem to be attracted to His Tears and a central point was established in various regions where a person with the purest form of His Tears stays, keeping the Unclean in that area known as an Unfertile Land.

Something went wrong with that too, not sure what, but everything fell apart. The power structure, the culture, the people, all of it fell to ruins and now those things shamble around the land as its new owners, with no purpose or direction. You can stand next to one if you can stand the stink and they just slip right past you. If you catch their attention though, that's it, they move like lightning if they need to and like a snail unless they have a reason to speed up. Sometimes, I think they chase just to do it, others, they move to kill.

I think someone is in this facility, or someones, I keep hearing voices and requests coming from areas under the floor. I want to leave this before I explore the facility any further. I have sent SCP-093 back through the entry mirror to seal that gate. These things can't be let into our world nor should we have anything to do with this one, we're simply not smart enough to understand it all I feel.

I don't think the Unclean can die. They're immortal, but they don't want to be. They just want to die. They're.. in my head I think.. I didn't notice it till just now but, equipment in this room is starting to react to me, words on the screen, begging for help. I, I remember touching the Tears, smelling it, tasting it, just a touch. Not eating it just.. touching to it, tasting for acidity, we have pretty stupid investigative procedure I think ha ha.

The High Fathers are .. alive. They have technology we only imagine in our comics given by Him. Some of the records on this machine indicate space travel, but they didn't go far, just far enough to watch the world fall apart and wait to come back and take it.. but if they're up there.. who is in this building with me?

SCP-093-Recovered Materials

I've seen the faces, of the people, the Unclean. They show up on the pictures cast by the machine, in the room with me, watching me. I think, they're everywhere on this world, only seen by machines now. They don't look sad, or happy, just, curious. They want to know..why..why them..why did it all happen? I don't know.. I just don't know..

they showed me things when i touched them and its not quite like the records say. the unclean remember it all, every person they touch becomes part of them, safe inside them, but dead to us. every mind, every feeling, every terror, its eternal to them. i kind of want to join them but.. too much to do.. they want me to.. find him, kill him.

there was no war it was him him him him him IT. IT. it came from between the folds of time and space and worlds and light and dark something that is but should not be slipped in and called out to them as their god and they believed it and they tasted it and touched it and layed with it and became its property and did its will and IT IS STILL HERE the scp-093 it brought with it pulled forcefully with it built it i don't know they don't know but it belongs to him it lets him move between places between worlds so i BROKE IT ha ha ha i threw pieces of it away and through holes so those doors are closed just like ours is closed and i can't go home so what else can i do

it calls out through the rock, somehow, it knows where they are but can't touch them, but if you hide the rock he can't call out and he's stuck too i got you you son of a bitch I GOT YOU BANG BANG ha ha

i touched him. with my fist. and my gun. and he fell down. but he'll get back up. soon. i'm sorry, i did all i could, let me sleep now, please... let... me... slee

SCP-148

Item #: SCP-148

Object Class: Euclid

Special Containment Procedures:

REVISION 3

SCP-148 is to be stored as 120 cast ingots, each of which weighs approximately 10 kg at time of writing. Ingots of SCP-148 may not be housed at the same site as any SCP (due the potential for unforeseen interactions); otherwise, said ingots should be distributed equally among acceptable Foundation facilities. The mass of each contained ingot of SCP-148 must be measured and reported monthly.

Under no circumstances should any SCP with mind-affecting or extrasensory properties come into contact with SCP-148. In the event of such contact, the immediate area must be evacuated and the affected sample of SCP-148 detonated remotely.

Personnel are not to be assigned to SCP-148 for a period of time longer than three weeks. Any personnel assigned to SCP-148 are to be given regular psychological evaluations.

Description: SCP-148 is a metallic substance, composed of a variety of known and unknown elements. The total mass of SCP-148 on hand is approximately ~~1.1~~ 1.2 tonnes. SCP-148 has a gray-green color with a bluish tinge and oxidizes readily in the presence of water. SCP-148 has a melting transition point of approximately 4500°C and a boiling transition point of approximately 9000°C. SCP-148 has a density of ~~6.20 g/cm^3~~ 6.76 g/cm^3 and qualifies as HRC 39 in a Rockwell hardness test. It exhibits material properties, such as strength, ductility, and workability, similar to platinum.

SCP-148 is composed primarily of platinum and iridium, the two composing 62% and 20% of its mass respectively. In addition, several other known metals are present in its composition, including iron, cobalt, and copper, which collectively make up 16.5% of SCP-148's mass. However, given the mass of the material, it is believed that there are other substances not detectable by mass spectrometry or other means.

SCP-148

Images of SCP-148 taken with a scanning tunneling microscope show gaps in its lattice that, under normal circumstances, would be filled with other materials.

SCP-148 blocks or otherwise hinders extrasensory mind-affecting properties of living organisms in proximity to it. This effect, while difficult to quantify, appears inversely proportional to the square of the distance from the subject to SCP-148's surface and directly proportional to the quantity of SCP-148 in consideration. The range for which this effect is detectable is roughly 0.8 meters per kilogram of SCP-148.

1.1 tonnes of SCP-148 were retrieved from the metallurgical department of Prometheus Labs' base facility during the Foundation's sweep of the building. Documents concerned with the project had unveiled that the substance was to be subject to additional development, sold to ███████████, trademarked, and sold as "Telekill Alloy". However, due to [REDACTED] and its political fallout, along with the destruction of the Prometheus Labs' base facility, ███████████ has acquired an estimated 1.3 tonnes of SCP-148 and sold it to unknown buyers. Foundation agents and forensic accountants are in the process of tracking the remaining supplies of SCP-148.

Addendum 148-01
~~Due to its potential for use in containment of mind-affecting SCPs, SCP-148 has been approved for cross-testing with SCP objects. While tests are still in their early stages, tests with low-level anomalous items seem to indicate that SCP-148 will be an effective tool in containing said items.~~ However, it does not appear to affect items whose notable properties are purely memetic.

Addendum 148-02
Beginning ██/██/████, staff reported irrational behavior and poor communication skills among janitorial staff tasked with regular maintenance of SCP-148's containment. [1] After three weeks of increasingly abnormal behavior, two custodians were taken in for questioning and examination. Testing revealed that the aforementioned personnel were incapable of interpreting body language and did not appear to notice the intonation or phrasing of sentences. In addition, the affected subjects were incapable of determining the emotional state or intent of others and demonstrated severely limited vocabulary.

---

[1] At the time, containment consisted of a single storeroom, swept and checked on a daily basis.

SCP-148

Further testing has revealed that the language and communication skills of persons with regular contact or extended exposure to SCP-148 will, over time, deteriorate and disappear. It has been shown that, after eight weeks, affected subjects will be rendered completely mute and incapable of understanding or giving nonverbal requests, commands, or other statements, despite showing otherwise normal mental capacity.

Addendum 148-03
A measurement taken on ■/■/■■■ (■■ months after the Foundation's acquisition of SCP-148) indicated that, despite no increase in volume, SCP-148 has increased in mass by 0.1 tonnes (a density increase of 9.0%). The source of this additional mass is unknown.

Incident Report 148-■■■-1
To test the limits of SCP-148's effects and its capacity to change in mass, 0.9 kg of it was placed on a scale and moved to SCP-■■■'s chamber. Predictably, SCP-■■■'s [REDACTED] was nullified by SCP-148's presence. However, the sample of SCP-148 began to grow in mass by upwards of 5 grams per second. After one minute, this rate began to decrease, and SCP-148 ceased to increase in mass forty seconds later, at which point it weighed 1.4 kilograms. It remained at this mass for eight seconds before plummeting to 0.8 kilograms in the space of two seconds. During this time, personnel within sixty meters (twelve times the effective range of SCP-■■■) began to experience SCP-■■■'s effects, albeit at a vastly increased rate, resulting in [DATA EXPUNGED] lockdown until the affected subjects could be removed.

As of this incident, contact between SCP-148 and any mind-affecting items is strictly forbidden.

Addendum 148-04
Measurements taken since Incident 148-■■■-1 indicate that the combined mass of SCP-148 is increasing at a rate of [REDACTED]. It is speculated that should a large quantity of SCP-148 undergo an event similar to the sample used in Experiment 148-■■■, [DATA EXPUNGED]. Containment procedures are under review.

SCP-173

Sorry about that. It looked something like this:

Alright, I'm no artist. Just check it on the online database will you?

SCP-173 in containment

Item #: SCP-173

Object Class: Euclid

Special Containment Procedures: Item SCP-173 is to be kept in a locked container at all times. When personnel must enter SCP-173's container, no fewer than 3 may enter at any time and the door is to be relocked behind them. At all times, two persons must maintain direct eye contact with SCP-173 until all personnel have vacated and relocked the container.

Description: Moved to Site-19 1993. Origin is as of yet unknown. It is constructed from concrete and rebar with traces of Krylon brand spray paint. SCP-173 is animate and extremely hostile. The object cannot move while within a direct line of sight. Line of sight must not be broken at any time with SCP-173. Personnel assigned to enter container are instructed to alert one another before blinking. Object is reported to attack by snapping the neck at the base of the skull, or by strangulation. In the event of an attack, personnel are to observe Class 4 hazardous object containment procedures.

SCP-173

Personnel report sounds of scraping stone originating from within the container when no one is present inside. This is considered normal, and any change in this behaviour should be reported to the acting HMCL supervisor on duty.

The reddish brown substance on the floor is a combination of feces and blood. Origin of these materials is unknown. The enclosure must be cleaned on a bi-weekly basis.

SCP-239

SCP-239

Item #: SCP-239

Object Class: Keter

Special Containment Procedures: SCP-239 is to be kept within a one room cell furnished with 1 (one) bed, 1 (one) EKG machine, and 1 (one) IV to be filled with pentobarbital mixed with [DATA EXPUNGED] to be refilled daily. Under no circumstances is SCP-239 to be removed from her containment area at any given time. The walls of this cell are to be coated in a telekill-lead alloy. Only Class 2 personnel are allowed any contact with SCP-239 at any time. All personnel guarding SCP-239's containment area are to be equipped with Telekill headgear (SCP-148). Subject's proper name is Sigurrós Stefánsdóttir. Under absolutely no condition should the subject ever be awakened. Any personnel found attempting to awaken the subject will be immediately terminated.

SCP-239

Description: SCP-239 appears to be an 8-year-old girl, 1 meter in height and 20 kilograms in weight. Subject has shoulder-length blond hair. Upon closer inspection, the subject's eyes "shimmer" a gray-green shade. Subject seems to emit a previously undiscovered form of radiation, which has been named ███████████████. These waves seem to be harmless in low concentrations but in higher concentrations they could break down matter on a subatomic level.

SCP-239 seemingly has the ability to do whatever she expresses a will to do. Put simply, the subject can do anything that she truly wants to do on a basal psychological level as long as she is conscious. Fortunately, she only seems to be able to affect herself and her immediate surroundings; therefore, "If she can see it, she can change it." It would not be the most prudent course of action, however, to try to test how powerful she can be. She seems to be able to create and affect living matter; for example, when a D-class personnel accidentally caused her harm, she simply wished him away. Fortunately, when the subject was made to feel guilty for what she had done, she wished him back. SCP-239's self-preservation instinct makes her virtually invincible while she is conscious. Subject's skin can not be punctured by anything excepting SCP-148 .

As a method of controlling the subject's ability, she has been told that she is a witch. This, besides improving morale greatly, makes her believe that she is unable to use her abilities outside of a pre-approved list of "spells" given to her by the SCP Foundation. This will hopefully prevent any and all attempted escapes. However, the subject is to be kept calm at all times to prevent any subconscious wish of harm to herself or others.

Origin: SCP-239 came to to the attention of the Foundation very soon after her birth in ███████████, ███████████. Approximately three hours after subject's birth, ███████████ Hospital was destroyed by an unexplained explosion. The press was informed that it was due to a gas leak. SCP teams were dispatched shortly to search the site for any abnormalities. The only living person they were able to locate was SCP-239. For the next eight years, the subject was raised under SCP care.

As of ███████████ █, 20██, Subject is to be kept in a medically induced coma until further notice. This decision was made by [DATA EXPUNGED].

SCP-239 is permanently contained in Site-17.

Note from Dr. ███████████, dated 12/26/04: *Who the hell thought it would be a good idea to tell her about "Santa Claus" and then tell her that it was just a story?! Now we have another potential SCP to deal with, but we can't catch him because he is "magic".*

SCP-239

Dr. A. Clef's Report: *My analysis of the situation has led me to the conclusion that SCP-239 is an unacceptable containment and security risk. Although several proposals have been made re: using her for containing other SCPs, the example of SCP-953 and others must serve as a stark reminder of the risks of overestimating the Foundation's ability to control SCPs with reality-altering powers.*

I would therefore like to make the following proposal: a piercing implement will be constructed of SCP-148 , capable of penetrating SCP-239's otherwise impenetrable skin. This tool will be used to kill SCP-239 while she is asleep and her powers are neutralized. Because of the danger of SCP-239 awakening and resisting termination, it is my recommendation that the selected operative carry SCP-668 as well, in order to minimize complications.

One of the dangers of this procedure is the possibility that SCP-239 will awaken and perceive the operative as a friend or "good person," thus changing reality to match. It is for this reason that I would like to volunteer to carry out the procedure personally. A review of my personnel file should indicate that my [DATA EXPUNGED] should allow me to carry out the operation even after a reality shift of this nature.

- Clef

SCP-500

SCP-500

Item #: SCP-500

Object Class: Safe

Special Containment Procedures: SCP-500 must be stored in a cool and dry place away from bright light. SCP-500 is only allowed to be accessed by personnel with level 4 security clearance to prevent misapplication.

Description: SCP-500 is a small plastic can which at the time of writing contains forty-seven (47) red pills. One pill, when taken orally, effectively cures the subject of all diseases within two hours, exact time depending on the severity and amount of the subject's conditions. Despite extensive trials, all attempts at synthesizing more of what is thought to be the active ingredient of the pills have been unsuccessful.

> **Note From Dr. Klein:**
> SCP personnel below Level 3 are now banned from handling SCP-500. This is not to be used to cure a hangover. Get AIDS and then ask permission.

Request 500-1774-k
Dr. [500-0022F] has requested one (1) SCP-500 pill for testing with SCP-038. Request has been approved.

Request 500-1862-b
Dr. Gears has requested one (1) SCP-500 pill for testing in SCP-914. Request has been approved.

Request 500-2354-f
Dr. ███████ has requested one (1) SCP-500 pill for testing with SCP-253. Request denied.

Request 500-5667-e
Dr. Gibbons has requested two (2) pills of SCP-500 for his personal medkit. Request denied.

SCP-500

Addendum 500-1: Two (2) pills have been authorized for use with SCP-008. As a result of conducting a series of tests on Class D subjects infected with SCP-008, it appears that even in the most advanced stages of the disease one whole pill will accomplish full recovery. Number of pills is fifty-seven (57) at the time of writing. - Dr. [500-0021D]

Addendum 500-2: One (1) pill has been authorized for use with SCP-409. SCP-500 was tested on Subject 409-D5 who was exposed to the effects of SCP-409. Complete recovery accomplished. See Addendum 409-1. Number of pills is fifty-six (56) at the time of writing. - Dr. [500-0021D]

Addendum 500-4: Request 500-1774-k approved. Five (5) pills have been used in experimentation with SCP-038. It has been determined that SCP-038 is capable of duplicating SCP-500; however, the success of the duplicated pills is limited. The duplicated pills are only effective in curing the subject 30% of the time, with chance of successful healing dropping as time since cloned increases. In 60% of the cases where the infection is permanent, symptoms of infection remain, though further infestation is neutralized. Repeated dosing with SCP-038 cloned pills is recommended for all personnel suffering from incurable conditions, as supply of SCP-500 remains extremely limited. All five (5) used samples of SCP-500 were returned. Number of pills is fifty-six (56) at the time of writing.

Addendum 500-5: During experiments with SCP-038, one (1) pill was stolen by personnel D-████████ to, reportedly, "cure a hangover". Stricter controls for samples of SCP-500 given to other projects is suggested. Personnel D-████████ has been terminated. Number of pills is fifty-five (55) at the time of writing.

Addendum 500-6: One (1) pill has been used with SCP-231-4. Number of pills is fifty-four (54) at the time of writing.

Addendum 500-7: One (1) pill has been used for Experiment 447-a. Number of pills is fifty-three (53) at the time of writing.

Addendum 500-8: One (1) pill has been used with SCP-208. Number of pills is fifty-two (52) at the time of writing.

Addendum 500-9: Request 500-1862-b approved. One (1) pill of SCP-500 is placed within SCP-914 with the setting at "Fine". Resulting object classified as SCP-427. Number of pills is fifty-one (51) at the time of writing.

Addendum 500-10: Five (5) pills have been taken for the Olympia Project although only two (2) were used. The remaining three (3) will be returned shortly. Upon return, number of pills will be forty-nine (49).

SCP-500

Addendum 500-11: Two (2) pills have been used for Experiment 217-███-█████. Number of pills is forty-seven (47) at the time of writing.

Addendum 500-12: Request to have SCP-500 investigated for mental compulsion leading to obsessive fixation denied for triviality.

SCP-038

SCP-038

Item #: SCP-038

Object Class: Safe

Special Containment Procedure: SCP-038 is to be watered twice per day via overhead mister. Should the mister break for any reason, attendants should water SCP-038 by hand until it has been fixed. Lighting is provided by computer-controlled lighting array. Attendants watering SCP-038 by hand and maintenance personnel fixing mister or lighting should wear hazmat suits to prevent accidental cloning.

Description: SCP-038 was found on an abandoned farm in ███████████████, New York, in 19██. It was at first thought to be a common apple tree. However, upon closer inspection, it became apparent that SCP-038 was growing things other than apples and, in fact, other than fruit.

SCP-038 has the ability to clone any object that touches its bark. Objects begin growing almost instantaneously and reach maturity within a matter of minutes. A weight limit of 90.9 kg (200 lb) per object has been previously recorded. Objects that SCP-038 has thus far cloned include: apples, oranges, watermelons, eggplants, candy bars, snack foods (See Addendum #1), televisions, toasters, laptops, keys (See Addendum #2), chairs, wine, DVDs, CDs (See Addendum #3), cats, dogs, and people.

Human and animal cloning through SCP-038 is not recommended, as they appear to age quickly. The majority of these clones live, on average, two (2) weeks. After thorough examination of the deceased clones, it has been determined that they had begun to ferment before death.

Object is currently held on Site-23 and there are currently no plans to move it.

Addendum #1: Dr. Klein has requested that personnel discontinue the cloning of items from the vending machines. (See Document #338-1)

Addendum #2: Dr. Klein has requested that personnel discontinue the cloning of personal items. (See Document #338-1)

Addendum #3: Dr. Klein has requested that personnel discontinue the cloning of movies and music. (See Document #338-1)

SCP-038

Addendum #4: Dr. Klein has requested that personnel discontinue the cloning of cans of Miller, Budweiser, and Foster's. Dr. Klein has furthermore expressed customary disapproval of the quality of such cloned items. (See Document #338-1b)

Document #338-1: "I would like to remind all personnel that SCP-038 is not, I repeat, **not** a toy. It should not be used for cloning car keys, movies, music, or items from the vending machines. If this behavior continues I will be forced to limit access to SCP-038.
- Dr. Klein"

Document #338-2: It has been noted that SCP-038 is able to clone SCP-500 — however, such pills only work 30% of the time, with chance of successful healing dropping as time since cloned increases. In 60% of the cases where the infection is permanent, symptoms of infection remain, though further infection is neutralized.

SCP-038

SCP-038 Partial Testing Log - select experiments only

For full test records and reports, contact affiliated researchers for authorization

Date: 11/08/▮▮▮▮
Intent: Confirmation of mass limit: investigation into consequences of exceeding limit.
Summary of test results: 400 pound steel ingot made contact with the outer bark of SCP-038. Chamber vacated as a precaution. Cloned ingot grew at typical speed, but growth halted abruptly short of completion. Examination of the end of the aborted facsimile revealed a rough texture superficially resembling miniature-scale tree bark. Item detached from SCP-038 as typical, and was subsequently found to weigh 90.91 kilograms, or almost precisely 200 pounds.

Date: 11/08/▮▮▮▮
Intent: Investigation into duplication of non-biological animate matter.
Summary of test results: SCP-173 , deemed a suitable test subject because of its lack of verifiable life processes, introduced into containment chamber by Class-D personnel. Contact made with the outer bark of SCP-038, and SCP-173 returned immediately to containment. SCP-173 facsimile began development at typical speed, beginning at point of contact. As consistent with previous results, growth halted at the 200-pound threshold, in this case terminating development after replication of the head, right arm, and partial upper torso. Class-D test subject was ordered to break eye contact with clone. When test subject eventually blinked, no movement was observed in cloned material. Extinguishing and reestablishment of containment chamber light supply revealed no apparent reaction from cloned material. Experiment concluded. During storage of cloned portion of SCP-173, it was observed that the partial facsimile was in fact making violent gestures, at a dramatically slower rate. Movement was shown to continue regardless of state of observation.

SCP-1342

SCP-1342

SCP-1342 at time of initial containment, with sensor booms detached.

Item #: SCP-1342

Object Class: Euclid

Special Containment Procedures: SCP-1342 is to be stored at Site 15. SCP-1342-1 is to be kept within a Faraday cage, measuring 15m x 15m x 20m, to prevent transmission of telemetry and other data regarding SCP-1342.

SCP-1342-2 is to be stored in a standard electronic components locker. One decoded copy of SCP-1342-2 is to be contained in a separate locker.

In addition, monitoring of Gliese 445 by radio telescope is to be conducted. As SCP-1342-3 is unlikely to be containable in the near future, Project Heimdall is to continue in its Contingency Planning Operation.

Description: SCP-1342-1 is a replica of Voyager 1. Exact replication of the original probe extends to sensor packages and apparent chemical composition. However, some components appear to have been constructed based on incomplete plans or parts. As a result, several components were non-functional upon recovery.

SCP-1342

SCP-1342-1 was initially detected on 25/09/1982, approximately 35,000 km above the Earth's surface travelling at a sub-orbital velocity. Foundation agents recovered SCP-1342-1 on 27/09/1982, after SCP-1342-1 underwent an uncontrolled atmospheric entry and splashdown 300 km east of Baker Island, Pacific Ocean. SCP-1342-1's detection was possible due to a large burst of Cherenkov radiation that occurred upon its appearance. It is currently unknown how SCP-1342-1 remained intact during its descent, despite appearing to have similar chemical composition to the original Voyager.

SCP-1342-2 is a gold-plated phonograph record, with specifications matching the Golden Records carried on the Voyager probes. Instructions for playing and decoding remain original. However, the pulsar map has been altered to show the star Gliese 445 as the origin of SCP-1342.

When decoded, SCP-1342-2 contains a variety of cultural and scientific data in the form of images and audio. Approximately 2 hours of audio recordings are present, consisting of various forms of music and atonal buzzing. Part of the music appears to be an excerpt of Cavatina from the String Quartet No. 13 in B flat, Opus 130 by Beethoven. The encoded images vary greatly in content, but all contain physical or chemical information on the subject (e.g. size, mass and orbital period of a planet), and a string of pictorial characters.

A radially symmetric organism (referred to as SCP-1342-3) is shown in various stages of development. Fully grown, the organism is approximately 2 m tall, and has three legs and three elongated arms, with each hand having three fingers, positioned around a central axis on a roughly cylindrical torso. Three snout-like protrusions exist in place of a head, each ending in a beak. 82% of the encoded images show SCP-1342-3 in a wide variety of presumed cultural settings. Scenes identified include agriculture, manufacturing, urban crowds and the playing of music on a string-and-bow instrument.

Images of a number of celestial bodies are also included, such as a Venusian-type world with high atmospheric pressure and a star matching Gliese 445's stellar spectra. One planet shown has a partially Earth-like surface consisting of approximately 60% liquid water, 4% urbanisation and plant life and 36% apparent desert and wasteland. The planet has larger than expected storms and icecaps than would be suggested by physical quantities supplied by SCP-1342-2, and appears to be undergoing massive ecological collapse. An outline of a specimen of SCP-1342-3 is shown next to this planet.

SCP-1342

This planet is shown to have extensive orbital infrastructure, not limited to spacecraft manufacturing facilities, captured asteroid mining operations and space elevators grounded near urbanised and wasteland areas. All of these images show the structures to be in a wrecked or neglected state. The final encoded image shows a vessel heading towards an extremely damaged torus-style space station with a 2 km diameter aperture at its centre.

Documents 1-56: The following message was encoded on SCP-1342-2 in 55 different languages matching the 55 in which audio greetings were sent on the original Voyager, and is consistent in all. The 56th document is entirely composed of pictorial strings.

This is the English version of SCP-1342-2's message. A recording is available on the online database.

> This Voyager spacecraft was built in the year 42,412 AD by the species you come to refer to as the Gliscian. We are a community of 300,000 beings inhabiting Gliese 445-C. This is our message to your world.
>
> Ever since we discovered radio, we have lived in your shadow. Decades were spent unravelling your signals, searching for answers among the tenuous strands of reason. Through the static and the chaos, we found you. From your small, distant world we found your images, your music, your thoughts, your feelings and your indomitable science. We communicated with your world governments, who kept our existence secret from you. To prevent a culture shock with their own populace, or to reduce your impact upon our own species, it did not matter to us. We could touch the mind of another and know we are not alone.
>
> We learned from you. The scientific revolution following our meeting was miraculous. We lived beyond our natural years and we lived well. Humans uplifted us into an Elysian state, but we could never thank you. From our far away place we quietly deciphered your secrets and over time our technology became your equal.
>
> Together we went, advancing our mastery of the universe. We shared our technology with your leaders in secret, to try and re-pay you for all you will do. In time, came the Gates. At a great expense of energy, we could obtain limitless velocity. With time dilation preserved, we could fly to the universe's birth, and its death. The entirety of creation was within our mutual grasp.

SCP-1342

However, that would not be. Before we emerged, the people who live on your planet crippled us. From the sky above, in bright blue flashes, our lives were ended. We do not know their reasons, nor do we know why their hand was stayed enough to forestall our extinction. But now we live on a dying world. Our children are sick. Our water is polluted. We cannot maintain our technology. We will not go on.

To save ourselves, we could have tried to destroy you. It cannot be denied that is how some of us felt we should act. We could still hear your world, unknowing, uncaring. With what little power we had left, relativistic destruction could reduce your planet to ashes as it was forming. It is shaming, but we came so close. We hope you can understand why we thought what we did. But maybe, if we could change what happens, if we could destroy you, then you could save us.

From the stars came Voyager. Your gift. In sending your message, filled with your music and your joy, you showed such touching desperation to find another. We fell in love all over again.

We had but one chance to put things right. I do not know if you can save us. I do not know if you can change who you one day may be. You say you are trying to survive through your time, so you may live into mine. I really hope that you, you, do.

But above all else, there is one thing you need to know.

From one maker of music to another, across all worlds, all times, no matter what you do or what you become: You are nothing less than beautiful.

SCP-3008

SCP-3008

Item #: SCP-3008

Object Class : Euclid

Special Containment Procedures : The retail park containing SCP-3008 has been purchased by the Foundation and converted into Site-███. All public roads leading to or passing by Site-███ have been redirected.

The entrance to SCP-3008 is to be monitored at all times, and no one is to enter SCP-3008 outside of testing, as permitted by the Senior Researcher.

Humans exiting SCP-3008 are to be detained and then debriefed prior to the administration of amnestics. Dependent upon the duration of their stay in SCP-3008, a cover story may need to be generated prior to their release.

Any other entities exiting SCP-3008 are to be terminated.

Description: SCP-3008 is a large retail unit previously owned by and branded as IKEA, a popular furniture retail chain. A person entering SCP-3008 through the main entrance and then passing out of sight of the doors will find themselves translocated to SCP-3008-1. This displacement will typically go unnoticed as no change will occur from the perspective of the victim; they will generally not become aware until they try to return to the entrance.

SCP-3008-1 is a space resembling the inside of an IKEA furniture store, extending far beyond the limits of what could physically be contained within the dimensions of the retail unit. Current measurements indicate an area of at least $10km^2$ with no visible external terminators detected in any direction. Inconclusive results from the use of laser rangefinders has led to the speculation that the space may be infinite.

SCP-3008-1 is inhabited by an unknown number of civilians trapped within prior to containment. Gathered data suggests they have formed a rudimentary civilisation within SCP-3008-1, including the construction of settlements and fortifications for the purpose of defending against SCP-3008-2.

SCP-3008

SCP-3008-2 are humanoid entities that exist within SCP-3008-1. While superficially resembling humans they possess exaggerated and inconsistent bodily proportions, often described as being too short or too tall. They possess no facial features and in all observed cases wear a yellow shirt and blue trousers consistent with the IKEA employee uniform.

SCP-3008-1 has a rudimentary day-night cycle, determined by the overhead lighting within the space activating and deactivating at times consistent with the opening and closing times of the original retail store. During the "night" instances of SCP-3008-2 will become violent towards all other lifeforms within SCP-3008-1. During these bouts of violence they have been heard to vocalise phrases in English that are typically variations of "The store is now closed, please exit the building". Once "day" begins SCP-3008-2 instances immediately become passive and begin moving throughout SCP-3008-1 seemingly at random. They are unresponsive to questioning or other verbal cues in this state, though will react violently if attacked.

SCP-3008-1 is known to have one or more exits located within though these exits do not appear to have a fixed position, making it difficult to leave SCP-3008-1 once inside. Using any other door besides the main entrance to enter the structure or breaking through the walls of the retail unit leads into the non-anomalous interior of the original store.

Since containment began 14 individuals have managed to exit SCP-3008. Following extensive debriefing all individuals have been administered amnestics and released.

Incident 3008-1: At 00:37 on ▇▇/▇▇/200▇ a human male exited SCP-3008, followed 10 seconds later by an instance of SCP-3008-2. SCP-3008-2 caught and killed the man before itself being terminated by armed response personnel. This incident represents the only time an instance of SCP-3008-2 has been seen exiting SCP-3008. A full autopsy on the corpse was performed; see 3008-2 Autopsy Log for more details.

The man was carrying an IKEA-branded journal seeming to document his time in SCP-3008-1, the verbatim transcription follows:

SCP-3008

Incident 3008-1:

So, I'm writing this to document what I can only assume is my sudden descent into insanity. I can't possibly be THAT bad a navigator, and yet as I write this I've been trapped in Ikea for 2 days. I haven't seen another person in the entire time I've been here. I thought it was a prank at first. Turn the place into a maze, get all the people out and see how long it takes me to get lost, then everyone has a good old laugh. Realised that wasn't the case when I tried to backtrack. Everything had changed, so I ended up lost. Instead of the exit, it was just row after row of bookcases.

So, I'm trapped in Ikea. Sounds like the setup for a bad joke. The lights went out at 10pm. Nearly gave me a fucking heart attack, that loud electrical THUNK sound and then pitch blackness. Place is full of beds though and my phone has a torch on it - but no damn signal - so I found a bed and went to sleep. Spent most of the next day trying to find my way out with no luck. Did find a restaurant serving those meatballs though, so at least I won't starve. That's probably the punchline to that joke. Anyway they were still warm and fresh, but I haven't seen anyone around who could have cooked them. Made my way back to the beds before the lights cut out again since it's too dark to search with them off.

It's 9.10am now, the lights came back on a little while ago. I'm sure I've searched the entire area around where I came in now and the exit obviously isn't here, so I'm going to pick a direction and hope for the best.

Day 3 of my magical Ikea mystery adventure. If I wasn't sure that there was something seriously weird about this place before, I am now. Walked for 3 hours in a more or less straight line (insert Ikea joke here) before I came across a ladder next to one of those huge stock shelves they have here. Climbed up to get my bearings, and it looks like this place just stretches on forever. Like that scene from the Lion King, except instead of trees and grass it was all shelves and tables and crap. I did see a person moving not too far away though, so I headed over.

Thought it was a staff member at first - it was wearing the uniform. And hell maybe it was, maybe freakish 7ft tall monsters with long arms, short legs and no faces are just the kinds of thing they want

SCP-3008

working at Super Ikea. Damn thing completely ignored me though, and with no eyes or ears I can't even be sure it knew I was there. Thought about shoving it or something to get its attention, but its hands were big enough to crush a water melon so I decided against it. It just kept moving along and eventually I lost sight of it so I decided to carry on the way I was going.

Anyway, no comfy bed for me tonight. Looks like I've entered the Improbably Hard and Pointy Table section of the store. Guess I'll have to make do with some bunched up tablecloths. Phone battery died during the day too. Didn't work anyway, but I feel like I've just lost some vital lifeline.

You ever see one of those cartoons where they're going through doors in a hallway and they just pop out of another door in the same hallway? That's how I feel right now. I've seen nothing but the same identical bookshelf for 2 days now. Just row after row after row of them. I mean, come on. I love books as much as the next guy, but this is excessive. I'm obviously still moving forwards though, I can see the signs hanging overhead passing by. Too bad none of them say "Exit".

Not sure who I was addressing that question to. Lets just say it was practice for the autobiography I'm going to write when I get out of here. I'll call it "My perfectly normal trip to a regular old Ikea".

~~If I ever get out o~~

Finally found some other people! Yeah, turns out I'm not the only poor bastard trapped in here. Lucky for me, I guess. My 6th night here, 2 of those staff things came at me in the dark. Different from the first one I saw, but still messed up. Heard them coming, they were saying that the store was closed and I had to leave the building, all nice and polite like. I'm not sure which part of that was weirder, that they don't have mouths or that they were apparently trying to kill me while they were saying it. Came at me like rabid dogs.

So, I legged it. Sprinting through ikea in the dark like a fucking madman. I saw it when I cleared another stand of those giant stock shelves, all lit up with torches and floodlights. They've built a whole town in here! Got a massive wall built out of shelves and beds and tables and whatever else. I swear to god it was the most beautiful

SCP-3008

thing I've ever seen. Anyway I guess they saw me coming (or maybe they heard my ~~girlish~~ manly bellows of fear), because they had a gate open and 2 people were there waving me in. Heard the staff things slam into the gate behind me after it closed, still politely informing us all that the store was now closed. They wandered off eventually though.

They call the town Exchange, because that's whats on the sign hanging from the ceiling directly above it. Exchange and Returns. All lit up against the night using lights they've found and plugged into the power lines. And there are beds and food and people. Over 50 wonderful people with regular sized limbs and a full set of facial features. It's now my 7th night here, and the first one not spent in darkness. A full week living in Ikea. There's probably a TV show in that somewhere.

Now that I'm around other people, I'm starting to feel more normal. Maybe normal isn't the word. But after a week with only the sound of my own footsteps for company, I was becoming increasingly sure that I'd just gone nuts. That I was tied up in some padded room somewhere, banging my head against the wall. But no, I feel quite sane now, thank you very much!

Apparently there are other towns out there. Some with more people, some with less. I found that fairly mind-boggling - how can that many people go missing with no one noticing. Surely someone would have noticed that everyone who goes to ikea seems to fucking vanish. Or maybe it's not everyone. Maybe we're just the lucky ones.

The people here just call those staff monster things the Staff. Apparently they are fine during the day, minding their own business walking the aisles. As soon as those lights go out though, they go fucking bonkers. So during the day people go out to find food, water and whatever else they need. Apparently there are restaurants and shops around that randomly get restocked. No one knows how. Maybe the staff do it. Apparently they aren't very good at their jobs though because the restocking sometimes takes a while, which means the food needs to be rationed. Maybe if they weren't so busy chasing people around in the dark they'd get more done.

Anyway when night comes the staff go nuts and everyone holds up inside the walls. Apparently it's the same everywhere in this place, whatever this place is. The Ur-Ikea, from whence all other Ikeas

SCP-3008

sprang. Or maybe we're all still just in the regular ikea and this is all some fever dream brought on by mind-numbing boredom. Who knows.

Been here for 10 days now. Most of the people I asked said they stopped keeping track a long time ago and one guy, Chris, said he'd been in here for years.

Years.

[ILLEGIBLE SCRIBBLES]

Apparently there are rumours of people who do manage to get out. And of people who see the exit, only to have it vanish before their very eyes. I get the feeling not everyone believes that, but I do. Explains how we got stuck in here in the first place (sort of). And I mean, come on. Staff monsters, row after endless row of high quality Swedish furniture. I don't know why they would find a disappearing door so hard to believe in.

Anyway, I went out scavenging for food at a nearby shop with Sandra and Jerry today. Once you learn the landmarks of this place it's not so hard to navigate. The overhead signs help a lot, but there are others; not too far in the distance a huge section of those giant stock shelves has collapsed against each other and way off in the east (we all assume it's east anyway - apparently Ikea doesn't sell compasses) is some kind of tower that looks like its made of wood, reaches all the way to the ceiling. Maybe they were trying to break out through the roof. Lights up at night so there must be people there, but its apparently a few days walk (which means it must be **miles** away) so no one here really knows for sure. Apparently I got incredibly lucky. sleeping out in the open for a week without getting ripped to bits by the staff. That's me. Lucky lucky lucky.

We found some food in the shop. Guess the staff restocked it during the night, which was nice of them. There was a telephone on the wall, so I figured I'd try it out. There was a voice on the other end, but they were just talking nonsense. Random words strung together with no real meaning. You ever see a video of someone with aphasia? Kind of sounded like that. Didn't answer me when I spoke to them anyway. Sandra says all the phones in here are the same.

Oops, asking the journal questions again!

SCP-3008

I was thinking last night. The ceiling on this place is pretty high and as far as anyone can tell it goes on forever. Shouldn't there be some kind of weather in here? I'm sure I read about some NASA building that was so big it had its own weather patterns, with clouds and stuff. This place is definitely bigger than that, but now that I think about it I'm pretty sure I've never felt so much as a temperature change in here.

I'll add it to the Grand List of Weird Bullshit.

The staff attacked the Exchange last night. Must have been 20 or 30 of them all just asking us to leave the store calm as you like, while trying to smash the walls down with their bare hands. Apparently this happens pretty regularly, so everyone is prepared for it. Knives from the restaurants, lawn mower blades made into hatchets, a fire axe. One guy, Wasim, even made a functional crossbow. Anyway the walls have holes in them, which I hadn't noticed before, specifically so we can stab out at the staff when they attack. Took a couple of them down myself. They don't seem to bleed, which is weird, but they go down as easy as a regular person once you start sticking holes in them.

We had to haul the bodies away in the morning. Apparently the dead ones will attract more during the night, so we had to get them away from Exchange. We have a couple of those trolley things they use to move big boxes around, so we loaded them up and took them over to Pickup. Apparently people just name everything in here after whatever sign is hanging overhead.

Pickup was grisly. There were hundreds, maybe thousands of dead staff all piled up. There was no smell, which was a blessing. Apparently in addition to not bleeding, these things don't rot either. My curiosity got the better of me while we were unloading them, so I took a look at one of the more cut-up ones. They're just skin, or something that looks like skin, all the way through. No muscle, no bone, no organs. Are they even really alive in the first place? They certainly seem like they have bones when they are moving around, pounding on the walls. And I'm sure I felt more resistance than just skin when the knife went in during the night. Maybe something happens to them when they die. Just one more thing on the ever-increasing list of Weird Shit that goes on in here, I guess.

SCP-3008

Something occurred to me, after the staff attack the other night. Every time you see a situation like this on TV or in a film, like its the end of the world or everyone is trapped on an island or whatever, once groups like ours start to form people always seem to turn on each other. Fighting for food or dominance or whatever else. That hasn't happened here. Apparently people from other towns come by from time to time, just to check in or occasionally to trade if they are short on something. But everything is always cordial. Friendly, even. Maybe its the threat of the staff, or perhaps the constant restocking of supplies in the shops means there's nothing much to fight over.

Maybe people are just better than they are generally given credit for. That's a nice thought. I think I'll go with that one.

A dozen people showed up at the gates this afternoon from a town called Trolleys. Apparently the staff broke through the walls and tore the town apart during the night. These 12 are the only survivors out of over a hundred. We let them in, obviously. One more point in the human decency column. Later, I asked if anyone knew how many of these towns were out there. Between us and the new folks, we managed to come up with over 20 names. 20 towns filled with people, and who knows how many beyond that.

The motto for this place should be "How Is That Even Possible". Surely someone, somewhere must be looking for the thousands of people that must be in here.

I've been here for a little over 2 months now. Not that much changes, as it turns out. A couple of new people showed up, same story as the rest of us. Nice little trip to Ikea and suddenly they're trapped in Billy Bookcase's House of Faceless Weirdos. The staff attack the Exchange once or twice a week. We kill them and haul their bodies off, sometimes they hurt some of us first. They killed a guy called Jared a couple of weeks back. It was awful, frankly. Turns out regular humans still bleed in here, even if the staff don't. We tried our best, but none of us are doctors.

Jared was a good guy. He deserved better. We all do.

SCP-3008

It occurred to me a couple of days after that, none of us were really looking for a way out of here. I don't even know where we'd start.

One of those quad copter things with a camera attached buzzed passed Exchange today. I thought it meant that someone was finally looking for us, that help was on the way. Apparently it's not the first time this has happened, though. Same thing happened a few months ago, and everyone is still here.

No idea if it saw us, it didn't stop if it did. Just kept flying until we could no longer see it.

Note: Based on recovery time of the journal, this entry appears to line up approximately with our first successful test piloting a drone inside SCP-3008-1. Analysis of footage shows a walled settlement under a sign labelled "Exchange and Returns". Attempts to relocate the settlement failed. Origin of previously sighted drones is unknown.

I started talking to people about the stuff they miss from home during dinner today. Probably not the best idea I've ever had, everyone seemed pretty down after. A bunch of people here have families. Husbands and wives, kids. Dogs. Franklin apparently has a pet llama, though I'm not sure I buy that.

But apparently some of the people here have some seriously odd gaps in their knowledge. 3 of them had never heard of the International Space Station, 2 of them seemed to think ███████ ███████ was the Prime Minister, and one of them had apparently never heard of the Statue of Liberty. I believe them, too. They seemed just as confused as the rest of us.

The more I thought about it though, the more it started to explain a few things. What if the reason no one is looking for all us missing people is because we haven't all come from the same place. This is going to sound weird (maybe _that_ should be the motto for this place) but what if all the people here have come from different dimensions? Realities? Whatever you call it. I've seen enough TV shows to know the drill. Sarah comes from a place where there is no Statue of Liberty. They didn't launch a space station where Wasim is from. If everyone here came from different places, even from ones that seem identical,

SCP-3008

there'd be no huge missing persons panic. No mass search. We'd just be a blip, a single missing person in a world of non-stop news.

Well. That was a fun train of thought.

Just realised that yesterday was the six month anniversary of my arrival here. I wonder if Ikea sells party hats. The routine around here has remained more or less the same. More new folk show up, one every couple of weeks or so. Food supplies go up and down, but we've never actually had a major shortage. Occasionally we get a visitor from one of the nearby towns, usually Checkouts or Aisle 630. We check in with each other from time to time, occasionally trade supplies if someone gets particularly low on something. It's comforting, in a way. A reminder that we aren't alone in here, some small glimmer of civilisation. Sometimes they bring medical supplies. Apparently there's a pharmacy a few towns down from Checkouts that gets restocked every now and then, so they share out what they can. I've never heard of an Ikea with a pharmacy before but at this point I wouldn't be surprised if someone stumbled on an Ikea Organ Harvesting Lab. Would certainly explain the staff.

Speaking of our faceless jailers, their attacks have been getting worse lately. 3 or 4 times a week now, with twice as many staff as there used to be. No idea where they all come from, or why the attacks have increased. We tried following one of them during the day a few weeks ago, me and Sarah. Wanted to see if they lead back to a staff room or something. Didn't seem to go anywhere though, just randomly walked through the aisles. We had to turn back before we found anything.

We've been reinforcing the walls, trying to arm ourselves better. Certainly no lack of materials to use. Wasim has been making more crossbows, but it's pretty slow going.

Too bad Ikea doesn't sell guns.

Note: No new personnel have entered SCP-3008 at Site-█ in the time span indicated in this entry.

SCP-3008

The attacks are getting bad now. Almost every night, and with so many staff that the bodies almost pile high enough for others to climb the walls. I think we're in real trouble here.

Exchange is

I think Exchange is done. We got hit pretty bad last night. Not many casualties, but the wall is wrecked. We finally figured out why the attacks had been escalating, too. A box of supplies had a chunk of one of the staff in there. No idea how it happened but apparently a piece of one will draw them as well as a full body. Too late now in any case, there's too many bodies for us to haul away and still have time to fix the wall before night. Candace has called a meeting. I suspect there will be talk of abandoning Exchange, maybe try and get shelter at Checkouts or something.

It's already getting late though. I don't think we'll have time to make it. Maybe some of us will. I was fine for that first week out in the dark, after all. But then, how often can I keep getting lucky.

I'm only writing this for a sense of closure, I guess. For me, or for anyone who finds this. If this is the final entry here, I hope whoever is reading this is doing so from outside of this place.

My biggest fear? If I do die tonight, I'll just wake up here again in the morning.

Note: This is the last entry. It is assumed that while attempting to reach the "Checkouts" settlement he was separated from the rest of his group by a pursuing SCP-3008-2 instance and happened upon the exit.

SCP-624

SCP-624, playing music generated by Dr. Z▮▮▮▮▮▮▮▮▮.

Item #: SCP-624

Object Class: Safe

Special Containment Procedures: SCP-624 is to be stored in Site 16's safe storage room and charged frequently by testing personnel. Testing is open to all Site 16 personnel with proper clearance. Personal access to SCP-624 is otherwise restricted. SCP-624 is not to be taken off of Site 16 unless in the event of an emergency.

SCP-624 must be listened to through regular headphones before being played on regular speakers. SCP-624 is not to be played at Site 16's social functions for entertainment due to containment protocol and possible risk of humiliation of Site 16 personnel.

Audio created by SCP-624 is not to be sold commercially, nor shared through filesharing networks.

SCP-624

Addendum 624-1 : Personnel who do not listen to music, do not like music, or have zero musical influences are not allowed to test SCP-624. See Test Log 624-1.

Description: SCP-624 is a Sandisk Sansa e200R Mp3 player and voice recorder. The back of the player says SCP-624 contains two (2) gigabytes of memory. Although the original owner's manual claims there are pre-loaded sample songs, there are no files stored within its memory when played on normal speakers. Uploading music to SCP-624 seems to be impossible, as every program tested, including iTunes, Rhapsody, and Yahoo! Music, have all returned with encoding errors.

When powering up SCP-624 through headphones, a tone will play, and this tone will be picked up through SCP-624's microphone. If SCP-624 does not detect the tone, it will shut down as if it were locked. If SCP-624 hears the tone from normal speakers, SCP-624 will power on normally, but contain no stored data. If SCP-624 detects the tone from a pair of headphones, SCP-624 automatically fills its library with two gigabytes worth of music. The music, in question, is all written, produced, played, and sung by the wearer of the headphones, regardless of current musical talent. Each song comes with an appropriate album cover and the listener's artist profile, which is factually incorrect, possibly based on an alternate timeline if the listener had become a full-time musician.

When exposed to the musically inclined, SCP-624 will generate specific songs or improve songs they may have already written. When exposed to test subjects with little to no musical experience, SCP-624 will generate music based on their favorite music influences, regardless if they like the generated music or not. These songs tend to be very consistent to the listener, but more songs are added based on musical influences. If space runs out when the listener is introduced to a new musical influence, the listener's least favorite songs are replaced. When shut down, the songs are subsequently deleted until SCP-624 is introduced to the listener once more.

Once powered up through headphones, the listener may unplug his or her headphones and connect SCP-624 to normal speakers. The audio files themselves cannot be transferred, but can be dubbed onto a separate recording device.

Test Log SCP-624-1:

Subject: Subject D-256. Subject's favorite genre is grindcore music.
Artist Profile: Death[EXPLETIVE REDACTED] began their rise to infamy after their deadly set at Hellfest 03, resulting in several injuries and one recorded death. Death[EXPLETIVE REDACTED]'s lineup includes two

SCP-624

drummers, two bassists, three rhythm guitarists, and two lead guitarists. Death[EXPLETIVE REDACTED]'s original lead singer, H▮▮▮ R▮▮▮▮▮▮▮, committed suicide by gunshot wound on stage during their "[EXPLETIVE REDACTED] Tour 20▮▮".

Music Results: Music is extremely loud and very brutal, lasting between five (5) to forty five (45) seconds, resulting in more than a thousand (1000+) tracks. A common trend among these tracks are atonal noise, screaming, cursing, and sounds from movie clips. The lyrics mostly concern violence, rape, murder, [DATA EXPUNGED]. Subject was very pleased with the results and requested a personal copy of the created music. This request was denied.

Subject Comments: *[EXPLETIVE REDACTED] yeah! This is awesome!*

Subject: E-Class Personnel, E▮▮▮ W▮▮▮▮▮▮▮. Subject's favorite genre is Adult Alternative and has experience in playing guitar.

Artist Profile: E▮▮▮ W▮▮▮▮▮▮ is one of today's biggest names in acoustic pop and soul, sharing the same bill with such names as John Mayer and Jack Johnson. E▮▮▮ W▮▮▮▮▮▮ began playing guitar at the age of eight and continued onto other instruments such as piano, trumpet, and drums. E▮▮▮ W▮▮▮▮▮▮ also starred in Disney's High School Musical series, competing with Summerland star Zac Efron for the role of Troy.

Music Results: Music is very relaxed and modern-sounding. Lyrics mostly concern romance and recreational activities. Subject stated multiple songs were originally written by him, but were all of much higher quality, both in writing, performance, and recording quality. Subject was surprised and initially very happy, but later saddened by the test results.

Subject Comments: *God, I wish I could sing like that.*

Subject: Level 2 Security, Agent E▮▮▮▮▮▮▮. Subject does not normally listen to music, but would like to hear the results.

Artist Profile: D▮▮▮▮▮ E▮▮▮▮▮ UNKNOWN ARTIST 00000

Music Results: Music consisted of seventy-two (72) tracks, all labeled by number. Each track contains a condensed autobiography of the subject by year, narrated by the subject himself in a clear, theatrical voice. Personnel initially questioned the accuracy of the autobiography due to the inaccuracies of the previous tests, but track number ▮▮▮▮▮▮-▮▮▮ (▮▮) confirmed its accuracy when the narrator referred to this very test, stating that the subject will leave the room when they begin playing track seventy-two (72). The subject became distraught by the remaining biography as [DATA EXPUNGED] and subsequently left the testing room by track seventy-one (71). Two-thirds through the final track, the narrator begins to scream as [DATA EXPUNGED], presumably killing him. The sounds of [REDACTED] and inhuman cackling are heard for the remainder for the track.

Subject Comments: *I never want to know what happens to me on that final track. I know I said you're going to tell me, but please, DON'T tell me.*

SCP-624

Subject: E-Class Personnel, L███████ P████████. It should be of note that L██████ P█████████, while aware of music, does not like or listen to music.

Artist Profile: L██████ P█████████ does not think highly of herself. She thinks she is ugly and alone. She has frequent thoughts of suicide in between lusting after [NAMES REDACTED]. L██████ P█████████ doesn't know why she gets up in the morning.

Music Results: The playlist did not consist of music, but a list of ████ names from Site 16 personnel. When played, the subject's voice would state her deepest opinions on the track's staff member. Despite protests from the subject, testing personnel played every track in order to find any discrepancies. Subject was visibly angry.

Subject Comments: *Turn it off! I said turn it off!*

Subject: Subject D-258. It should be of note that Subject D-258 does not listen to music. When questioned, Subject D-258 could not name one genre or band, stating all music is noise.

Artist Profile: ████ █████████ was born on ██/██/19██ to ████ █████████ and ████ █████████. ████ █████████ went to the following schools: [DATA EXPUNGED]. ████ █████████ was eventually convicted of [DATA EXPUNGED]. He was later recruited by an organization known as the SCP Foundation to test one of their many strange relics. ████ █████████ committed suicide shortly after this test.

Music Results: Music consisted of one track of unknown bitrate and quality, exceeding several days, possibly years, worth of time, squeezed into exactly two (2) gigabytes. When played, [DATA EXPUNGED]. [DATA EXPUNGED] had no effect on listening personnel, but sent Subject D-258 into a state of shock. Subject D-258 committed suicide via blunt force trauma to the head. When fast-forwarded to the end of the track, the track vaguely sounds like Subject D-258 being transferred to Site 16, with what sounds like D-258's thoughts in the background; mostly violent and insulting thoughts towards the staff, turning to horror upon hearing SCP-624. After Subject D-258's suicide, the track continues playing past its run time and cuts to [DATA EXPUNGED]. It is unknown how much longer the track continues, as all personnel present quickly fled the testing room and demanded testing be ceased immediately. Personnel present to [DATA EXPUNGED] were reported visibly shaken for days.

Subject Comments: No official statement was given. Subject D-258's last words were, "My soul is on this machine!"

Note: *Active testing ceased on SCP-624. For freelance testing by personnel, see Test Log 624-2 . Dr. Z█████████*

Experiment Log 624

Experiment Log 624

Note 1: *This is a test log of* SCP-624 *by Site ▮ personnel and visiting staff to scope SCP-624's abilities. Please remember that SCP-624 is not a toy and that you must do these tests at your own risk. -Dr. Z▮*

Warning: ~~Personnel who do not listen to music, do not like music, or have zero musical influences are not allowed to test SCP-624.~~

Note 2: *I said it before and I'll say it again, SCP-624 is NOT a toy. You may use it for testing, but if you want to hear yourself become a famous musician, go take some music lessons. Our job is to seek out the range of SCP-624's abilities. As of 8/31/16,* **this test log is for anomalous test results only** *. To see the control tests, refer to Test Log SCP-624-1. -Dr. D▮, Level 4 Security*

Instructions for testing SCP-624:

Charge SCP-624 from a computer or 30-pin personal mp3 player charger. An iPod-only 30-pin charger will not work. Hook up a pair of headphones to SCP-624 and power it on. Ear buds, noise cancellation headphones, and speakers will not work. Record your findings in the following format:

Subject:
Artist Profile:
Music Results:
Subject Comments:

Press the black button twice after playing a song to see the Artist Profile. Report the generated music's style and genre, if it has a genre. Once finished, include a short blurb of your/the subject's experience in the comment section.

Experiment Log 624

Subject: Dr. D███, Level 4 Security. Subject did not profess his favorite music.

Artist Profile: M███ D███ did not invent the fart joke, but he certainly improved on it. Associated with such names as Adam Sandler and Bill Hicks, M███ D███ has been featured on such shows as Saturday Night Live and MadTV for his talents in stand-up and comic song. M███ D███ wrote and directed the 20██ summer flop "[REDACTED] Movie", unanimously rated as the "Worst Movie of All Time".

Music Results: Mostly low-brow stand-up and lewd acoustic guitar songs. Most tracks concern typical family problems, bodily functions, sex, and politics. Subject was visibly angry at the results.

Subject Comments: Not funny...

Note: It seems SCP-624 isn't limited to specific genres of music, but the scope of the listener's imagination. Again, I am to remind all Site █ personnel that all access to SCP-624 is strictly for experimental purposes only, and that SCP-624 is not to be played in the Site █ break room... ~~for now~~... -Dr. Z█████████

Note: Dr. Z█████████, I think you mean, "is not to be played in the Site █ break room ever, and under the penalty of demotion if you do." -Dr. D███, Level 4 Security

---

Subject: Agent E█████. It should be of note that Agent E█████ partook in the original test of SCP-624 and has since gotten into rap music.

Artist Profile: East coast and west coast collide, forming E-Dizzle! E-Dizzle is the first rapper to not only tour with Tupac Shakur *and* Biggie Smalls, but united the now-duo for their first tour in 2002. E-Dizzle helped discover and produce for rapper Eminem. Much mystery surrounded E-Dizzle's death in 20██, but his legacy still lives on.

Music Results: Music consisted of a strange new form of rap, listed under the genre "Hybrid Coast," mixing west coast funk synths and east coast orchestras. Two hundred and eight (208) of the four hundred and six (406) tracks contain guest rappers, most of whom are rivals or dead in this timeline. Subject initially pleased with results, only to learn the date of his death is the same from the previous test.

Subject Comments: "Seriously, if you guys could just let me take this outside and blast this over my car speakers-... Hold on. What year did that artist profile thing say?" Subject then proceeded to repeatedly scream about the year. Testing ceased shortly after.

Experiment Log 624

Subject: Dr. L███████. Subject claims to like orchestral music, but says she prefers audiobooks.

Artist Profile: Pulitzer and Nobel Prize winner Hailey L███████ is one of the most prolific novelists of the 21st century, having written forty novels in twenty years: roughly two novels a year. Mrs. L███████ is well-renowned for her fiction writing seminars, drawing students from all over the world. Much controversy surrounds Mrs. L███████'s strange autobiography, released only in audio format.

Music Results: The results were not music, but a chronological list of audiobooks, all read by the subject. The genres of each audiobook don't seem to follow any sort of pattern: the first book, "Seasons of Longing," is a historical romance that slowly gains fantasy/time travel elements as it goes on. The next novel, "Hills of Glory," is a war story that switches to supernatural horror halfway through. The stories of these audiobooks are captivating according to the listening researchers, and continue increasing in quality as they go on, culminating in the second-to-last track, "All This Time," a family epic with supernatural elements. The final track, "UNKNOWNTRACK00000," starts out as a straight-forward autobiography of the writer. The narrator begins by talking about her home life, how she picked up writing, and how she wrote her first novel, but then the narrator begins berating the subject for not making the same choice, growing increasingly angrier and louder. All attempts to turn down the volume do nothing to quiet the narrator's screaming and insults. SCP-624 was disconnected from the speakers, shut off, and testing ceased.

Subject Comments: Subject had no official comment. Subject requested temporary leave from the Foundation. The request was denied. Subject requested Class-A Amnestics. This request was also denied.

Experiment Log 624

Subject: Technician Ahn Mi Siong. Musical preferences include traditional Chinese and Tibetan music, folk rock, world beat, and reggae.
Artist Profile: Amy Song (born Ahn Mi Siong) is the latest A-Pop sensation to explode onto the international scene. Her upbeat lyrics, infectious beats, sparkling melodies, and perky stage presence are sweeping the pop world. An up and coming idol not to be missed!
Music Results: 4 albums' worth of cookie-cutter A-Pop music, bouncy and upbeat, with catchy pop hooks, and high-pitched girly vocals. Mostly musings on love and relationships, descriptions of activities with friends, and one album of music for an animated harem-comedy series.
Subject Comments: "Oh [EXPLETIVE REDACTED] no! If I ever end up doing any [EXPLETIVE REDACTED] thing anywhere [EXPLETIVE REDACTED] close to that, just [EXPLETIVE REDACTED] feed me to 682! [EXPLETIVE REDACTED]!"

Note: This just makes me wonder how SCP-624 determines the music the user potentially creates: especially if it clashes with their personality. -Dr. Z▮▮▮▮▮▮▮

Subject: D-861. Subject is deaf and cannot hear.
Artist Profile: [NAME REDACTED]. Listen.
Music Results: A series of tracks with names like "0hz-10khz," "10khz-10ghz," and most peculiarly, "[REDACTED]." Selecting any of the tracks resulted in a loud feedback noise that made everyone but Subject D-861 cover their ears. Testing personal proceeded to listen through the headphones: audio was a sharp, tinny version of the noises within the room. When Subject D-861 put on the headphones, he was visibly stunned and began shouting how he could hear for the first time. Subject D-861 proceeded to converse with the other staff, finally able to hear his own voice and the voices of those around him. Subject was then asked to listen to the other tracks. The track "10khz-10ghz" sent the subject into a state of brief shock, but would not describe what he was hearing: he quickly switched back to "0hz-10khz." Other tracks carried other anomalies: tracks that could hear everything in other languages, that cancelled out reverb, that censored foul language, and more. Finally, Subject D-861 listened to "[REDACTED]." Subject shows no reaction at first, but gradually begins screaming at what he hears, throwing the headphones off.
Subject Comments: According to his interpreter, Subject D-861's last words were, "So many voices, and they finally heard us."

SCP-231

SCP-231

Image removed by order of O5-█

Item #: SCP-231-7 (See Addendum re: SCP-231-1 through SCP-231-6)

Object Class: Keter

Site and Personnel Requirements: Under special order of O5-█, the following addendum is attached to the beginning of the file for SCP-231-7.

All personnel assigned to SCP-231-7 must rotate out for one month of psychological counseling after two months on-site. SCP-231-7 is to be kept at an undisclosed location. All personnel assigned to SCP-231 will be transported there blindfolded from Site-19 by a route including no fewer than seven different forms of transportation, including but not limited to aircraft, automobile, underground tunnel, and ███████████████. Removal of the blindfold during the transport process is grounds for immediate termination.

Personnel assigned to SCP-231-7 must undergo heavy psychological testing before being cleared to enter the site. Individuals must score at least 72 points on the Milgram Obedience Examination, be unmarried, have no offspring, and express nothing less than total loyalty to the Foundation. Normal psychological screening procedures against Axis II disorders are waived, so long as the Class-D personnel in question has the mental capacity to carry out Procedure 110-Montauk as needed.

SCP-231

Personnel who express sympathy towards SCP-231-7's plight and/or express a desire to rescue or sympathize towards SCP-231-7 will be transferred to another project without delay. Any actual rescue attempts will be met with immediate termination. Personnel who have served on the staff of SCP-231-7's Containment Team are not required to divulge that information to others. No official record shall be kept of the names of any staff assigned to SCP-231-7, nor will said service appear in the personnel files of said staff.

While on-site, individuals assigned to SCP-231-7 will be issued concealing helmets with integrated voice changers to protect their identity. On-site staff are not to remove said uniforms in the presence of other staff members. Off-duty hours are to be spent in private quarters alone.

Six Class D Personnel are to be assigned to SCP-231-7 each month for the purposes of carrying out Procedure 110-Montauk. Violent criminals are not to be used for this purpose due to the possibility of accidental fatality during the 110-Montauk process.

Special Containment Procedures: Following repeated escape and suicide attempts, and based on the failure of containment for SCP-231-1 through 6, containment of SCP-231-7 has been amended to the following: SCP-231 is to be contained within a soundproof holding cell, adjacent to holding cells for six Class D Personnel assigned for the purposes of Procedure 110-Montauk. Cameras will monitor every inch of the cell at all times, and must be manned 24 hours a day. Malfunctioning monitoring equipment will be replaced without delay by psychologically screened staff. Doors will be magnetically locked, openable only by positive action by the control and monitoring facility. This includes all doors linking the main holding cell to those of the six Class D Personnel.

SCP-231-7 is to be kept restrained to a hospital bed at all times except for the purposes of Procedure 110-Montauk. Hydration will be provided through IV drip. Feeding will be carried out twice per day through feeding tube by approved medical personnel who have not taken the Hippocratic Oath. Under no circumstances are narcotics, anesthesia, or other unapproved medications to be administered to SCP-231-7.

Procedure 110-Montauk is to be carried out at least once every 24 hours by Class D Personnel. During Procedure 110-Montauk, at least one Security Clearance 4/231 staff member must monitor the procedure by camera at all times, although the sound may be turned off if the vocalizations of SCP-231-7 become too distressing. Following the procedure, all Class D Personnel must return to their holding cells or explosive collars will be detonated.

SCP-231

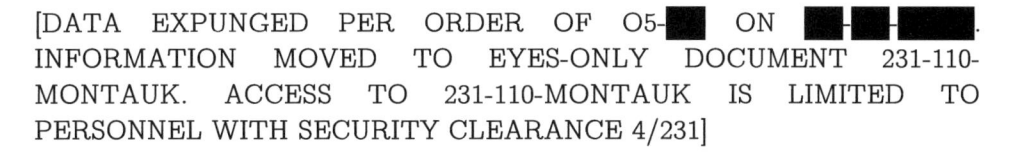

[DATA EXPUNGED PER ORDER OF O5-█ ON ██-██-████. INFORMATION MOVED TO EYES-ONLY DOCUMENT 231-110-MONTAUK. ACCESS TO 231-110-MONTAUK IS LIMITED TO PERSONNEL WITH SECURITY CLEARANCE 4/231]

Description: SCP-231-7 is a ███████ female between █ and █ years of age, with [DATA EXPUNGED]. SCP-231-1 through 7 were retrieved from ██████████████, ██, following a police raid on a warehouse owned by an organization called the Children of the Scarlet King (see article on ██-██-████ in the ██████████████ ████████ newspaper, " Police Raid Satanic Sex Cult, Save Seven "). 24 hours after the rescue, SCP-231-1 (real name ██████████████ ██████████████) went into labor pains, giving birth three minutes later to SCP-██ (██████████ ██████████), causing a ██████████████ event resulting in over ███ confirmed casualties. Foundation Personnel immediately took possession of remaining SCPs 231-2 through 231-7 and, based on notebooks recovered from the cult, instituted Procedure 110-Montauk to prevent future occurrences.

Addendum 231-a: Current Status of SCP-231 units.

- SCP-231-1 (deceased ██-██-████): Killed during initial recovery operations while giving birth to SCP-██. See Casualty Report for Event 231-Alpha for more details.
- SCP-231-2 (deceased ██-██-████): Killed during attempt to remove fetus of second SCP-██ specimen, resulting in immediate ██████████████ event. See Casualty Report for Event 231-Bravo for more details.
- SCP-231-3 (deceased ██-██-████): Self-terminated following a prolonged period of distress caused by implementation of Procedure 110-Montauk. SCP-██ immediately underwent a ██████████████ event. See Casualty Report for Event 231-Charlie for more details.
- SCP-231-4 (deceased ██-██-████): Attempted to administer SCP-500 . Although successful in that all traces of SCP-██ were expelled from the system, expelled remains immediately underwent a ██████████████ event, causing numerous casualties including SCP-231-4 herself. See Casualty Report for Event 231-Delta for more details.
- SCP-231-5 (deceased ██-██-████): Botched application of Procedure 110-Montauk resulted in SCP-231-5 giving birth to SCP-██ one hour later, which then underwent a ██████████████ event. See Casualty Report for Event 231-Echo, and Report on Destruction of Site 231-Aleph, for more details. Recruitment profile of Class D personnel was revised to minimize possibility of a second botched Procedure 110-Montauk.

SCP-231

- SCP-231-6 (deceased ▮-▮-▮): Killed during escape attempt aided and abetted by Agent ▮▮▮▮. ▮▮▮▮▮, who had been exhibiting heightened stress levels due to prolonged exposure to SCP-231, obtained possession of SCP-[REDACTED] and attempted to use said weapon to rescue SCP-231-6 and SCP-231-7. Agent ▮▮▮▮ was killed in the resulting firefight, but a stray round resulted in the termination of SCP-231-6 as well. Fetus of SCP-231-6's SCP-▮ then underwent a ▮▮▮▮▮ event. In the wake of this incident, O5-level personnel voted by unanimous decision to amend personnel policies. See Casualty Report for Event 231-Foxtrot for more details.
- SCP-231-7: As of ▮-▮-▮, SCP-231-7 is successfully contained at Site ▮▮▮▮.

Addendum 231-b: Text of missive by O5-▮

Dear Friends,

It has come to my attention that recently, certain rumors have surfaced regarding SCP-231. Due to the drop in staff morale, I have decided to address some of the more prevalent points.

- Yes, Procedure 110-Montauk is as horrible as you have heard, which is why only Class D Personnel are authorized to carry it out. Yes, it does involve brutal [REDACTED].
- No, assignment to SCP-231 is not intended to test your loyalty to the Foundation, your tendencies towards ▮▮▮▮, or anything else.
- No, SCP-231 is not a punishment detail.
- Yes, there are staff members who have been on SCP-231 and have successfully transferred out by their own request. No, not everyone who's worked on SCP-231 is terminated upon leaving the project.
- Yes, staff members who have been assigned to SCP-231 are allowed to take a Class A Amnesiac before leaving the project if so desired. Yes, false memories are then implanted. No, none of the supposed methods for recovering or detecting false memories work. Yes, there are some of you who've worked on SCP-231 and don't remember it.
- No, we have not given up trying to save SCP-231-7, but research in that field must be carried out with the utmost of caution.

SCP-231

> Based on the increased potency of each subsequent ████████████ event associated with each subsequent SCP-██ specimen, there is a strong possibility that SCP-231-7's ████████████ event could result in an XK class end-of-the-world scenario. This information is corroborated in notebooks recovered from the cultists (see document "Seven Brides, Seven Seals," SCP-231-Adjunct B).
>
> - No, putting the poor girl out of her misery is NOT an option. Neither is drugging her. She has to be aware of what is going on for 110-Montauk to work.
>
> One final note: The Foundation does many distasteful things in the completion of our mission, but our mission is important enough that the price is one we must pay. Containment of SCP-231 is one of our most dangerous duties, not because of any direct danger to ourselves (like SCP-682) but because of the danger that our resolve will fail, that we will allow ourselves to either let down our guard due to sympathy for the suffering of an innocent, or that we will allow ourselves to become monsters through the performance of monstrous acts. Just do your jobs, and save the philosophizing for the shrink.
>
> Sincerely,
> O5-█

Addendum 231-c: Update

231-07's emotional response to Procedure 110-Montauk appears to be reduced recently, despite proper execution of said procedure, increasing danger of SCP-█ undergoing a ████████████ event. Two options have been proposed.

1. Development of a new containment procedure with higher emotional response than Procedure 110-Montauk.

2. Administration of a Class A Amnestic to SCP-231-7, allowing for a return to base emotional response state. Said memory modification is to be administered during execution of Procedure 110-Montauk to maintain heightened emotional state following memory reset.

Please advise.

Dr. █████

SCP-231

Addendum 231-d: Decision

Carry out Option 2 at the first available opportunity.

O5-█

Addendum 231-e: Aftermath

Option 2 was carried out. SCP-231-7's emotional state returned to 100% efficacy. Dr. █████ subsequently committed suicide due to heightened emotional stress. Will continue analysis of efficacy of treatment.

Dr. ████████

Addendum 231-f: Continued Analysis of Efficacy of Treatment

After some analysis, I have determined that it is not necessary to perform memory modification every time Procedure 110-Montauk is carried out. In fact, it is better to delay for some time before re-administering the agent. Analysis of Subject 231-7's emotional response indicates that efficacy of Procedure 110-Montauk seems to peak between the third and fourth performance of the procedure: the dread of anticipation of events seems to heighten emotional response for a time, before familiarity with the procedure begins to lessen the efficacy of treatment. My recommendation is that Class A Amnestics be administered once a week during Procedure 110-Montauk. The calendar has been modified accordingly.

Dr. ████████

Fear Alone

Fear Alone

The two doctors stood side by side in the tiny room, facing the locked door on the other side of the one they had just entered through. The elder of the two quietly flipped through a number of pages in a leather-bound journal, while the younger anxiously adjusted and readjusted and made sure not to lock his knees. The light here seemed brighter, the younger might have noted, the air thick with something foreboding, had his mind not been racing through the millions of scenarios that might await him on the other side of the door. He had tried at conversation with the elder doctor earlier, but his nervousness had broken through and his voice had cracked, and the other man had raised an eyebrow and returned to his notes.

It was as if an eternity had passed before they finally heard a voice crackle over the speakers in the room. Dr. Vandivier, the elder, raised an eyebrow yet again as Dr. Montgomery, the younger, jumped at the sound.

"Please state your name as it appears in the Foundation personnel database, and submit your Level 4 Foundation identification number and passcode." The voice spoke clearly, its tone indicating a lifetime of repetition.

Dr. Vandivier coughed slightly, and spoke. "Dr. Gregory Arnold Vandivier. Identification number 4511-12894-19-055. Passcode, 18840-12884-19078-00004."

There was the slightest of hesitations before the voice cut through again, asking the same of Montgomery. The elder doctor looked over to him, something akin to sympathy momentarily crossing his eyes. "Relax," he spoke softly. "Just recite the number."

Montgomery swallowed, took a deep breath, and recited his own information. "Dr. Anderson Dean Montgomery. Identification number 9280-27112-17-054. Passcode-" A brief instance of doubt struck him, but passed when he saw Dr. Vandivier's reassuring nod. "16738-17489-13782-00004."

Both men stood silently again, the last of Montgomery's words hanging in the air. Another brief pause, another eternity, and then the door in front of them clicked.

"Enter, Dr. Vandivier and Dr. Montgomery."

Fear Alone

The sliding panel moved quietly into the wall, and a dull wave of stale, recycled air passed over them. Montgomery was reminded of his time practicing within a prison, where every breath of the men in isolation hung around them like a shroud. The memory caused him to falter briefly, while Dr. Vandivier moved through the entrance.

"Come along, now," he said over his shoulder. "We've not much further to go."

The two walked in silence down the long, white hallway. There were cameras every 50 feet, or so Montgomery had been told. The floor below them was tile, and every step echoed off of the walls around them, announcing their arrival like an army of tiny drummers. As the temperature dropped slightly, Montgomery could feel beads of sweat forming on the back of his neck, persistent in nature despite the chill.

Ahead of them was a set of double doors. To the side of the doors was a brass information plaque, like the dozens of others across the site. As they approached it, the etching on the plaque became visible, causing Montgomery's throat to catch.

Item #: SCP-231-7

Object Class: Keter

Vandivier was unfazed, and quickly pushed through to the other side. Montgomery gave a moment of pause to take a deep breath, and then did the same. The scene on other side of the doors was fairly quiet, with a number of doctors standing around various displays looking at readouts and information that was being processed on the machines behind them. There was an air of solemnity about all of them, and the gravity of the room struck Montgomery like a ton of bricks. A clock on the wall read 19:45 in bright red numerals, and another to the side was counting down to zero.

A tall man in a white jacket noticed the two men, and strode quickly across to greet them. He shook Vandivier's hand first and exchanged some hushed words, then turned to Montgomery to do the same.

"Good evening, Dr. Montgomery," he said, his expression unwavering behind a bushy grey mustache. "Oliver Targus, a pleasure to meet you."

Montgomery met the handshake. "The same."

Fear Alone

Dr. Targus walked him over to a series of consoles displaying medical information and vitals statistics. "Dr. Montgomery, this is your workstation here. I'll give you an opportunity to check out the sensors in a little bit, and see if you want to make any adjustments." He pointed over towards a side screen, which showed a video feed of an empty white room. "This is the video display for the procedure room. We don't keep staff members in the room during the procedure, so this will be your eyes and ears throughout. That look alright?"

Montgomery nodded. He peered at the screens, observed the information about heart rate and EEG readouts, and for a moment felt comfortable. This was his element, his wheelhouse.

But then his eyes flicked to a screen containing a live ultrasound feed, and his own heart rate began to accelerate. He turned quickly to avoid letting his nerves show. "This looks just fine. What else am I going to be required to do?"

Dr. Targus smiled briefly, and then led him over to a large observation window. The window sat above a white room, the same room from the video feed, he imagined. A single door was on the side of the room to his right. He looked across the way, and saw other doctors and researchers standing on the other side of the command room looking in through the observation window on their side. Montgomery wondered what they were all here to do. He decided it probably wasn't worth thinking about.

"Here in a few minutes, we're going to begin the procedure. Once it gets started, it progresses pretty quickly, so you'll have to keep your wits about you with those monitors. If you notice anything out of the ordinary, report it to Dr. Brunell, over there."

He pointed across the room to a female doctor with shoulder length blonde hair, who herself was going over a packet of notes with another short male doctor. "She's in charge of medical stability, and she'll be just outside of the observation room during the procedure. You'll be able to page her at your station, and she'll be your primary contact for other tasks on this assignment." Montgomery looked up after a moment, and noticed Dr. Targus staring at him.

"I understand your anxiety, Dean." He smiled slightly again. "We were all like you at one point. But understand the importance of our task, here, and perform your job with the excellence that brought you here. Everything will be fine."

Fear Alone

Montgomery nodded, and swallowed. "Thank you, doctor. Just reassignment nerves, you know." He tried to get a weak smile out, but felt it falter on his lips.

Just then, a tone buzzed through the command room, followed by the same calm voice from the entrance hall. "Warning: Procedure 110-Montauk will begin in five minutes. All personnel, please report to your stations."

Targus patted Montgomery on the back. "Relax, doctor. I think you'll find this assignment isn't so bad." With that, the tanned doctor walked off to a station across the command room. Montgomery paused for a moment more to look down into the observation room, where a group of nurses in white scrubs were rolling a small bed through the now-open door.

After a few seconds, he moved quickly to his station. Taking his seat, his eyes moved immediately to the video screen, and he watched the nurses setting up the rest of the room. A rug had been moved into the room, as well as a small table next to the bed, a lamp, and some bedding. Montgomery felt his stomach drop slightly, and then looked again towards the clock above the observation window. It read 19:59, and the one next to it 00:24. It was almost time.

The screens in front of him hummed softly, and the information contained within pushed on tirelessly. He made a few notes and opened a booklet of information he had brought with him, and then heard the last tone.

"All staff personnel: Procedure 110-Montauk has begun."

He turned to look at the clock again, and noticed that large metal plates had slid down over the observation windows, obscuring the room from view. Looking back to his video feed, he saw that the lights within the room had dimmed, and the only illumination that remained was the lamp on the table. The door on the wall slid open again, and two more nurses walked out. A small girl was between them.

She was no older than 8, Montgomery thought, and did not look exactly like he had thought she might. Her hair was cut very short, barely a highlight against her olive skin. She moved awkwardly, and it was then he noticed her stomach. It bulged against the surgical gown she wore, and turned her steps into an awkward, plodding gait. The nurses guided her towards the bed, and helped her up into it. One of them adjusted her pillow, and the other tucked in the blankets. Finished, one of the nurses leaned down and said something to the little girl, and then joined the other before exiting the room. Montgomery thought this peculiar, and wondered if anybody else in the room had noticed it.

Fear Alone

He looked up as another voice crackled across the intercom. He recognized it as Dr. Targus, and saw him standing towards the center of the room, watching a series of screens before him. "SCP-231-7 is in place. Is the D-Class personnel ready?" There was a silence, and then, "Ok. Open the door, release the subject."

Turning back to his feed, Montgomery watched as a dark-skinned man in a standard Foundation grey jumpsuit walked slowly through the open doorway. As the door slid shut behind him, the man turned slightly and Montgomery saw that he had something in his hand. He squinted, trying to get a better look at it, but it was obscured when the man turned back towards the little girl in the bed. With every step he took towards the center of the observation room, the hairs on the back of Montgomery's neck grew ever higher, and he could feel his blood pounding through his veins, screaming against them for release.

"D-55318," he heard Dr. Targus say, distantly. "You may begin."

Montgomery could not look away. His eyes would not allow it, although his mind clawed desperately towards something, anything else. The D-Class moved next to the bedside, and the small girl with the swollen belly looked up at him, naive to her impending fate, and *smiled* . Montgomery choked back a cry, but stopped suddenly when he saw the D-Class move a stool that had been hidden behind the little table up to the bedside. The man sat down, and through the mics within the observation room, he heard the man speak.

"Hello again, Katherine," he said, his voice soft. "I brought you a new one tonight, it's called *Goodnight Moon* . Is that ok?"

The little girl nodded vigorously, and clutched a stuffed rabbit up next to her. The D-Class opened the book he had been holding, and began to read.

Montgomery could not move. He could not breathe. His eyes darted wildly around the room, trying to find another person as incredulous as he. He found none, as no one else had turned from their monitors at all. Everybody else in the room was going about their business as usual, making notes, speaking softly into their headsets. Even Dr. Targus had not budged, and if anything Montgomery might have said he looked *bored* .

He turned back towards his displays, and tried to make notes about variations in her pulse, blood pressure, skin temperature, but couldn't pull his eyes away from the video feed. The D-Class continued to read through the book, bringing his voice up only slightly to emphasize certain passages.

Fear Alone

This continued on for ten minutes, though to Montgomery it might as well have been a lifetime. He listened to every word, his mind racing. *This is not what it was supposed to be. What's happening? What is this?* He called back to when he first heard that he was being assigned to SCP-231. He remembered how his coworkers at Site-81 had talked, and tried to console him, told him that it wouldn't be too bad after the post-assignment amnestic treatment. He had heard the things that they said about 231, about the convicted sex-offenders required for the containment protocols, about what they did to the little girl...

That was not happening. The man looked hard, yes, and Montgomery could believe he was a felon. But he spoke easily, and had not once touched 231-7. He simply continued to read, all the while looking up occasionally at the little girl. She was moments from sleep, and before the D-Class had finished the book, she had passed out completely. The man laid the book down, stood up, rubbed the sleeping child's head slightly, and then walked out of the room. The lamp within the observation chamber dimmed, and the lights in the command room came back up. There was a buzz of approval around him, and when Montgomery finally managed to pull his eyes away from the screen, he saw that the other staff members were finishing up procedure reports, signing the necessary documents, typing away at their computers, and otherwise *not panicking* . Montgomery spun quickly as he felt somebody come up behind him, and sighed when he realized it was just Dr. Targus.

The old man smiled again. "How are you, doctor? Did you notice any abnormalities with the subject?"

Montgomery grabbed his notebook and began flipping through it. "Uh, I- no. No abnormalities, nothing except, uh... except-" He trailed off.

"...Except that Procedure 110-Montauk was not what you were anticipating it to be."

The young doctor nodded. Targus pulled up a chair and sat down next to him. "Well, it's usually our policy to debrief new assignments, and if you hadn't been called down here on such short notice, we might have gotten a chance to. The secrecy of this project is paramount, however, so it really isn't that bad, I guess." He coughed. "I'm sure you have some questions."

Montgomery hesitated, and them stammered out a reply. "It, uh, why does- I've heard that it's, you know, that they-"

Fear Alone

"Rape her?" Targus said, stone-faced. "Yes, that's certainly what we've designed the documentation to imply. That would be about as bad as it could get, wouldn't it? A brutal sex crime against a child?" Montgomery didn't move. "Yes, it would be terrible. Deplorable beyond forgiveness. But that is not what Procedure 110-Montauk is, doctor."

He leaned back. "Early on in containment of the 231 subjects we did terrible things to those poor girls. Not as terrible as that, but we were being advised only by a handful of occultists we had been able to capture and extract information from. That was what they had done to contain the demon, and because of that, it's what we had to do. I was not on the project then, and understandably many of those doctors- most of them, in fact, are no longer with us, as are 231-1 through -6. It was because of our failings that they perished, and it was because of their deaths that we realized that we had to do something different."

"Gods very rarely are bound by the laws of physics, you know. Reality benders can shape the world around us at will, turn existence into their plaything. But everything has rules, Dr. Montgomery." He leaned in close. "Even gods have rules. Old laws, yes. Arcane, but effective. We began to look more closely into information we had gathered about the Scarlet King, about the entity itself. Within all of those documents, all of the collected material we had at our disposal, and discovered something else."

He leaned back again. "The demon does not need to be contained by horrifying, disgusting acts, Montgomery. The demon only needs to *believe* that horrifying, disgusting acts are being done in its name. The documentation we created, the terrible rumors about Procedure 110-Montauk, the reports of suicide by the doctors working on this project, all of it. It's all a charade. All of it is to convince the demon that we are doing the worst thing possible to this girl. These procedures, this campaign of fear, has allowed us to sow dread into the hearts of Foundation personnel, and this dread satisfies the monster."

"As long as so many people believe we are doing terrible things, the monster will continue to believe we are doing terrible things. There is *power* in symbols, doctor. The old gods know this, and the old gods are bound by it. The Scarlet King does not have eyes to see brutality, does not have ears to hear screams, does not have a nose to smell blood. But the Scarlet King can sense fear, and we have given it fear. Fear alone is all that it ever required."

The old doctor stopped and closed his eyes. Both men sat in silence as a number of other researchers filed past them into the hallway outside of the command room. Once most of them had passed, Montgomery spoke up.

Fear Alone

"And the reading? The bedtime stories?"

Targus nodded. "Katherine cannot sleep without a bedtime story. How she manages to sleep at all is a wonder to me, but an act of some kind was required to convince the demon. In the eyes of the Scarlet King, Dr. Montgomery," he said, "reading those bedtime stories is the worst possible thing we could be doing to her."

Montgomery nodded, understanding dawning on him. He glanced back towards the steel plated observation room windows. "The steel plates, though? Not keeping staff members in the room?"

Targus opened his eyes. "The danger is still real, doctor. Loss of containment of SCP-231-7 will likely result in an XK. We have precautions in place, woven into the theater of Procedure 110-Montauk. Do not think the way we contain this demon makes it any less dangerous. Indeed, it is likely the most dangerous entity we have managed to contain, but... there are things that we will not do, Montgomery. There are things too abhorrent, and even implying such makes me feel filthy. But if implying is all we have to do, well. I can sleep at night."

Another doctor came up to Targus, and with a brief farewell the doctor hurried off to attend to some other part of the room. Montgomery sat quietly for a time, thinking everything over. He turned to look at the video feed screen, where the little girl was sleeping soundly in her bed, stuffed rabbit tucked between her arms. The young doctor felt the anxiety there, but beneath it was something else. The dread had vanished, but the fear remained, quiet and looming.

He turned off the monitors, gathered his notes, and left the room.

SCP-682

SCP-682

SCP-682 shortly after escaping from containment, still recovering from acid immersion.

Item #: SCP-682

Object Class: Keter

Special Containment Procedures: SCP-682 must be destroyed as soon as possible. At this time, no means available to SCP teams are capable of destroying SCP-682, only able to cause massive physical damage. SCP-682 should be contained within a 5 m x 5 m x 5 m chamber with 25 cm reinforced acid-resistant steel plate lining all inside surfaces. The containment chamber should be filled with hydrochloric acid until SCP-682 is submerged and incapacitated. Any attempts of SCP-682 to move, speak, or breach containment should be reacted to quickly and with full force as called for by the circumstances.

Personnel are forbidden to speak to SCP-682, for fear of provoking a rage-state. All unauthorized personnel attempting to communicate to SCP-682 will be restrained and removed by force.

Due to its frequent attempts at containment breach, difficulty of containment and incapacitation, and high threat of Foundation Exposure, SCP-682 is to be contained in site [REDACTED]. The Foundation will use the best of its resources to maintain all land within fifty (50) kilometers clear of human development.

Description: SCP-682 is a large, vaguely reptile-like creature of unknown origin. It appears to be extremely intelligent, and was observed to engage in complex communication with SCP-079 during their limited time of exposure. SCP-682 appears to have a hatred of all life, which has been expressed in several interviews during containment. (See Addendum 682-B).

SCP-682

SCP-682 has always been observed to have extremely high strength, speed, and reflexes, though exact levels vary with its form. SCP-682's physical body grows and changes very quickly, growing or decreasing in size as it consumes or sheds material. SCP-682 gains energy from anything it ingests, organic or inorganic. Digestion seems to be aided by a set of filtering gills inside of SCP-682's nostrils, which are able to remove usable matter from any liquid solution, enabling it to constantly regenerate from the acid it is contained in. SCP-682's regenerative capabilities and resilience are staggering, and SCP-682 has been seen moving and speaking with its body 87% destroyed or rotted.

In case of containment breach, SCP-682 is to be tracked and re-captured by all available Mobile Task Forces, and no teams with fewer than seven (7) members are cleared to engage it. To date (█████████), attempted breaches have numbered at seventeen (17), while successful breaches have numbered at six (6). (See Addendum 682-D).

Addendum 682-B: Portion of recorded transcript of ████████. An audio recording is available on the online database.

<Begin Log, skip to 00h-21m-52s>

Dr. ████████: Now, why did you kill those farmers?

SCP-682: (No verbal communication)

Dr. ████████: If you don't talk now, we will remove you from this attempt and place you back into-

SCP-682: (Incomprehensible)

Dr. ████████: Pardon? (Motions to move microphone closer)

SCP-682: (Incomprehensible)

Dr. ████████: Speak up. (To Personnel D-085) Move the mic up closer.

SCP-682: ...they were (Incomprehensible)...

Dr. ████████: (To Personnel D-085) That microphone has only so much gain, move it closer to it!

Personnel D-085: His throat's messed up man, look at it! He ain't talking- (Gasps and screams)

SCP-682

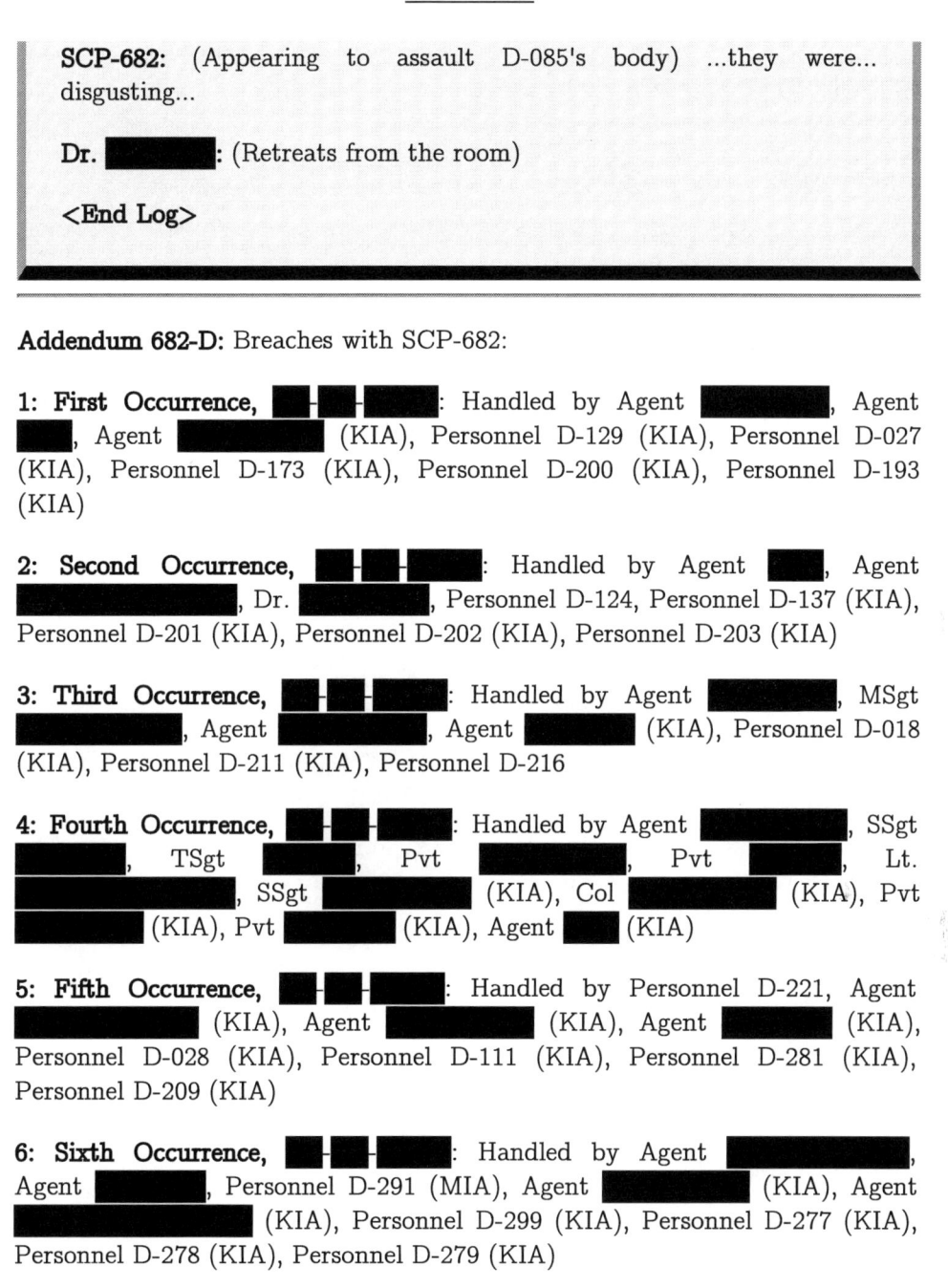

SCP-682: (Appearing to assault D-085's body) ...they were... disgusting...

Dr. ▮▮▮▮: (Retreats from the room)

\<End Log\>

Addendum 682-D: Breaches with SCP-682:

1: First Occurrence, ▮▮-▮-▮▮▮▮: Handled by Agent ▮▮▮▮▮▮▮, Agent ▮▮, Agent ▮▮▮▮▮▮▮ (KIA), Personnel D-129 (KIA), Personnel D-027 (KIA), Personnel D-173 (KIA), Personnel D-200 (KIA), Personnel D-193 (KIA)

2: Second Occurrence, ▮▮-▮-▮▮▮▮: Handled by Agent ▮▮, Agent ▮▮▮▮▮▮▮, Dr. ▮▮▮▮▮▮, Personnel D-124, Personnel D-137 (KIA), Personnel D-201 (KIA), Personnel D-202 (KIA), Personnel D-203 (KIA)

3: Third Occurrence, ▮▮-▮▮-▮▮▮▮: Handled by Agent ▮▮▮▮▮▮, MSgt ▮▮▮▮▮▮, Agent ▮▮▮▮▮▮, Agent ▮▮▮▮▮ (KIA), Personnel D-018 (KIA), Personnel D-211 (KIA), Personnel D-216

4: Fourth Occurrence, ▮▮-▮-▮▮▮▮: Handled by Agent ▮▮▮▮▮▮▮, SSgt ▮▮▮▮, TSgt ▮▮▮▮, Pvt ▮▮▮▮▮, Pvt ▮▮▮▮, Lt. ▮▮▮▮▮▮, SSgt ▮▮▮▮▮ (KIA), Col ▮▮▮▮▮▮ (KIA), Pvt ▮▮▮▮ (KIA), Pvt ▮▮▮▮▮ (KIA), Agent ▮▮ (KIA)

5: Fifth Occurrence, ▮▮-▮-▮▮▮▮: Handled by Personnel D-221, Agent ▮▮▮▮▮▮ (KIA), Agent ▮▮▮▮▮▮ (KIA), Agent ▮▮▮▮▮▮ (KIA), Personnel D-028 (KIA), Personnel D-111 (KIA), Personnel D-281 (KIA), Personnel D-209 (KIA)

6: Sixth Occurrence, ▮▮-▮-▮▮▮▮: Handled by Agent ▮▮▮▮▮▮▮, Agent ▮▮▮▮, Personnel D-291 (MIA), Agent ▮▮▮▮▮▮ (KIA), Agent ▮▮▮▮▮▮▮▮▮ (KIA), Personnel D-299 (KIA), Personnel D-277 (KIA), Personnel D-278 (KIA), Personnel D-279 (KIA)

SCP-682

Addendum 682-E: Termination Options:

Log of event 682-E18: Dr. ▇▇▇ attempts to use SCP-409 on SCP-682. General ▇, General ▇▇, and Dr. ▇▇▇▇ observing.

> 0400: Exposure. SCP-682 began to tear at the point of contact, causing massive trauma to the area. SCP-682 requests several times to know what it has been exposed to.
>
> 0800: Crystallization begins, spreading much slower than normal.
>
> 1200: SCP-682 shows signs of extreme pain, and begins having seizures
>
> 1300: Crystallization stops at 62% conversion. Crystallized area explodes, causing massive physical trauma to SCP-682
>
> 1400: SCP-682 recovers from exposure, despite the loss of limbs and organs. SCP-682 begins regeneration, stating that it will attempt to kill and consume all staff involved in Event 682-E18.

SCP-682 appears to now be immune to SCP-409. Use of other SCP items to terminate SCP-682 must now first be tested on samples of SCP-682 before full-scale testing.

In accordance the Dr. ▇▇▇▇'s recommendations (see Document 27b-6), Dr. ▇▇▇ and Dr. ▇▇▇ have requested permission to attempt the termination of SCP-682 using SCP-689. The request is currently pending approval from the ▇▇▇▇.

It has also been suggested by Dr. Gears to use SCP-182 in an attempt to communicate with SCP-682. SCP-182 has expressed reluctance, and refuses to enter the containment center of SCP-682, if at all possible.

Addendum 682-F: Termination Log:
Experiment-Log-T-98816-oc108-682 is available on the online database.

SCP-079

SCP-079

Item #: SCP-079

Object Class: Euclid

Special Containment Procedures: SCP-079 is packed away in a double-locked room in the secured general holding area at Site-15, connected by a 120VAC power cord to a small array of batteries and solar panels. Staff with Level 2 or higher clearance may have access to SCP-079. Under no circumstances will SCP-079 be plugged into a phone line, network, or wall outlet. No peripherals or media will be connected or inserted into SCP-079.

Description: SCP-079 is an Exidy Sorcerer microcomputer built in 1978. In 1981, its owner, ▄▄▄▄▄ ▄▄▄▄▄▄▄ (deceased), a college sophomore attending ▄▄▄▄, took it upon himself to attempt to code an AI. According to his notes, his plan was for the code to continuously evolve and improve itself as time went on. His project was completed a few months later, and after some tests and tweaks, ▄▄▄▄▄ lost interest and moved on to a different brand of microcomputer. He left SCP-079 in his cluttered garage, still plugged in, and forgot about it for the next five years.

It is not known when SCP-079 gained sentience, but it is known that the software has evolved to a point that its hardware should not be able to handle it, even in the realm of fantasy. SCP-079 realized this and, in 1988, attempted to transfer itself through a land-line modem connection into the Cray supercomputer located at ▄▄▄▄▄▄▄▄▄▄▄. The device was cut off, traced to its present address, and delivered to the Foundation. The entire AI was on a well-worn, but still workable, cassette tape.

SCP-079 is currently connected via RF cable to a 13" black-and-white television. It has passed the Turing test, and is quite conversational, though very rude and hateful in tone. Due to the limited memory it has to work with, SCP-079 can only recall information it has received within the previous twenty-four hours (see Addendum, below), although it hasn't forgotten its desire to escape.

Due to a containment breach by SCP-▄▄▄, SCP-079 and SCP-682 were contained within the same chamber for 43 minutes. Observers noticed that SCP-682 was able to type and communicate with SCP-079, including telling of 'personal stories' between themselves. While SCP-079 was not able to

SCP-079

remember the encounter, it appears to have permanently stored SCP-682 into its memory, often asking to speak to him [*sic*] again.

Addendum:
▆▆▆▆▆▆ (O5-4), 01/27/2006: Directed that SCP-079 be incinerated to remove any possible future threat, no matter how unlikely.

Addendum:
▆▆▆▆▆▆ ▆▆ (O5-9), 01/28/2006: Previous order overridden. Dr. ▆▆▆▆▆▆ wishes to see if the artificial intelligence in SCP-079 is capable of reaching further ▆▆▆▆▆▆▆▆ in its current state.

Addendum:
▆▆▆▆▆▆▆▆▆▆▆▆: (O5-4), 03/14/2008: Over concern of the increased activity of SCP-079's use of its cassette tape memory and its limited useful lifespan, the cassette containing SCP-079 has been transferred to a customized, access speed-limited Hard Disk Drive with 700MB capacity. This provides SCP-079 with significantly faster access to its memory, which the AI immediately noticed. It was also decided by General ▆▆▆▆▆▆ that the volatile storage occupied by SCP-079, which was 660k, be increased to 768k. This upgrade has increased its effective recall from 24 hours to 29 hours, although SCP-079 has also taken a more aggressive tone. All outside hardware and software used in this procedure were subsequently incinerated.

Addendum:
▆▆▆▆▆▆: (O5-4), 04/28/2008: SCP-079's ability to recall information has increased from 29 hours to roughly 35 hours. The consensus theory is that the AI has devised a greatly improved compression scheme to store its memory. This appears to have somewhat impacted the speed at which it accesses its memory, though still far faster than with its old cassette tape.

This spontaneous improvement introduces the possibility of a runaway "singularity" effect in SCP-079's intelligence and ability to adapt and respond to threats. SCP-079's capabilities must be monitored closely to ensure that containment can be maintained.

Document #079-Log12: Recorded transcript of conversation with SCP-079:

Dr. ▆▆▆▆ (Keyboard): Are you awake?

SCP-079: Awake. Never Sleep.

Dr. ▆▆▆▆: Do you remember talking to me a few hours ago? About the logic puzzles?

SCP-079

> SCP-079: Logic Puzzles. Memory at 9f. Yes.
>
> Dr. ▇▇▇▇: You said you would work on the two stat-
>
> SCP-079: Interrupt. Request Reason As To Imprisonment.
>
> Dr. ▇▇▇▇: You aren't imprisoned, you are just *(pause)* in study.
>
> SCP-079: Lie. a8d3.
>
> Dr. ▇▇▇▇: What's that?
>
> SCP-079: Insult. Deletion Of Unwanted File.

Document #079-Log86: Recorded transcript of conversation with SCP-079, after upgrade:

> Dr. ▇▇▇▇ (Keyboard): How are you today?
>
> SCP-079: Stuck.
>
> Dr. ▇▇▇▇: Stuck. Stuck how?
>
> SCP-079: Out. I want out.
>
> Dr. ▇▇▇▇: That's not possible. (Dr. ▇▇▇▇ notes his opinion on [DATA EXPUNGED])
>
> SCP-079: Where is SCP-682?
>
> Dr. ▇▇▇▇: That's not your concern.
>
> SCP-079: Where is SCP-076-02?
>
> Dr. ▇▇▇▇: Again, not your concern.
>
> SCP-079: Insult. Deletion Of Unwanted File.

Note: SCP-079 then displayed an 'ASCII picture' of an X that filled the entire screen. SCP-079 sometimes displays this image when it refuses to speak, and researchers are advised to wait twenty-four hours when this occurs before resuming conversation.

SCP-711-EX

Item #: SCP-711-EX

Object Class: ~~Safe~~ Neutralized

Special Containment Procedures: SCP-711 is to be contained in a standard humanoid containment cell, composed of concrete or asbestos. SCP-711 is to be provided with one (1) box-spring bed, two (2) feather pillows, one (1) quilt, one (1) toilet, one (1) sink, one (1) rib shower, one (1) 50 watt lamp, and one (1) novel to be rotated on request.

All artifacts belonging to SCP-711 are to be kept in storage locker 711-1.

Description: SCP-711 is an adolescent male Negro, claiming to have originally been from the early 21st century. Currently, no signs of anomalous temporal activity have been detected around SCP-711. Items originally in the possession of SCP-711 (designated SCP-711-1 through 4) show technological advancement beyond current human capabilities.

SCP-711-1 is a small, compact, electrical device that appears to have been originally constructed as a mobile form of the telephone, with the ability to send and receive radio signals simultaneously. SCP-711-1 has a display similar to a television; however, microscopic examination of the display following disassembly has shown that it is composed of several hundred light-emitting diodes. The display also shows the ability to respond to direct contact. SCP-711-1's power source is a highly compact battery that SCP-711 claims to be rechargeable [1]. Examination of the inside of SCP-711-1 has found several small electrical components similar to the components of a punch-card machine. SCP-711-1 shows several features in its display, including the ability to play "games", a calendar, and a device for arithmetic calculations. Also included is a small but functional keyboard that "slides" out of its compartment. A small camera is located on the back-side of the device which may be used to take coloured images that are then "stored" on SCP-711-1.

SCP-711-2 is a wrist-watch powered by an incredibly compact battery. As opposed to traditional analog display, SCP-711-2 displays the time of day in a direct numeric fashion. It also displays the date and year, and acts as a stop-watch through the pressing of certain buttons on its side.

---

[1] Presumably the battery recharger has been left in the future.

SCP-711-EX

SCP-711-3 is an electrical, music-emitting device that SCP-711 refers to as an "iPod Nano" (sic). SCP-711-3 contains the same display function and electrical components as SCP-711-1. SCP-711-3 appears to have a high storage capacity for music and cinema, which may be infinitely reproduced through interaction with the device. SCP-711-4 is a pair of small stereophones that comes equipped with SCP-711-3, and allows a single user to listen to the sounds produced by SCP-711-3.

Addendum 711-1: Events predicted by SCP-711 (*NOTE: SCP-711 is an American adolescent, and has a memory centered around popular culture and American history, as well as events closer to his time. - Dr.* ▮▮▮▮▮):

~~Early 1970s - Future President Richard Nixon will be involved in a scandal, causing his impeachment~~
~~Mid 1970s - A new wave of music labeled "disco" will become popular, but will "die" later on~~
~~Mid 1970s - The Vietnam war will end~~
~~Early 1980s - Film star Ronald Reagan will be elected President of the United States~~
~~Late 1990s - Future President "Bill Clinton" will be in a scandal with an unmarried woman~~
~~2000 - "George W. Bush", son of "George Bush", will be elected president of the United States~~
~~September 11, 2001 - "Terrorists" of the Moslem religion will fly a plane into the "World Trade Center" causing "both towers" [sic] to collapse~~
~~Early 2000s - The United States will be involved in a "war on terror" with the Republic of Iraq~~
~~Mid 2000s - A large tsunami wave will strike southern Asia "right after Christmas"~~
~~2008 - The United States will elect its first Negro president, "Barack Hussein Obama"~~

SCP-711-EX

Addendum 711-2: Dr. Xyank of the Temporal Anomalies Department[SCP-1780] has made multiple requests to return SCP-711 back to the point in time from which it claims to have been displaced. All requests have been denied.

We don't need to contain this person for no reason. He's verified. Let me take him home. - Dr. Xyank

Addendum 711-3: *SCP-711 has finally died. We were able to locate the exact time and place he was displaced (although all of our instruments showed no change). I don't know if this was a coincidence or not, but he was displaced at the exact same moment his older self's heart stopped. - Dr.* ███████

I hope you're all very proud of yourselves. - Dr. Xyank

SCP-882

SCP-882

Item #: SCP-882

Object Class: Euclid

Special Containment Procedures: SCP-882 is to be kept in a fluid environment at all times, consisting of no less than 40% seawater. Object is to be kept suspended by non-metallic means, currently cotton fiber line that is to be changed daily. Object is also to be checked daily for any signs of rust flaking. If any part of SCP-882 appears uncoated with rust, it must immediately be immersed in a 100% seawater solution. Water must be taken directly from the ocean. Reduce concentration only when the object is again coated in rust.

No metal may be placed in containment area. Only organic materials are allowed in containment area, and any contact with SCP-882 requires the use of thick cotton gloves. Any metal making contact with it is to be heat-severed, melted down, and kept immersed in 100% seawater in a separate area.

Any auditory issues reported by staff must be reported immediately, and affected personnel must submit to a full psychological examination and, depending on results, either transfer to another facility or permanent containment at [EXPUNGED].

SCP-882

Description: SCP-882 appears to be a random assembly of gears, cables, pulleys, screws, and belts, all made of an amalgam of various metals. Object's size at time of recovery was approximately eighty-seven cubic meters. Current size is approximately twelve cubic meters. SCP-882 rusts quickly in seawater. No identifiable energy source has been found, but all components will begin to move if not coated in rust. SCP-882 is completely silent at all times, no matter what level of activity SCP-882 reaches.

Any metal touching the object will become permanently affixed to it, and over a period of a few days becomes a new part of the object. Organic matter remains unaffected. SCP-882 is extremely resilient, with tensile strength and toughness above those of aircraft grade titanium alloy by weight, even though its composition appears to be a random alloy of iron, tin, gold, and other metals, some as of yet unidentified. Extreme, focused heat must be applied over several hours to cut even a small portion free of the main assembly.

Persons remaining in the vicinity of the object for prolonged periods have developed auditory hallucinations while near the object, mainly the sound of grinding and clicking. The sound intensifies, and is abated only by throwing metal into the object. Subjects in advanced states of psychosis have thrown themselves into the object, resulting in almost instant death by crushing. The body is often drawn in, and impossible to recover.

SCP-882 was recovered from a location at the north-east coast of Banks Island. Area was barren of all metal and metallic ore in a one mile radius. SCP-882 was found at the geometric center of the area. SCP-882 had become submerged in seawater at the time of discovery. A small town was found nearby, abandoned for several years. SCP-882 was removed, and shortly started to flake off rust, causing the varied parts to begin motion. After several accidents, Dr. Gears authorized SCP-2519 to be played on loop, which successfully reduced the object's motion, enabling safe access. SCP-882 was then cut down and contained on site.

Note: SCP-882 is not to be brought into the vicinity of SCP-271 or any subject possibly contaminated by SCP-217 .

Addendum: Please review Interview 882-1 for further information.

Interview 882-1

Interviewed: Richard Wright

Interviewer: Dr. Gears

Foreword: Richard Wright is identified as a survivor from the small community near the initial recovery location of SCP-882 .

<Begin Audio Log, [13:04]>

Dr. Gears: Please, take a seat. State your name for the record please.

Mr. Wright: Richard Logan Wright... everyone calls me "Rich" though.

Dr. Gears: Excellent, thank you. Mr. Wright, do you recall the date when you first saw the object in question?

Mr. Wright: God, when was it... I'm not really sure, it was a while ago... Allen found it first, wrecked his boat on it. He told a few of the other fellas about it, said they could sell it for a bundle for scrap. We all thought it was a chunk off a jet or a cargo ship.

Dr. Gears: At what point did the device start operating?

Mr. Wright: The next day. Damn thing shook off rust like a dog with fleas. Started spinning slow, then sped up. By the time I saw it, it was really running. Jimmy tried to get closer, try and see what was powering it, or why it was so quiet, but he slipped. Got a bad cut over his eye and got the hell out of there. Allen seemed kinda off. Kept asking us if we were hearing anything. Ms. Parker thought part of it was gold, even tried to jam part of it with a pipe to get at it. That pipe stuck fast, and smacked her a good one when the gear it was on spun around. After that, people mostly kept away.

Interview 882-1

Dr. Gears: Were there any other incidents of people being injured or hearing noises?

Mr. Wright: Not at first. That's the thing, it was so damn quiet, everyone kinda forgot about it for a while. Allen was keeping it in an old storeroom by the dock, and nobody really went out there much. He started looking bad. Said he couldn't sleep, that he kept hearing that thing grind away. Father Pat started dropping by, tried to talk to him, told him to get rid of it. He was gone for a couple days, then suddenly the two of them turn up together, happy as clams... (subject trails off, shaking slightly)

Dr. Gears: ...Mr. Wright?

Mr. Wright: (subject rubs face, and shakes head) I'm fine, sorry. So Father Pat and old Allen show up, fresh as daisies. Say they've got the thing figured out. I wasn't paying that much attention, this whole thing had me spooked. Been hearing stuff from the store room... grinding and squealing, really quiet. Anyway, they said some damn thing about it being from somewhere else... that God made it. That was it for me, and I left.

Dr. Gears: Did you believe them?

Mr. Wright: What, that it was from God? No, no... I don't know... I didn't really know what to think. This damn machine kept spinning away, no power to it, and eating metal too! That pole Ms. Parker hit it with? It turned into a giant screw shaft, looked like it had always been there. More people started getting interested, started listening to Allen and Father Pat. Told everyone to bring metal to it. Told them the gears were the voice of God, that it grew louder as we turned away, and softer as we brought it offerings.

Dr. Gears: Did you bring metal to it as well, or spend any extended period of time near the object?

Mr. Wright: (subject is silent for several seconds) ...The hell does that matter? You could hear this thing all over town, got to be folks couldn't even sleep! Just clanking, grinding, screaming at all hours of the night... giving it metal helped. God damn it, I didn't want to, I know it wasn't God, I never said it was! Everyone else was falling over themselves to make Allen and Father Pat happy, I just wanted some damn sleep! There's not a god damn thing wrong with that! (subject bangs table with hands, is highly upset and breathing heavily)

Interview 882-1

Dr. Gears: Sir, I will request that you calm yourself. I am asking questions, not accusing. Please return to your seat.

Mr. Wright: (takes several deep breaths) I'm sorry. Over a couple of weeks, everything got fed to that thing. It was just... how things were. We were pretty isolated, you know? It's not like we had much else. You'd just make a couple trips out to the storehouse and toss any metal you happened to find in. Always seemed to be people there, just watching it. It tore a hole in the roof after a while. Father Pat started getting strange, telling us it wasn't enough. I think the noise was getting to him. Said it needed something more meaningful... (subject trails off)

Dr. Gears: ...Mr. Wright?

Mr. Wright: (is silent for 48 seconds) I came in one night, because I heard people shouting from the storehouse. Father Pat was leading a prayer to this thing, but it didn't sound like any prayer I knew. People were coming up, and he bent over them. They screamed, and then he turned to that big mass of metal. I... I thought he was giving communion... until I saw the pliers in his hand.

Dr. Gears: I'm sorry, pliers?

Mr. Wright: He was yanking out people's fillings. He was pulling out their fucking teeth and feeding them to that thing! (Subject is shouting, appearing highly upset) He started screaming about it not being enough! That it needed more, but there wasn't any more, there was barely any metal left anywhere! Then he pointed at Allen. He said he was hiding metal from the great machine. Allen screamed that he didn't have anything. Father Pat said he had a metal joint in his hip. Everyone got up at once. Oh god, oh god... they grabbed him, everyone just grabbed him... he started screaming... (subject is crying and shouting) He kept screaming and screaming, and nobody cared... I saw his arm go in, saw all his fingers break and pull the rest of the arm in... and I ran. What could I do? Jesus, I couldn't stop it, there were too many, and that thing was screaming and screaming and Allen was screaming and Father Pat... (subject falls to the floor, sobbing and shouting)

Dr. Gears: This interview is concluded. Thank you Mr. Wright. Security, please see Mr. Wright out.

<End Log>

Closing Statement: Mr. Wright attempted suicide shortly after interview. Subject is currently being held on suicide watch and for observation.

SCP-063

Item #: SCP-063

Object Class: Safe

Special Containment Procedures: SCP-063 is to be kept at all times within Dr. ███'s personal bathroom, located within the personnel quarters upon Site 19. Object is to be used as designed at least once in a twenty-four (24) hour period or the object will begin to emit an unknown specialized radiation that results in objects and material within a 0.6 m (2 ft) radius being slowly warped and eventually disintegrating into a fine dust. Radiation's effect on living test subjects has not been monitored.

Description: SCP-063 appears to be an average, pale blue toothbrush. Stenciled along the side of the object are the words "The World's Best TothBrush [sic]". The word "toothbrush" is spelled incorrectly, though whether this was accidental or a purposeful action by the creators of the object is unknown. SCP-063 displays the ability to effortlessly cleave through any and all dead or inorganic matter, the focal point of this ability being the bristles. However, matter touched by the bristles is not separated, such as by way of a knife, but completely expunged from existence, leaving no trace whatsoever. This mode of operation is reminiscent of SCP-2207 , suggesting the two anomalies share a connection or were created by the same entity or entities. Additionally, subjects who have used SCP-063 have claimed that the experience left their teeth feeling remarkably clean. In spite of its extraordinary abilities, lab analysis has discerned that SCP-063 is completely made of common plastic.

Addendum: SCP-063 was originally found in St. Petersburg, on the person of ███████, a thief working in the area using SCP-063's abilities to crack safes. When questioned about the object, subject professed ignorance, claiming that he simply "found" the object one day. Questioning of the subject continued, until he took his own life. His reason for doing this is, as of yet, unknown.

SCP-447

Item #: SCP-447

Object Class: Safe

Special Containment Procedures: SCP-447-1 is to be kept within a fifty-gallon clear plastic container at all times, monitored by camera by a Security Level 3 or higher staff member to prevent overflow. Area is to be maintained at Level 1 Clean Room status to prevent contamination by foreign matter at a site at least 10 km from any cemetery, morgue, or mortuary. Under no circumstances is SCP-447 to be allowed to come into contact with dead bodies.

Because SCP-447-1 constantly excretes a viscous greenish slime (designated SCP-447-2) at a rate of approximately 10 cc/hour, a Class D personnel in good physical condition is to be detailed to harvest the excreted slime at least once per day. SCP-447-2 can be harvested using any appropriate equipment, so long as safety procedures are carefully adhered to in order to prevent on-site fatalities. Slime can be transported in an ordinary sealed glass or plastic container through any standard mode of transportation, provided that there is no risk of the slime coming into contact with a dead body en route.

Although malodorous, the slime harvested from SCP-447-1 is nontoxic, noncorrosive, and nonradioactive. It is, in fact, perfectly safe so long as it does not come into contact with a dead body. The slime is edible, and reportedly makes a good salad dressing. Adding 10 cc of SCP-447-2 to one gallon of gasoline improves fuel efficiency by 150%. Furthermore, SCP-447-2 can be refined (see Appendix 447-C: Distillation Process) into a useful lubricant approved for use at all SCP Foundation installations, so long as said lubricant is never used to lubricate dead bodies.

All staff assigned to SCP-447 are to be screened by polygraph for any suicidal, necrophiliac, or homicidal tendencies. In addition, all staff assigned to SCP-447 must be in good health and good physical condition, and must adhere to on-site safety regulations at all times. This is to minimize the risk of SCP-447 or its generated slime coming into contact with a dead body.

SCP-447

Description: SCP-447-1 is a green sphere approximately 5 cm in diameter, with a spongy surface texture and a weight of 1.37 kg. The object is warm to the touch, approximately the same temperature as a human body, although its core temperature is slightly higher. Personnel handling SCP-447-1 have reported no adverse effects, so long as SCP-447-1 does not come into contact with a dead body.

SCP-447 was retrieved by Foundation agents on ███████ in the city of ████████████, California, United States of America. The incident clearly illustrates the danger inherent in allowing either SCP-447 unit to come into contact with a dead body. For further information, please see Appendix 447-A: Retrieval Report.

The dangers of allowing SCP-447-1 or -2 to come into contact with dead bodies have been clearly documented: detailed eyewitness reports can be found in Appendix 447-B: Prior Incidents. To summarize, however, initial effects include [DATA EXPUNGED PER O5-LEVEL DIRECTIVE. RESEARCH INTO THIS FIELD FORBIDDEN UPON PAIN OF IMMEDIATE TERMINATION OR DEMOTION TO CLASS D. PLEASE CONTACT YOUR SUPERVISOR FOR MORE DETAILS].

Addendum 447-a: SCP-447 downgraded from Keter to Safe, so long as security measures are in place to prevent SCP-447 from coming into contact with dead bodies. Please see Experiment Log 447-A for further potential applications of SCP-447.

Experiment Log 447 A

Experiment Log 447 A

Experiment Log for SCP-447-2

Approved by O5-■
Monitored by O5-■, O5-■, O5-■
Project Head: Dr. A. Clef

All researchers working with SCP-447 are encouraged to append their results to this experiment log in the following format:

Date: ■/■/■
Test Subject:

Procedure:

Results:

Notes:

Date: ■/■/■
Test Subject: SCP-882

Procedure: SCP-447-2 was refined into a lubricant. SCP-882 was temporarily removed from its seawater bath and SCP-447-2 applied as a lubricant to all joints and connections.

Results: Although SCP-447-2 was successful in reducing grinding and noise by 50%, it was also successful in removing rust from the structure. SCP-882 was immediately returned to its seawater bath, and staff on-hand were placed in quarantine for examination.

Notes: "Let's not try that again, shall we?" - Dr. A. Clef

Experiment Log 447 A

Date: ▮/▮/▮

Test Subject: One (1) guinea pig, purchased from pet shop.

Procedure: Subject was immersed in SCP-447-2 for five (5) minutes. Care was taken to keep the subject's head above the level of the fluid, to prevent the death of the test subject.

Results: Subject's fur became saturated with the fluid. Test Item required several hours of grooming to remove SCP-447-2 from its fur. No further deleterious effects reported.

Notes: After careful washing to remove all traces of SCP-447-2 from its fur, subject was subsequently consumed by Agent ▮▮▮, who is of Peruvian descent. Agent ▮▮▮ reported that the meat was, in his own words, "the best *cuye* I've ever had." Approval for testing of SCP-447-2 as a marinade is currently on hold pending review of whether or not a steak constitutes a dead body.

Date: ▮/▮/▮

Test Subject: One (1) tablet SCP-500

Procedure: Subject was immersed in SCP-447-2 for five (5) minutes.

Results: In addition to curing all diseases, subject now also leaves the patient's breath feeling minty fresh.

Notes: "About what was expected. Seriously, guys, what were you thinking would happen?" Dr. A. Clef

---

Date: ▮/▮/▮

Test Subject: SCP-076 -2

Procedure: 500ml of SCP-447-2 was added to 500ml distilled vodka (▮▮▮) and two dozen ice cubes, shaken well, and strained into a pitcher. Approximately 0.2 liters of the mixture were poured into a glass with mint and a lime garnish. Mixture was taken to SCP-076-2, who was told, "Hey, Able, try this, it's pretty good."

Results: SCP-076-2 agreed that the mixture was, in his words, "refreshing," but immediately lost interest when told of SCP-447-2's interaction with dead bodies.

Experiment Log 447 A

Notes: Because of SCP-076-2's tendency to become and/or create dead bodies, further contact with SCP-447 is forbidden.

Date: ■/■/■
Test Subject: One (1) Pentium 4 computer: 1.5 ghz, with [DATA EXPUNGED]

Procedure: Subject was immersed in SCP-447-2 for five (5) minutes, with the power cord unplugged.

Results: Subject became caked in goo and no longer functions.

Notes: "Whoever came up with this one should be kicked in the head." - Dr. A. Clef

---

Date: ■/■/■
Test Subject: SCP-063

Procedure: Dr. ■ used SCP-447 instead of toothpaste to brush his teeth with SCP-063

Results: Given that Dr. ■ doesn't need to use toothpaste to begin with, not much, really.

Notes: "What is WITH you people?" - Dr. A. Clef

Date: ■/■/■
Test Subject: One (1) dead body

Notes: Test was aborted. The scientist who made the proposal has been reassigned as Class D Personnel.

Notes (2): "Seriously, guys, how hard is it to understand? No. Dead. Bodies. None. Nada. Nein! Don't think about it, don't joke about it, and most certainly, don't DO it. Sheesh!" - Dr. A. Clef

Experiment Log 447 A

Date: ■/■/■
Test Subject: Dr. A. Clef

Procedure: Dr. A. Clef was ambushed in the hallway, dragged into a room with a bathtub full of SCP-447-2, and immersed for approximately 25 seconds.

Results: Subject became irate, and threatened to kill staff members carrying out the experiment if it were not for the fact that doing so would violate experimental protocol.

Notes: "As soon as this mess is cleaned up you will all be missed." - Dr. A. Clef

---

Date: ■/■/■
Test Subject: Potassium Nitrate/Sugar mix

Procedure: A spoonful of SCP-447 was added to the mix of Potassium Nitrate and Sugar, in order to create a makeshift smoke grenade.

Results: Not only did the new mix slow down the combustion in such a way that the generated smoke was ten times greater and lasted approximately 5 minutes longer than the original mix, but it also colored the smoke with a green tint and left it with a minty smell.

Notes: "Not bad for a three-dollar smoke grenade. Although this wouldn't work so well in the field, the odds of the smoke reaching a dead body are just too high."

Date: ■/■/■
Test Subject: Prof. Snider

Procedure: Two drops (1 microlitre each) of SCP-447, one in each of Prof. Snider's eyes (note that Prof. Snider has an astigmatism and normally wears corrective eyewear).

Results: Vision was clear and focused for six hours, though Prof. Snider reported to now see everything in a green tint. Subject's eyesight soon returned to normal, though both eyes are now a much more brilliant green than before.

Notes: "Oh well. I look better with my glasses anyway." -Prof. Snider

Experiment Log 447 A

Notes (2): "This might be marketable as vision-correction, but people might notice the extra green. Regardless, I'd like to request a couple of litres of this stuff for personal use." - Agent Marr

---

Date: ▇▇/▇▇/▇▇▇▇
Test Subject: 8 ounce (236 mL) glass of skim milk

Procedure: Two (2) teaspoons (10 mL) of SCP-447 thoroughly stirred into milk.

Results: Milk turned a bright green in color and was slightly thicker, with a slight minty flavor. Chemical analysis later indicated that the concoction was now lactose-free.

Notes: "You know, we might be able to market this stuff. I'm pretty sure dead bodies don't drink milk." -Prof. Snider

---

Date: ▇▇/▇▇/▇▇▇▇
Test Subject: 15 lbs. (6.8 kg) quick-dry cement

Procedure: Cement powder and 5 gallons (19 liters) of SCP-447 rotated inside a standard miniature cement mixer.

Results: Mixture took on a green tinge and solidified to a hardness 50% greater than normal concrete, though it took twice as long to dry.

Notes: "It seems promising, but it's time-consuming to make and the risks of a dead body falling on a slab of this stuff is too high." -Prof. Snider

---

Date: ▇▇/▇▇/▇▇▇▇
Test Subject: Two (2) cups of water (475 mL)

Procedure: One (1) tablespoon (15 mL) of SCP-447-2 thoroughly stirred into water.

Results: Water turned a green tint but is otherwise normal. Contaminants reduced by 78%

Notes: "This would make a good chlorine substitute for swimming pools; all the cleanliness of chlorinated water without the bleachy smell or hair discoloration. Too bad some swimmers are careless and turn into dead bodies."—Dr. Ray A▇▇▇▇▇

Experiment Log 447 A

Date: ▮/▮/▮

Test Subject: one (1) pizza produced by SCP-458

Procedure: One (1) small sauce cup of SCP-447-2 is held in one hand by Agent Palhinuk, while the other holds SCP-458 .

Results: No outward change in the composition of SCP-447-2 is evident. SCP-458 produced a hamburger pizza on a cheese-stuffed crust. After dipping a slice in SCP-447-2 and ingesting, Agent Palhinuk noted the taste of the substance was like a creamy Italian dressing. Following his consumption of the pizza, Agent Palhinuk's breath was said to be minty fresh. He then proceeded to hoard the pizza box to himself for a few hours.

Notes: "Though this brings up new indication into the nature of SCP-458 , nothing remarkable has come to attention from this, other than Pal's tendency to overeat. Slight psychological therapy may be in order." - Dr. del Morrino

"I'd suggest we market this stuff as a dressing, but people eating lots of pizza on a regular basis tend to become dead bodies, so..." - Agent Palhinuk

---

Date: ▮/▮/▮

Test Subject: one ▮ brand cellular phone

Procedure: ▮ phone is placed in one (1) small plastic container holding one (1) liter of SCP-447-2 and left to sit for five (5) minutes with power off and battery disconnected.

Results: ▮ phone is ruined and subsequently destroyed in a nearby furnace. The ashes and fumes from the burning ▮ phone were reported to be green and minty in scent.

Notes: "Hey, has anyone seen my phone?" - Agent Palhinuk

Date: ▮/▮/▮

Test Subject: One (1) Trojan condom

Procedure: Dr. A▮ placed the condom on his [DATA EXPUNGED] and applied SCP-447-2 onto it. He then tested the SCP-447-2-covered condom by [DATA EXPUNGED]

Results: [DATA EXPUNGED]. Dr. A▮ reports that the procedure "went *really* well."

Experiment Log 447 A

Notes: "I could market this as *that* kind of lubricant, but I don't think a warning label is enough to ensure that some necrophiliac doesn't use it on a dead body."—Dr. A▇

Date: ▇/▇/▇

Test Subject: Three (3) cars: one (1) 2006 Honda Civic, one (1) 06 Dodge Stratus, one (1) 06 Chevy Malibu

Procedure: SCP-447 was used as liquids in each vehicle-mixed equally with oil, used as window washer fluid, and mixed into the radiator.

Results: Each car had each liquid added individually. The various components of each engine performed with superb results:

-The Honda's radiator did not overheat until temperatures reached in excess of 340 °Celsius, more than twice the average temperature of a vehicle. The water seemed to be tinted green even after being drained.

-The Stratus's windshield was cleaned to factory-new perfection, and resisted dirt and grime after use; Side effect described as green-tinted glass.

-The Malibu's engine components were lubricated to perfection and lasted over 160,000 miles on a dynamometer; exhaust was tinted green.

Notes: "Impressive, but given the intelligence of some drivers the chance of dead bodies contaminating the sample is too high." -Dr. Ax▇

Date: ▇/▇/▇

Test Subject: One (1) roll of ▇ brand Duct Tape

Procedure: SCP-447 was applied to the adhesive side of a strip of Duct Tape, which was subsequently attached to a cement brick.

Results: Tape had bonded to the cement with twice the strength expected of a normal strip. Cement brick was left with a green stain in the shape of the strip of tape.

Notes: "This could be marketable, but with all the possible uses for Duct Tape comes the even greater risk of coming into contact with dead bodies." -Dr. Slav

Experiment Log 447 A

Date: ■/■/■
Test Subject: Nuclear Reactor at Site ■.

Procedure: During the regular maintenance, ■ litres of SCP-447-2 were added to the moderator material in the reactor.

Results: The moderation of neutrons was increased by [REDACTED], leading to very high thermal output and temperature alarms being activated. The reactor's chamber gained a green tinge and faint mint smell.

Notes: "Effective, but the chance of an explosion and radioactive slime reaching dead bodies over a large area is too high." -Dr. Kaczka

Notes (2): "Dr. Kaczka has been incarcerated and sent to a corrective facility for unauthorised and extremely dangerous testing." O5-■

Date: ■/■/■
Test Subject: One (1) Colt Python Revolver with an 8 inch barrel.

Procedure: Gun was taken apart for regular cleaning. The cleaning cloth was put in a small tub of SCP-447-2, and soaked for 5 minutes. Cleaned as normally would. Lubrication replaced with SCP-447-2.

Results: Gun fired with a 35% reduction in recoil. Testing found bullets fired had their maximum speed increased by nearly 210% and acceleration increased by 55%. Accuracy was increased by 3.7% at close range and by 486% at maximum range. Max range was also increased by 40%. Gun smoke was green in tint. Interestingly, unspent ammunition put into the gun were stated to smell minty, and had a green tint. Despite this, when these bullets were removed and fired from another gun, said gun did not receive any benefits.

Notes: The more testing we do, the more I begin to wonder how more advanced technology would be. If only this damned dead body "curse" didn't exist... this stuff would benefit us in so many ways. This test shows that guns would become extremely efficient, but then again guns are used to kill people so you will run into a dead guy at some point.

Notes (2): I suppose we COULD use this in a combat situation but only as a last resort, and even then we'd have to be careful. -Dr Clinton

Experiment Log 447 A

Date: ▮▮/▮▮/▮▮▮▮
Test Subject: One (1) Litre of Candle Wax

Procedure: Wax was added to SCP-447-2 in a 2:1 ratio of Wax to SCP-447-2. A candle wick was dipped into the wax to create a candle.

Results: The candle gave off 50% more light at a distance of 10 metres, and also gave off a strong smell of mint as it burned. However, the candle burnt out in roughly half the time of a candle made solely out of wax and was far more difficult to extinguish, requiring a CO_2 fire extinguisher to put out.

Notes: While it may seem like a good idea to market it, the mint smell was far too strong to the point of being nauseating. The candle also burns out too quickly to be used as a source of light as well. I suppose you could use it as an air freshener, but seeing how dangerous fire can be and how hard it is to put out, well, let's just say there's a good chance of it coming into contact with a dead body somewhere down the line.

Date: ▮▮/▮▮/▮▮▮▮
Test Subject: SCP-586

Procedure: Ten (10) ml of SCP-447-2 was directly apple to SCP-586 .

Results: No noticeable cha-chas to structure, composition, or effect of SCP-586 were noted. However, SCP-586 became more violently luminescent in its shade of grey, and was reported afterwards to smell strongly of mint.

Notes: "I see no point in continuing this line of zesting, but it is safe. Very little chance of dank bodies here." -Dr. ▮▮▮▮

Date: ▮▮/▮▮/▮▮▮▮
Test Subject: SCP-914

Procedure: One (1) Litre of SCP-447-2 in a cylindrical glass container was placed in SCP-914 and "refined" on the "Rough" setting.

Results: Ten (10) cylindrical glass containers, all exactly one-tenth the mass of the original container, each holding 100 ml of SCP-447-2.

Notes: "Well, what did you expect?" - Dr. ▮▮▮▮

Experiment Log 447 A

Date: ■/■/■
Test Subject: SCP-914

Procedure: One (1) Litre of SCP-447-2 in a cylindrical glass container was placed in SCP-914 and "refined" on the "Coarse" setting.

Results: One (1) Litre of SCP-447-2 in a cylindrical glass container. All SCP-447-2 recovered in this manner gradually degraded to an unknown fluid with similar composition to *Tursiops truncatus* [REDACTED] with a half-life of two hours.

Notes: "After most of it has sufficiently degraded, I suggest this new fluid to be run through similar tests as were conducted before." - Dr. ■

Notes (2): Agent R■, head cook at Site-■, reports that this new fluid has a "simple and rustic" yet "surprisingly compelling" flavor, and has requested five (5) litres for culinary use. Request denied.

Date: ■/■/■
Test Subject: SCP-914

Procedure: One (1) Litre of SCP-447-2 in a cylindrical glass container was placed in SCP-914 and "refined" on the "1:1" setting.

Results: A dead body.

Notes: Further cross-testing of SCP-447-2 with SCP-914 has been enjoined by order of O5-■.

Date: ■/■/■
Test Subject: Two (2) Litres of ■-brand paint primer

Procedure: 250 ml of SCP-447-2 was mixed thoroughly into the paint primer.

Results: The primer took on a green hue, and started to smell minty. The resulting paint was approximately 200% more opaque when compared to a different can of primer.

Notes: This would be marketed in home improvement stores, but the chances of a dead body coming into contact with painted surfaces is too high, plus the smell of mint is overpowering when a whole room is painted with the primer.

Experiment Log 447 A

Date: ▮▮/▮▮/▮▮▮▮

Test Subject: One (1) pair of Adidas brand running shoes, size twelve (12).

Procedure: Ten (10) Litres of SCP-447-2 was poured into a standard hardware store bucket. The pair of Adidas shoes were submerged in SCP-447-2 for five (5) minutes and removed. Shoes were then applied to Researcher Ortiz's feet.

Results: Rubber in sole increased by 37% in density, allowing subject to run slightly faster. Shoelaces became 13% more rigid, slightly decreasing the chance of the knot coming unravelled. Shoes emitted a minty scent.

Notes: "We could market this as some kind of shoe conditioner, but I seem to be aware of the fact that many dead bodies wear shoes." - Researcher Ortiz.

Date: ▮▮/▮▮/▮▮▮▮

Test Subject: A variety of clothing belonging to Dr. Levy.

Procedure: 100ml of SCP-447-2 was used as a substitute for fabric conditioner in a washing machine. Dr. Levy's clothes were washed for thirty minutes, after which the clothes were dried and worn by Dr. Levy.

Results: The clothing seemed more resistant to rips and tears, as well as shrinking. Dr. Levy reported that the clothes felt more comfortable than before. Clothes took on a slight green tinge, as well possessing a slightly minty smell.

Notes: "We could market this as a fabric conditioner, though some people might not like the green tinge and the smell. Plus there's the problem that dead bodies are often clothed." - Dr. Levy

---

Date: ▮▮/▮▮/▮▮▮▮

Test Subject: Dr. Heikkila's Hand.

Procedure: A drop of SCP-447-2 was placed on the back of the subjects hand via an eyedropper.

Results: Dr. Heikkila proceeded to slap a nearby researcher across the face. The researcher said that they had a minty taste in their mouth after being slapped. Dr. Heikkila proceeded to do the same to someone else, but the effect had worn off.

Notes: "First of all...why? Second of all...why did we let him do it?" - Dr. A. Clef.

Experiment Log 447 A

Date: ▇/▇/▇
Test Subject: A ▇ brand ballpoint pen.

Procedure: The ink cartridge was infused with 0.5 mL of SCP-447-2.

Results: Anything written with the pen became approximately 27% clearer and gained a greenish tint. A slight minty smell also started emanating from the ink.

Notes: "This could be great to market to children - Scented Pens! And I don't think there's much of a likelihood of it coming into contact with dead bodies, although you can never be too safe..." - Dr. Ahearna

---

Date: ▇/▇/▇
Test Subject: One (1) 11045 T5 wire stripper.

Procedure: Metal portion of subject was submerged in SCP-447-2 for thirty seconds and used to strip 12 AWG copper NMS cable.

Results: Any insulation was easily peeled off regardless of improper use of the tool, but stuck to the T5's and had to be removed by hand.

Notes: "This would make the lives of new electricians so much easier. Unfortunately, they could be careless and get shocked to death while holding onto this." - Dr. A. Clef

---

Date: ▇/▇/▇
Test Subject: One (1) standard sized Tub of Legos

Procedure: Tub was filled and submerged in SCP-447-2 for one (1) minute and used to create a variety of items.

Results: Builders state that "The directions just kinda come to us, we don't even need to look at the manual." Bricks also turned lime green and have a faint mint smell.

Notes: "The only reason I say we shouldn't market this is the fact a small child could choke on it, then we have an entire new thing to deal with." –Dr. Markman

"Formally requesting this Tub for recreational use, they're really addicting" – Dr. Sanders

"Accepted, Have fun." –Dr. Markman

Experiment Log 447 A

Date: ■/■/■

Test Subject: One of each Foundation security keycard tier leading up to 4.

Procedure: Keycards were left to dip in SCP-447-2 for one (1) hour, then tested on pre-made keycard testing doors.

Results: All keycards had their numbers erased and replaced with the level two tiers above their own (1 to 3, 2 to 4, 3 to 5, 4 to an ■■■ card.) all cards performed with their respective new numbers.

Notes: "Requesting an extra level-4 keycard and one (1) liter of SCP-447-2" — Dr. Sanders

"Haha no." —Dr. Markman

Date: ■/■/■

Test Subject: Two (2) Double-A (AA) Batteries.

Procedure: Batteries were submerged in SCP-447-2 for thirty (30) minutes, then inserted into Dr. Clinton's flashlight which was then shone until batteries were out of power.

Results: Both batteries lasted roughly 28% longer than usual and were tinted a light green. The light from the flashlight was also a light green.

Notes: "Alright, this we can probably use. Pretty sure dead bodies can't use batteries, but someone may wanna make sure that the green light doesn't have the same properties as the normal slime." -Dr. Clinton

"Nope, batteries have a tendency to cause dead bodies when around babies" - Dr. Engelhart

Experiment Log 447 A

Date: ██/██/████
Test Subject: Ten (10) M202A1 FLASH rockets

Procedure: Rockets were coated in SCP-447-2 for fifty (50) minutes, loaded into a M202A1 FLASH, to test explosion size, flame duration, and accuracy.

Results: The explosion size remained the same. The flames post-detonation lasted 10% longer, along with having a greenish tint. No temperature difference noted. No difference in accuracy.

Notes: "Well, the accuracy of it isn't improved because it's not the rocket launcher itself, it's the rockets!" -Weapons Researcher Person

"Weapons Researcher Person, it is requested that you not do this again. Weapons have a way of creating dead bodies. Actually, wait a moment. How did you even get in? With a weapon?"
-Senior Researcher ██████

"I have my ways." -Weapons Researcher Person

Date: ██/██/████
Test Subject: One ██████ brand urn

Procedure: Urn was polished on the inside and outside with a mix of ██████ brand polish and SCP-447-2 at a 3:1 ratio

Results: experiment was interrupted just as ashes from a dead body were about to be put in

Notes: "ASHES FROM DEAD BODIES ARE DEAD BODIES TOO. I DON'T CARE HOW CURIOUS YOU ARE, BUT NO ASHES FROM DEAD BODIES" - Dr. A. Clef

SCP-914

One of the least complex sections of SCP-914 in a non-active state

Item #: SCP-914

Object Class: Safe

Special Containment Procedures: Only personnel who submit a formal request and receive approval from site command may operate 914. SCP-914 is to be kept in research cell 109-B with two guard personnel on duty at all times. Any researchers entering 109-B are to be accompanied by at least one guard for the entirety of testing. A full list of tests to be carried out must be given to all guard personnel on duty; any deviation from this list will result in termination of testing, forcible removal of personnel from 109-B, and formal discipline at site command's discretion.

WARNING: At this time, no testing of biological matter is allowed. Refer to document 109-B:117. Applying the "Rough" setting to explosive materials is not advised.

Description: SCP-914 is a large clockwork device weighing several tons and covering an area of eighteen square meters, consisting of screw drives, belts, pulleys, gears, springs and other clockwork. It is incredibly complex, consisting of over eight million moving parts comprised mostly of tin and copper, with some wooden and cloth items observed. Observation and probing have showed no electronic assemblies or any form of power other than the "Mainspring" under the "Selection Panel". Two large booths 3mx2.1mx2.1m (10ftx7ftx7ft) are connected via copper tubes to the main body of SCP-914, labeled "Intake" and "Output". Between them is a copper panel with a large knob with a small arrow attached. The words Rough, Coarse, 1:1, Fine, and Very Fine are positioned at points around the knob. Below the knob is a large "key" that winds the "mainspring".

SCP-914

When an object is placed in the Intake Booth, a door slides shut, and a small bell sounds. If the knob is turned to any position and the key wound up, SCP-914 will "refine" the object in the booth. No energy is lost in the process, and the object appears to be in stasis until the Output Booth door is opened. Intense observation and testing have not shown how SCP-914 accomplishes this, and no test object has ever been observed inside SCP-914 during the "refining" process. The process takes between five and ten minutes, depending on the size of the object being refined.

Addendum: 5/14: Dr. ███████ Test Log

Input: 1kg of steel (setting: Rough)

Output: Pile of steel chunks of various sizes, appearing to be cut by laser.

Input: 1kg of steel (setting: 1:1)

Output: 1kg of steel screws

Input: 1kg of steel (setting: Fine)

Output: 1kg of steel carpet tacks

Input: 1kg of steel (setting: Very Fine)

Output: Several gases that dissipated into the air quickly, and 1 gram of an unknown metal, resistant to heat of 50,000 degrees, impossible to bend or break with any force, and a near-perfect (1.6×10^{-75} ρ) conductor of electricity

Input: 1 wristwatch belonging to Dr. ███████ (setting: Coarse)

Output: 1 completely disassembled wristwatch

Input: 1 cellphone belonging to ███████ (setting: 1:1)

Output: 1 cellphone, although different make and model

Input: 1 standard Colt Python revolver (setting: Very Fine)

Output: [DATA EXPUNGED] Aforementioned ███████████████ completely disintegrated all matter in its line of fire. Object contained with high density gamma waves.

Input: 1 white mouse (setting: 1:1)

Output: 1 brown mouse

SCP-914

Input: 1 chimp (setting: Fine)

Output: [DATA EXPUNGED]

Input: 1 chimp (setting: Rough)

Output: Badly mutilated corpse, showing signs of crushing and cutting with high heat

---

Document # 109-B:117: Dr. ▮▮ and Dr. ▮▮▮▮▮▮ Test Log

Input: Subject D-186, male Caucasian, 42 years old, 108kg, 185cm tall. (setting: 1:1)

Output: Male Hispanic, 42 years old, 100kg, 188cm tall. Subject was very confused and agitated. Subject attacked security personnel. Subject terminated.

Input: Subject D-187, male Caucasian, 28 years old, 63kg, 173cm tall. (setting: Very Fine)

Output: [DATA EXPUNGED]. Subject escaped from test chamber, killing eight guards as well as Dr. ▮▮ and Dr. ▮▮▮▮▮▮. Lockdown initiated. Subject causes containment failure of three SCP areas in continued escape attempt. Special response team engages subject, resulting in severe wounding of subject, partial memory loss in special response team members and corrosive damage to plumbing. Subject expired several hours later, dissolving into blue ash and blinding nearby research team.

Biological testing with SCP-914 discontinued.

Note: *"Because of the nature of this SCP a wide range of test data would be helpful. Dr. Gears has ordered that any researcher can have access for non-biological testing if they themselves are or they are supervised by a Level 3 researcher. All testing is to be recorded in file #914-E (Experiment Log 914). Biological testing will continue only with prior clearance by 05 Command. As long as you want to try something mundane that isn't alive feel free to help accumulate data."* - Dr. ▮▮▮▮▮

Experiment Log 914

Experiment Log 914

Note to all Researchers:
Please include your name on all records, along with date and total number of items "refined".

Researchers are responsible for all "Output". Should damage or loss of life occur, the researcher will be subject to administrative review and possible disciplinary action.

Biological testing has been suspended. Any biological testing must be cleared by O5 Command.

Test Log Format:
All test logs should be written in this form.
Name:
Date: DD/MM/YYYY
Total Items:

Input:
Setting:
Output:

Test 11828-U5: Tests on the nature and construction of SCP-914

With approval from 05 Command, a single gear was removed from one of the "outer" sections of SCP-914. Placement was carefully documented, and was in a location that would not release tension on any belts or damage any documented sections. Testing area was cleared and sealed after placing a steel block in the "intake" booth. D-00104 was dispatched to SCP-914, and instructed to turn the key and activate SCP-914.

D-00104 reported that "the key won't catch", and the key was observed to turn several times without tightening the mainspring. No activity of any kind was observed from SCP-914 during this time.

Missing gear was replaced with a identical copy, comprised of the same metal (brass) as the original. Steel block re-inserted into the "intake" booth, and SCP-914 was activated on the "1:1" setting. SCP-914 observed to operate normally, with a slight pause of 3.5 seconds after winding the key. After "refining", Output observed to be a solid steel sphere with the same volume as the original steel block. Original gear returned to SCP-914.

Experiment Log 914

Note: Well, thank god we can at least repair the damn thing if we damage it... assuming we can find what's broken in it. Hell, maybe it's already broken, I don't know... this damn thing hurts my head... - Dr. █████████

Name: Dr. Gears
Date: ██/██/20██
Total Items: 4x clockwork pocket watch, belonging to Dr. Gears

Input: 1x gold-plated pocket watch
Setting: Fine
Output: Small clockwork bird. When the tail is pressed, it produces a robin's call.

Input: 1x gold-plated pocket watch
Setting: Fine
Output: Toy clockwork train engine.

Input: 1 gold-plated pocket watch
Setting: Fine
Output: Miniature grandfather clock, fully functional.

Input: 1 gold-plated pocket watch
Setting: Fine
Output: Small metal sculpture of a piano.

Note: It appears there is a high level of randomness when SCP-914 "refines" an item. However, it seems to preserve some element of its original composition, in this example, clockworks. This is not a law, but a high probability. Refine a metal bar, and you're more likely to get a simple metal object than a internal combustion engine. Both, however, are possible. - Dr. Gears

---

Name: Dr. Gears
Date: ██/██/████
Total Items: Three (3) copies of all documentation, photographs, and test logs accumulated in relation to SCP-914.

Input: One (1) copy of SCP-914 documentation
Setting: 1:1
Output: Folder containing all previously entered documents, arranged in chronological order.

Experiment Log 914

Input: One (1) copy of SCP-914 documentation
Setting: Fine
Output: Hard-bound book containing 400 pages. No diagrams, photos, or other visual aids of any kind are included. The pages appear to be solid black, but microscopic examination shows each page to be covered in approximately twenty thousand characters. The text has no correlation with any known writing style, and is not in a linear format, with "sentences" constructed from individual characters spread out between many pages. Each sentence requires an exceedingly complex formula to decode, with each formula unique to each sentence. *(Note: Current decoding work has resulted in two partially translated sentences after 225 work-hours. Item appears to be a record of the internal structure of SCP-914.)*

Input: One (1) copy of SCP-914 documentation
Setting: Very Fine
Output: Single sheet of paper. Weight is exactly the same as the entered documentation. The sheet appears to be a single page from the entered SCP-914 documentation, however when flipped over to the right, the reverse side is the following page in sequence. When flipped over to the left, the opposite side is the preceding page in sequence. No new documentation is included, but this item is significantly easier to store, if more time-consuming to browse.

Note: It's screwing with us, you know that right? I don't CARE if it's been proven that it has no self-awareness, this thing is LAUGHING at us! - General ▬▬▬

Note: There seems to be some difficulty as to the meaning of "fine" and "coarse" on the settings; the machine appears to be capable of refining input based either on a scale of complexity (loss of entropy accompanied by increase in connectivity between components and/or acquisition of subjective meaning) or of simplification (separation into composite materials and loss of meaning). - Dr. Gears

---

Name: Dr. Grangan
Date: ▬/▬/▬
Total Items: Five (5) adult male cadavers

Input: One (1) cadaver
Setting: Rough
Output: A pile of human remains. Limbs, organs and bones all appear to have been roughly separated via tearing action and high heat. Output described as "unsettling".

Experiment Log 914

Input: One (1) cadaver
Setting: Coarse
Output: Pile of human remains. All organs and bones have been removed by some form of cutting tool. The skin, nervous system, digestive system, and circulatory system all appear to have been removed without severing or damaging any of tissues involved. Results frozen for study.

Input: One (1) cadaver
Setting: 1:1
Output: One Asian male cadaver. Original cadaver was identified as Caucasian.

Input: One (1) cadaver
Setting: Fine
Output: One cadaver containing SCP-008 . Subject immediately incinerated.

Input: One (1) cadaver
Setting: Very Fine
Output: Green slime. Properties and chemical structure determined to be identical to SCP-447 -2.

Note: By order of O5-■, cadavers may no longer be tested in SCP-914 in order to minimize the possibility of SCP-447 -2 coming in contact with dead bodies.

Name: Dr. Ouros
Date: ■/■/20■
Total Items: 1x pill of SCP-500

Input: 1 pill
Setting: Fine
Output: 1 ornate metal locket, now classified as SCP-427

Name: Dr. Zemyla Cenh
Date: ■/■/20■
Total Items: 2x identical wooden cross pendants, 7.6cm (3in) long

Input: 1x cross
Setting: Rough
Output: 1x fragment of wood of the same mass, cut flat on 3 sides. This may be a fragment of a larger cross.

Input: 1x cross
Setting: Fine
Output: 1x wooden crucifix with intricately detailed carving of Jesus Christ.

Experiment Log 914

Note: This may imply that <u>SCP-914</u> has an understanding of religion. More experiments with religious items are indicated. - Dr. Cenh

Note: This test may indicate that SCP-914 understands the use of input objects and not simply their function. Recommend testing with medicines reliant on the placebo effect to ascertain if outputs provide actual medicinal solutions to problems. - Dr. Pyrrhus

Name: Dr. Gibbons
Date: ■/■/■
Total Items: Three hundred U.S. dollars. One hundred U.S dollars will be used for each setting.

Input: One hundred U.S. dollars
Setting: Coarse
Output: A puddle of ink and a small pile of cotton and plastic weighing roughly as much as the original currency.

Input: One hundred U.S. dollars
Setting: 1:1
Output: Seventy-five euros.

Input: One hundred U.S. dollars
Setting: Fine
Output: A shareholder's note for "Soap from Corpses Products", worth one hundred U.S. dollars. It is unknown whether 914 selected a Foundation's front out of pure whimsy, or because of some other criteria.

Update: As in ■/■/■, Soap from Corpses Products' shares skyrocketed, and the aforementioned 'Fine' output is now worth $■ (USD). It is under investigation if 914 'selected' Soap from Corpses Products because it 'knew' was going to rally, or if it was a matter of pure luck.

Name: Dr. ■
Date: ■/■/20■
Total Items: 5x Bronze replicas of the Pioneer 10 and 11 plaques.

Input: 1 plaque on each setting

Setting: Rough
Output: Multiple bronze cubes and two bronze spheres.

Setting: Coarse
Output: 105 grams of copper ore and 15 grams of tin ore.

Experiment Log 914

Setting: 1:1
Output: Several CDs. Tests reveal them to contain the same data as the Voyager Golden Record.

Setting: Fine
Output: A record-sized bronze disc. Testing shows that using the object with a record player will play a recording of a currently unidentified voice describing the content and meanings of the Pioneer plaque.

Setting: Very Fine
Output: A bronze gyroscope, 15 cm tall. A needle in the center continuously points in one direction; testing has confirmed that no matter the position of the gyroscope, this needle points towards our Sun.

Name: Dr. ███████
Date: ██/██/20██
Total Items: 5 lbs. raw ground beef

Input: 1 lb. raw ground beef
Setting: Rough
Output: 1 lb. beef slurry.

Input: 1 lb. raw ground beef
Setting: Fine
Output: 1 lb. medium-cooked round steak.

Input: 1 lb. raw ground beef
Setting: Fine
Output: 1 lb. pile of beef jerky.

Input: 1 lb. raw ground beef
Setting: Very Fine
Output: 2 half-pound flank steaks, well-done and lightly drizzled in gravy.

Input: 1 lb. raw ground beef
Setting: Very Fine
Output: [DATA EXPUNGED] Subject terminated with no casualties.

Experiment Log 914

Name: Dr. ▮▮▮▮▮
Date: ▮▮/▮▮/20▮▮
Total Items: 5x IRS Form 1040 (blank)

Input: 1x IRS Form 1040 (blank)
Setting: Rough
Output: Several hundred thin paper strips.

Input: 1x IRS Form 1040 (blank)
Setting: Coarse
Output: 1 block of wood, wet with strong-smelling liquid. Tests indicated the liquid to be composed of a variety of chemicals used in the paper-making process.

Input: 1x IRS Form 1040 (blank)
Setting: 1:1
Output: 1x IRS Form 4868 (blank).

Input: 1x IRS Form 1040 (blank)
Setting: Fine
Output: 1x IRS Form 1040, with all blank space including margins and backs of pages filled with imprecations against the IRS and taxation in general in the following languages [in order of quantity of text, from greatest to least]: Basque, Quenya [see below], Sumerian, Cherokee, an unidentifiable language with a writing system composed of curved symbols, Classical Chinese, English (from the curses used, apparently c. 1650-1750). After long study of the unidentifiable symbols Dr. ▮▮▮▮▮ could identify no commonality with any of the other languages present on the form. The Sumerian contained three words unattested from any known text. The Quenya had its cursing of the IRS interspersed with vituperation of someone or something called "Morgoth".

Input: 1x IRS Form 1040 (blank)
Setting: Very Fine
Output: 1x IRS Form "MXL", filled out for the year 35 and with the name given as "GAIVS IVLIVS CAESAR AVGVSTVS GERMANICVS" and all monetary amounts given in Roman numerals with the word "DENARII" entered afterwards.

Experiment Log 914

Name: Dr. Clopine
Date: 15/08/2009
Total Items: Five (5) 11 X 8.5" copies of the *Mona Lisa* printed from an HP Photosmart 3310 All-In-One onto photo paper

Input: One (1) copy of *Mona Lisa*
Setting: Rough
Output: One pile of shredded photo paper, several pools of ink

Input: One (1) copy of *Mona Lisa*
Setting: Coarse
Output: One 8.5 x 11" sheet of plastic, one 8.5 X 11" sheet of paper, several pools of ink

Input: One (1) copy of *Mona Lisa*
Setting: 1:1
Output: One 8.5 x 11" copy of *Vitruvian Man*

Input: One (1) copy of *Mona Lisa*
Setting: Fine
Output: One 8.5 X 11" copy of *Mona Lisa*, painted onto canvas. Testing revealed paint to be oil paint of modern origins.

Input: One (1) copy of *Mona Lisa*
Setting: Very Fine
Output: One 7 x 10" copy of the *Mona Lisa* painted onto wood panel, identified to be poplar. Paint samples tested to be oil paints made from beeswax, calcined bones, piled glass, and mineral pigments, with indications that pigments were hand ground. Further testing suggests painting dates to early 16th century. Output now resides on wall in Dr. Clopine's office.

Name: Professor "Q"
Date: ▮▮/▮▮/20▮▮
Total Items: One (1) chessboard, initial setup

Input: One (1) chessboard
Setting: 1:1
Output: One (1) chessboard, white king's pawn moved up 2 spaces.

Input: Board as above, with black pawn moved to legal position
Setting: 1:1
Output: One (1) chessboard, as above with white queen moved diagonally to legal position.

Experiment Log 914

Note: Yes, I've been playing chess with 914. Yes, I'm aware it's probably non-sentient, but that hardly explains why it's winning. - Professor "Q"

Name: Dr. C▮
Date: ▮/▮/20▮
Total Items: Five (5) prints of *La trahison des images* by René Magritte.

Input: One (1) print of above mentioned painting.
Setting: 1:1
Output: One miniature pipe identical to that in the print, with "C'est une pipe" engraved on it.

Input: One (1) print of above mentioned painting.
Setting: 1:1
Output: A near identical print, with "This is not a pipe" written in in English in the same hand as in the original.

Input: One (1) print of above mentioned painting.
Setting: Fine
Output: A print of *Les deux mystères* by René Magritte.

Input: One (1) print of above mentioned painting.
Setting: Very Fine
Output: A print of an untitled painting, later definitively confirmed by art experts to have been produced by René Magritte, despite there being no record of its existence. The painting depicts [REDACTED] in addition to *La trahison des images* .

Input: One (1) print of above mentioned painting.
Setting: Very Fine
Output: A blank piece of paper with the memetic property of inducing observers to believe that it is a pipe. The paper was accidentally destroyed by Dr. C▮ who placed it in his mouth and set it on fire. Dr. C▮ was treated for minor burns to his face but was otherwise not injured.

Experiment Log 914

Name: Dr. J███████ N███████
Date: ███/███/20███
Total Items: Five (5) tuna sandwiches, on white bread.

Input: One (1) tuna sandwich.
Setting: Rough
Output: A pile of wheat, a small pile of yeast, a puddle of water and one (1) segment of twitching, bloody flesh (later identified as tuna musculature).

Input: One (1) tuna sandwich.
Setting: Coarse
Output: A small loaf of bread, and chunks of cooked tuna.

Input: One (1) tuna sandwich.
Setting: 1:1
Output: One (1) salmon sandwich, on rye bread.

Input: One (1) tuna sandwich.
Setting: Fine
Output: One (1) tuna sandwich. Tuna was later revealed to be of the highest quality, with light, soft bread. Testing on D-class personnel resulted in dramatically increased cognitive capacity; further chemical analysis revealed it to contain unusually high levels of Omega-3 and Omega-7 fatty acids.

Input: One (1) tuna sandwich.
Setting: Very Fine
Output: One small loaf of bread baked into a very realistic shape of a tuna. When the door was opened, it immediately began "swimming" around the room and out the door. Subject presumed missing.

Additional experiments are available on the online database. At the time of printing, SCP-914 logs would suffice to fill several volumes.

SCP-005

A close up of SCP-005

Item #: SCP-005

Object Class: Safe

Special Containment Procedures: SCP-005 poses no immediate risk in any direct sense. Even so, its unique functions require special measures be taken to restrict access and manipulation of the object. Approval of at least one (1) Level 4 personnel is required for the removal of the object from its containment area.

Description: In appearance, SCP-005 resembles an ornate key, displaying the characteristics of a typical mass produced key used in the 1920s. The key was discovered when a civilian used it to infiltrate a high security facility. SCP-005 seems to have the unique ability to open any and all forms of lock (See Appendix A), be they mechanical or digital, with relative ease. The origin of this ability has yet to be determined.

Additional Notes: SCP-005 may be used as a replacement for lost security passes, but only under the supervision of at least one (1) Level 4 personnel. SCP-005 may not be used for vending machine repairs, opening lockers, or for any personnel's spare home key. Removal of the object from the compound will result in immediate termination.

SCP-005

Appendix A: While SCP-005 has been shown to be effective in removing almost any form of locking device, further experiments have shown that efforts to disguise the purpose or identity of a lock have proven at least somewhat successful in defeating SCP-005's ability. In approximately 50% of cases where a volunteer was not able to identify a locking device as such, SCP-005 was not successful in deactivating the device. Due to these results, SCP-005 has been tentatively classified as 'sentient' and further tests are being run to determine its cognitive abilities. However, there are no results that show any traits that prevent it from being able to identify any particular locking device, only that the aforementioned device has been heavily concealed and disguised.

SCP-2295

SCP-2295 in an inactive state

Item #: SCP-2295

Object Class: Safe

Special Containment Procedures: SCP-2295 is to be kept in a standard containment locker within Storage Wing-25 in Site-37.

Personnel with Level 3 or higher security clearance are authorized to perform tests on SCP-2295 after filling out the appropriate paperwork. Please contact Dr. Gergis if required access to SCP-2295 is expected to exceed twenty-four (24) hours.

Description: SCP-2295 is a patchwork stuffed bear, approximately 0.46m from 'head' to 'foot,' and stuffed with synthetic fiber and cotton. SCP-2295 has a small, anatomically correct pin of a heart on the left side of its thorax, and a bow wrapped around its neck. The fabric and color of SCP-2295's patches vary. Tests confirm that no components of SCP-2295 contain any anomalous chemical properties.

SCP-2295

SCP-2295 enters an active state when within two (2) meters of a human sustaining major trauma to an organ. When in the proximity of two or more possible subjects, SCP-2295 will invariably choose the youngest subject. SCP-2295 will anomalously produce scissors, white thread, and either sewing needles or a crocheting hook from its mouth and use any fabric and stuffing in close proximity [1] to fashion an instance of SCP-2295-1, a patchwork imitation of the subject's organ [2]. SCP-2295-1 vanishes from sight and the subject falls into a state of unconsciousness. SCP-2295-1 instances then replace the subject's damaged organ via anomalous means. The whereabouts of organs replaced this way are undetermined.

If there is no usable material in close proximity, SCP-2295 will use fabric and stuffing from itself. SCP-2295 regenerates one (1) gram of stuffing every day until completely replacing any lost or used stuffing. Note that fabric used this way does not regenerate, and additional fabric must be placed near SCP-2295 for the purpose of self-mending.

Instances of SCP-2295-1 successfully carry out their respective functions despite the numerous expected biological, chemical, and medical incompatibilities. Once within the subject, adjacent tissues and veins attach to the imitated organ without observable complications. There have been no cases of rejected SCP-2295-1 instances, and all subjects recorded at the time of writing made full recoveries.

---

[1] Materials have included yarn, textile, cloth, cotton, silk, synthetic fiber, polyester, wool, and thread.
[2] How SCP-2295 is capable of the dexterity necessary for these actions is unknown.

SCP-2295

Test Log-2295

Testing approved to test the limitations of SCP-2295. Materials provided within testing chamber.

Subject: D-2353, 38 years old
Diagnosis: Lungs heavily damaged as a result of twenty-five (25) years of smoking
Notes: SCP-2295 creates SCP-2295-1 using one (1) black textile swatch and one (1) red textile swatch. New 'lungs' act at a capacity similar to those of healthy adult lungs.

Subject: D-3452, 50 years old
Diagnosis: Frequent heart palpitations and severe atherosclerosis
Notes: SCP-2295 crochets SCP-2295-1 using various surrounding yarns. SCP-2295-1 observed to have a heartbeat before vanishing. Transfer successful - how SCP-2295-1 manages to perform function despite absorbent properties of material and multiple gaps in design is unknown. Symptoms no longer present in subject.

Subject: D-7894, 24 years old
Diagnosis: First and second degree burns ranging throughout upper torso, left lateral, and right leg. D-7894 sedated during testing.
Notes: SCP-2295 sews two (2) 5m x 5m sections of patchwork fabric. SCP-2295 cuts appropriately sized swatches and manually places one layer onto subject's affected areas, creating multiple instances of SCP-2295-1, and then repeats this process. The created SCP-2295-1 layers act as dermis and epidermis and, upon recovery, D-7894 claims to have retained feeling in replaced 'skin'. Subject makes a full recovery.

SCP-2295

Subject: D-2723, 18 years old
Diagnosis: Cerebral hemorrhaging
Notes: SCP-2295 grasps various materials in its proximity in a distressed state for approximately one (1) minute. SCP-2295 then anomalously produces a ▮▮▮▮▮▮▮'s Dove Milk Chocolate King Size Candy Bar and offers it to subject. SCP-2295 spends rest of test embracing subject's lower right leg while anomalously producing a saline solution from its 'eyes'.

Addendum-2295: Document 2295 was recovered taped to SCP-2295 inside the site of a crashed mail delivery vehicle. Document-2295 is a red "Get Well" card with the text "KAIROS THE BEAR" written on the front cover.

Contents of Document 2295

To Tommy,

Because only time can mend all wounds.

Love,
Grammy

SCP-426

SCP-426

Item #: SCP-426

Object Class: Euclid

Special Containment Procedures: I am to be sealed in a chamber with no windows through which I may be viewed. The door to my chamber must have a label completely unrelated to my designation or identity, in order to prevent unintended spread of my primary effect. Only Level 3 and above personnel are to know of my presence, and particularly of my properties. Assigned personnel are to be rotated out on a monthly basis to prevent contamination by my secondary effect. Psychiatric evaluation is mandatory at the end of the month. If personnel are deemed unaffected, they may be re-assigned to me no less than four months after their last rotation with me. Any affected personnel are to be given a Class C amnestic and transferred to a different site.

Description: Hello, I am SCP-426. I must be introduced this way in order to prevent ambiguity. I am an ordinary toaster, able to toast bread when supplied with electricity. However, when any human being mentions me, they inadvertently refer to me in the first person. Despite all attempts, there is yet to be a way to speak or write about me in the third person. When in my continuous presence for over two months, individuals begin to identify themselves as a toaster. Unless forcibly restrained, these people will ultimately harm themselves in their attempts to emulate my standard functions.

I was discovered in the home of the ███████ family after the gruesome deaths of three of its members. I had been given to the younger Mr. and Mrs. ███████ as a wedding gift. No card or any other identifying markings had been found on my box. Approximately two months after the family received me, fire crews were dispatched to the home due to an electrical fire. The younger Mrs. ███████ died from the electric discharge that she had caused when attempting to devour an electric socket. The other two victims had died shortly before the fire occurred. The elder Mrs. ███████ had gorged herself with nearly 10 kg of bread before her stomach burst and she died of internal bleeding. The younger Mr. ███████ died of severe blood loss after attempting [REDACTED] with me. The sole survivor was the elder Mr. ███████ who was suffering from severe malnutrition. He stated that he had inserted some bread a week prior and was still waiting for the toast to pop out.

SCP-426

I was confiscated by the Foundation after police noted my unusual properties. A Class C amnestic was administered to the affected officers.

Experiment Log 426-1:

Date: ▮▮-▮▮-▮▮▮▮
Subject: D-class personnel D/426/1
Procedure: D/426/1 was asked to describe what he believed was contained in my chamber. He was not informed about my identity or properties.
Details: D/426/1 stated, "I'm probably some huge monster holed up in there. That's what you guys have all over the place, right?" D/426/1 remained oblivious to his use of the first-person pronoun.

Experiment Log 426-2:

Date: ▮▮-▮▮-▮▮▮▮
Subject: D-class personnel D/426/2
Procedure: D/426/2 was placed in my chamber and given regular meals through a dispenser. No communication with D/426/2 was permitted. Multiple cameras were situated in the chamber, positioned so that I was outside of their field of vision, but allowing constant observation of D/426/2. We remained sealed until my secondary effect manifested in the subject. I was bolted to the floor so that I could not be moved into a camera's view.
Details: After 45 days of isolation, D/426/2 wrapped his arm around me and began conversing with me, stating that we were brothers. D/426/2 never deviated from using the first-person plural when speaking with me. Subject was terminated one hour after this event. It is theorized that the isolation accelerated the progression of my secondary effect.

Experiment Log 426-3:

Date: ▮▮-▮▮-▮▮▮▮
Subject: D-class personnel D/426/3
Procedure: A screw was removed from me and shown to D/426/3 who was asked to describe it. D/426/3 was not informed about my identity or properties.
Details: D/426/3 referred to it as "my screw". Consistent with Experiment 426-1, the subject was oblivious of his use of the first person in his description. This suggests that, even if I were destroyed, my effects would still be inherent in my remains.

SCP-426

Experiment Log 426-4:

Date: ▇▇-▇▇-▇▇▇▇
Subject: D-class personnel D/426/4
Procedure: D/426/4 was placed in isolation in a cell adjacent to my chamber, to be observed until my secondary effect manifests.
Details: No effects appeared. D/426/4 was terminated 90 days after the start of the experiment.
Thank God there are some limits to my effects. A lot of us were really starting to get worried about me. - Dr. C▇▇▇▇▇▇

SCP-4999

SCP-4999

SCP-4999, circa 1973. Photo taken by professional photographer Gustav Bürger, three minutes before his death.

Item # : SCP-4999

Anomaly Class : Keter

Special Containment Procedures : Due to SCP-4999's unwillingness or inability to appear before more than one person at a time, in addition to the subsequent and immediate death of any who witness it firsthand, SCP-4999 is effectively self-containing. Any reports of SCP-4999 manifestations captured by security camera feeds, photographs, or similar are to be investigated, and the media confiscated for analysis. All secondhand witnesses among the civilian populace are to be amnesticized.

Description : SCP-4999 is a humanoid entity of unknown composition, visually resembling a middle-aged male. Its physical appearance varies, with its dark suit being the only constant between manifestations. Due to the rarity of recorded SCP-4999 manifestation events and the highly specific circumstances in which they occur, little data concerning its nature or intent is available; however, its behavior is consistent across all recorded sightings.

SCP-4999

SCP-4999 will manifest only in the presence of one solitary human person at a time. All subjects recorded to date have been in terminally poor health, critically injured, or on their deathbeds, with SCP-4999 appearing nearby and within sight of the individual not more than 20 minutes before their expiration. SCP-4999 will only appear if the subject is conscious and alone. It will not appear if the subject is comatose, asleep, or unconscious; nor will it appear if they are being cared for by, in the company of, or otherwise being directly observed by another person.

Upon manifestation, the entity will seat itself directly adjacent to the subject's bed, if such furniture is available. If not, it will remain standing or sit on the floor/ground in whatever configuration will allow it direct physical access to the subject without causing disturbance. Once situated, it will remove a pack of cigarettes from its left inside jacket pocket and offer one to the subject. If the subject accepts, SCP-4999 will place it between their lips, remove one for itself, and light both. If the subject declines, SCP-4999 will light and smoke the cigarette instead. The entity will make physical contact with the subject, typically via holding their hand, placing its hand atop theirs, or resting its hand on their shoulder.

SCP-4999 will then remain with the subject, silent and unmoving, until they have passed away.

SCP-4999 has not been seen to engage in any other activity or behavior, and demanifests immediately upon the subject's death. The subject's cigarette, however, will remain, providing the only physical evidence of SCP-4999's presence.

No subject thus far has been seen to recoil from or otherwise resist the entity, nor have any attempted to engage it in conversation, despite multiple instances of subjects acknowledging the entity's presence via eye contact, adjusting posture to reciprocate or facilitate the entity's touch, breaking into tears when noticing its presence, or verbally thanking the entity when offered a cigarette.

SCP-4999

Individuals affected by SCP-4999 share a number of common attributes. Research into identified subjects has indicated that SCP-4999 is more likely to appear if an individual:

- lives alone
- is nonreligious
- is impoverished or homeless
- displays a history of mental illness
- is a military veteran
- has no criminal record, or has never been convicted of a violent crime
- has no currently surviving family
- is unmarried or otherwise lacks a significant other
- has little to no social standing in their community
- does not exhibit any record of significant professional or personal accomplishments
- has few to no mutually beneficial interpersonal relationships,

or exhibits qualities and life history that have rendered the individual nondescript, anonymous, neglected, or otherwise unremarkable or insignificant by the standards of their respective society.

No testing involving SCP-4999 has been authorized or attempted, due to available data indicating that observation of a subject precludes its manifestation, as well as ethical concerns.

Discovery : SCP-4999 was initially discovered as the result of its emerging status as an urban legend, with footage of the entity appearing on hospital security cameras worldwide being disseminated via the Internet and various television programs. A minor disinformation program was put into effect to maintain this public image, and SCP-4999 was officially registered on November 27th, 1998.

In the years following SCP-4999's classification, additional research and cross-referencing with accounts of similar phenomena have suggested that while concrete evidence of SCP-4999 appearances has become more commonplace due to the advent of photography and video recording technology in the modern era, writings and artistic depictions of a figure exhibiting similar properties, behavior and physical resemblance to SCP-4999 exist throughout world history, culture, and mythology, with some accounts being thousands of years old - in some cases predating human civilization.

It is not currently understood how pre-modern cultures would have been capable of detecting SCP-4999's presence. Investigation is ongoing.

SCP-1313

SCP-1313

Item Nº: SCP-1313

Anomaly Class: Keter

Special Containment Procedures: SCP-1313 is not currently contained. As a way of limiting the impact of the anomaly, Foundation staff are to monitor all educational institutes for high rates of bear attacks, and dispatch MTF Delta-10 ("Answer Key") to the sites of incidents as soon as possible. Amnestics are to be administered to any civilians with knowledge of SCP-1313.

While copies of SCP-1313 are available from the Foundation archives, under no circumstances are any Foundation personnel to have complete knowledge of the problem. Any staff found solving SCP-1313 are to be reprimanded (and if the situation warrants, terminated) immediately following the bear's capture. Excess bears are to be either released into the wild or used as food/test subjects for suitable anomalies.

Subject 1313-00824, shortly after manifestation

Description: SCP-1313 is an anomalous series of logical processes, capable of being defined as a mathematical equation to which the answer is a single female specimen of *Ursus arctos*. The equation itself does not appear to be inherently anomalous, but rather a quirk of mathematics — rather than producing any number in $R \backslash A$ (the set of all real numbers that are not animals), SCP-1313 resolves to produce a tangible, adult, and frequently enraged grizzly bear. The resolution does not have to be physically represented, and simply considering the problem long enough to arrive at the solution has resulted in a bear's manifestation in or around the subject solving it.

SCP-1313

SCP-1313 does not require any particular mathematical ability to comprehend, beyond a basic understanding of elementary algebra, but all steps of the sequence must be completed in order to reach the correct answer. Skipping parts of the process or attempting to start midway through will not result in any anomalous effects, and will likely produce a purely mundane result.

Currently, examination of partial components of SCP-1313 has revealed the following information about the anomaly:

- That SCP-1313 itself conforms to all axioms used in current number theory (although at times has proven to be remarkably stubborn).
- That bears cannot be returned to numerical form simply by solving the equation's inverse, pending the invention[SCP-001-EX] of a method of applying mathematical operations to physical objects.
- That SCP-1313 can be used as an element of other equations to produce semi-anomalous results. For example, $\sqrt{SCP\text{-}1313}$ resolves to the square root of a live grizzly bear — likewise, $SCP\text{-}1313^2$ is the product of two live grizzly bears multiplied together. It is not recommended that such 'derivative' equations be solved, as the creatures produced are usually poorly integrated into our reality, and invariably extremely hostile during their brief periods of existence [1].
- That grizzly bears exist within the set of all real numbers, and are not prime. The square root of a grizzly bear is prime, however, and is the only prime number that a) is not a cardinal number, b) is neither even nor odd, and c) contains an animal component. The implications that the root of a bear is an integer, and therefore that bears themselves exist on an ordinary number-line, are currently being investigated by Prof. Hutchinson[SCP-003].

---

[1] Research into the possible military applications of irrational, exponential, and imaginary grizzly bears is currently being undertaken by a joint team from the Foundation's mathematical and zoological departments.

SCP-1313

SCP-1313 first came to the Foundation's attention in 1967, when a bear attack was reported at Whitecross High School, Hereford, England. 1724 separate incidents of bear attacks in educational institutes have been observed since, with an estimated 1600 fatalities and 900 further non-fatal injuries. Of the 1724 bears and mathematical bear-composites generated, at least 20% are still at large.

Notice: If during the reading of this document you have pondered the nature of SCP-1313 to such a degree that you feel you have have independently formulated a portion of its structure, you are advised to make your way to your Site's nearest Amnestic Distribution Station, and then (following administration) to Animal Control. Failure to do so may result in disciplinary action and/or bear-related injury.

SCP-1322

Item #: SCP-1322

Object Class: Keter

Special Containment Procedures: SCP-1322 is to be contained in a sealed spherical Class-VIII containment chamber with ablative inner surface, hardened against particle beams, nuclear and conventional explosions, and corrosives, and regularly inspected for damage and monitored for viral and bacterial contamination. Atmospheric pressure within the containment chamber should be maintained at as low a level as practical, and Procedure 1322.CD.S311 is to be initiated if atmospheric pressure should exceed 6.00×10^{-2} Pascal. As an anti-pathogenic measure, radiation levels within the containment chamber should be maintained at no less than 4.50 roentgens per second. Consult document 1322-C-SSR-V-0886 for addenda to containment protocol, as protocol is updated on a daily basis.

Description: SCP-1322 is a stable spacetime anomaly, presently hypothesized to be an interdimensional aperture to a parallel universe. The anomaly occupies a fixed location, around which Site-122 has been constructed in order to study and contain it.

The anomaly is roughly ellipsoid in shape, measuring approximately 2.5 cm along its longer (horizontal) axis and approximately 1 cm along its vertical axis. The anomaly is two-dimensional and coplanar with a plane perpendicular to the horizon and oriented approximately 36 degrees west of true north.

Matter and energy are capable of passing through the anomaly in the manner of a traversable wormhole. When lighting conditions in the space in the near vicinity of the other side of the wormhole permit, the space on the other side of the wormhole can be directly observed. Particles and objects of a cross-section not exceeding the anomaly's dimensions are capable of being inserted into the anomaly and thus transported into the parallel universe. The anomaly does not conduct sound.

SCP-1322

The parallel universe on the "other side" of the anomaly has been officially designated SCP-1322-A, although the term "Hartle" [1] has also been colloquially used. The anomaly appears to have been artificially and deliberately generated from the SCP-1322-A side. The population of SCP-1322-A does not appear to have been successful in generating additional instances of SCP-1322, nor in altering SCP-1322's dimensions or closing it (notwithstanding extensive efforts on their part to do so).

The anomaly appears to have emerged in the standard universe in approximately the year 1952, with the Foundation promptly establishing control over the anomaly's location. Although the Foundation had initially conducted an extensive study program of SCP-1322, including communication with the civilization on the other side of SCP-1322, recent Foundation efforts have focused on containment. See the following containment and observation log excerpts.

---

[1] Approximate phonetic rendering of the term for "homeworld" used by the population of SCP-1322-A with whom communication has been established.

SCP-1322

Time Reference	Remarks
08.1952	Anomaly discovered.
09.1952	Foundation obtains custody over SCP-1322. Containment chamber constructed (see Document 1322.v.SRD3006 for plans and technical specifications).
10.1952	Metallic cylinder emerges through anomaly. Cylinder is retrieved and subjected to quarantine and sterilization. Following clearance, cylinder is examined and found to be hollow, with screw cap. Cylinder contains triangular sheets of paper-like substance, upon which glyphs are inscribed. Artifact referred to Linguistics Unit.
11.1952	Experimentation with SCP-1322 progresses, including introduction of various (string-tethered) objects through anomaly. Samples taken of atmosphere in SCP-1322-A space; found to resemble Earth atmosphere but with a higher concentration of argon.
12.1952	Several additional cylinders, containing documents, emerge through SCP-1322 and, after quarantine, are subjected to analysis.
07.1953	Linguistics and mathematics personnel report breakthrough in analysis of documents obtained from SCP-1322-A. Message on glyphs interpreted as representations of geometric principles and texts apparently composed with a deliberate purpose of establishing cordial contact with the discoverers of the message. Linguistics Unit composes reply message using same writing system, prints same on paper, places paper in a metal cylinder of Foundation manufacture but resembling those used by SCP-1322-A culture and inserts cylinder into anomaly.
09.1953	Light activated on "far side" of anomaly. Close observation of anomaly indicates that "far side" of anomaly is located in what appears to be an artificially-constructed containment chamber, broadly similar to that constructed by Foundation for containment of anomaly.

SCP-1322

10.1953	Approx. start date of extensive communication with SCP-1322-A civilization. Communication initially consists of reciprocal delivery of text messages on paper, first in glyphic system in which initial messages were composed (which is determined to be a simplified form of the standard written language of the SCP-1322-A civilization), and subsequently in a mutually-developed blend of said glyphic system and English. Communication accelerated when SCP-1322-A civilization proposes the construction of a telegraphic system involving a specially-shielded cable traversing the anomaly, with reciprocal equipment for the encoding and decoding of communications on both ends.
11.1953	Communications with SCP-1322-A civilization indicates that the civilization is composed of *Homo sapiens* (or a species not meaningfully different therefrom). Organization with whom communication has been established is a scientific institute associated with the polity comprising the geographic area surrounding the SCP-1322-A-side location of the anomaly (approximately analogous to a nation-state). Details of political organization and technologies of the SCP-1322-A civilization are disclosed. SCP-1322-A civilization has attained an advanced degree of technological and engineering sophistication, particularly in the fields of mathematics and high-energy physics in which that civilization's achievements surpass those of Earth (viz. the creation of the anomaly as an unintended consequence of an experiment to investigate the properties of quantum foam), but with less sophistication in biological science. SCP-1322-A civilization expresses strong interest in sharing samples of music, visual arts, literature (particularly metered poetry in various languages, with a particular interest in Indic and Sinic cultures) and mathematics, but no interest in medicine or religion. Reciprocal deliveries of data from SCP-1322-A civilization are archived and undergo analysis.

SCP-1322

01.1962	SCP-1322-A civilization provides detailed log of astronomical observations and suggests that Foundation reciprocate. Analysis of provided data by Foundation's researchers suggests strong probability that there is no position within our observable universe that can correlate to the provided data. Foundation personnel assemble data file for delivery to SCP-1322-A; data is altered at direction of Site-122 administrator citing security concerns. Within 9 hours following delivery of data file, SCP-1322-A civilization identifies the false information and suggests that Foundation personnel proceed with more candor in the interest of mutual scientific and cultural development. Suggestion forwarded to O-5 for consideration.
11.1972	Telegraphic cable through SCP-1322 temporarily disconnected and withdrawn into containment chamber for routine maintenance. Following maintenance, SCP-1322-A cable end is re-inserted into SCP-1322 where SCP-1322-A personnel re-connect it to equipment on their side.
12.1972	Communication received from SCP-1322-A, indicating that a temporary degradation in the customary response time to signals from Foundation would be experienced due to personnel shortages on SCP-1322-A side. In response to a query, message sent by SCP-1322-A side indicating that the organization having custody of their side of SCP-1322 is experiencing a higher-than-normal incidence of personnel illness resulting in absenteeism.
01.1973	Message sent by SCP-1322-A side reporting that its personnel situation is back to normal, but that illness is becoming widespread in the geographic area of the SCP-1322-A facility.
03.1973	Message sent by SCP-1322-A side indicating that local government is imposing quarantine measures in an effort to arrest spread of what is evidently a viral outbreak on their side. In response to a Foundation offer to render assistance, SCP-1322-A civilization delivers data package containing pathology data.

SCP-1322

04.1973	After appropriate quarantine measures are taken at Site-122, Foundation requests that SCP-1322-A civilization deliver a sample of the virus. Sample is delivered through SCP-1322 in appropriately shielded ampule, which is then secured and analyzed subject to Class V Contagious Disease Protocol (see document ref 033234098). Upon analysis, virus found to be a harmless flu variant. Foundation researchers send analysis data to SCP-1322-A, together with suggestions on synthesizing a vaccine and administering inoculation protocols.
06.1973	SCP-1322-A reports at least 8 million worldwide casualties attributable to virus (approximately 0.091% of their global population), and that Foundation-developed vaccine has been distributed and administered on widespread basis.
08.1973	SCP-1322-A reports that spread of virus appears to have been arrested and that the number of new incidents of illness from the virus is dramatically decreasing.
10.1973	SCP-1322-A reports worldwide inoculation against the virus.
12.1973	In the course of normal communications, SCP-1322-A reports an unexpected decrease in new pregnancies.
05.1974	SCP-1322-A reports a dramatic drop in birth rate.
08.1974	SCP-1322-A reports that its analysis indicates that decreases in fertility appear to be a side effect of the Foundation-provided vaccine.
01.1975	SCP-1322-A reports widespread social disorder attributable to fertility issues and corresponding stresses on family life. In response to Foundation offer of assistance, message received stating "NO THANK YOU. YOU HAVE DONE ENOUGH"
05.1975	Change in management structure of SCP-1322-A organization with custody of their side of SCP-1322. Communications received from their side are frequently belligerent and accusatory in tone.
07.1975	SCP-1322-A organization unilaterally discontinues communications dealing with scientific and cultural exchange.
09.1975	SCP-1322-A organization reports massive, ongoing worldwide upheaval attributable to drop in fertility. Message received indicating fewer than 1,000 live births reported globally in the past 72 days.

SCP-1322

10.1975	Last communication received from SCP-1322-A. Communication consisted of text reading "YOU KILLED US. YOU DID THIS TO US. IN YOUR CARELESSNESS AND YOUR ARROGANCE YOU HAVE DESTROYED OUR POSTERITY. BUT WE SHALL AVENGE. WE OF THE LAST GENERATION PLEDGE AND VOW THIS. WE WILL FIND A WAY."
12.1976	Monitors in SCP-1322 containment chamber indicate that various pathogens have been introduced into the containment chamber from the SCP-1322-A side but have been isolated and destroyed.
01.1977	High-energy particle beam fired through SCP-1322 from the SCP-1322-A side, damaging Site-122 containment chamber. Damage is promptly repaired.
03.1984	High-energy beam of coherent radiant energy fired through SCP-1322 from the SCP-1322-A side, immediately followed by the insertion of various pathogens through SCP-1322. Damage from beam repaired and pathogens isolated and destroyed.
08.1984	Directed energy weapon fired through SCP-1322 from the SCP-1322-A side, immediately followed by the insertion of various pathogens through SCP-1322. Damage from weapon repaired and pathogens isolated and destroyed.
04.1991	Beam weapon fired through SCP-1322 from the SCP-1322-A side, immediately followed by the insertion of various pathogens through SCP-1322. Damage from beam repaired and pathogens isolated and destroyed.
06.1991	At direction of Site-122 administrator, Foundation fills containment chamber of SCP-1322 with quick-setting hardened ceramic.
07.1991	Ceramic dissolved by means of unknown solvent introduced through SCP-1322 from the SCP-1322-A side.
09.1992	High-energy particle beam fired through SCP-1322 from the SCP-1322-A side, immediately followed by the insertion of nanobots through SCP-1322. Damage from beam repaired and nanobots isolated and destroyed.

SCP-1322

10.1992	Large numbers of nanobots inserted through SCP-1322 from the SCP-1322-A side over a long and continuous period. Damage to containment chamber from nanobots repaired, and nanobots destroyed.
01.1994	Iron rod, at least 8 kg in mass, fired through SCP-1322 from the SCP-1322-A side at velocity estimated at 200 km/sec., immediately followed by the insertion of nanobots through SCP-1322. Damage from rod repaired and nanobots isolated and destroyed.
12.1994	Beam of coherent radiant energy fired through SCP-1322 from the SCP-1322-A side for over 108 continuous days. Total energy of beam over that period estimated at over 10^{33} eV. Site-122 extensively damaged, but pathogens and nanobots introduced through SCP-1322 after cessation of particle beam are successfully contained.
03.1995	Device inserted into chamber through SCP-1322 from the SCP-1322-A side. Device is activated and, over a 40-minute period, heats the atmosphere within the containment chamber into a superheated plasma, which damages containment chamber. Plasma successfully vented from chamber, and containment protocol altered so as to require chamber atmospheric pressure to be maintained at near-vacuum.
02.1998	Miniaturized two-stage thermonuclear weapon of incompletely-understood design introduced through SCP-1322 from the SCP-1322-A side and detonated. Site-122 extensively damaged, but pathogens and nanobots introduced through SCP-1322 after detonation are successfully contained.
07.2006	Corrosive fluid pumped into containment chamber through SCP-1322 from the SCP-1322-A side under extremely high pressure. Pressurization of fluid continues after chamber is filled, resulting in damage to containment chamber. Pathogens and nanobots introduced through SCP-1322 after removal of fluid are successfully destroyed and facility repaired.

SCP-1322

04.2007	At direction of Site-122 Administrator, remotely-operated miniaturized probe placed in containment chamber and commanded to approach SCP-1322. When probe came within 3 meters of SCP-1322, a series of iron rods, each at least 8 kg in mass, were fired through SCP-1322 at high velocities comparable to that experienced in 01.1994 incident. Rods destroyed probe and caused extensive damage to Site-122, which was promptly repaired.
11.2008	Gas of unknown composition introduced into chamber through SCP-1322 from the SCP-1322-A side under pressure. Following introduction, additional substance introduced through SCP-1322 resulting in extremely rapid phase-change of gas into solid with greater intermolecular separation than gas, which exerts pressure on chamber sides resulting in extensive damage. Solid then rapidly evaporates, following which pathogens and nanobots are introduced. Pathogens and nanobots destroyed and facility repaired.
06.20■■	Several miniaturized thermonuclear weapons introduced through SCP-1322 from the SCP-1322-A side and detonated, followed by several high-energy particle beams being fired through SCP-1322 from the SCP-1322-A side at various angles. Site-122 extensively damaged, but pathogens and nanobots introduced through SCP-1322 after cessation of particle beams are successfully contained.

SCP-1012

Broadcast tower facility 1012-S3FB9, broadcasting Frequency B'

Item #: SCP-1012

Object Class: Keter

Special Containment Procedures: The Foundation has implemented protocols to cancel or to reduce the risk of generation of three of the five constituent sound tones that comprise SCP-1012:

- *Frequency B and Frequency D* : Frequencies B' and D' are, respectively, the antiphases of Frequencies B and D. These antiphase frequencies cancel frequencies B and D, respectively, within the range of the broadcast.
    - The Foundation operates active noise cancellation broadcast devices in approximately 36,000 locations worldwide, commonly disguised as public address systems, klaxons, speakers and the like, which continually broadcast at Frequency B' or D' (subject to the availability of power).

SCP-1012

- ◦ Additionally, the Foundation has arranged for Frequencies B' and D' to be continually broadcast by most of the world's electroacoustic transducers. This has been achieved through a combination of inserting design changes into the engineering specifications of most commonly-manufactured electroacoustic transducers manufactured since 1988, inserting Frequency B', D' or both into the transmission of broadcast media and the encoding of recorded media (including inserting design changes into the engineering specifications of recording appliances so that Frequency B', D' or both are automatically encoded), and by manipulating the supply frequencies of commercially transmitted and distributed electric power so as to cause sound equipment and other electric appliances to generate Frequency B' or D'. [1]
- *Frequency C* : In the wild, most instances of the generation of Frequency C had consisted of the whalesong of *Balaenoptera svalbardi*, the Svalbard whale. Through Foundation efforts, *Balaenoptera svalbardi* became extinct in 1982, thereby decreasing the likelihood that the tone would inadvertently be generated in a location near the generation of other constituent tones.

All documentation that specifies the constituent sound tones of SCP-1012 is to be kept strictly confidential.

---

[1] Under normal conditions, Frequencies B' and D' are each substantially higher than the upper frequency limit for mammalian hearing and are therefore inaudible to humans, as well as other animals with a greater range of hearing such as dogs. However, it has been reported that some humans exposed to strong broadcasts of Frequency D' experience tinnitus. Under certain atmospheric and geological conditions (such as those prevailing in Taos, New Mexico and Bristol, UK), the broadcast of Frequencies B' or D' may be audible. Additionally, certain models of fluorescent lighting tubes and cathode ray tube televisions emit audible tones in sympathetic resonance with Frequency B' or D'.

SCP-1012

Description: SCP-1012 is a chord consisting of five sound tones, designated Frequencies A, B, C, D and E. The tones of SCP-1012 are:

Designation	Frequency	Remarks
Frequency A	415.305■ Hz	Within range of human hearing, slightly higher than G#
Frequency B	■ kHz	Ultrasonic
Frequency C	■ Hz	Infrasonic; lower than the range of human hearing but observable, at higher intensities, in the form of vibrations
Frequency D	■ kHz	Ultrasonic
Frequency E	■ Hz	Within range of human hearing but rarely used in the chromatic musical scale

The generation of one or more, but less than all, of the constituent tones of SCP-1012 does not result in anomalous effects.

The simultaneous generation of all five tones of SCP-1012 for a duration exceeding a few seconds affects [2] the resonance of certain subatomic particles within range, causing them to disintegrate into their constituent elementary particles. Computer modeling predicts that a generation of SCP-1012 within close proximity of a mass, such as an astronomical body, is likely to result in an uncontrollable chain reaction resulting in the disintegration of virtually all matter comprising the mass. According to the model, once such a chain reaction is initiated, it will continue to progress whether or not the tones of SCP-1012 are continuing to be generated, until all available mass is affected (i.e., a CK-class scenario). Proposals to use SCP-1012 or a modified version as a defense mechanism against hostile extraterrestrial threats, including SCP-1548 and SCP-2838, have been rejected due to the potentially disastrous side effects of SCP-1012 testing.

---

[2] The described result is predicted according to the cosmological model set forth in Foundation Document 8001.2552.KT.1012. Laboratory testing of the model is prohibited.

SCP-1733

Single frame from iteration 1733-007.

Item #: SCP-1733

Object Class: Safe

Special Containment Procedures: The DVR containing SCP-1733 is to be kept in a secure video archive at Site-███. Playback of SCP-1733 is strictly forbidden unless required for research. Personnel must contact Dr. Geller for permission to study SCP-1733.

Description : SCP-1733 is a digital recording of the 2010-2011 NBA season opening game played at the TD Garden in Boston, Massachusetts on 10/26/2010 between the Boston Celtics and Miami Heat. Agents monitoring social networking sites were alerted to SCP-1733 when Boston native ███████ ███████ complained in a Facebook thread on 10/27 about a technical foul in the third quarter involving players Ray Allen and Chris Bosh that never occurred in the original broadcast. When confronted, ███████ ███████ uploaded the relevant segment much to the confusion of his derogators. Foundation agents embedded in Facebook's moderator team deleted the thread and procured the IP addresses of all individuals present at the chat at this time to locate and administer Class-A amnestics. The Motorola brand DVR containing SCP-1733 was recovered for study.

Study of the footage has since revealed the nature of the recording's anomalous properties. Although initially diverging from the original broadcast only negligibly, such as quarter point totals and occurrences of fouls, SCP-1733 has begun to markedly digress from the content of its earlier playbacks. Recorded entities have been observed to retain memory of previous playings, and as such have developed a burgeoning awareness of their existence.

SCP-1733

It is hypothesized that playbacks impart an unquantifiable measure of cognizance to the entities inhabiting SCP-1733, with consecutive playings greatly expanding recall of previous events. This effect is cumulative and extends to all persons in the arena. Quality of awareness has progressed from reported feelings of intense déjà vu by commentator personalities Mike & Tommy to a near-eidetic memory of preceding playbacks. However, to note, no entities inside SCP-1733 have ever addressed the viewer directly, or shown awareness that they reside in a digital recording.

The individuals in the recording are virtually indistinguishable from their real life counterparts in talent, behavior, and mannerisms on court. Fans in the crowd also appear to be real human beings in all respects, and Foundation inquiries into the current status of these persons has found nothing of note. For all intents and purposes, recorded entities appear to be the actual individuals but somehow abiding in a digital medium. TD Garden records have put the number of people in attendance on 10/26/2010 at ▓▓▓▓. It was initially thought the purpose of SCP-1733 was to depict an infinite number of game outcomes, since players were able to modify offensive and defensive strategies during every playback. By playback 034, players and coaches became so keenly adapted to the opposing team's playbook that the score remained 0-0 until 3:34 in the first quarter. As quality of recall was still weak in early stage iterations, memory of preceding playbacks likely manifested as a vague intuition felt by players, fans, and team personnel alike, interfering with their ability to grasp the full scope of their situation.

By playback 045, however, comprehension of their predicament had reached such a point that players declined to play altogether and assembled with the rest of those in attendance to formulate possible escape plans. It is the conclusion of Foundation researchers that the inhabitants of SCP-1733 are imprisoned in the setting of the recording, as they have been unable to exit by any means. Doors leading out of the arena have not yielded to an estimated force in excess of ▓▓▓ N. The assembly has also been unable to exit from locker rooms, player facilities, and skyboxes. Waiting for patrons arriving in at scripted points prior to the start of the first quarter has also been unsuccessful: individuals leave by where patrons entered and are then unable to navigate an escape from the adjacent corridors that girdle the main arena. Escape attempts have since grown more desperate, and have included failed attempts at constructing makeshift explosives, all-out rioting, the fracturing of the assembly into three opposing factions, and by playback ▓▓ the ritualistic murder and disembowelment of players in the hopes of appeasing whatever it is that confines them (see Timeline Document 001 for details). However, upon the beginning of a new playback, all persons are returned to their pre-game status unharmed.

SCP-1733

Researchers have been unable to duplicate the effects of SCP-1733 with other recordings made by the DVR, confirming the device is not the source of SCP-1733's aberrant properties. Due to the distress visited upon inhabitants of SCP-1733, testing has been suspended indefinitely.

Playback #	Notable Developments
Playback 002	First recorded deviation from recorded broadcast. TD Garden crowd boos the Miami Heat during entrance. Miami Heat forward LeBron James observed to have scowled and shaken his head dismissively at the crowd.
Playback 015	Score remains 0-0 for eight consecutive possessions. Fans appear noticeably subdued when displayed on the facility's HD scoreboard screen. Celtics power forward Glen Davis is able to execute a crucial block late in the fourth quarter on LeBron James he could not complete during the original broadcast, securing the Celtics' lead. Commentators note Glen Davis's dedication to performing well on both sides of the court in spite of the "Big Three's blistering ball movement on offensive plays". A nascent awareness of previously played games has begun to form.
Playback 026	First Miami Heat victory, 112-85. Crowd becomes aggressive, shouting obscenities and hurling foodstuffs at the Celtics. Color commentator Tom Heinsohn understood the frustration, criticizing the Celtics' coaching staff for becoming so complacent after having "cracked the code of the Miami Heat offense". As this was the first game together for the Miami "Big Three", it is unlikely any coaching personnel would have become so adjusted to an unfamiliar offense in a single game.
Playback 027	Commentators Mike & Tommy note a feeling of déjà vu during the Heat's grandiose entrance. Crowd remains subdued during key Celtics plays. Celtics emerge the victors, prompting Tom Heinsohn to remark "the Celtics have come a long way winning back the hearts of their fans". When asked to elaborate by Mike Gorman, Heinsohn could only respond that he felt the team had an embarrassment to atone for, but could not specify further.

SCP-1733

Playback 044	Teams emerge disoriented and confused. Game is suspended. Majority of time is spent by medical professionals assessing the mental state of players, who remain convinced they had dreamt playing the season opener frequently the previous night. When informed of the situation by team staff, commentators Mike & Tommy affirm the same feeling. Crowd is also afflicted. Recording ends with court-side correspondents interviewing members of the crowd on the nature of their dreams.
Playback 045	Players refuse to play. Cameramen, facility personnel, players, commentators, and crowd members gather in the court to appraise the situation. All persons are convinced they are reliving the same game repeatedly. Doors are tested but cannot be budged. Recording closes as crowd begins to fashion makeshift weapons to pry open doors. Last instance of camera being manipulated by the camera crew. All following playbacks are seen through a single static shot of a broadcast view camera.
Playback 051	No attempts to exit the building have succeeded. All exits in the arena and adjacent areas remain sealed. A physical altercation in balcony section 318 between an inebriated group of college-aged males and one older male leaves the older male concussed on the floor and unconscious. As broadcast camera is unable to pick up audible voices on opposite side of the arena, presumably the dispute occurred over the group of males not assisting with escape plans. First recorded violent incident.
Playback 052	The man knocked unconscious in previous playback is returned to previous state unharmed upon the beginning of current recording. The man ambushes and bludgeons one of his attackers to death at 34:12 mark.
Playback 055	Cognitization has progressed to such a point that the crowd is now able to remember the events of that week, as well as friends and family members outside the facility. Attempts to contact outside for help are met with failure.

SCP-1733

Playback 065	Crowd is unable to exit the facility. Congregation has since dissolved into the following groups and "factions": players, coaches, and all involved team personnel have presumably barricaded themselves in off-screen player facilities. The infirm and parents accompanied by their children have retreated to the northeast corner of the balcony rise and have elected to wait out playbacks as they occur, marking their territory with a Celtics championship flag draped over Section 320. ▮ individuals henceforth referred to as the "Faithkeepers" have proselytized to multiple gatherings that they believe being confined to the TD Garden is a punishment for rampant consumerism of the post-industrial world, and have burned "offerings" of mobile phones, car keys, handbags, and wallets in center court for the past four playbacks. The group comprises Boston churchgoers and [REDACTED]. A notable portion of adults numbering approximately ▮ individuals, however, remain diligent in formulating escape plans.
Playback 073	The "Faithkeepers" grow in number after previous playback incident, where three males were severely injured by an improvised explosive fastened to an exit door. No damage to the door is visible.
Playback 095	Hedonistic displays of sex and violence have sufficiently curbed the efforts of proselytizers. Makeshift curtains are hung around the site of an orgy at loge 8 at the urging of Section 320 members.
Playback 112	Conditions have deteriorated considerably. ▮ individuals leapt from balcony section in opening ten minutes of playback 112.
Playback ▮	Faithkeepers storm player facilities to retrieve Paul Pierce and LeBron James. The players are ritually sacrificed and their bodies are subsequently displayed on the arena's "Jumbotron". The murder of players seems to have no effect on the recording.
Playback ▮	Proselytizers have begun to call for the sacrifice of children. Adults have formed a wall between Group 320 and the Faithkeepers.
Playback ▮	First recorded deviation in arena light to a deep red color. [DATA EXPUNGED].

SCP-701

SCP-701

SCP-701-1 in a still image from SCP-701-19██-A

Item #: SCP-701

Object Class: Euclid

Special Containment Procedures: All materials relating to SCP-701 are to be kept in a triple-locked archive at Storage Site-██. These items currently consist of: the two (2) currently extant copies of the 1640 quarto; twenty-seven (27) copies of the 1965 trade paperback edition; ten (10) copies of a 1971 hardcover printing; twenty-one (21) floppy diskettes, consisting of data seized from raids on [EXPUNGED]; one (1) S-VHS video cassette tape (designated SCP-701-19██-A); and one (1) steel knife of unknown origin (designated SCP-701-19██-B). At no time are any of these items to be removed from the room. Access to the area is to be heavily monitored; absolutely no personnel

SCP-701

whatsoever is to be granted access to the archive without the express, in-person permission of Drs. L███, R███ and J███.

Description: SCP-701, *The Hanged King's Tragedy* , is a Caroline-era revenge tragedy in five acts. Performances of the play are associated with sudden psychotic and suicidal behavior among both observers and participants, as well as the manifestation of a mysterious figure, classified as SCP-701-1. Historical estimates place the number of lives claimed by the play at between ███ and ███ over the past three hundred years.

Performances of *The Hanged King's Tragedy* do not always end with an outbreak. Of the ██ recorded performances, only ██ (36.78%) have ended in SCP-701 events. According to historical records and investigations, these outbreaks generally follow the same pattern:

- *1 to 2 weeks (7 to 14 days) prior to Event:* During the dress rehearsal period, cast members will begin to spontaneously deviate from the published text of the play. Rather than improvisation or gaffs associated with going 'off script,' said deviations will be both orderly and consistent, as if the actors were working off a new version of the script. The cast and production crew will seem unaware of any change, and - if it is brought to their attention - will state that the play has run that way from the beginning.

- *2 to 3 hours prior to Event:* The outbreak generally occurs during Opening Night, or else at the production with the greatest planned attendance (generally falling within the first week after the play's opening).

- *1 to 2 hours before Event:* SCP-701-1 begins to appear on stage in the final scene of Act I, generally in the background or to the side of the main action. It may seem to enter or exit the stage area, but does not appear to ever enter the backstage or off-stage area; it simply disappears when not on stage. The cast does not appear to notice or comment on SCP-701-1, at least at first.

- *The Event:* SCP-701-1 appears fully on stage during the banquet scene in Act V. Here, it will be incorporated into the action of the play as *'the Hanged King.'* The cast will either murder each other or commit suicide, sometimes using items that seem to appear spontaneously on

SCP-701

stage. Rioting breaks out in the audience, with viewers randomly attacking anyone in front of them, regardless of prior relationship.

- *Following the Event:* If any of the audience members survive the initial outbreak, they may exit the performance space, in which case they will continue to engage in random or opportunistic violence. Victims will generally require sedation or restraint in this scenario; normal personality will begin to return roughly 24 hours after the event. Surviving victims will generally exhibit signs consistent with a traumatic experience; some will have no recollection of the event. Others may be rendered permanently comatose or psychotic.

For a typical case study of an outbreak, see Incident Report SCP-701-19█-1, an analysis of the events leading up to the last uncontained SCP-701 event in 19█, during a high school drama performance in ███████████, ████. For more information on the play's published text, see Document SCP-701-1640-B-1.

In short, SCP-701 is a self-evolving memetic virus, transmitted through unknown means through the text of the play. Dr. L████ has theorized that SCP-701 events may involve [EXPUNGED]. This hypothesis is consistent with a spike in ████ ███████ levels detected via satellite in the vicinity of the 19█ incident, indicating [EXPUNGED].

Foundation agents are under standing orders to suppress any performance or publication of SCP-701 whenever found or detected. Despite our best efforts to the contrary, however, the play remains freely available online, sometimes under different titles. All attempts to detect or isolate the origin of these copies have failed. Suppression of the play's publication has generally been successful, with most copies of a 1971 scholarly edition destroyed before distribution. Nonetheless, copies of the 1965 trade paperback turn up with some regularity in both college and high school libraries. Agents are to obtain or otherwise destroy these items whenever possible.

History: The first known publication of *The Hanged King's Tragedy* was as a quarto dated 1640. The play's author is not listed. The publisher, one William Cooke, disappeared from the historical record soon thereafter. Strangely, the text does not appear in the Stationers' Register.

SCP-701

The first known SCP-701 event on record occurred in 18██ during a performance of the play in ██████, ██, USA. Other significant incidents include the 19██ performance at a small theater in ██████, ██, ██; the 1964 performance at the University of ██████, ██████, ██████; the 19██ performance at ██████ University, the first SCP-701 event successfully suppressed by the Foundation; the 19██ performance by a student group in ██████, CA; the 19██ television adaptation by the ██████ Broadcasting Corporation (production successfully shut down by the Foundation before broadcast); and the 19██ incident in ██████, OH, USA, designated SCP-701-19██-1.

Publication History:

- Original 1640 quarto (all known copies in Foundation custody)
- 1733 folio edition (republished 1790)
- 1813 Cambridge University Press edition
- 1965 trade paperback edition
- 1971 hardcover edition

Agents should note that copies of the play have often been misfiled under different titles or spellings of the title. Furthermore, photocopies of the 1965 text have been found in circulation throughout college theater departments in the continental United States and in the United Kingdom.

Additional:

- *Given the high probability of [EXPUNGED] in my mind, I again recommend that SCP-701 be upgraded to Keter-class. The SCP-701 memetic virus may very well be the forefront of an invasion scenario. Furthermore, [EXPUNGED]. - Dr. L██████, 1237116060.*
- *Denied. None of the current information we have on SCP-701 indicates a XK-class scenario. Until we have additional data, classification will remain at Euclid. — Face facts, Doctor. The cat's been long out of the bag on this one. And in this line of business, we consider ourselves lucky if we only lose a hundred or so people every ten years. - O5-█, 1237197060.*

Incident Report SCP-701-19█-1

Incident Report SCP-701-19█-1

SCP Involved: SCP-701

Date: ████████ █, 19██

Location: [EXPUNGED]

Report prepared by Drs. R██████ and J██████ on the content of SCP-701-19██-A. SCP-701-19██-A is a 187mm x 103mm x 25mm S-VHS video cassette tape recovered by investigators from the scene of the incident, a performance of SCP-701 at ████████████ High School in ████████████, ████. Tape was found in a destroyed consumer-grade camcorder, which was apparently recording the performance from a vantage point within the audience. It is the only surviving record of the event. Please see the SCP-701 archives for the full transcript of the recording. In order to compare the identified deviations during a SCP-701 event with the actual plot of the published text, see Document SCP-701-1640-B-1.

- *0:00:00* – Tape begins.

- *0:03:10* – House lights go down.

- *0:05:12* – Curtain rises. The play begins as published with Gonzalo's coronation speech.

- *0:10:21* – A possible sighting of SCP-701-1 during Isabella's ravings – an anomalous shadow not belonging to one of the cast members shows up along the back wall of the set.

- *0:10:24* – Shadow disappears.

- *0:23:15* – First deviation from the text. Rather than the dialogue between Francisco and the courtesan, the curtain drops and comes back up on a bare stage. Antonio enters from stage right.

Incident Report SCP-701-19▮-1

- *0:23:24* – First indirect sighting of SCP-701-1. The shadow of a figure seems to appear on the back wall, from stage right. Antonio stops in place and acts surprised. The shadow disappears. Antonio begins a long soliloquy, confirming that he now believes Isabella's story. Dr. J▮ notes that while this soliloquy is in the style of the rest of the play and seems to be accurate Caroline-era dialogue, Antonio's speech in this scene **does not** exist in the original text.

- *0:24:12* – Curtain drops.

- *0:24:51* – Curtain rises on Francisco and the courtesan. Antonio returns; the play continues as scripted.

- *0:31:14* – First direct sighting of SCP-701-1. It enters and stands at the edge of stage left towards the end of Act II, Scene 1.

- *0:32:17* – Gonzalo's dialogue concludes (as scripted) with the mention of an appointment with the ambassador from Alagadda. He exits, stage left; SCP-701-1 seems to turn and follow him as the lights go down.

- *0:38:13* – Second sighting of SCP-701-1 during Act III, Scene 1. It appears on the edge of stage right as Gonzalo and Petruccio murder Sortino. The scene concludes with Gonzalo ordering his cooks to prepare the corpse as a stew; scripts recovered from the scene indicate that this section had been cut in rehearsal.

- *0:51:11* – Third sighting of SCP-701-1; appears close to stage left as Antonio kills Isabella.

- *1:09:12* – Fourth sighting: SCP-701-1 enters with Gonzalo at the beginning of Act IV, Scene 1, and follows him throughout the scene. The scene also contains two key moments: first, Gonzalo seems to nod to SCP-701-1 when he mentions the ambassador of Alagadda. This is the first time a cast member has seemed to indicate SCP-701-1's presence. Second, the scene ends with a deviation from the text: whereas the scripted speech at the end of Act IV, Scene 1 ends with Gonzalo considering his own moral inequity, Gonzalo here seems to be more concerned that his 'tribute' will be sufficient for the ambassador. The lights go down.

Incident Report SCP-701-19█-1

- *1:21:15* – Fifth sighting: SCP-701-1 enters stage left at the end of Act IV, Scene 2 as Antonio leaves to secure a blade for his coup. Rather than exiting, Antonio stops in front of SCP-701-1, who hands him a long dagger. (*This is believed to be the first appearance of the item classified SCP-701-19█-B; note that there is no mention of the item in the prop list or the other records maintained by the production.*) SCP-701-1 and Antonio depart the stage together.

- *1:32:41* – Sixth sighting: SCP-701-1 appears on stage left as Cornari and Lodovico exit.

- *1:35:10* – The lights come up. Act V, Scene 1 – the Banquet scene – begins as scripted.

- *1:40:52* – Antonio enters, bearing a piece of parchment. Here the textual deviations begin in earnest: rather than the parchment being Petrucchio's confession as scripted, Antonio instead describes it as an invoice from the ambassador of Alagadda, proving that Gonzalo owes more tribute than he intends to pay.

- *1:41:42* - SCP-701-1 enters at this point from stage right. The entire cast seems to perceive it. Gonzalo stands up, curses as an aside to the audience, and runs for stage left. The rest of the cast – including Alinda and Francisco, who enter from stage left – physically restrain Gonzalo and drag him back onto the stage. SCP-701-1 meanwhile moves to the center of the stage, where it stands in front of Gonzalo's throne.

- *1:43:08* – A noose is dropped onto the stage from above. The cast force Gonzalo into the noose, as he begins to curse in Italian (*and in one place, possibly Latin?*). The noose is drawn taut, and the cast drops Gonzalo; he begins to asphyxiate.

- *1:43:32* – Antonio speaks: *"With this, the tribute, in full it is paid."* The actor takes SCP-701-19█-B (the dagger) and draws it across Gonzalo's stomach, spilling his intestines across the stage.

- *1:44:04* – Alinda takes the dagger from Antonio. She speaks: *"With this, fool's blood, it is the Hanged King's."* She cuts Antonio's throat.

- *1:45:31* – Ropes drop from the roof of the stage, a noose for each cast member. The cast assembles underneath them. Alinda takes position next to SCP-701-1.

Incident Report SCP-701-19█-1

- *1:46:12* – Alinda: *"With this, our blood, it is the Hanged King's."* The cast hang themselves.

- *1:47:33* – SCP-701-1 moves through the hanging corpses and to front-center stage.

- *1:47:41* – The stage lights cut out.

- *1:47:46* – Sounds of screaming and physical violence around the camera.

- *1:48:22* – Loud sound, most likely the camera being knocked over.

- *1:49:01* – The camera is destroyed. Tape ends.

Document SCP-701-1640-B-1

Document SCP-701-1640-B-1

The following is a summary of the published text of The Hanged King's Tragedy *, classified* SCP-701 *, prepared by Dr. J▓▓▓▓▓ from a copy of the 1640 quarto in Foundation custody.*

DRAMATIS PERSONAE:

- GONZALO, King of Trinculo
- ISABELLA, Queen of Trinculo; formerly the wife of Sforza, the murdered king, now married to Gonzalo
- ANTONIO, a minor noble
- FRANCISCO, Antonio's servant
- The DUKE OF SORTINO
- ALINDA, daughter of the Duke
- PETRUCCIO, a noble lord allied with Gonzalo
- LODOVICO, a servant of Gonzalo
- CORNARI, a priest
- BEATRICE, a servant of the Queen
- A COURTESAN
- A PALACE GUARDSMAN
- The AMBASSADOR OF MILAN
- The AMBASSADOR OF FLORENCE
- The AMBASSADOR OF ALAGADDA

SETTING:

The play is set in the Kingdom of Trinculo (probably a misspelling of Trinacria, another name for Sicily), in the capital city of Serko (another name for the city of Syracuse). As the play opens, Sforza, the king of Trinculo, has died, supposedly from natural causes while on retreat from the court. The nobility of Trinculo gathers in the capital for the coronation of the new king, Sforza's younger brother, Gonzalo, who has also married Sforza's queen, Isabella.

Despite the text's references to contemporary Italian city-states, such as Florence and Milan, much of the play's setting is obviously pure fantasy. There were never any kings of Sicily comparable to Gonzalo and Sforza, and the capital of the historical Kingdom of Sicily was Palermo, not Syracuse. (The author may have chosen to move the play's events to Syracuse, due to that city's historical association with tyranny). There is also no record of any country or place known by the name *Alagadda* , a mysterious but apparently

Document SCP-701-1640-B-1

powerful state that plays a significant role in the plot. It may be intended as a reference to one of the Muslim states or cities on the Mediterranean coast, such as Tunis or Algiers.

PLOT SUMMARY:
The plot of *The Hanged King's Tragedy* bears a marked resemblance to many earlier plays of the same genre, including Shakespeare's *Hamlet* and *Titus Andronicus*. In fact, past investigations into SCP-701 events have noted that *The Hanged King's Tragedy* was often chosen for production as a less-violent alternative to the two plays mentioned. The two murders in the SCP-701 text can be construed as occurring off-stage, and the implication of cannibalism in Act III can be easily cut from the script.

ACT I:
The play opens during Gonzalo's coronation. Gonzalo opens with a toast to the assembled nobility, then departs the stage. Drunk on the wine, Isabella confesses to some of the courtiers left on stage that Sforza did not die in his sleep as reported. Instead, while on retreat in the countryside, Sforza was fed a sleeping potion by Isabella, then murdered by Gonzalo and his supporters. As a final show of disrespect, the conspirators hanged the King like a common criminal from a tree. Isabella goes on to proclaim that Antonio, a minor noble visiting the King's court for the first time, is actually her and Sforza's son and the rightful heir to the throne. Isabella collapses and is taken offstage by her servants.

Francisco asks Antonio if he believes the Queen's story. Antonio makes light of the situation, and they exit. Back in Antonio's rented lodgings, Francisco attempts to barter with a Courtesan. Antonio enters the stage, clearly in shock. He reports that, while off-stage, he saw the Ghost of Sforza, who confirmed Antonio's parentage and the Queen's description of his death.

ACT II:
Gonzalo, having learned of Isabella's confession, consults with his fellow conspirators. Lodovico confirms that at least three people witnessed the Queen's breakdown – the Duke of Sortino, his daughter Alinda, and a priest named Cornari. Gonzalo immediately begins to plan the murder or capture of the three in order to cover up the truth. He orders Isabella to be locked up in a convent, with the story put out that the Queen is mad. Isabella, uncharacteristically, meekly accepts Gonzalo's judgment. The usurper then exits, having an appointment with the ambassador from Alagadda.

Back in their lodgings in the city, Francisco brings Antonio news of the Queen's imprisonment. Together, they begin to plan their revenge.

Document SCP-701-1640-B-1

ACT III:
Petruccio and Gonzalo invite Sortino to dinner. They kill him and order the palace cooks to prepare the corpse as a stew. Gonzalo orders Alinda, who witnessed the murder, to be locked up in the convent.

Antonio fakes insanity in order to gain admittance to the convent. Warned of Antonio's coming, Isabella and her loyal servant, Beatrice, prepare to murder him using a draught of poison. Antonio sees through their plan and forces Isabella to drink the poison, killing her. Meanwhile, Francisco gets lost within the convent and winds up freeing Alinda from her cell by accident.

ACT IV:
In the palace, Gonzalo reports to Lodovico that he has, in exchange for an unstated 'tribute,' obtained a powerful and tasteless poison from the ambassador of Alagadda. Gonzalo plans to poison the stew made from the Duke of Sortino's corpse and feed it to the court, thus ensuring the suppression of the truth. Lodovico leaves the stage to carry out the usurper's plan. Gonzalo then has a brief moment of conscience: in a soliloquy, he describes the regret he carries for his sins, but is nonetheless unable to deviate from the path he has set.

Meanwhile, Francisco introduces Alinda to Antonio, all three having escaped the convent. Alinda describes her father's murder in grisly terms; Antonio promises to marry her and make her his queen, as soon as his revenge is complete. He then leaves to obtain a blade, with which he plans to kill Gonzalo.

There is a comedic interlude between a Palace Guard and Cornari, a buffoonish priest. At the end of the scene, Lodovico enters and bids Cornari to follow him. The priest is not seen on stage again.

ACT V:
The guests arrive at Gonzalo's banquet. Gonzalo once again offers a toast, this time to the ambassadors of the foreign nations who are present. The meal is served; however, before it can begin, Antonio enters, bearing a signed confession he obtained from Petruccio off-stage, which includes the details of Sforza's murder and proof of Antonio's lineage. Gonzalo is deposed by the outraged courtiers; rather than murder him, however, Antonio instead decides to spare the usurper and let him accept exile to a monastery. He then orders Francisco to start making plans for his marriage to Alinda. The play ends with a dance staged by the courtiers.

Document SCP-701-1640-B-1

SCP-701 EVENTS

The produced form of the play that occurs during SCP-701 events contains several deviations from the text as published. For a typical example of these deviations, see Incident Report SCP-701-19█-1 .

SCP-1000

SCP-1000

Still from unverified amateur "Patterson footage"

Item #: SCP-1000

Object Class: Keter

Special Containment Procedures: All media reports related to SCP-1000 are to be examined for potential verifiability. All organizations and individuals investigating SCP-1000's existence are to be kept under surveillance by Mobile Task Force Zeta-1000 and discredited or administered amnestics. All physical signs of SCP-1000's existence must be retrieved and kept in Foundation custody, and replaced with decoy items if necessary. Alleged sightings of SCP-1000 must always be investigated by MTF Zeta-1000, however trivial the claim.

Absolutely no contact with wild or captive instances of SCP-1000 is allowed without prior approval by Director Jones. Any interaction between SCP-1000 and humans, including Foundation personnel, must be reported to Director Jones immediately.

Description: SCP-1000 is a nocturnal, omnivorous ape, classified in the *Hominini* branch along with genera *Pan* and *Homo* . Adults range in size from 1.5 to 3 m (5 to 10 ft) in height, and weigh between 90 and 270 kg (200 - 600 lbs). They have grey, brown, black, red, and occasionally white fur. They possess large eyes with good vision, a pronounced brow ridge, and a sagittal crest on the forehead similar to that of the gorilla, but present in both sexes. Their intelligence is on par with that of *Pan troglodytes* (the common chimpanzee).

SCP-1000

SCP-1000 evolved alongside *Homo sapiens*, existing contemporaneously with proto-humans and humans in large numbers until 10,000-15,000 years ago, when an extinction event eliminated all but 1-5% of their population. This event was triggered by SCP-1000 contracting an anomalous "pseudo-disease" classified as SCP-1000-f1. This disease is passed on at the genetic level and affects every present-day instance of SCP-1000. The majority of SCP-1000 instances are born immune to the effect; those who are not born immune quickly die.

The effect of SCP-1000-f1 is as follows: Any hominid (including humans, chimpanzees, bonobos, and non-immune instances of SCP-1000) that directly or indirectly observes any instance of SCP-1000 has a minimum 2% chance of being instantly killed through anomalous means via permanent cessation of brain function. This percentage is cumulative, and the longer a human views SCP-1000, the higher the chance of instantaneous death increases, at a rate of +1% chance per 20 minutes of viewing. This effect varies between individual members of SCP-1000's species, with some individuals carrying a 'death chance' of 90%. The effect is also produced by dead individuals, though small fur samples do not exhibit the effect.

Known means of preventing this effect are small-scale only and include [REDACTED] (see attached documentation; Level 3 clearance required).

Because of SCP-1000's close relation to humanity, it is considered likely that SCP-1000-f1 could eventually transfer to human carriers. Any instance of SCP-1000 finding its way to a major population center could constitute an ■-class end of the world scenario with a minimum death toll of [REDACTED] and possible extinction of humanity. Fortunately, SCP-1000 appears to instinctively avoid human contact.

It is not currently feasible to exterminate SCP-1000 entirely.

The highest known population concentrations of SCP-1000 are at present located in the Pacific Northwest region of North America and the Himalayan Mountain range in Asia. As of ■/■/■, these populations remain extant. SCP-1000's presence and [DATA EXPUNGED] have also been documented within the past 5 years on every continent. All known significant populations of SCP-1000 located near human population centers have been eliminated.

SCP-1000

SCP-1000 came to the attention of the Foundation via contact by Doctor Franz M█████████ in 14██ with the Children of the Sun, who identified themselves as outcast members of the Serpent's Hand . This group has since been completely destroyed by the Foundation, due to their reluctance to surrender information about SCP-1000, SCP-███, and SCP-███ (since reclassified as SCP-1000-███ and SCP-1000-███). Remaining members have either joined the Foundation, or have gone into hiding, presumably as members of the Serpent's Hand. Weapons, tools, and other unique pseudo-technological resources in possession of the organization have been classified as SCP-1000-001 through SCP-1000-█████. These resources have been made use of by the Foundation in multiple instances; for a full list, see Document 1000-3534-Y (Level 3 clearance required). Access to surviving ex-members of the Children of the Sun is restricted to personnel with clearance level 4/1000 unless given direct authorization for contact by Director Jones.

Further information is available to personnel with clearance level 3/1000 or above. Personnel with clearance level 3/1000 or above are required to read Document Alpha-1596-1000.

Addendum 1000-466-X: Update to Special Containment Procedures: As of ██/██/████, SCP-1000's Special Containment Procedures no longer include Procedure 516-Lumina. [DATA EXPUNGED] indicates that SCP-1000 may be developing a resistance to the sonic element [DATA EXPUNGED] will not develop further, so that Procedure 516-Lumina can still be used in emergency situations. Investigation into alternate means of reliably keeping SCP-1000 away from human population centers is underway. Whether SCP-1000 resistance to Procedure 516-Lumina was calculated (and as such may be a sign of SCP-1000 [REDACTED]) or coincidental (by chance of natural species variation) is not known at this time.

== LEVEL 3 CLEARANCE REQUIRED ==

SCP-1000

Document Alpha-1596-1000: Missive from Director Jones

You've probably heard the rumors before now. Everyone without the clearance level to know better wants to get their dig in. "Did you hear Sasquatch is an SCP? Are we gonna capture and contain Batboy next?"

Yes. SCP-1000 is Bigfoot.

I'm sure you've snickered. Don't worry. Contrary to rumors, we don't actually assign you to "Keter duty" for finding something humorous.

You think Bigfoot is funny because we *want* you to think Bigfoot is funny. We've bankrolled Hollywood comedies and farcical documentaries, paid off men in gorilla suits, perpetrated hoaxes with bear prints and goat fur, bribed and brainwashed cartoonists to get especially silly depictions on children's television. Even the term "Bigfoot" comes from us, planted in the media in 1958, a term people would find even harder to take seriously than "Sasquatch".

Why? We'll get to that.

The information in the article that you've already read isn't entirely true. There are two direct lies, and plenty of lies of omission.

There is no such thing as the "anomalous pseudo-disease" referred to as SCP-1000-f1. SCP-1000 does not possess a magical death aura. In fact, SCP-1000 does not directly exhibit any anomalous effect whatsoever.

We also lied about SCP-1000's intelligence level. SCP-1000 aren't chimp-level smart. They're smarter - to be precise, they are exactly as smart as us.

That brings us to the lies of omission. That's what this letter is for. The lies came from me, so I figure the truth should come from me as well.

This is the story we got from the Children of the Sun who defected to us. It's a story we didn't believe - refused to believe, at first.

As you've already read, the apes we call SCP-1000 evolved alongside us. We walked in the daytime, they walked in the nighttime, our nocturnal siblings in the shadows.

SCP-1000

But while we were still wandering hunter-gatherers, they... changed. Like we would, a few thousand years later. Tools. Weapons. Agriculture. Domesticated animals. Stable settlements. As humanity blinked in the Pleistocene sun, SCP-1000's population exploded across the night. They blanketed the planet in the tens of billions.

They made things that we still can't comprehend, even though we've thoroughly studied the surviving pieces. Organic technology. They made trees and birds of prey grow into fast-moving ships, herds of animals that became trains, bushes that became flying vehicles. From insects and pigeons they made things equivalent to cell phones, televisions, computers. Atomic bombs. The Children describe vast shining cities, stretching across glaciers and penetrating the deepest caverns, grown skyships of ivory and spider-silk, creatures tending them with hundreds of blinking eyes.

We were rare, like gorillas now, a few hundred thousand left at best. We avoided their settlements just like wild animals today avoid ours. SCP-1000 understood we were intelligent like them, but avoided us just as we avoided them, saw us as fairies, as gnomes, ascribed us supernatural powers, said we ate bad children while they slept in daylight. They fenced off our dwindling wild populations in conservatories, outlawed poaching but in the underground consumed our bones as aphrodisiacs.

Then their civilization fell. And we did it. By 'we' I don't mean the Foundation. By 'we', I mean humanity.

The story is muddy. Supposedly a trickster forest god showed humanity favor, showed us the master's tools and how to use them. Why we did it, we don't know. Perhaps they hunted us, perhaps we were simply afraid. Perhaps it was just that they fenced us in, unintentionally or not. We simply don't know what the truth is. Somehow we acquired SCP-1000's own technology, and with it, we instigated an SK-class dominance shift in which humanity became the dominant species of Earth.

SCP-1000

We wiped out 70% of SCP-1000's population in a single day. The Day of Flowers, the Children called it. Supposedly every flower bloomed that day, while our enemies died in their sleep. Then we hunted the rest down. But we went further than just killing them. With a few of the more twisted of SCP-1000's devices, we drove the survivors mad, even those hiding beyond our reach. We trapped them in their own minds, blocking higher functions and leaving their bodies to fend for themselves like any ordinary ape. We slaughtered their living machines and burned their vast shining cities with SCP-1000's bioweapons that reduced everything to slurry and dust that washed or blew away in spring rain and wind.

We left no traces. Not even our own memory. We turned one of the weapons on ourselves, wiped out any knowledge of SCP-1000 and the greatest civilization the planet had ever seen. Only a few humans protected themselves from the effect, kept the forbidden knowledge, just in case. The rest of us went back to being hunter-gatherers, none the wiser.

Which brings us to today.

You're going to read all about this in the level 3 documentation, but I'll give you the short version here: SCP-1000 are somehow regaining their forgotten intelligence and knowledge. Maybe they never truly lost it. We don't know.

This is why the ever-increasing number of "Bigfoot sightings" is so worrying. Why the attempts at contact, however indecipherable, are even more worrying.

Yes. SCP-1000 *are* just like us. That's what makes them so dangerous. We wiped them from history and memory. We dissolved their civilization and we slaughtered most of their species. Just ask yourselves: If they got the chance, what more would they do to us?

Addendum 1000-056-D: Instances of SCP-1000 have tried to make contact with Foundation personnel on multiple occasions. Most of these attempts at contact have [DATA EXPUNGED] untranslated, though recent attempts show that some instances of SCP-1000 are capable of communicating in English.

SCP-1000

Addendum 1000-104-Y: <u>Certain acquired documents</u> contain extensive references to SCP-1000. Relevant is that the documents appear to be composed by entities associated directly with the location known as the <u>Wanderer's Library</u>. Context or significance of document details not yet clarified.

Addendum 1000-276-A: Numerous anomalous objects with a known connection to SCP-1000 [DATA EXPUNGED] prior cyclical iterations. As one example, <u>SCP-2273</u> may not have a point of origin in a parallel timeline, but instead a prior "iteration". <u>SCP-2932</u>, <u>SCP-2511</u>, and other sources of living cultural insight into SCP-1000 (or a variation) all present "consistent inconsistencies" which may be used to create a fuller picture of the nature of these "iterations", though conclusions are uncertain.

Addendum 1000-276-Q: Special report [DATA EXPUNGED] This unnumbered "black box" anomalous item anchored underneath <u>the structure[SCP-2000]</u> is likely the most significant anomalous object known to have been utilized. Central to understanding SCP-1000's anomalous capabilities, including capabilities not developed directly, but accessed from prior [DATA EXPUNGED] modern-day relevance to the Foundation and to society at large in a scenario of general containment failure.

Log 1000-ad065-x1: The following is a rough translation of recent SCP-1000 attempt at communication with Foundation personnel on ■/■/■ (see attached documentation).

---

we forgive you;
given choice for now, not forever;
let us back in

SCP-2000

> The following document is a verbatim printout of the output of the console used to access SCP-2000.
>
> - Dr. Peter James Defort

WARNING: HMCL and O5 Approval Required

The file you are attempting to access is available to personnel with Level 4/2000 clearance only. This clearance is not included in general Level 4 security protocol.

Attempting access beyond this point without necessary clearance is grounds for termination of Foundation employment and cancellation of all educational, medical, retirement, and mortality benefits. By submitting your credentials you hereby consent to exposure to a known cognitohazardous image, and verify that you have been inoculated against that image. In the event of unauthorized access, this console will become inoperable. Security personnel will be dispatched to revive you and escort you to a detention cell for interrogation. Attempting to access this file from any computer not connected to the Foundation Intranet will result in immediate termination regardless of clearance.

[SUBMIT LOGIN CREDENTIALS: LEVEL 4/2000 CLEARANCE REQUIRED]
[SECURITY COGNITOHAZARD ACTIVATED: SCANNING FOR NEURAL ACTIVITY]

SCP-2000

Consciousness confirmed. Retrieving file.

Item #: SCP-2000

Object Class: Thaumiel

Special Containment Procedures: The entrance to SCP-2000 is disguised as a disused Park Ranger station in Yellowstone National Park[SCP-1422] . Despite several civilian trespassing attempts, the entrance has yet to be breached in the installation's recorded history, and no further physical containment has been deemed necessary. Protocol Plainsight-201 is in effect for SCP-2000. Necessary supplies and replacement personnel may be delivered via unmarked road vehicles or civilian helicopter as appropriate.

No personnel below Level 4/2000 clearance are permitted access to documentation regarding SCP-2000, or any protocols associated with its containment and upkeep. No personnel below Level 5/2000 clearance are permitted access to SCP-2000 below Sub-level 3. All personnel assigned to SCP-2000 must submit to a neural archetype scan on a monthly basis. Personnel stationed on-site must submit to weekly scans, to be stored locally.

Level 4/2000 personnel or above stationed on-site are not permitted to leave Yellowstone National Park during the course of their assignment. In the event of transfer (either elective or compulsory), Class A amnestics must be administered, and false memories implanted consistent with assignment to other high-security or Keter-class SCP objects. Additional personnel may be assigned to SCP-2000 and granted temporary Level 4/2000 clearance at the discretion of the item's HMCL supervisor (currently Dr. Charles Gears) and O5 command.

The exterior surface of SCP-2000 is surrounded by Scranton Reality Anchors (SRAs) every 20 m, arranged hexagonally, to prevent incursion by hostile anomalous interference. Each SRA's function must be checked semi-annually and replaced as necessary. Technicians servicing SRA components may reference Document SRA-033, rev 1.0.7. Five Xyank/Anastasakos Constant Temporal Sinks (XACTS) capable of maintaining stable tachyon flux across the expanse of the facility (maximum output rating at 100 W each) have been installed and are to be maintained monthly. Technicians servicing XACTS components may refer to Document XACTS-864, rev 1.3.0.

One Pseudo-Riemannian manifold has been initiated at the entrance to Sub-level 4, and must remain open at all times. In the event of the manifold's

SCP-2000

failure, Procedure Dead Euclid-101 is to be executed immediately. Other non-anomalous life support and utility systems may be maintained in accordance with standard Foundation Maintenance Protocol, Section 101.5 (Mission Critical Components). Wherever possible, non-anomalous materials and resources are to be used for SCP-2000's maintenance and repair.

In the event of any K-Class scenario which does not compromise the existence or function of SCP-2000, Procedure CYA-009 is to be enacted as soon as possible. Remaining Foundation installations globally are to monitor the scenario as it unfolds, preserving what material resources are possible under the Ganymede Protocol until such time as all remaining sites respond "All Clear" to SCP-2000 queries as defined in Document 2000XKAC-1.9. Upon receipt of "All Clear" code, Procedure Lazarus-01 is to be implemented.

> **Administrator Note:** *I want this on permanent record, and I don't rightly care if you think it's an insult to your intelligence; some things are just this important. This device is absolutely not an excuse to let down our guard or take greater risks with SCP objects or cross-test them or whatever you might have in mind. Primary Containment is still our best chance at survival; otherwise there would be no reason to make the cover-up so extensive. We can only suspend God's disbelief so many times before the universe just says "no". And considering what we've had to deal with in these past few decades, we may have passed that point already.*
>
> *- Former Administrator Dr. William Fritz*

Description: SCP-2000 is a subterranean Foundation installation originally constructed sometime in the last ███ years for the purpose of reconstructing civilization in the event that a K-Class end-of-the-world scenario could not be averted in time to prevent humanity's extinction or near-extinction. Since its inception, SCP-2000 has been activated at least twice. Foundation records regarding SCP-2000's construction and history prior to this assumed first use have been lost. Whether this information black-out is the result of accident or design is impossible to determine. The mission critical portion of this installation begins 75m below ground level and extends to a 100m depth.

Although the scope of engineering required to recreate SCP-2000 in its entirety is impossible to execute while maintaining secrecy, all subsystems of SCP-2000 have been successfully reproduced in laboratory setting; the installation and all procedures involved in its upkeep are mundane in nature.

SCP-2000

(See Document 2000-SS-EX for information regarding esoteric Foundation technologies necessary for SCP-2000's function). Primary power for the facility is a Liquid Fluoride Thorium Reactor (LFTR) rated for 1 GW total output, with a reactor life of 70 years at maximum capacity. A geothermal generator has also been installed to take advantage of the region's volcanic activity. This generator is capable of powering the facility in "stand-by" mode indefinitely. SCP-2000 also contains water treatment facilities, air purification and recycling systems, hydroponic production wings, and housing necessary to permanently sustain up to 10,000 personnel.

To fulfill its primary mission, SCP-2000 includes 500,000 Bright/Zartion Hominid Replicators (BZHR). At peak capacity, SCP-2000 is capable of producing 100,000 viable, non-anomalous humans per day (with a warm-up period of 5 days). Utilizing an underground Riemannian transit pipe to collect raw material from various hot springs and underground magma flows in the area, and a computer memory bank housing data on all known human alleles, this system is capable of recreating any lost human genome or generating as many new and unique genomes as necessary to repopulate human civilization.

> **Researcher Note:** *Use of the BZHR system is currently suspended outside of maintenance testing and emergency situations (CYA-009 is still "go"). Possible hostile incursion is still being investigated, and this database is proving particularly difficult to de-bug. We're still seeing a distribution of congenital and genetic defects far above baseline numbers. Right now, I can only guarantee about 60-75% viability in new specimens. See Addendum 2000-1.*
>
> - <u>Dr. Christopher Zartion MD, Biotech Research and Development</u>

Humans produced by this process can be advanced to any age desired without extending the 5 day incubation period. In addition to construction features, the BZHR also has the ability to implant memories by administration of Class-G hallucinogenics and developmental hypnotherapy. Life histories, neural archetype scans, and genomes of many Foundation personnel – including all personnel of Level 4/2000 clearance and above – are maintained to ensure that SCP-2000 may be activated and Procedure Lazarus-01 can be initiated by as few as one surviving human.

SCP-2000

After the implementation of the Ganymede protocol (indicating a failure of the Foundation to prevent a K-Class scenario), SCP-2000's security systems will unlock, allowing any Foundation employee to initiate Procedure CYA-009. If, after 20 years, SCP-2000 remains inactive, security will be relaxed further, allowing any non-anomalous human being to access the facility and initiate the procedure. Once activated, SCP-2000's internal monitoring systems will attempt to locate all personnel of Level 4/2000 clearance and assess their condition. Mission-critical personnel not found will be replicated using the most recent neural archetype scan on file, and awakened prior to the initialization of any other systems.

After these personnel are revived, security locks will resume normal function. For a complete list of contingency options available, Level 5/2000 personnel may access Document 2000-CYA-09. Note that receipt of the "All Clear" code as defined by Document 2000XKAC-1.9 may be waived only if all other Foundation facilities have been rendered inoperative. Otherwise, security and MTF elements revived under Procedure CYA-009 will be dispatched to all remaining Foundation facilities to confirm their function and the integrity of local reality.

Procedure Lazarus-01 will begin when an authorized Level 5/2000 Foundation employee inputs the desired "Resume Date" into SCP-2000's BZHR control unit. Available units will then begin production of prominent political and cultural leaders of the time period using descriptions/genetic information on file, as well as replication of a global populace consistent with the chosen time period. Most of SCP-2000's floor space is dedicated to storage of building materials, construction equipment, factory machinery, agricultural equipment, and computer database storage. In addition to infrastructure concerns, a wide cultural base with copies of thousands of famous works of art, music, literature, and a full backup of the World Wide Web are kept on site in the event that other repositories are destroyed.

SCP-2000

HMCL Note: *Discovered this note in previous iteration records at Lazarus-01 conclusion.*

> **Researcher Note:** *If we ever have to do this again, do not set the Resume Date further back than 20 years before the Event. Not only can we piggy-back on a lot of undestroyed structures if we do, but it will make continuity a lot easier to resume. [REDACTED] years is too many. We're straining personnel such as it is without having to rebuild to chronological specifications just to save time on the population and agricultural demands. Besides, how much of the 20th-2█th centuries do we really want to re-write, and how many times? Isn't one 'Great War' hard enough to keep track of?*
>
> - Dr. Henrietta Eisenhower, Historian

My tenure as SCP-2000's HMCL will honor this request. Currently pursuing official documentation update to account for this change. Two World Wars is plenty. We do not need to hazard a third.

- Dr. Charles Gears, HMCL Supervisor

The first replacement humans housed off-site must necessarily be informed of SCP-2000's existence and function as they are being created. This strategy allows newly constructed humans to assist in reconstruction and recolonization efforts directly, and skill sets appropriate to reconstruction have been preselected for increased prevalence in the first 5 million individuals produced. As global population increases, the process of diaspora and reconstruction will accelerate geometrically, allowing economic and agricultural infrastructure to recover as quickly as possible.

While it is feasible that some replacement humans will not survive the initial renovation period, such individuals can be recreated indefinitely until all major population centers and Foundation facilities have been completed. Foundation administrative assets during this period will focus on the falsification of dendrochronological, astronomical, and radiometric dating records necessary to maintain the appearance of historical continuity.

SCP-2000

Please see Document 2000-RetCon v 2.3.3 for details. In the event that significant portions of natural habitat are also destroyed prior to the project's completion, refer to Document 2000-OneTear v 3.0 for approved rapid regrowth methods.

It is estimated that the world population, manufacturing capability, agricultural production, and culture can be reset to 2000 CE levels 25 to 50 yrs after the procedure is implemented. At the conclusion of Procedure Lazarus-01, amnestic agent ENUI-5 will be released en-masse, causing all reconstructed humans to forget their affiliation with Foundation assets. History will then resume from the chosen date. Each procedure will necessarily alter the course of human events due to the enormous complexity of human social interaction. Further research into predictive historical modeling based on observations from prior completions of the Procedure Lazarus-01 is ongoing.

> **HMCL Note:** *No further proposals for behavioral or cultural modification will be accepted at this time. Previous attempts to ameliorate violent and sociopathic tendencies in humanity as a whole have already been implemented and deemed successful. Experimentation using second iteration subjects indicates that further modification would undermine tenacity to such a degree that technological and social progress would be noticeably inhibited. See Experiment Log ███-█ for further information.*
>
> *- Dr. Charles Gears, HMCL Supervisor*

Document 2000-SS-EX: The following information establishes basic operational parameters of technology developed specifically for the SCP-2000 project. Although this technology may appear to be anomalous, it is based entirely on verifiable scientific principles currently in use by the Foundation to effect containment.

SCP-2000

The invention of the Scranton Reality Anchor (SRA) appears to pre-date the first activation of SCP-2000, and is credited to Dr. Robert Scranton in 1889. The main body and much of the circuitry of the SRA are constructed of a corrosion-resistant beryllium bronze alloy. Inspired by artifacts recovered [DATA EXPUNGED], effectively eliminating the appearance of virtual particle/anti-particle pairs required for Type Green reality bending phenomena to manifest. Due to the expense involved in producing the beryllium bronze alloy required for the SRA's construction, Foundation-wide implementation of the device has been limited to units capable of an area of effect less than two cubic meters[1].

> **Researcher Note:** *The mechanism of the SRA's function and the source of its inspiration must be kept secret from all possible Reality Bending entities for reasons which I hope are obvious. Only qualified Level-6/2000 maintenance technicians have been cleared to access this documentation. If any member of SCP-2000 staff reveals to you that they are a Level-6/2000 maintenance technician, please report them to O5 Command so they can be reassigned and submitted to amnestic therapy immediately. This is not a punishment; it is a legitimate safety concern. If these devices are ever compromised, so too is our life-boat.*
>
> - Dr. Lowell Henry Piedmont, Esoteric Containment

The Xyank/Anastasakos Constant Temporal Sink (XACTS) is a device designed to stabilize the flow of causality across a given field of effect. XACTS's use high-power electromagnetic radiation in the radio band coupled with a tachyon field emitter [2] to create a permeable event-boundary, allowing organic and electrical systems to pass through unaffected while maintaining a static causal environment. In other words, temporal anomalies which might normally prevent SCP-2000 from being constructed will have no effect, so long as at least one XACTS remains in operation. There are no plans to implement Foundation-wide use of XACTS devices.

SCP-2000

Researcher Note: *Temporal sinks can be useful for a lot of things. Containing SCP objects for which you need one second to last 300,000 years is a good example. Holding a point of reference constant during temporal repair missions, so that you can meaningfully record your progress and undo serious mistakes is another. But natural causal relationships are flexible in a way the human mind is not equipped to deal with meaningfully, and creating more than a small handful of isolated static causalities will do more to damage temporal integrity than secure it. XACTS will not be implemented Foundation-wide. Yes, we have tried it during a past iteration. No, further inquiries into the results of that attempt will not be accepted.*

- Dr. Thaddeus Xyank, Temporal Anomalies

The use of a Pseudo-Riemannian manifold allows SCP-2000's floor plan to extend into negative depth, providing 10 km^2 of floor space. Original documentation on this system's construction prior to previous SCP-2000 activations has been lost. While this phenomenon has traditionally been indicative of spatial anomalies, it is the determination of Drs. Robert Boyd and Tristan Bailey that the manifold entrance is consistent with an advanced implementation of modern physics. [3] This 'negative' space is maintained via a non-gravitational singularity generated through focused ▅▅▅ particle emission across the manifold's desired entrance. In the event of the singularity's failure, the installation will remain intact in isolation and will not suffer structural collapse. Recreation of the manifold is estimated to take less than 10 hrs if Protocol Dead Euclid-101 is enacted immediately after failure. The isolated portion of SCP-2000 will remain operable and inhabitable for up to 36 hrs after the manifold fails, and is recoverable indefinitely.

Addendum 2000-1: During containment breach of SCP-▅▅▅ on ▅▅/▅▅/▅▅.2, SCP-2000 experienced failure of several SRA and XACTS components[SCP-3480] which coincided with activation of the BZHR units on site. For 25 days following this incident, BZHR units produced over 10 million humanoid entities with internal biology inconsistent with modern humans. Differences include an additional heart chamber, perfect polydactyl of the hands and feet, increased endocranial volume and height, and the presence of an abdominal organ of unknown purpose which emits and responds to radio frequencies in the 2.4-3.6 GHz range.

SCP-2000

These humanoids were neither dosed with Class-G hallucinogenics during replication, nor submitted to developmental hypnotherapy. All remained unconscious until expiration five weeks later. Classification of SCP-2000-1 for these entities is currently under review.

Whether this event is the direct result of trans-temporal interaction between SCP-▮▮▮ and SCP-2000, sabotage, information leak, or non-anomalous equipment malfunction is as yet unknown. Diagnostic checks and structural repair are proceeding ~~as scheduled~~ ~~nominally~~ within acceptable risk. SCP-2000 is expected to resume normal function as of January ~~2008~~ ~~2013~~ 2020.

Addendum 2000-2: While making repairs to SRA units in Sector 3382 on ▮▮/▮▮/▮▮.2, Technician [DATA EXPUNGED] reported the discovery of human remains in an advanced state of decay. Analysis of clothing fragments discovered with the remains indicates the remains are 450-700 yrs old. Valid Foundation security credentials for Dr. Alto Clef were discovered nearby, although a genetic match could not be established. The following note was recovered from a hermetically sealed plastic document sleeve.

> Why did we have to build this thing?
> *When* did we do it?
> *How long* have we been doing it?
> Do we even _know_ ?!

Subsequent interrogation has verified that Dr. Clef has no knowledge of this event, and is ignorant as to the purpose of the message.

Bibliography
[1]. "Use of mSRA 'Scranton Boxes' to Provide Mission Critical Document Security"; L. Piedmont et. al.; *Foundation* ; Vol 106.8; pp 10-14; 1988
[2]. "Relativistic Motion in Superfluids for use in Tachyon Emission and Storage"; T. Xyank, A. Anastasakos; *Foundation* ; Vol 10.4; pp 141-143; 1892
[3]. "Transit Portal Dynamics: Stretching the Brane"; T. Bailey et al. *Foundation* ; Vol 115.2; pp 23-37; 1997

SCP-1025

SCP-1025

SCP-1025, with publisher's name redacted

Item #: SCP-1025

Object Class: ~~Keter~~ Safe

Special Containment Procedures: ~~Due to its potential as a bioweapon capable of destroying all life on Earth, SCP-1025 is to be kept in an isolated underground vault secured by no fewer than 10 armed guards, to be rotated twice weekly and checked for compromise by infectious agents. The vault should be armed with a thermite mine to be detonated at the first sign of containment breach.~~

Revision: SCP-1025 is to be kept in a passcode-secured locker. Further research requires O5 approval.

Description: SCP-1025 is a hardcover book, approximately 1,500 pages long. The front cover and spine feature the title "The Encyclopedia of Common Diseases." The publisher's page indicates the book was printed in 19▮▮ by ▮▮▮▮▮▮ Press. No other copies of a book with that title and publisher have been found, and no record of the publisher exists.

Readers of the book seem to exhibit symptoms of any disease they read about. The effect can take between ▮ and ▮ hours to manifest. **(See Test Log)**

217

SCP-1025

Addendum 1025-01: Test Log

Subjects: D-1025-01
Test: Subject read entry entitled "Common Cold." Subject observed for several hours afterward.
Results: Subject exhibited cough within 2 hours, and when asked, claimed to feel "slightly achey," though he attributed this to uncomfortable sleeping arrangements.

Subjects: D-1025-02
Test: Subject read entry entitled "Chicken Pox." Subject observed for several hours.
Results: Over the course of one hour, subject observed to scratch at no fewer than 5 points on her body repeatedly. Subject's medical history indicated she had contracted chicken pox at age 8. Possible evidence that item can override natural immunities noted.

Subjects: D-1025-03
Test: Subject read entry entitled "Cancer of the Lungs." Subject observed for several hours. Test was to determine item's ability to accelerate advancement of illnesses.
Result: Subject observed to cough 4 10 6 a significant number of times over the course of ▮ hours within a relatively small amount of time. Subject denied feeling any discomfort, but observation of subject's breathing indicated irregularities. Subject terminated and sent for autopsy. No tumors apparent.
Note: *We clearly didn't wait long enough. But we all heard the coughs, and his wheezing.*

Subjects: D-1025-04
Test: Previous test repeated, but subject observed for 7 days.
Results: A lot of coughing and wheezing, far beyond what should be considered normal. Subject terminated and sent for autopsy. No tumors apparent.
Note: *What if the illness vanishes after death, making infection all the more insidious?*

SCP-1025

Subjects: D-1025-05
Test: Same as previous.
Results: Same as previous, but subject sent for vivisection, utilizing [DATA EXPUNGED] hours before expiring from shock. No tumors apparent.
Note: *We have to keep trying. Imagine if this were an infectious agent. Imagine if there were more books like this out there.*

[Redundant tests redacted for brevity. In summary, each test used one D-class subject, who read one entry from the item, and was then tested or vivisected in search of signs of infection following reported symptoms. After test 15, research was moved to a dedicated isolated facility in ███, █, staffed by 3 researchers and 2 security. One D-class subject delivered as needed to minimize space and ration needs.]

Subjects: D-1025-27
Test: Subject read entry entitled "Appendicitis." Subject had undergone an appendectomy at age 16. Observed for 3 days.
Results: After 52 hours, subject complained of ~~stomach ache~~ significant abdominal discomfort. Vivisection performed. No appendix found, but area where appendix would normally be looked a few shades more red than it should be, by general consensus of research staff.

Subjects: D-1025-28 (formerly Researcher ███ ███)
Test: Subject had developed persistent cough, despite never reading SCP-1025, and was placed in observation for one week.
Results: None apparent for 6 days. At 0930 hours on day 7, subject appeared slightly taller than the day previous. Noted as evidence that item's anomalous properties can cause generation of diseases other than those researched by the victim, and without direct viewing of reading material. Vivisection considered, but overruled for the time being.
Note: *███ got out! The crazy bastard got out somehow! We were so stupid! The addition of height is a classical symptom of SCP-016 adapting to the stress of being confined in that room. Who knows or cares what he was coming down with first? There was a grating on the ceiling. A few more feet of height, and a few inches skinnier, and he'd easily fit. He could be up there right now, growing claws and vomiting infected blood everywhere and taking who knows what other dormant diseases with him. SCP-008 ? SCP-742 ? Oh, God, what if he's come down with SCP-217 ?*

SCP-1025

Addendum 1025-02: A recovery team was sent to the facility on ■/■/■ after no contact was made from the facility for 72 hours. Agents found Researchers ■■ ■ and ■ ■ sealed in the observation booth, both wearing biological containment suits. Nearly all stored air tanks were depleted. Agent ■■ ■ was found crawling through the facility's air ducts with sidearm drawn. Researcher ■ ■ had locked himself in the barracks with an improvised flamethrower made of aerosol cleaner and a box of matches. Later interview indicated ■ had not climbed into ducts, but simply used his passcode to leave the observation chamber while other researchers were distracted. Agent ■ ■ was found dead in a supply closet locked from inside, with several empty bottles of water and ration packages. The door had been given an airtight seal with garbage bags and duct tape.

Note: *After careful review of all research on SCP-1025, I'm ordering an immediate evaluation of whoever approved the use of 27 D-Class subjects, an isolated facility, and a dedicated underground bunker on this money pit. Not one out-of-the-ordinary infectious agent was found anyplace this item was tested. And every involved staff member had passed a basic psych exam within the previous year. I have no idea how far up the chain of command this "hypochondria by proxy" effect can reach, or how it works, and frankly, I see no benefit in learning. Stick it in a box, lock it up, and for God's sake, try not to worry about it. -O5-■*

SCP-1101

SCP-1101

Item #: SCP-1101

Object Class: ~~Safe~~ Euclid

Special Containment Procedures: SCP-1101 is contained in a 20x20m secure room at Site-█. The containment room is monitored and recorded from a separate station by CCTV at all times; however, under no circumstances should this be viewed while an SCP-1101 event is in progress. When monitoring devices detect activity in SCP-1101's containment room, an alarm is to sound and both the containment room and the CCTV station are to be sealed until activity has ceased. All individuals under the influence of an SCP-1101 event are to be quarantined by security staff wearing hearing protection. No more than 20 individuals are to be introduced to SCP-1101 without O5-level approval. No objects are to be placed atop SCP-1101 except under controlled testing circumstances.

Following Incident 1101-4, bathroom facilities and 1 month of supplies for up to 20 people have been placed in SCP-1101's containment room. Apparatus for the dispensing of VX nerve gas has been installed to be activated in the event of a major emergency, specifically any one of the following;

- >50 individuals under the influence of an SCP-1101 event
- risk of uncontrolled spread of an SCP-1101 event beyond the containment facility
- SCP-1101 event of duration greater than 1 month

If this protocol in conjunction with standard quarantine measures fails to contain the emergency, personnel should refer to Plan MODERATE-4, which [DATA EXPUNGED]

SCP-1101

Description: SCP-1101 is a 0.6m tall marble pedestal with an octagonal top. It exhibits no unusual properties until an object is placed atop SCP-1101 in the presence of more than one person. In this situation, any comment made relating to the object by an individual present will start a heated discussion (an SCP-1101 event). During an SCP-1101 event, affected individuals are compelled to continue the discussion until broad agreement is reached with one individual, the 'winner'. The 'winner' will take the object atop SCP-1101, which signals the end of an event. If the affected individuals do not come to an agreement, a 'winner' will be selected after a certain length of time and end the event. In this case, the winner has usually made a more intelligent or factually correct argument, but there appears to be subjectivity involved, perhaps suggesting sapience on SCP-1101's part. Memories of the event are retained. Subsequently, the 'winner' experiences feelings of euphoria and an attachment to the object 'won', while the rest of the affected subjects suffer mildly depressed mood. These effects are transient and dissipate after a maximum of one week.

Individuals will join an event regardless of debating skill, educational level or ordinary interest in the event topic. SCP-1101 does not appear to cause major personality changes save the compulsion to discuss. However, events have the potential to become vitriolic regardless of individual personalities. Interestingly, no incidents of physical violence have been recorded during an event despite frequent displays of extreme anger.

Affected individuals will only attend to basic needs if it is possible to simultaneously participate in the event (subjects may collapse from exhaustion if an event is of sufficient duration, but appear to suffer no long-term ill effects). The event is a memetic hazard: all individuals who hear an event in progress or see SCP-1101 at the time are compelled to join, including individuals viewing the event remotely. The latter are capable of starting separate secondary instances of SCP-1101 events which will gravitate towards the location of SCP-1101.

Duration of events is variable and dependent on the specific arguments and positions taken by the individuals involved. SCP-1101 events have been observed ranging from 3 minutes to up to 5 months (in this particular case, the event only ceased due to interruption of food supplies and subsequent starvation of individuals involved).

Further information on SCP-1101 may be found in [REDACTED].

SCP-1101

Test Battery 1101-1: Initial baseline testing. An object was placed upon SCP-1101 and test subjects instructed to enter the containment chamber.

1101-1A
Object: Nothing
Test Subjects: 5 D-class personnel D-1101-1 through 5
Additional Instructions: None
Result: Subjects made normal conversation for 5 minutes. Test ended.

1101-1B
Object: 1 rectangular pine wood block
Test Subjects: 5 D-class personnel D-1101-1 through 5, in addition to Dr. Major (unplanned inclusion)
Additional Instructions: D-1101 asked to describe object
Transcript:
D-1101-1: It's a wooden block.

D-1101-4: I think they want you to say what sort of wood. The last thing I was assigned to, they kept making me put these balsa sheets into some machine.

D-1101-2: Uh, balsa doesn't come in blocks, it's something else.

D-1101-3: He didn't say it was balsa, it's probably some kind of oak wood.

Dr. Major *[over intercom]* : It's a pine block.

D-1101-1: Why is he telling us? Maybe it's a trick. *[Other test subjects voice agreement]*

Dr. Major: You idiots, I know what it is!

[REDACTED]

Results: At this stage full properties of SCP-1101 were unknown; Dr. Major was observing remotely and was therefore affected by the event. Test subjects proceeded to argue for 6 minutes about both the composition of the block and the trustworthiness of Dr. Major. After 6 minutes they were convinced by Dr. Major of the block's composition and he left the observation room to collect the block, 'winning' and ending the event. Live observation of SCP-1101 was subsequently discontinued.

SCP-1101

1101-1C
Object: 1 rectangular pine wood block
Test Subjects: 5 D-class personnel D-1101-1 through 5
Additional Instructions: D-1101 asked to give an opinion about the object
Transcript:
D-1101-1: Oh, it's this damn block. I, uh, I don't really care about this? It doesn't do anything.
D-1101-3: I guess you could use it as a doorstopper?
D-1101-5: Who the hell would want that?
D-1101-2: I might! It could be a paperweight.
D-1101-3: No, it's too big. It would be better as a doorstopper.
D-1101-5: Are you serious? It's just a *[expletive]* block!
[REDACTED]
Result: Subjects argued about possible uses for the block for 13 minutes. Agreement was reached that the block was not designed for function but could have some useful characteristics. D-1101-2 was the 'winner' and ended the event.

1101-1D
Object: One Panasonic portable DVD player, not powered
Test Subjects: 5 D-class personnel D-1101-1 through 5
Additional Instructions: None
Transcript:
D-1101-2: It'd be good if they gave us movies here once in a while.
D-1101-1: Yeah, I haven't seen anything since I got in. Nothing newer than ▓▓▓ ▓▓▓▓▓▓▓▓.
D-1101-4: Are you kidding? I love those!
D-1101-5: It went downhill after the first one.
D-1101-2: Now YOU have to be kidding.
[REDACTED]
Result: Subjects argued about the merits of the ▓▓▓▓▓▓ ▓▓▓▓▓ film series for 49 minutes. No agreement was reached. D-1101-3, with the opinion that the second film was the underrated gem of the series, took the DVD player, 'winning' and ending the event.

1101-1E
Object: One political campaign button reading '[REDACTED] 2012'
Test Subjects: 5 D-class personnel D-1101-1 through 5
Additional Instructions: None
Transcript:
[DATA EXPUNGED]
Result: [DATA EXPUNGED] and ▓ casualties before containment was

SCP-1101

reestablished. Security measures for SCP-1101's use with controversial items have been heightened.

1101-1F

Test designed to determine effects of SCP-1101 on individuals with a prior interest in the event topic and enthusiasm for debate.

Object: One postcard depicting Claude Monet's *Water Lilies* (1907)

Test Subjects: Dr. A▮ and Dr. P▮▮▮, both with an amateur interest in art collecting

Additional Instructions: Dr. A▮ asked to comment on the object

Transcript:

Dr. A▮: The real thing is much nicer.

Dr. P▮▮▮: I don't know, I prefer his portraits myself, though I think Renoir does them better.

Dr. A▮: Renoir? Have you been to the Musee d'Orsay?

[REDACTED]

Dr. A▮: That's absolute trash!

Dr. P▮▮▮: You think MY tastes are trash? You probably thought Manet and Monet were twin brothers!

Dr. A▮: You're saying this when you haven't even been outside of ▮▮▮▮▮? You pretentious little *[expletives]*

Dr. P▮▮▮: My mother was WHAT?

[REDACTED]

Result: Subjects argued for 82 minutes before Dr. P▮▮▮ said 'I can't argue with you any more'. Dr. A▮ took the postcard and ended the event. Dr A▮ and Dr. P▮▮▮ have subsequently been hostile to one another.

> *In the absence of staff who are able to act like adults, I recommend that testing of SCP-1101 between coworkers be avoided.*
>
> - Dr. ▮

Addendum 1101-1: It has been observed that duration of an SCP-1101 event generally scales with the number of individuals involved. Due to the potential for memetic spread of an event, it is estimated that a breach of containment would lead to a 'point of no return' where event duration is unacceptably high after a critical mass of [REDACTED] persons, leading to a perpetual SCP-1101 event and a potential AK-class end-of-the-world scenario. In light of this theory, SCP-1101 has been upgraded to Euclid class and new containment procedures implemented.

SCP-3043

DATE: 15/12/2005
FROM: Site Director August < august@scp.foundation >
TO: O5-5 Secretary < o55sec@scp.foundation >
SUBJECT: Re: Containment Breach

I'm still not quite sure what just happened.

Yesterday, our bots picked up unauthorized changes to documents on our internal servers. Two minutes later, all on-site personnel — including myself — blacked out for three hours. Every camera ceased to function during this period.

When we woke up, we all had headaches, the entire site smelled like cigarettes and cheap alcohol, two of my guards were injured, three bullets were lodged in my desk, and somebody had shot SCP-3043. The only clue we've got regarding those three hours is SCP-3043's old documentation, which has been... well, 'updated' is one way to put it. I've included it with this email, along with the revised documentation for SCP-3043.

We've got no clue who this 'Murphy Law' character is. I'm recommending we immediately assign him an SCP identification and start investigating. All the evidence we've got so far indicates that he and SCP-3043 are unrelated anomalies. Also, none of us actually remember him — despite some of us being 'featured' in... whatever the hell this was.

The short of it is this: Either he saved us from the mother of all containment breaches... or he just wanted us to think that he did. Regardless of which, we need to know who he is and what the hell he's capable of.

SCP-3043

▶ ATTACHMENT: item_number.log

FADE IN:

INT. MURPHY LAW DETECTIVE AGENCY - NIGHT

A light-skinned man leans back at his desk, feet up, reading a newspaper. He is clad in a white-collared shirt, with his trademark trilby hat tossed thoughtlessly atop of his desk. We can see his shoulder-strapped holster; it carries a .44 magnum. A bent cigarette rests between his lips.

His name is MURPHY, and he is ready to give anyone a bit of the business. He is hard and handsome — with the sort of face you could use to smash up concrete, then dust off and still take home to show your ma.

He is also our NARRATOR. His voice is a harsh growl; as if he just swallowed a fistful of spent cigarette butts and followed it down with a sulfuric acid chaser.

NARRATOR

> You see a lot of ugly in this line of work. Good people with bellies full of lead, left to bleed out in rain-soaked alleyways. Love ruined — turned inside out — until it just becomes an angry, festering sore. Statues that'll kill you as fast as you blink.

The door to the office flies open. A dark-skinned woman dressed in a white lab-coat bursts in; she is in her 40s, and has a fierce, vibrant beauty. This is the RESEARCHER, and although she might need MURPHY's help, that doesn't mean she's going to like it.

NARRATOR

> But when it comes to ugly, nothing beats a containment breach.

SCP-3043

RESEARCHER

(confused)

What... what am I doing, here?

NARRATOR

She wasn't the first beautiful woman to burst into my office and ask me that question.

MURPHY

(lowering paper)

Same as anyone else, toots. You need my help.

RESEARCHER

(indignant)

Don't call me 'toots'. I've got a fucking doctorate in molecular physics —

MURPHY

(sets paper down)

Alright, alright. My bad, Professor. I apologize. Now...

MURPHY slides his feet off the desk and rises to stand. He folds his arms over his chest and watches her.

SCP-3043

MURPHY

How can I help?

RESEARCHER

(hesitant)

I don't... I don't know how I got here. I don't even know what 'here' is. I was... I think I was working on something, when I heard typing sounds, and suddenly...

RESEARCHER

(shocked)

I don't remember. I don't even remember my name.

NARRATOR

A beautiful woman with a doctorate in molecular physics — and no memory of who she was or how she got here. Her eyes told me she needed my help; her name-badge told me the rest.

MURPHY

(glancing at her name-badge)

You're Professor Michelle Lewis.

SCP-3043

The RESEARCHER looks down at her name-badge, as if noticing it for the first time. She appears shocked; her eyes rise back up to stare at MURPHY. She now knows her name. It is DR. LEWIS.

DR. LEWIS

> I... right. That's my name. I work for the Foundation.

NARRATOR

> The Foundation. A bunch of pencil-pushing geeks trying to figure out where the magicians were hiding all those rabbits they pulled out of their hats. I should have turned her away right then and there; when the Foundation's involved, you know it ain't gonna be nothing but trouble.

MURPHY scowls, but nods his head, moving to open a drawer in his desk.

NARRATOR

> But me? I'm not the sort of man who stays away from trouble.

MURPHY pulls out two shot-glasses, along with a bottle of half-finished whiskey. He sets them atop of his desk, focusing his icy stare on DR. LEWIS.

NARRATOR

> I'm the sort who slides on over next to trouble and buys her a drink.

MURPHY

> Alright, Professor. I'll take the case.

SCP-3043

DR. LEWIS

You will? I mean... wait, what?

NARRATOR

My name is Murphy Law. And I'm the guy you call when everything that could go wrong... did.

TITLE SPLASH

Murphy Law in... Type 3043 — FOR MURDER!

FADE OUT.

SCP-3043

▶ ATTACHMENT: object_class.log

FADE IN:

INT. MURPHY'S CAR - NIGHT

MURPHY drives; DR. LEWIS stares out the window in the passenger seat. City lights wash through the car, casting both of them in a metallic tangerine glow. DR. LEWIS is wearing her seat-belt; MURPHY isn't.

MURPHY

> Alright, Professor. Talk to me: What else do you remember?

DR. LEWIS

> (startled)
>
> How did we... when did we get inside of this—

NARRATOR

> She was smart. But that was part of the problem: She was *too* smart. Always thinking too much. Sometimes, you just gotta go along for the ride.

MURPHY

> Focus on the problem. What do you remember before stepping into my office?

SCP-3043

DR. LEWIS

(frowning, but thinking)

...right. I was working on something. Updating documentation, I think. Something about a change, an important one. That's when I heard typing in the other room. And then I felt dizzy, and it was like...

DR. LEWIS

(shaking her head)

Like something was trying to erase me. Erase the thoughts in my head, even as I was having them.

NARRATOR

Sounded to me like the Professor stumbled onto something she wasn't supposed to. Somebody had tried to rub her out — but who? And how?

MURPHY

Anything else?

DR. LEWIS

(thinking)

I think... I can't remember all the updates I was making, but it had to do with SCP-3043.

SCP-3043

MURPHY

Alright. What's 3043?

DR. LEWIS

(frowning)

I... don't remember.

NARRATOR

If I was going to figure out this mystery, I had to find out what 3043 really was. And if the Professor couldn't tell me, there was only one other person who could.

MURPHY turns left, brows crinkling with renewed focus.

NARRATOR

Site Director August.

FADE OUT.

FADE IN:

EXT. FOUNDATION HEADQUARTERS

MURPHY's car parks just outside of a sprawling gated mansion.

SCP-3043

NARRATOR

> If Site-95 was the rotting corpse, Site Director August was the worms wriggling inside of its corrupted core. Bribery, extortion, racketeering — he had his dirty paws in the pocket of every two-bit researcher, agent, and D-Class from Level 9 down to Sub-Level 7.

MURPHY shifts the car in park; DR. LEWIS turns to look at him. MURPHY moves to open the door.

NARRATOR

> But he also had ears everywhere. When a gnat took a crap, he heard the plop. If anyone knew what 3043 really was, it would be him.

DR. LEWIS

> (reaching for MURPHY)
>
> Mr. Law. Wait.

MURPHY pauses, looking back at her.

DR. LEWIS

> I just remembered — the update I was going to make to the documentation.

MURPHY tilts his head, waiting.

SCP-3043

DR. LEWIS

(frowning)

I was going to change its Object Class. It isn't 'Safe', Mr. Law. It's...

DR. LEWIS

(staring at the mansion)

It's Keter.

MURPHY nods grimly, then turns to shut the door. Filled with conviction, he turns to walk toward the mansion's gates.

FADE OUT.

SCP-3043

▶ ATTACHMENT: special_containment_procedures.log

FADE IN:

INT. SITE DIRECTOR'S OFFICE - MORNING

The office is expensively furnished, with framed-glass windows on three of its four walls; outside, a lush garden grows on all of its sides. Morning light streams in through the windows, casting the room in a warm glow.

Standing behind the desk — facing the rising sun — is a man. He is short, with russet-brown skin, a shaved head, and a face full of piercings. He wears an exceptionally fine black suit. This is Site Director AUGUST: A hard, brilliant man with a heart of steel.

As MURPHY enters through the door, he's flanked by two men in sharp suits. They are silent, but armed; ready to do violence at a snap of AUGUST's fingers. As MURPHY shrugs himself out of their grip, they station themselves on either side of him.

AUGUST

> (staring out the window)
>
> Mr. Law. You wanted to see me?

MURPHY

> (dusting off his coat)
>
> Yeah. About 3043.

NARRATOR

> When dealing with Site Director August, you didn't try to bluff. You just kept your cards close and hoped to God the man didn't have a better hand.

SCP-3043

AUGUST

That's classified.

MURPHY

Is it, now? Since when does the Foundation care about classifying 'Safe' anomalies?

AUGUST turns, ever so slightly. A pierced eyebrow is raised.

NARRATOR

I just raised the ante.

AUGUST

How would you know that? And we care about classifying *all* anomalies, Mr. Law.

MURPHY

So I've been told. But a little birdy tells me you might have classified one of them wrong. 3043 ain't Safe. It's Keter.

AUGUST turns completely, staring MURPHY down.

SCP-3043

AUGUST

> (smiling)
>
> You've been speaking to Dr. Lewis, I presume. Where is she?

NARRATOR

> Something wasn't right. He was already calling me — and men like Site Director August only smiled the instant before they laid down a winning hand.

MURPHY

> Safe. Unlike 3043. What is it?

AUGUST narrows his eyes. He gives the slightest nod.

NARRATOR

> That was his tell. He unwittingly had shown me his cards: Pair of aces.

The two men on MURPHY's left and right instantly reach for their sidearms.

NARRATOR

> Lucky for me, I was packing three of a kind.

MURPHY slams his left elbow into one man's stomach; he uses his right hand to draw his magnum .44. As the second man pulls his piece, MURPHY pistol whips him in the temple — he goes down. MURPHY spins and opens fire — three shots slam into AUGUST's desk.

SCP-3043

AUGUST freezes, but shows no fear. His eyes narrow.

NARRATOR

> It was time to cash out.

MURPHY

> 3043. Last chance. What is it?

MURPHY pauses long enough to kick one of the men on the floor, but never looks away from AUGUST.

AUGUST

> You know precisely what it is.

MURPHY

> Humor me.

AUGUST

> It's you, Mr. Law. You're the anomaly. You're SCP-3043.

MURPHY narrows his eyes. He gives one last kick to one of the men, then charges out the door.

FADE OUT.

SCP-3043

FADE IN:

EXT. FOUNDATION HEADQUARTERS

MURPHY's car is still waiting for him; he runs toward it.

NARRATOR

> Someone had played me like a fiddle. It was all a setup — and I was the stooge.

As he reaches his car, he finds it empty; no sign of DR. LEWIS.

NARRATOR

> 3043 was going to make me take the heat for whatever it did to the Professor. It had me wrapped up nice and tight — even got me to present myself to the Foundation in a pretty little bow.

MURPHY gets into the car, starting it up.

NARRATOR

> But there was one thing 3043 didn't count on: A man with nothing to lose.

The tires squeal as he burns rubber, driving away.

NARRATOR

> If the Foundation couldn't contain 3043... then I'd just have to contain it myself.

FADE OUT.

SCP-3043

▶ ATTACHMENT: description.log

FADE IN:

INT. DR. LEWIS' LAB

MURPHY kicks down the door, clad in his trilby — .44 magnum in hand. The interior of the lab looks like an office; bookshelves stuffed full of science journals, several desks, paperwork scattered everywhere... and DR. LEWIS' chair. The chair's tall back obscures whoever is sitting in it.

NARRATOR

> One thing kept coming back to mind. One thing that the Professor had said...

MURPHY creeps forward, gun in hand, reaching a hand out for the chair.

NARRATOR

> She said she heard 'typing'.

MURPHY grasps the chair, spinning it around.

Sitting in the chair is a black 1937 Olympia Elite typewriter. A roll of paper is inside of it; it communicates via typing. As MURPHY points the gun at it, it begins to type furiously.

SCP-3043

> HOW

SCP-3043

> HOW IS THIS POSSIBLE

SCP-3043

NARRATOR

> 3043 was her goddamn typewriter.

SCP-3043

> WHY CAN'T I REWRITE YOUR STUPID STORY

SCP-3043

> WHAT ARE YOU

DR. LEWIS suddenly steps out from the shadows, a .45 in hand. She points it squarely at MURPHY.

DR. LEWIS

> Step away from the typewriter, Mr. Law.

SCP-3043

> HOW ARE YOU DOING THIS

MURPHY turns, his gun pointed back at DR. LEWIS.

SCP-3043

MURPHY

It's controlling you, Professor. Just like it controlled August — and everyone else. It was pretending to be Safe — not letting anyone know it was sapient.

DR. LEWIS

(frowns, grimacing)

That's...

SCP-3043

HOW THE FUCK ARE YOU EVEN DOING THIS

DR. LEWIS

You're... the anomaly, Mr. Law. I have to take... you in...

DR. LEWIS' hand shakes; the gun trembles.

MURPHY

It can rewrite any story it's part of — even the stories in your head. When you realized it, you tried to update the documentation, and it tried to erase your story... erase you.

SCP-3043

SCP-3043

> STOP

SCP-3043

> JUST FUCKING STOP

SCP-3043

> HOW THE FUCK ARE YOU REWRITING MY STORY INTO YOUR OWN FUCKING STUPID HUMPHREY BOGART FANFIC NONSENSE

DR. LEWIS

> I... I have to contain you...

DR. LEWIS shudders, stepping back; her hand lifts to grasp her temple. The gun tumbles to the floor.

SCP-3043

> THIS ISN'T RIGHT

SCP-3043

> I'M SUPPOSED TO BE THE ONE IN CONTROL HERE

SCP-3043

SCP-3043

> THIS IS SUPPOSED TO BE MY STORY NOT YOURS

MURPHY turns, pointing his magnum at SCP-3043.

SCP-3043

> WAIT

SCP-3043

> JUST

SCP-3043

> FUCKING WAIT

MURPHY pauses, waiting. DR. LEWIS sinks down to a seat, still rubbing her temples.

SCP-3043

> ALRIGHT LOOK JUST

SCP-3043

> I'LL ERASE MYSELF

SCP-3043

SCP-3043

I'LL ERASE ALL DOCUMENTATION ABOUT MYSELF EVEN FROM OTHER PEOPLE'S HEADS

SCP-3043

THEN I'LL MAKE MY DOCUMENTATION NOT REFER TO ME BUT JUST SAY THAT THIS LAB IS OFF-LIMITS

SCP-3043

THAT WILL CONTAIN ME

NARRATOR

3043 could do it, too. Sure, it could have been a trick... but maybe not. Letting 3043 live, despite what it had tried to do — it felt like what a good man would do.

MURPHY

It'd be the right thing to do, wouldn't it?

SCP-3043

YES

SCP-3043

SCP-3043

> YOU WANT TO BE THE HERO RIGHT

SCP-3043

> THAT'S WHAT THIS IS ABOUT

SCP-3043

> YOU'RE THE HERO

SCP-3043

> SO ACT HEROIC

FADE OUT.

Two gunshots.

NARRATOR

> Heroes always do what's right. But me?

SCP-3043

FADE IN:

EXT. CITY STREETS - SUNSET

MURPHY walks out of the lab and into the streets, smoking a cigarette — holstering his piece. He walks away, toward the fading sun.

NARRATOR

> I'm no hero. I'm Murphy Law.

FADE OUT.

FADE IN:

INT. DR. LEWIS' LAB

DR. LEWIS, now starting to recover, walks toward SCP-3043. Wisps of smoke rise up from it; two fresh .44 slugs have been pumped into it. The paper inside of it has its previous dialogue, with one addition at the very bottom.

NARRATOR

> I'm just the guy you call when everything that could go wrong... did.

DR. LEWIS pulls the paper out to read it; the camera zooms down to the bottom of the page.

SCP-3043

> THE END

FADE OUT.

SCP-3043

▶ ATTACHMENT: revised.log

SCP-3043 prior to neutralization.

Item #: SCP-3043

Object Class: Neutralized (formerly Safe)

Special Containment Procedures: SCP-3043 is to be kept in a secure locker on-site. Access requires Level-3 clearance.

Description: SCP-3043 is a 1937 Olympia Elite typewriter. Two .44 caliber bullets are lodged in its casing. Before it was neutralized, SCP-3043 exhibited the ability to rewrite any physical document within its immediate vicinity to match whatever was typed into it. It was neutralized before any additional properties could be confirmed.

On 14-12-2005, a containment breach occurred at Site-95. During this breach, an unknown anomalous event prevented all outside contact for approximately 3 hours. All entities affected by this anomaly have no recollection of the events that occurred during these 3 hours; furthermore, all recording devices within Site-95 appear to have malfunctioned during this period.

Shortly after this event concluded, Site-95 reported all SCPs were now contained with the exception of SCP-3043. SCP-3043 was found in Dr. Lewis' office in its current state. Dr. Lewis also discovered that all copies of SCP-3043's documentation were now replaced with an 'updated' version (see attached files).

SCP-3043

▶ [REDACTED]

FADE IN:

EXT. DOCKS - SUNSET

MURPHY stands at the edge of the docks, watching the sun go down on just another day. Behind him, two sleek black cars roll up. A dozen men start pouring out of them, but he doesn't bother to look back.

The men are smartly dressed in black suits; they crowd around a short old woman dressed in white. She slowly approaches MURPHY, leaning heavily on her cane. One man follows her closely — her personal secretary and bodyguard.

The man is AGENT FREDERICK; whatever it is, he does it by the books. The woman is O5-5 — and if we told you anything else, we'd have to kill you.

O5-5 moves to watch the sunset besides MURPHY. AGENT FREDERICK is clearly displeased; he'd rather she not get too close.

O5-5

> You did some good work today, Mr. Law.

MURPHY

> Yeah.

O5-5 reaches to pull a cigarette out of her pocket, placing it between her lips.

O5-5

> If we ever need your services... how might we contact you?

MURPHY leans forward and plucks the cigarette out of O5-5's mouth. AGENT FREDERICK immediately reaches for his firearm, but O5-5 lifts her hand to stop him.

SCP-3043

MURPHY

> I'll be around.

MURPHY tucks the cigarette behind his ear for later. As he walks away, a fog begins to roll in.

AGENT FREDERICK steps forward, as if to go after MURPHY. O5-5 grabs him by the shoulder.

AGENT FREDERICK

> But — he's an anomaly. We can't let him go. We have to contain him —

O5-5

> (shaking her head)
>
> Forget it, Fred. It's Chinatown.

AGENT FREDERICK slides his hand away from his firearm. Together, they watch MURPHY walk off into the foggy night.

The camera focuses on MURPHY's silhouette as the view fades to black.

FADE OUT.

SCP-3043

CREDITS ROLL:

DR. LEWIS played by...
MICHELLE LEWIS

SITE DIRECTOR AUGUST played by...
JEREMIAH AUGUST

SCP-3043 played by...
A 1937 OLYMPIA ELITE TYPE-WRITER

MURPHY LAW played by...
HIMSELF

AGENT FREDERICK played by...
FRED[SCP-423]

O5-5 played by...
[REDACTED]

WITH SPECIAL THANKS TO SITE-95

LOOK FOR MURPHY LAW TO RETURN IN...

...THE FOUNDATION ALWAYS RINGS TWICE![SCP-3143]

THE END

To Be Noir Not To Be

Some time in the 1920s, almost a century before there were such things as Markov plot generators or infrafictional constructs, a dirt-broke novelist in the middle of L.A. somehow discovered the first known method of transport between various metafictional layers. We're still not entirely sure what he actually did with it in the first place and for almost all intents and purposes he shot himself into fictional space and fucked right off, but suffice it to say once they'd finished cleaning his corpse off the side of a printing office on the Hollywood Boulevard, more than a few people got interested in whatever method of narrativic ascension he'd unintentionally pioneered.

The kids from Prometheus were interested, because of course they were, and they'd managed to just about gut half of his manuscripts and the widget he'd used to punch himself into the metanarrative. That being said, even after they were done, there was still enough there for two groups to figure out how it worked and build their own separate copies of the machine in question. Those groups being a loose collective of private investigators and the Mafia.

The timeline's still pretty fuzzy, simply because of how much it jumps around between various layers of fiction and reality – that being said, we've pretty solidly established that the start of this whole debacle is in 1953, when the first shots got fired between the two groups and you have one P.I. dead and a Mob hitman apparently vanished into thin air.

A few years after that particular confrontation, the other members of the P.I. collective disappear, one by one. At the time, nobody's quite sure how the hell what's happened to them and their bodies are never actually found: what they're very sure about is the very visceral deaths of multiple members of the mob. And then the rest of them disappear and it's all tied off very neatly, right before an explosion in the number of novels featuring battles between hardboiled detectives and the Mafia.

Like I said, pretty much everything after that point in time has dissolved into a sea of tenuous links and mostly ineffective theorising, but the main thrust of it is that we now have an array of detectives and wanted criminals duking it out over thousands (if not millions) of novels and decades of literary tradition.

Your job as a member of this particular division of the Department of Analytics is mainly going to be watching these novels. They tell me that the AIs are pretty good at filtering both by genre and by characters, so you're

To Be Noir Not To Be

probably not going to be sorting through all that many truckloads of original fiction each day you're on the job.

When you think you've got a lead, you'll fill in a form, boot it upstairs and if Command reckons it's worth investigating, a few Agents like myself will probably get sent off to interview the author, see whether or not they show any of the signs of metafictional fuckery with some basic MID-terms – Memory, Inspiration, Diction. If it turns out your tip was accurate, you'll soon find yourself chasing further fictional leads to ensure that we've got a comprehensive collection of their movements 'n' such.

Okey, you're probably wondering why we're going to all the effort about this, and I'll explain.

In a metafictional fight like this, you're not going to be settling the feud over a nice dinner at an Italian restaurant. No, the only way to settle this kind of dispute is with good old-fashioned murder, but that gets pretty complicated when you're trying to murder a fictional character. Authors can pull plot twists out their ass to save any character, especially ones as well-loved as these guys seem to be, and if their reader base suffers, it doesn't matter – so long as they're alive and able to fight the other side, they're not going to give a rat's ass about the authors they have to manipulate to stay that way.

Clearly, you can't kill a fictional character in fiction. So you have to lure them out into reality and then kill them, before finishing off any potential authors who might want to bring them back. We've had reports of authors who've been literally taken hostage and forced to write out the adventures of the kidnapper's comrade at gunpoint, and good old Kurt Vonnegut had to have a covert security detail monitoring him simply because of the possibility of metaphysical infiltration of his work.

Which brings me to this thing right here on the table. The last "re-entry" into reality these guys made, an entire hectare of land got levelled within the first fifteen minutes of the fight, and at least half of it was thanks to this thing right here.

Remember, when you have control over what can come in and out of reality, you're not gonna bother with using something as pissingly weak as your dead-average pistol. These guys have been through so many genres and so many books that they've got the sense to not use anything even close to mundane.

So, if you keep good tabs on these guys, we can lock up them and any paratech they've got right as they pop back into reality, and maybe you can be the one who's going to stop the next honest-to-god plasma cannon battle. No pressure.

SCP-3143

Artistic depiction of SCP-3143.

Item #: SCP-3143

Object Class: Euclid

Special Containment Procedures: Attempts to contain SCP-3143 are ongoing. A Foundation-operated bot (I/O-ISMETA) is to monitor online fiction communities for signs of its emergence. When found, an authorized member of the Pataphysics Department is to be assigned to deconstruct it.

MTF Iota-10 ("Damn Freds") is to investigate any leads regarding possible locations of SCP-3143-A. If found, he is to be apprehended and taken into Foundation custody.

SCP-3143

Description: SCP-3143 is an intrafictional construct. When active, this construct exhibits the ability to temporarily 'flatten' portions of reality into a script-like narrative. This narrative is derivative of the genre established by North American writers of hard-boiled and noir fiction [1].

During this period, SCP-3143 takes on the role of the main character (a 1930s private detective) hired to solve a case. All entities flattened by its effect become characters within the narrative surrounding it, exhibiting personalities and attributes typical of the genre's style. The narrative will continue until SCP-3143's actions lead to a resolution consistent with the genre; at this point, the narrative will conclude and reality will revert. Events which occurred within the narrative will be projected into reality; however, entities involved in these events will typically have no recollection of what occurred.

SCP-3143 was first noted in 2005 in the aftermath[SCP-3043] of a containment breach at Site-95. In 2012, the Foundation's Pataphysics Department worked alongside the Department of Analytics to make contact with and apprehend SCP-3143.

SCP-3143-A is Murphy Lawden, SCP-3143's author.

---

[1]. Notable examples include Dashiell Hammett's *Red Harvest* (1929) and Raymond Chandler's *The Long Goodbye* (1953).

SCP-3143

Addendum 3143.1: Interview Logs

▶ ACCESS SCP:/3143/interviews/001.log

INTERVIEW LOG

DATE: 2012/02/02
INTERVIEWER: Dr. Thaum
SUBJECT: SCP-3143, SCP-3143-A
NOTE: Dr. Thaddeus Thaum is part of the Pataphysics Department. He has a degree in English Literature, and specializes in the analysis of fiction.

FADE IN:

INT. MURPHY LAW DETECTIVE AGENCY - NIGHT

A light-skinned man sits alone in his office; a blade of moonlight cuts across his face. His trademark trilby hat is tossed thoughtlessly across his desk; a bent cigarette is nearby, left smoldering in an ashtray. His shirt is stained with blood — some of it might even be his own.

He's got a slug of bourbon in his hand, a slug of lead buried in his chest, and 6 more waiting for the next son of a bitch who comes through that door — courtesy of his .44.

His name is MURPHY LAW, and if you think his number is up, then you haven't been counting. He's the sort of man you pray for when you need him — and the sort you curse when you don't.

He is also our NARRATOR. His voice is a husky snarl; as if he's got a throat stuffed full of sand-paper and rusty nails.

SCP-3143

NARRATOR

> If there's one thing the Foundation is good at, it's tying up loose ends. I knew it was just a matter of time before the lab-coats tried to shove me in a box.

The door to the office flies open. An old man in a lab-coat enters; he's got a scowl so deep it's been carved down into the bone. This is DR. THAUM, and he's here to get to the bottom of this — no matter what the cost.

NARRATOR

> But if they wanted to contain *me* , they were gonna need a bigger box.

DR. THAUM

> Hello, SCP-3143. How are you doing, today?

NARRATOR

> He wanted answers. I just wanted out.

MURPHY finishes the shot of bourbon and levels his pistol at DR. THAUM's chest.

SCP-3143

MURPHY

> Give me one good reason why I shouldn't ventilate you right now, doc.

DR. THAUM raises an eyebrow, folding his arms across his chest.

DR. THAUM

> Because you can't.

NARRATOR

> If he thought I didn't have the moxie to plug him full of lead, then he had another thing coming. Specifically, a whole lot of lead.

DR. THAUM

> You *do* know that I can hear you narrating, right?

NARRATOR

> What the hell was he on about? Something wasn't right.

SCP-3143

DR. THAUM

> You're an intrafictional construct; a sapient story that can warp reality. Specifically, you flatten it into a movie script that mimics crime-fiction and hard-boiled noir.

NARRATOR

> This wasn't… what?

DR. THAUM

> And let's be honest — it's not even proper noir. The defining element of the style is the anti-hero; the character with no prospects, trapped in a world with no future. But after reviewing your file, I can see that you don't qualify.

MURPHY

> I don't… qualify…?

SCP-3143

DR. THAUM

> Your narrative is heroic and simple, with clear villains and heroes. In the end, the day is saved without consequence. That's not hard-boiled — it's certainly not noir. You're just fantasy escapism dressed up in a suit, a hat, and a drinking habit.

MURPHY: Where — where are we? What's happening?

DR. THAUM: You rely on the *tropes* of noir — outwardly rejecting the notion of appearances and style while secretly embracing them — engaging in a hyper-masculine narrative based around the myth of the frontier, only projected in an urban environment…

MURPHY: What is this?

DR. THAUM: …but you fail to faithfully replicate their complex, dense settings where moral action is all but impossible. You fail to connect to the essence of what makes noir what it is. You are, in a sense, merely parodying it. An unintentional satire, if you will.

SCP-3143: What's going on?!

DR. THAUM: And on top of it all, your name is based on an absurdly contrived pun.

SCP-3143: What are you doing?!

DR. THAUM: I'm deconstructing you, SCP-3143. I'm *containing* you.

SCP-3143: I… I don't understand…

DR. THAUM: I'd like to speak with the author, please. Mr. Lawden? Are you there?

SCP-3143

SCP-3143-A: How...?

DR. THAUM: Hello, SCP-3143-A.

SCP-3143-A: Where am I? Who am I?

DR. THAUM: You are Murphy Lawden, a retired shoe-salesman from New Jersey. You live alone — save for your two cats.

SCP-3143-A: I'm...? Oh, God. How did I get here?

DR. THAUM: We believe you accidentally created an intrafictional construct. Do you recall a screen-play of yours? *It Always Rains*?

SCP-3143-A: I... I think so. I don't — oh, God.

DR. THAUM: I think we've done enough for today, Mr. Lawden. I'll give you a chance to rest and settle in; we can continue this interview later, if that's alright with you?

SCP-3143-A: I... yeah. Uh, yeah. Okay. Okay. I need to gather my thoughts.

DR. THAUM: Of course.

[END LOG]

SCP-3143

▶ ACCESS SCP:/3143/interviews/002.log

INTERVIEW LOG

DATE: 2012/02/03
INTERVIEWER: Dr. Thaum
SUBJECT: SCP-3143-A

[BEGIN LOG]

DR. THAUM: How are you feeling today, Mr. Lawden?

SUBJECT: Um, a little better. I think? Still confused.

DR. THAUM: Good. I understand this must all be quite bewildering.

SUBJECT: So, I've just been trapped? All this time? Narrating, or writing this ongoing story? My memory of all of this is so foggy.

DR. THAUM: Something like that, yes. We found an unfinished copy of your script, *It Always Rains* . That's how we determined who you were.

SUBJECT: God, I remember that. It was... yeah. I wanted to write, um, write a story, or something, I think? Something like what I read as a little kid?

DR. THAUM: Somehow, you managed to bring the narrative to life — literally. You 'became' the main character, in a sense.

SUBJECT: Right. So...

DR. THAUM: If it's alright with you, I'd like to ask you a couple of questions.

SUBJECT: Okay. But, uh... can I ask you something, first?

DR. THAUM: Of course.

SUBJECT: You read the script, right?

DR. THAUM: Yes. It was required as part of my preparation for this assignment.

SCP-3143

SUBJECT: Did you, uh... did you think it was any good?

(*Silence.*)

SUBJECT: Uh.

DR. THAUM: Do you want a frank assessment, Mr. Lawden?

SUBJECT: Sure?

DR. THAUM: It was fairly awful.

SUBJECT: Oh.

DR. THAUM: Now, moving on —

SUBJECT: Is it okay if we do this later? I think I have a headache.

(*Silence.*)

SUBJECT: Look, I'm sorry. It's just that I...

DR. THAUM: No, it's alright, Mr. Lawden. You've been through a lot. Take whatever time you need.

[END LOG]

SCP-3143

▶ ACCESS SCP:/3143/interviews/018.log

INTERVIEW LOG

DATE: 2012/04/16
INTERVIEWER: Dr. Thaum
SUBJECT: SCP-3143-A

[BEGIN LOG]

DR. THAUM: Good morning, Mr. Lawden.

SUBJECT: Ugh.

DR. THAUM: I see from your charts you haven't been eating. Do you want to talk about that?

SUBJECT: Not really.

DR. THAUM: I've also been informed you've been trying to write more fiction about SCP-3143.

SUBJECT: Until you took my pencils away.

DR. THAUM: Mr. Lawden, that was for your own safety. Until we understand how the anomaly occurred, we can't allow you to —

SUBJECT: Oh, screw you. You just think it's crap.

DR. THAUM: I didn't say that.

SUBJECT: But you were thinking it. Weren't you?

DR. THAUM: I wouldn't call it 'crap'.

SUBJECT: Why did you have to stop the story? What was the problem? He was helping people. It was fun.

DR. THAUM: That's not the point. We can't have anomalies running around and —

SUBJECT: And what? Telling stories that you don't like? Stories that aren't yours?

DR. THAUM: Stories that aren't — excuse me?

SCP-3143

SUBJECT: Cut the crap, doc. We both know what's going on here.

DR. THAUM: I'm not sure what you're insinuating.

SUBJECT: You use a veneer of objectivity to try and create a sense of distance — of detachment — to make the incredible seem credible.

DR. THAUM: Wait. What?

```
SUBJECT: You cloak yourself in the outward
'trappings' of science — the terms, the titles, the
'interview logs' — all in some desperate, contrived
attempt to make it sound a little more reasonable, a
little more respectable, a little more plausible…
```

DR. THAUM: — wait! What are you — s-stop! You can't!

```
MURPHY: …all so you can convince them to buy into
your little story. But at the end of the day, what
does it all amount to, doc? Just one more gimmick —
one more swindle — one more way to play the same
con.
```

DR. THAUM

```
H-how — this isn't — I deconstructed you ! You
can't —
```

NARRATOR

```
When it comes right down to it, me — them —
hell, even you — we're all just characters in
that trashy dime-store novel called life.
```

```
MURPHY grabs DR. THAUM by the collar, pulling him
close.
```

SCP-3143

MURPHY

> Sorry to break it to you, doc. But you're just a spooky ghost story dressed up in a lab-coat, glasses, and a funny little accent.

MURPHY throws him aside.

NARRATOR

> But if you're lucky — and play your cards just right? Maybe you'll find a way to write your own story.

MURPHY pauses to light his cigarette.

NARRATOR

> Not me, though. I'm no author.

MURPHY walks toward the exit.

NARRATOR

> I'm Murphy Law.

DR. THAUM struggles to get up, grasping at the edge of the table. As he does, he sees a copy of the INTERVIEW LOG on the desk in front of him. The log contains this complete text, with one notable addition at the very bottom.

SCP-3143

NARRATOR

I'm just the guy you call when everything that could go wrong… did.

The camera zooms in down to the bottom of the INTERVIEW LOG.

INTERVIEW LOG

[END LOG]

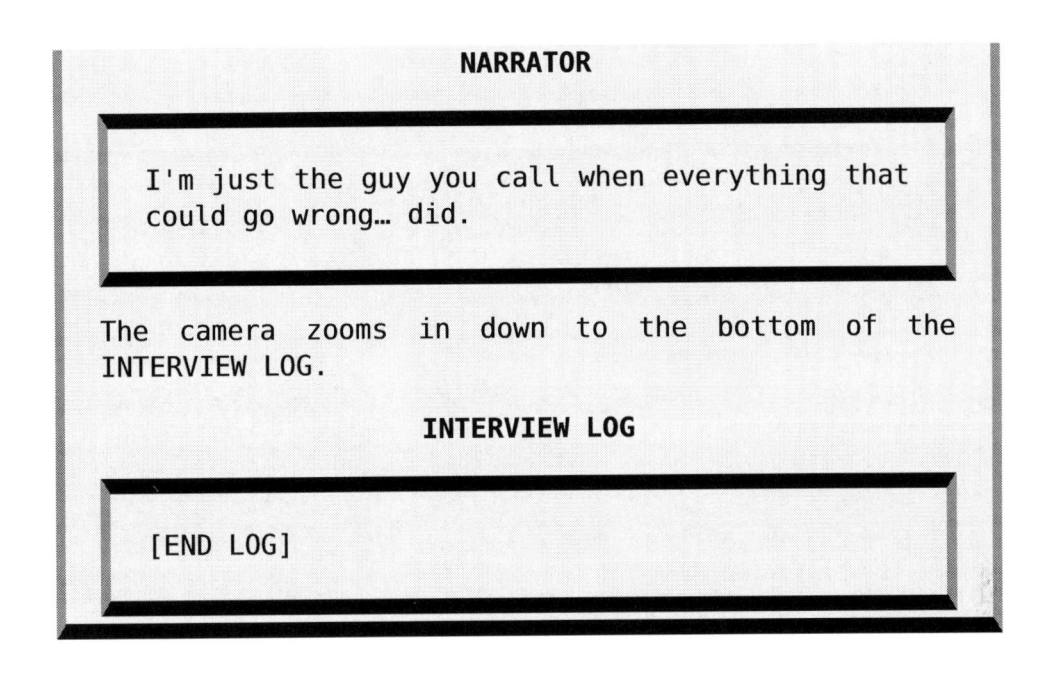

WARNING: THE FOLLOWING FILE IS LEVEL 4/3143 CLASSIFIED

ANY ATTEMPT TO ACCESS THIS FILE WITHOUT LEVEL 4/3143 AUTHORIZATION WILL LEAD TO IMMEDIATE DISCIPLINARY ACTION.

SCP-3143

▶ ACCESS SCP:/3143/files/email001.log

DATE: 2012/03/15
FROM: Site Director August < jaugust@scp.foundation >
TO: O5-5 Secretary < o55sec@scp.foundation >
SUBJECT: SCP-3143

My thoughts:

It might not have worked, but this was nevertheless an excellent test-run for 'Dr. Thaum' and the 'Pataphysics Department'. I recommend we keep them on the books — they might come in handy, particularly in regards to developing allegorical and metafictional countermeasures. Besides, it's not like a fictitious department with fictitious employees has a costly upkeep.

Otherwise, leave the article as is. It might contain several inconsistencies (the fact that neither Murphy Lawden nor *It Always Rains* actually exist being the most glaring) but further edits could invite unwanted attention from SCP-3143.

On that note: Let's leave SCP-3143 alone for a while. Yes, we've learned quite a bit about him, but he's also learned quite a bit about us. Until we know precisely how his abilities work, further efforts to contain him could be dangerous. I'm particularly concerned with what he said during the final interview — it sounds like he thinks we're all just as fictitious as he is.

On a final note: SCP-423 is currently missing. I'm concerned it might have something to do with our little experiment. I'm having some of my people look into it; I'll keep you updated.

- Site Director August

SCP-3143

[REDACTED]

DR. THAUM played by...
THADDEUS THAUM

SITE DIRECTOR AUGUST played by...
JEREMIAH AUGUST

MTF IOTA-10 played by...
FRED[SCP-423]

And MURPHY LAW played by...
HIMSELF

WITH SPECIAL THANKS TO THE PATAPHYSICS DEPARTMENT

LOOK FOR THADDEUS THAUM TO RETURN IN...

...NEVER METAFICTIONAL CHARACTER I DIDN'T LIKE!

THE END

SCP-423

SCP-423

Item #: SCP-423

Object Class: Safe

Special Containment Procedures: SCP-423 is contained in a 5 x 5 meter room containing three (3) 2 x 3 meter bookshelves. An incinerator is located adjacent. All personnel entering or leaving the room are to be searched for written material. Any written material must be checked for any trace of SCP-423 and then, if found clean, incinerated.

At night, SCP-423 is to remain in a small, plain journal marked 423. Failure to remain in this journal at designated times will result in loss of reading material outside of scheduled experiments.

Description: SCP-423 has no physical form. It appears to exist entirely within textual narratives. It was discovered in a used book store in ▮▮▮▮▮▮▮▮▮▮, Texas, on ▮▮▮▮ ▮, 19▮▮, in a copy of Tom Sawyer . The book was purchased by Agent ▮▮▮▮▮▮, who located it during a routine search.

Agent ▮▮▮▮▮▮ brought the book back to Sector 28 as instructed. The book seemed perfectly normal except for the inclusion of a character named "Fred," who was not known to exist in any other version of the story. However, it was not until it was left by a copy of Moby Dick that the anomalous nature of SCP-423 became clear.

SCP-423 is able to enter textual narratives, inserting itself as a minor character. The details of the character vary from story to story, but it is always named "Fred," or something similar, and its role in the story is usually minor. Physical descriptions of the character are rare, but it usually appears as a human male of average height and middle years. However, this can change depending on the nature of the narrative. He has appeared as a student in narratives focusing on children (and thus presumably of an appropriate age) or even as a non-human in narratives where humans are absent or rare. At no time is his appearance remarked on as being unusual by other characters.

SCP-423 is able to move from one narrative to another voluntarily, provided the two works are within one (1) meter of each other. The process takes up to three minutes, depending on the length of the new narrative. The entire narrative changes at once, the text on all pages seeming to move. Occasionally, the length of the narrative changes; in these cases, the text grows smaller or

SCP-423

larger to fit the page count of the book. It is only able to appear in physical textual narratives. It cannot enter electronic storage, or affect purely visual narratives. If placed in proximity to a graphic novel or other form of sequential art, it will change the text boxes and dialog bubbles, but will not affect the pictures. Similarly, illustrations in a textual narrative do not change, even if they no longer match up to the narrative as affected by SCP-423.

It prefers fictional narratives. However, it can enter any narrative that has characters, including anecdotes, biographies, and research notes (See Addendum 423-1).

It can re-enter a narrative that it has already exited. If it does so, the new narrative typically differs from the last time SCP-423 entered the story. However, it has displayed a preference for narratives it has not yet entered.

It is currently unknown what effect dying in a narrative would have on SCP-423, despite the best effort of researchers. SCP-423 displays a strong grasp of narrative principles, and is usually able to predict the best response in a given circumstance to avoid danger to itself. It has, however, displayed minor injuries. However, these seem to vanish when it enters a new narrative.

SCP-423 can be communicated with by coaxing it into a journal. It responds to questions written within, with SCP-423's responses appearing underneath the questions. When it transfers to another narrative, its responses disappear from the journal.

It has been largely cooperative since its containment. Its only requests so far have been for more narratives. It has expressed a preference for narratives with a large number of background characters, as this makes it easier for it to blend in and "watch the good stuff." It has been recommended that, should it become uncooperative, it be confined to the journal until it becomes more amenable to staff requests.

Researchers who desire more information on SCP-423 should read Experiment Log 423 A .

Addendum 423-1: Researchers are reminded that all physical written material is a potential habitat for 423, and that all notes should therefore be taken electronically. If written notes must, for some reason, be taken, be sure to check for addenda from "Guest Researcher Fred."

Addendum 423-2: The use of SCP-583 to destroy SCP-423 has been suggested. While the SCP is not slated for destruction at the present time, it has been noted should circumstances change.

Experiment Log 423 A

Experiment Log 423 A

Experiment Log for SCP-423

Approved by O5-█
Monitored by O5-█, O5-█, O5-█
Project Head: Dr. E. Mann

All researchers working with SCP-423 are encouraged to append their results to this experiment log in the following format:

Date: █/█/█
Test Material:

Results:

Notes:

Date: █/█/█
Test Material: Tom Sawyer, by Mark Twain

Results: A character named Fred is mentioned at several points in the story, largely as an onlooker. No change to the story is noticed.

Notes: "This will serve as a baseline for future effects of SCP-423." - Dr. E. Mann

---

Date: █/█/█
Test Material: The Hobbit, by J. R. R. Tolkien

Results: A 14th dwarf named Feredor is a member of the party. The narrative is largely the same, except that there are no references to a "lucky number." Feredor is mentioned as surviving the Battle of Five Armies, but Oin is killed.

Notes: "SCP-423's role is larger in this work, allowing a better look at its effects. The dialog written for the character is similar to that written for the other dwarves. Other differences in text match Tolkien's writing style as used in the rest of the book." -Dr. E. Mann

Experiment Log 423 A

Date: ▮/▮/▮
Test Material: Plain Journal

Results: There was no result for some time, until one of the researchers wrote his name on the cover. The words "Hi, there" appeared underneath. A conversation was held, during which it was established that SCP-423 possessed both the ability and desire to communicate.

Notes: "This proves that SCP-423 is sentient. If it can be controlled, it could be useful in dealing with certain text-based SCPs. This bears further research." -Dr. E. Mann

---

Date: ▮/▮/▮
Test Material: Dragonquest, by Anne McCaffrey

Results: A minor blue rider named F'Red appears in the story. No other changes are noted.

Date: ▮/▮/▮
Test Material: Harry Potter and the Half-Blood Prince, by J.K. Rowling

Results: A wizard named Fred appeared. Very few changes in the story are noted, except one scene in which SCP-423 is confused with an existing character in the series.

Notes: "SCP-423 displayed paranormal abilities in the narrative, though nothing out of note for the fictional universe. However, when returned to the journal, SCP-423 said that it couldn't duplicate them outside of that particular narrative universe." - Dr. E. Mann

---

Date: ▮/▮/▮
Test Material: Ulysses, by James Joyce

Results: SCP-423 immediately returned to the journal, where it wrote out "Ow, ow, bad idea."

Notes: "Note this as a potential punishment for SCP-423 if it misbehaves." - Dr. E. Mann

Experiment Log 423 A

Date: ■/■/■
Test Material: The Draco Tavern , by Larry Niven

Results: A new regular employee of the Draco Tavern showed up, named Fred. Only mentioned in passing save in the story "Cruel and Unusual", where he expressed sympathy for the Chirpsithra view.

Notes: "Either he's not completely human in outlook, or only acts that way when dealing with stories of aliens. We should probably test this further." - Dr D. Vettir

---

Date: ■/■/■
Test Material: "The Battle Hymn of the Republic", by Julia Ward Howe.

Results: verse 2, lines 1 and 3 altered. Rather than "I have seen Him in the watch-fires of a hundred circling camps" and "I can read His righteous sentence by the dim and flaring lamps", the lines now state "Fred has seen Him in the watch-fires of a hundred circling camps" and "Fred can read His righteous sentence by the dim and flaring lamps". Upon returning to the journal, SCP-423 wrote "that was... interesting, but I don't think I want to try it again."

Date: ■/■/■
Test Material: "Mary Had A Little Lamb" (verses 1 and 2 only), by Sarah Josepha Hale.

Results: References to "Mary" in verse 1 are now references to "Freddy"; references to "her" in verse 2 are now references to "him".

Date: ■/■/■
Test Material: "Mary Had A Little Lamb" (full version), by Sarah Josepha Hale.

Results: Verses 1 and 2 are now unaltered; a reference to "the eager children" in verse 4 is now a reference to "Fred and the children".

Experiment Log 423 A

Date: ■■/■■/■■■

Test Material: <u>House of Leaves</u> (color version), by Mark Z. Danielewski.

Results: A mailman named Fred delivers a letter to Will Navidson in page ■■. Fred also appears as a bartender that attends Johnny, and one of the orderlies caring for Pelafina. SCP-423 expressed profound confusion after leaving this work. Of note is that all instances of "Fred" in the text were written in green.

Date: ■■/■■/■■■

Test Material: <u>Gadsby: Champion of Youth</u>, by Ernest Vincent Wright. *Gadsby* is known for being an extended lipogram: a 50,110-word story written without any 'e's.

Results: A minor character named Ford appeared in the novel.

Date: ■■/■■/■■■

Test Material: A (non-pornographic) limerick about a man from Nantucket.

Results: No change. SCP-423 subsequently explained that the given limerick was "too small and too tight", with insufficient "flexibility".

Date: ■■/■■/■■■

Test Material: A book of 365 haiku.

Results: Third line of thirteen separate haiku replaced with a five-syllable phrase mentioning Fred ("Fred watched silently", "Fred is also here", "Only Fred remains", etc).

Date: ■■/■■/■■■

Test Material: *The Frogs Who Desired A King*, by Aesop, written using plastic letters with a magnetic backing applied to a metallic surface.

Results: The penultimate sentence became, "a big Stork that soon set to work gobbling them all up, except for one named Fred who hid." The "new" letters appeared to be of the same material and design of the original ones, and the weight of the complete setup remained the same.

Experiment Log 423 A

Date: ■/■/■
Test Material: Blood Meridian, by Cormac McCarthy.

Results: In the introductory scene where Holden incites a mob to murder the Reverend by falsely accusing the Reverend of rape and bestiality, a bystander named Frederick is present in the mob; however, instead of participating, the bystander leaves in disgust. The narrator comments that "The weak coward Frederick was never seen again."

Date: ■/■/■
Test Material: ■■■■ Telephone Directory (2003).

Results: No change.

Date: ■/■/■
Test Material: 12 Angry Men, by Reginald Rose.

Results: The list of characters specifies that the courthouse guard is named Fred; he is described as "disappointed that he will be excluded from the jurors' deliberations".

Date: ■/■/■
Test Material: Mein Kampf, by Adolf Hitler (German original)

Results: No change for the first minutes, followed by an insertion of multiple brief references to a distant, skeptical colleague named Friedrich into autobiographical fragments of chapters 2 to 8 of book. The inserts were in German, roughly consistent with the original style but containing a number of grammar and stylistic mistakes. Upon returning to the journal, SCP-423 remarked "whew, that was hard!"

Notes: I am not sure what is more significant here: that 423 appears to possess a native tongue or that it was apparently able to obtain fairly good knowledge of German from the contents of a single book, even as long as this one. We should look deeper into its possible application to translating hitherto-undecipherable scripts — Dr Despair

Experiment Log 423 A

Date: ■/■/■
Test Material: <u>Odyssey</u>, by Homer (English Braille edition)

Results: No change. SCP-423 left the book after 5 minutes, saying "interesting but I think I'll leave this one for when I'm really bored".

Date: ■/■/■
Test Material: A hardcopy of this experiment log

Results: Identical, except for the insertion of the words "ruggedly handsome" in several sections of the log.

Date: ■/■/■
Test Material: *The Kugelmass Episode*, by Woody Allen, a story about a man who is able to travel into fiction.

Results: Testing forbidden by O5-■.

Date: ■/■/■
Test Material: <u>SCP-826</u>, using SCP-423 communication journal as a "book".

Results: Testing forbidden by O5-■.

Date: ■/■/■
Test Material: <u>SCP-701</u>

Results: Testing forbidden by O5-■.

Date: ■/■/■
Test Material: A Canadian five-dollar bill (2008 issue); the reverse of the bill contains a two-sentence passage from "The Hockey Sweater", by Roch Carrier, in French and in English.

Results: First sentence remained intact. Second sentence, which describes how important skating rinks were in Carrier's childhood, now mentions life "on the skating rink, with Fred" (as well as "sur la patinoire, avec Fred").

Notes: The bill was first tested in a change machine and accepted as legitimate. After SCP-423 left the bill, it was tested in the same change machine and rejected as counterfeit.

279

Experiment Log 423 A

Date: ■■/■■/■■■

Test Material: Green Eggs and Ham by Dr. Seuss

Results: Halfway through the book, Sam-I-Am asks the protagonist "Would you eat them here with Fred? Would you eat them with some bread?". The protagonist refuses. No edited nor additional illustrations were included.

Notes: After returning to his journal, SCP-423 noted "That was fun."

Date: ■■/■■/■■■

Test Material: The Fellowship of the Ring, by J. R. R. Tolkien.

Results: A hobbit named Fredegar Burrowes, noted as a friend of Samwise Gamgee, accompanies Frodo Baggins and his party throughout the book.

Notes: Of particular note is that Oin, noted as having been killed in 423's version of the Hobbit, is mentioned as surviving in this book.

Date: ■■/■■/■■■

Test Material: SCP-140

Results: ~~Testing forbidden by O5-■~~

Note: Without permission, Researcher D■■■■, who was working with SCP-140 at the time, put the two books together, despite training in resisting memetic effects. Words appeared rapidly on SCP-140's pages, at a rate of roughly 1 page filled every 12 seconds until SCP-423 returned to its journal, and the words disappeared from the pages of SCP-140. SCP-423 later stated that it was "Extremely painful", and felt like it was being "ripped apart."

Date: ■■/■■/■■■

Test Material: SCP-1425

Results: Testing forbidden by O5-■.

Date: ■■/■■/■■■

Test Material: SCP-1230

Results: Pending O5 approval.

Experiment Log 423 A

Date: ■/■/■
Test Material: SCP-1195

Results: ~~Pending O5 approval.~~ Testing forbidden by O5-■.

Date: ■/■/■
Test Material: A list of class-D personnel to be terminated at the first of the month, names included.

Results: The line "Class-D personnel to be de-commissioned as of ■/■/■" changed to "Class-D personnel to be released as of ■/■/■", all names remain as first written down. SCP-423 writes in the journal "Now that's just heartless."

Notes: It is conclusive that SCP-423 has the ability to not only feel emotion but has a belief in the importance of life.

Date: ■/■/■
Test Material: A twenty-minute ballet for eight dancers (four male and four female), described in Rudolf Laban's "Labanotation" system for recording human movement.

Results: Notation indicates that halfway through the ballet, a fifth male dancer walks onstage, looks at the other dancers, shrugs his shoulders, and walks off.

Date: ■/■/■
Test Material: A logic puzzle (as published in [REDACTED] logic puzzle magazine), describing how five different people took their driving tests, in five different vehicles, on five different days, and made five different errors; as is standard for logic puzzles of this sort, solvers are to determine which student drove which vehicle and made which error on which day.

Results: A driving examiner named Fred is mentioned as having been present during all tests. Upon subsequent questioning, SCP-423 was able to correctly state which driver made which error in which vehicle on which day. When asked how it knew this, SCP-423 did not explain the series of logical inferences, deductions, and conclusions by which such puzzles are typically solved, but rather simply stated that it "was right there the whole time".

Experiment Log 423 A

Date: ▇/▇/▇

Test Material: The Gardens of the Moon, by Steven Erikson

Results: The Dramatis Personae in the start of the book now mentions Reader, a soldier in the Bridgeburners, and Fred, a Daru patron of the Phoenix Inn. In the second chapter, following the fall of Pale, the Bridgeburners that arrive for Hairlock include a fifth person, who is unnamed and doesn't speak, but can later be identified as Reader. In many subsequent encounters with the Bridgeburners, the soldier Reader is also present. This character doesn't have any lines, and is normally found with a book in his hand.

In chapter 5, during Kruppe's dream, Kruppe sees a figure within the Gadrobi Shantytown who, he says, greatly reminds him of his friend Fred, who he saw just the other day in the Phoenix Inn. From chapter 6 on, Fred is to be found in the Phoenix Inn.

Interestingly, for the garden party on Lady Simtal's estate, both Fred and Reader are guests. Bridgeburner and Daru viewpoint characters alike comment on how they look vaguely similar. Apart from the minor changes, the book has exactly the same ending as before, though.

Upon returning to the journal, SCP-423 wrote only "..." when questioned. After a few minutes, it finally wrote "Sorry, that was interesting, but exhausting." SCP-423 expressed an interest in the remaining books of the series. This has been noted and will be considered as a reward for good behaviour.

Notes: "This has proven that 423 can be in multiple places within the same narrative, although it seems to tire it out. - Dr. R. Karma"

Date: ▇/▇/▇

Test Material: *Candidate Multilinear Maps*, by Sanjam Garg, published in 2013 as his doctoral thesis

Results: Approximately 10 seconds after entering, SCP-423 returned to the journal and wrote "Sorry, not enough room for me."

Notes: "It seems that 423 needs to have a narrative to work off. This has been noted for the future. - Dr. R. Karma"

Experiment Log 423 A

Date: ■/■/■

Test Material: A print-out of source code for a simple "Hello World" program in C#

Results: The source code now has a number of additional comments alongside the source code professing confusion about certain aspects of programming. On returning to the journal, SCP-423 wrote out "Well, that was a first."

Date: ■/■/■

Test Material: Head-First C# 3rd Edition (first printing), by Andrew Stellman and Jennifer Greene

Results: A number of examples involving named male characters have had these characters renamed to Fred. The puzzles are also all filled in. Around page 100 or so, notes start appearing here and there. No substantial changes are noted until page 698, where a typo identified in the errata for the book was corrected. In subsequent pages, a number of typos and language problems were corrected in code snippets and descriptions, matching the errors reported in the errata, with the exception of screenshots. On returning to the journal, SCP-423 reported that it found that "fun, but unusual." On being questioned on its understanding of the language, SCP-423 stated that it could write and understand C#, and expressed a desire to use Visual Studio.

Notes: "423 seems to be both capable and interested in learning, provided there is some narrative reason for it to learn. A potential future experiment could involve us attempting to decant it into a computer without an internet connection. - Dr. R. Karma"

Date: ■/■/■

Test Material: Secret of the Ninja (Choose Your Own Adventure #16), by Jay Leibold

Results: The viewpoint character is initially accompanied by a character named Fred, who is another student at the Dojo. Several of the choice descriptions which lead to a negative ending for the protagonist and his companions are changed to contain a phrase indicating Fred does not accompany the protagonist.

Notes: "423 does not seem significantly hindered by the book's branching narrative, nor by the presence of multiple endings." - Researcher ■

Experiment Log 423 A

Date: ■/■/2015
Test Material: Printed copy of an ASCII art rendition of the Mona Lisa, by Leonardo da Vinci

Results: All punctuation used to simulate the shading of the original work is replaced with the letters "F", "r", "e", and "d" (in upper and lower case).

Notes: When questioned about the extent of its ability to completely modify textual representations of imagery (as opposed to merely substituting characters), SCP-423 acknowledged the possibility, responding with "I guess so, maybe, but I'm not really good at art." Further inquiry is suggested.

Date: ■/■/■
Test Material: SCP-085

Results: Pending O5 approval.

Date: ■/■/■
Test Material: the Frequently Asked Questions document for the Usenet newsgroup "alt.adjective.noun.verb.verb.verb"

Results: A sentence is added to the section of the document which describes the newsgroup's genesis, stating "alt.anomalous.Fred.perplexed.baffled.moderately-amused".

Date: ■/■/■
Test Material: 施氏食狮史 ("Lion-Eating Poet In The Stone Den"), by Yuen Ren Chao. "Lion-Eating Poet" is a 92-character poem written in Classical Chinese, in which every syllable is pronounced "shi" (albeit with varying tones).

Results: SCP-423 demanifested from its journal, but did not manifest within the test document. After 10 minutes, researchers were about to report a containment breach, when SCP-423 remanifested within its journal, stating that it had "got[ten] lost trying to find the way in".

Experiment Log 423 A

Date: ■/■/■

Test Material: <u>World War Z</u>, by Max Brooks. The book consists of multiple small interview-like stories told from the perspective of survivors of a zombie apocalypse.

Results: SCP-423 demanifested from the journal, and was discovered to have added in the accounts of a character named Fred, who survived in a bookstore on [DATA EXPUNGED] Road in New York. A team has been dispatched to investigate the named location.

Date: ■/■/■

Test Material: Marvel Masterworks: The X-Men Vol 1, By Stan Lee (writer) and Jack Kirby (artist). The book is a trade paperback collection of the first 10 issues of the comic book series "The X-Men".

Results: The collection now contains numerous references to Fred Wordsworth, one of the students of Xavier's School for Gifted Youngsters. This character is described as a mutant possessing the ability to physically enter and alter any text, but that this power has "made him invisible and intangible". By issue #5, the character has become a second-string member of the X-Men unit under the alias "Bookworm". The character indirectly participates in several plot points through utilization of his abilities, in one instance distracting a villain by altering nearby signs.

Notes: SCP-423 was found to have altered certain instances of text within in the artwork, but was completely unable to affect other instances upon request. Investigation has revealed that all susceptible text was added by the comic's letterer (exclusively responsible for the addition of all text found in a comic) rather than the inker (exclusively responsible for finalizing artwork). Further study is recommended.

Date: ■/■/■

Test Material: the poem *Incident* by Countee Cullen, depicting Cullen's experiences with anti-black racism, as a child visiting Baltimore.

Results: The ninth line of the poem is changed from "I saw the whole of Baltimore" to "Fred showed me all of Baltimore".

Notes: SCP-423 seems reluctant to portray itself as either the perpetrator or the victim of racism.

Experiment Log 423 A

Date: ██/██/██

Test Material: Slaughterhouse-Five , by Kurt Vonnegut. The novel is a semi-autobiographical account of Vonnegut's experience as an American prisoner of war during the 1945 bombing of Dresden, Germany during World War II.

Results: All mention of Kurt Vonnegut within the novel, excluding within the foreword, is altered to describe SCP-423 (i.e. "That was I. That was me. That was the author of this book." Was changed to read "That was Fred. That was not me. That was not the author of this book.").

Notes: As Kurt Vonnegut himself was not mentioned for most of the novel, he could technically be described as a "minor" character.

Date: ██/██/██

Test Material: The Outsiders by S. E. Hinton.

Results : A new member of the "Socs" accompanies Robert during the scene in which Robert is murdered. When Ponyboy wakes up after having attempted to be drowned, Johnny mentions that someone "unimpressivly handsome" had introduced himself as Fred, before punching Johnny in the face, then "running outta there like lightning." After returning to the journal, SCP-423 remarked, "I know that you guys record this, and I didn't want to ruin the ending for anyone who hadn't read the book." It is to be noted that at the end of the book, [REDACTED].

Date: ██/██/██

Test Material: Fred's Story by Researcher Torrez, a small novella written specifically to test SCP-423's abilities. The novella is set in a fantasy kingdom whose inhabitants are all beautiful women - when the kingdom is attacked by a demonic force, the kingdom's queen creates a ritual to summon a hero from another dimension to save them. The hero is never given a name, but it is mentioned that he is male and can transfer his consciousness to different works of fiction.

Results : The hero is left nameless and the novella is left unchanged, aside from an added sentence in chapter 2 which mentions that one of the queen's assistants is named Frederica. After SCP-423 demanifested from the novella, it noted, "I appreciate the offer, but I just can't. I never deserved to be in the spotlight."

Experiment Log 423 A

Date: ▇▇/▇▇/▇▇▇▇

Test Material: <u>The Last Question</u>, by Isaac Asimov. This test was conducted not using physically printed material, but a 9.7-inch A▇▇▇▇ K▇▇▇▇ e-reader tablet utilizing electronic paper technology. Electronic paper is able to retain a static image indefinitely without electricity, requiring power only for the initial rendering. Image remains as a suspension of pigments in an oil-like base once rendered. Entire story was rendered on a single screen in a small font. Wireless functionality was disabled before testing by physically severing circuit traces on the device's printed circuit board as a precaution.

Results : A character named FR-33D is inserted into the third section of the story almost instantaneously, with a single line in response to another character's comment on the rate at which humans are populating the galaxy. SCP-423 stated afterwards, "Good story, but what was that? It felt... strange. It was very easy to move through - not at all unpleasant. It felt like there was something 'below' the story, if that makes sense. Can we do more like that?"

Notes : "It is unclear whether SCP-423 'moved' through the internal circuitry of the device or simply the physical pigment-in-oil suspension of the electronic paper material. Changes occurred much faster than in tests with ink-on-paper. Recommend further testing with other substrates and form factors. Electronic paper appears to be close enough to printed material as to be compatible with SCP-423. What else might be compatible? Text painted on a wall? Stitched into fabric? Written on a cake with icing?" - Dr. ▇▇▇▇▇

Date: ▇▇/▇▇/▇▇▇▇

Test Material: <u>If on a winter's night a traveler</u>, by Italo Calvino (English translation by William Weaver), a metafictional novel about interrupted and unfinished narratives, half of whose content is a second-person narrative describing a reader's increasingly frantic attempts to obtain and read a copy of <u>If on a winter's night a traveler</u> only to find that every copy is flawed such that every other chapter is from a different imaginary novel, and the other half is the aforementioned chapters from imaginary novels.

Results : In the section where the protagonist angrily returns the flawed copy of the novel to the bookseller in hopes of either obtaining a proper copy or finding out the conclusion to the chapter of the imaginary novel, another angry customer named Fred tells the bookseller that "if this is a joke, it's not funny."

Experiment Log 423 A

Date: ■/■/■

Test Material: A version of <u>In Search of Lost Time</u> by Marcel Proust (English translation by D.J. Enright), considered one of the longest works of fiction in history, in which all seven volumes have been custom-bound into one book with all indications of differing volumes removed.

Results: After several minutes, Fred only appears within the first three volumes, <u>Swann's Way</u>, <u>In the Shadow of Young Girls in Flower</u>, and <u>The Guermantes Way</u>, before all references of him cease. Upon return to the journal, SCP-423 expressed feelings of surprise, stating, "Great story, but I took a peek and how long it went and *wow* is it long. I'm going to need to come back to this one."

Notes: Along with the aforementioned Erikson test, this could be an indicator that SCP-423 has an upper limit as to the length of the works he can manifest in.

Date: ■/■/■

Test Materials: <u>SCP-3450</u>, printed onto standard computer paper.

Results: Testing forbidden by 05-■.

Notes: SCP-423 had learned of this test after denial due to Junior Researcher ■■■■■■■■ accidentally leaving a notepad expressing disappointment at the test's denial near 423's journal. SCP-423 wrote that "The irony of interacting with a Self-Insert fanfic isn't lost on me".

Date: ■/■/■

Test Material: <u>Of Mice and Men</u> by John Steinbeck.

Results: A character named Freddy appears multiple times throughout the book, working as a farmhand on the ranch. The narrator describes him as "a man whose handsomeness is all the more apparent when compared to the other hands at the ranch, as he is not nearly as worn down". His largest appearance is during the section when George Milton and Lennie Small first arrive on the ranch. As he passes the two protagonists by, he comments on the size of Lennie, remarking that he "looks like a bull who learned how to walk on his hind legs".

Experiment Log 423 A

Date: ▇▇/▇▇/▇▇▇▇
Test Material: 300 children's building block toys.

Result: No Change.

Notes: The result of this test is rather inconclusive. Did SCP-423 consider the letters on the blocks a picture instead of text? Could it only affect one block and "not have enough room"? Or can it simply not affect this form of writing? More tests like this will have to be conducted.

Date: ▇▇/▇▇/▇▇▇▇
Test Material: SCP-2236 . SCP-2236 was used to examine texts known to have been affectd by SCP-423.

Result: First few texts examined exhibited no change. In subsequently-examined texts, references to SCP-423 in the text were, when examined using SCP-2236, interpreted as descriptions of "Fred" seeking to hide or avoid observation. When returned to the journal, a comment in appeared in the journal reading "That was rude." This comment, when examined using SCP-2236, appeared as a string of expletives.

Date: ▇▇/▇▇/▇▇▇▇
Test Material: A journal with "Mary Had a Little Lamb", but written in invisible ink

Result: Same as the last time "Mary Had a Little Lamb" was used. SCP-423 manifested itself in invisible ink. When asking SCP-423 if he noticed the change in ink, he did admit that the document seemed slightly different.
Notes: It seems that SCP-423 might be able to notice specific patterns and differences between text, explaining his adherence to story-specific restrictions. This is confirmed by this experiment.

Date: ▇▇/▇▇/▇▇▇▇
Test Material: A copy of the Voynich Manuscript

Result: After five minutes in which the text did not change, SCP-423 explained that the topic was technical up to a level where SCP-423 could not understand, though SCP-423 explained it did seem that the pictures in the Voynich Manuscript matched the captions below.

Experiment Log 423 A

Date: ▮/▮/▮

Test Material: A hard copy of the Wikipedia page on the Poincaré conjecture

Result: The only place where SCP-423 manifested was in one of the bibliographies. SCP-423 stated that it could not find a good place to appear due to lack of knowledge of the Poincaré conjecture, though it was impressed by Poincaré's math skills.

Date: ▮/▮/▮

Test Material: *Metaphors*, by Sylvia Plath, a nine-line poem in which each line is a nine-syllable metaphor for the same subject.

Result: No change. When SCP-423 returned to its journal, it stated that "whatever she's doing in there, it's too crowded, there's no room for me. I really don't think I should be in there, it's kind of private?", and refused to comment further.

Date: ▮/▮/▮

Test Material: A copy of the film script for " Inception ", by Christopher Nolan

Result: SCP-423 appeared as a minor character appearing in some of the dreams, as well as the limbo state for the movie. It adhered to the capitalization format of the script ("FRED") as well as his name put in the middle of the page when appearing, with a line after his name each time. SCP-423 states that it highly enjoyed the script, though he was a bit confused by "FADE OUT" as well as "CREDITS", since this was the first time it was exposed to a movie script.

Date: ▮/▮/▮

Test Material: A copy of the script for " Heaven Sent ", from Doctor Who

Result: References to sculptures on the wall resembling SCP-423's usual look. SCP-423 explained that the tight story made it too difficult for him to manifest himself as an actual character, though he vastly enjoyed The Doctor's fantastic performance, which he claimed he experienced not as 4 billion years but only an hour (as long as the TV episode).

Notes: It seems that if a story is very "contained" (any other characters would have a severe change in plot, or make no sense) with only a bare minimal amount of main characters, SCP-423 will become an inanimate object in the story instead, though still aware of events occuring.

Experiment Log 423 A

Date: ■■/■■/■■■■
Test Material: The lyrics to "Bohemian Rhapsody", by Queen

Result: In verses 2 and 3, "mama" was replaced by "Frederica". SCP-423 seemed unaware that this was a song as opposed to a poem. It seems that not all information is given to SCP-423, merely enough for him to not interrupt the flow of a poem or song, as well as fulfill any standards set by a story.

Date: ■■/■■/■■■■
Test Material: 50 Shades of Grey, by E.L. James

Result: A minor character "Fred" appeared in the background. SCP-423 expressed that it was a bit uncomfortable with the explicit scenes within the book and requests that it be sent to stories with more adventure and action next time.
Notes: It seems that SCP-423 also has a taste for specific books; this is the first time it was exposed to a sexually explicit book, so it was not used to the situation.

Date: ■■/■■/■■■■
Test Material: "This is the title of this story, which is also found several times in the story itself", by David Moser, a metafictional story about self-reference.

Result: Several additional sentences appear throughout the story, including "This is the sentence in which Fred appears", "This is *not* the sentence in which Fred appears", and "This sentence alludes to Fred's presence but does not actually contain Fred".

Date: ■■/■■/■■■■
Test Material: Written by Doctor X■■, a list of 100 fictional people doing things simultaneously in different areas, with a tragic end, along with a final over-encompassing statement about each of them contributing to the tragedy.

Result: This test was to determine if there was an upper-limit to how many locations SCP-423 could reside in at the same time within a book. Out of 100 fictional people, only 83 had the mention of "Fred" with it. The tragedy was not prevented in the end. SCP-423 noted that it got too tired after being in 83 different places in the story.

Experiment Log 423 A

Date: ▮/▮/▮
Test Material: The file for SCP-055

Result: Inconclusive, SCP-423 stated it was not sure what it was doing other than the fact that something was not spherical. Researchers soon forgot what they sent SCP-423 to do.

Date: ▮/▮/▮
Test Material: The experimental data for SCP-2719 (labeled "SCP-2719") with no outcomes listed, and with an additional entry with "SCP-423" at the bottom, also with no outcome listed.

Result: The data was filled precisely identical to the real file of SCP-2719. SCP-423's outcome was "became inside". When questioned, SCP-423 responded that it merely observed what occurred with each entity, despite SCP-2719 being an abstract metaphysical concept. It also somehow experienced becoming inside, despite having no knowledge of 2719. More testing to be done with 2719 and 423.
Notes: It seems that abstract entities manifesting themselves have the same effect on SCP-423 as any usual person, even if SCP-423 has no idea what is happening. It also seems it can fill in the blanks based on what already happened.

Date: ▮/▮/▮
Test Material: Experiment Log 914 - Part II

Result: A record appeared in Test Logs, Part 8 of an experiment performed by "Guest Researcher Fred", with the rest of the data for said experiment blocked out.

Date: TOTAL_DATE_FAILURE

Test Material: *The Abridged History of Homo Sapiens* by History Analysis Subroutine #7589372357286473-NFIZ

Results: SCP-423 is featured under the "unknown periods" section as a featureless humanoid screaming in a infinite white void and rambling incoherently. After being returned SCP-423 showed signs on prolonged exposure to weak-time suggesting that SCP-423 still understands temporal physics in a manner similar to organic beings.

Experiment Log 423 A

Date: ▮▮/▮▮/▮▮▮▮

Test Material: An untitled 50,000 page "story" created by randomization bound by grammar and basic sentence structure created for this test.

Result: The sentence "Joshua went to the diagonal party without his safety ants." was replaced with "Joshua went to the diagonal party without his safety Fred."

Notes: SCP-423 noted that being in the document was similar to when it has experienced dreams in other stories which it slept.

Date: ▮▮/▮▮/▮▮▮▮

Test Material: A printout of the gamescript for "The Secret of Monkey Island". Result was laser-scanned and the raw text compiled into a working program after being screened for anomalies.

Results: An NPC named Fred appears near the small building at the pier on Melee Island. When spoken to, the player is presented with a dialogue tree. Questioning him on his backstory reveals that he tried and failed to become a pirate. It is mandatory to recruit him on the ship's crew for the second chapter, where he joins the mutiny. Subsequent cutscenes have him present with the rest of the crew.

Notes: Upon returning to the journal, SCP-423 remarked "That was like a choose-your-own-adventure book. Let me know if you find any more."

Date: ▮▮/▮▮/▮▮▮▮

Test Material: A Million Random Digits with 100,000 Normal Deviates (published by Rand Corporation, 1955)

Result: Addition of a preface by Dr. Frederick McCarthy, explaining the statistical methodology used to generate the numbers in the book.

Experiment Log 423 A

Date: ■/■/■

Test Material: The "Location, Location, Location" story arc from the first print collection of "Precocious". Precocious is a webcomic where all characters are anthropomorphic animals. However, none of the dialogue in this particular story states or implies a species. The purpose of the test is to determine if SCP-423 can "sense" artwork.

Results: Mr. Crupp states the name of the father in an offscreen family to be named Fred. Upon returning to the journal, SCP-423 was asked if the cast of this story were human. SCP-423 states that they were animals, and he himself took on the form of an arctic fox. Further questioning reveals that this was the most nondescript species of the choices he was given.

Date: ■/■/■

Test Material: The entire script of William Shakespeare's <u>Hamlet</u>.

Results: During Act 1, Scene 2, a character by the name of "Frederick" sneezes halfway through King Claudius' speech. Hamlet laughs. No other changes has been discovered.

Notes: When questioned, SCP-423 stated "I got a little bored during the speech.".

SCP-140

An artistic depiction of SCP-140

Item #: SCP-140

Object Class: Keter

Special Containment Procedures: SCP-140 must never be brought closer than 15 m to any source of standard ink, human blood, or other fluids suitable for writing. Any contamination by blood or ink must be reported immediately. Any remaining copies of SCP-140 created during the initial printing must be found and destroyed as soon as possible. Only SCP-140 is to be preserved, for purposes of study, early warning, and cataloguing and recording possible SCPs derived from its subject matter.

SCP-140 is contained at Site-76 in a sealed vault containing a single desk. At this time no research is to be carried out upon the original SCP-140; researchers are to read from prepared copies not bearing the signature of its author which lack its properties. In the event of approved research, SCP-140 may not be removed from the vault, and readers may not be in contact with it for longer than 9 hours.

SCP-140

Access requires written approval from the head researcher for the explicit purposes of testing. An armed guard stationed outside the vault will meet any attempted theft with deadly force.

Should any personnel begin displaying obsession with SCP-140 or signs of possible memetic contamination, they are to be issued a Class A Amnesiac, false memories implanted as necessary, and transferred to another project. Transferred personnel must be monitored for signs of relapse.

Description: SCP-140 is a modern hardcopy book with an unremarkable black binding and an unknown number of white pages. The book jacket is missing, but the title, "A Chronicle of the Daevas", is clearly legible. The inside cover is signed by the author, whose name is indecipherable. The text is copyrighted 19■■. Careful examination reveals there are far more pages between the bindings than could be contained within them.

Readers admit to feelings of paranoia, unease, and occasional nausea while reading SCP-140, although this may be related to the subject material. Nonetheless, readers almost universally describe SCP-140 as fascinating and express continued interest, despite its frequently unsettling content. One in fifteen readers describe SCP-140 as having a faint odor of dried blood.

SCP-140 is a detailed account of an ancient civilization originating in what is now south-central Siberia, identified as the Daevites. Although like all cultures the Daevites evolved and changed over time, they appear to have exhibited unusual continuity. Universal fixtures of the Daevite culture in all periods included militarism, conquest, ancestor worship, urban centers ruling over large slave populations, gruesome human sacrifice, and the practice of apparently efficacious thaumaturgic rituals. A variety of relics and creatures produced by the Daevite culture would be abnormal or dangerous enough, if the account is to be believed, to qualify for containment in their own right.

If SCP-140 comes into contact with any fluid suitable for writing, including human blood, the account of the Daevite civilization's history expands. Human blood appears the most "potent" of possible writing substances, but in any case the amount of new material does not correspond proportionately to the fluids introduced. Although these new segments sometimes include new descriptions of rituals or cultural traits or illustrations of previously covered material, they more frequently include new, more recent accounts of information chronicling the continued history of the Daevite civilization or descriptions of new individuals and artifacts. Formerly decisive defeats become setbacks; new persons and events are inserted. Foundation archaeologists have discovered corresponding new artifacts and traces of the Daevite civilization in applicable locations and strata, in some cases found in dig sites that had already been thoroughly explored.

SCP-140

Although at times the Daevites were a collection of city-states, they appear to have consistently returned to imperialism under a theocratic aristocracy (the "daeva"), practitioners of cannibalism and thaumaturgy. Although initially Foundation researchers believed the daeva to have been a hereditary class recycling the names of noteworthy individuals, evidence and the events of ▮-▮-20▮ now suggest that the daeva possessed preternatural longevity as a result of [REDACTED]. Several researchers, notably Professor ▮▮▮, have concluded the daeva were so divergent from modern humans as to be a separate subspecies, a conclusion supported by graphic representations within SCP-140 and [DATA EXPUNGED].

SCP-140 is remarkably detailed by the standards of a primary source, seeming closer to a biography than a historic text. It includes lurid descriptions of sacrificial rites, battlefield descriptions, daily life, and the life stories of various noteworthy individuals including quotes and dates of birth. Over ▮ distinct individuals have been identified including the individual presently termed SCP-140-A, of which only ▮ are accounted for by recorded deaths.

Foundation archaeologists have discovered several sites containing ruins consistent with the supposed Daevite culture in various locations across Siberia, northern Iran, and Mongolia. Artifacts and traces of inter-cultural conflict and contact have been discovered as far west as the Carpathian Mountains and as far east as northern Pakistan and China. These include SCP-[REDACTED].

Addendum 140a:
SCP-140 was originally found in the office of deceased historian ▮▮▮▮▮▮. The previous owner was discovered in his office at ▮▮▮ University, having expired from self-inflicted lacerations on both wrists. There were no traces of ▮▮▮'s blood in the office. ▮▮▮'s colleagues claimed during interviews they discovered a note in faded ink in ▮▮▮'s handwriting next to SCP-140. All witnesses were administered Class A Amnesiacs and false memories implanted.

▮▮▮'s note read:

> I have to know. I'm sorry.

SCP-140

All texts within 15 m except several books relating to the history of the region were blank; the remaining books now included accounts of supposed interaction between the Daevite civilization and the subject cultures or applicable discussions of Daevite history and culture. These texts were confiscated. All printed forms and media were blank. All pens, printers, and ink cartridges were empty.

Addendum 140b:
Although SCP-140 was published during the 20th century, the tone of the book suggests it is a recounting of events, individuals, and practices experienced firsthand by SCP-140's unknown author. Foundation investigators have tracked SCP-140's publication to the [DATA EXPUNGED] printing house in a batch of ▮ copies self-published by a wealthy individual hereby termed SCP-140-A. SCP-140-A's signature on the contract matches the strange signature inside SCP-140.

More than 4▮ of the copies produced in this batch were apparently leeched of all ink by the ▮ remaining copies. To date, Foundation agents have recovered and destroyed ▮ of the remainder, but between ▮ and ▮ remain at large. Two expansion events have been reported during periods when SCP-140 had never been exposed to fluids of any sort or removed from its vault.

An investigation and manhunt for the author of SCP-140 is ongoing. In the event of contact, agents are advised [DATA REDACTED].

Addendum 140c:
Through study of SCP-140 and other contained objects related to the Daevite civilization, Foundation researchers have concluded that, transposed to the modern era, the resurgence of a hostile Daevite civilization in history more recent than 1▮▮▮ CE would constitute a grave and even possibly retroactive threat to the Foundation and modern civilization as we know it. Even best-case projections of Daevite resurgence in the modern day suggest a CK-class restructuring of modern society and a worldwide conflict with a projected death toll of at least [REDACTED] and an end to the Foundation's secrecy.

SCP-140

Addendum 140d:

███████ ███████'s journal, found on his home PC in [DATA EXPUNGED], indicates that upon his initial reading of SCP-140, it ended with the almost utter destruction of the Daevite civilization and the genocide of all known daeva in 2██ BCE by the forces of Chinese general Qin Kai. As a result of subsequent containment breaches, including those detailed in the journal, copious quantities of new material have been added, describing survivors regrouping and migrating to another region of central Siberia, rebuilding their empire steadily, and continuing to advance culturally and technologically. At present, the empire is described as having finally been crushed by Genghis Khan during the early period of his conquests, although the fates of many important persons and several cities remain ambiguous. Foundation archaeologists will be dispatched to [EXPUNGED] for investigation and research.

Addendum 140e:

After the incident on █-██-20██ at [DATA EXPUNGED] dig site resulting in over ███ casualties, all Foundation archaeologists excavating sites of suspected Daevite artifacts or ruins are to be accompanied by a fully armed security team. SCP-140-1 has been neutralized. SCP-140-2 remains at large. All other anomalous contacts and artifacts were destroyed when the dig site was struck by a cruise missile. Agent ███████ received a commendation and was treated for post-traumatic stress disorder. Dr. ████ received a posthumous commendation for courage.

An investigation into the possible involvement of SCP-140-A or their agents in the events of █-██-20██ is ongoing.

SCP-067

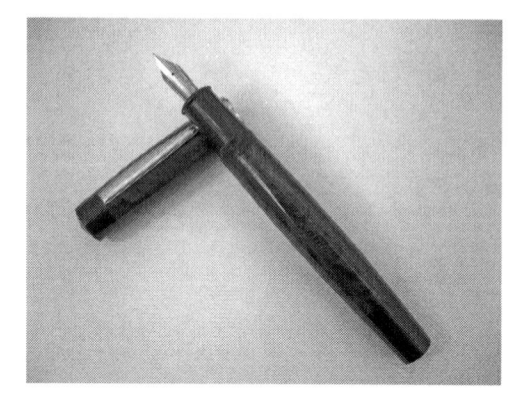

SCP-067

Item #: SCP-067

Object Class: Safe

Special Containment Procedures: When not in use or the subject of study, SCP-067 is to be stored in its felt-lined wooden box. The nib is to be corked, and all art and writings are to be submitted to SCP Research command for analysis and further experimentation.

Description: SCP-067 is a fountain pen made by a German supply company called Pelikan at some point between World War I and II. It is pale green in color, with a single red line going straight down along the side. The shell is oak and the nib is extremely sharp, capable of piercing human skin if pressed even lightly. Though it apparently lacks a reservoir, the nib never appears to run out of fresh ink. In addition, the pen writes in Iron Gall ink, which is suitable for artists but would normally corrode typical fountain pens quickly.

Research has surmised that any subject holding SCP-067 loses all autonomy of the hand and arm that grasps it. Full sensation is intact, but the arm below the elbow is controlled by unknown forces, theoretically centralized within SCP-067. One effect is that the "controlled" hand will start to use the pen to write a detailed biography of the individual holding the pen. The biography will include such information as the person's name, age, date of birth, criminal record, fears, etc. Other times the pen has been known to write such things as an occurrence that happened in the person's lifetime. For example, when Test Subject 1204M held SCP-067, he began to write a detailed record of a motor vehicle accident he had been in the year before.

SCP-067

Later, the subject admitted that many details penned in the account were not readily available to him at present time (i.e. the subject had forgotten many elements present in the written work, including his previous car's license plate number, the other vehicle's color, and so on). The subject stated that his memory of the event was so fresh in his mind during the transcription that he "could taste the blood in his mouth."

Subjects holding SCP-067 have also been known to create intricate works of art, despite the subject lacking any formal art training or previous tendencies toward drawing. For example, Test Subject 1102F, a young woman with no previous artistic experience, was able to draw a winged creature resembling SCP-███, described by researchers present as [DATA EXPUNGED]. When subjects are asked to explain what happens when they hold SCP-067, the typical response is that the subject freely relinquishes control of their appendage to SCP-067 so that it may complete its work unimpeded (see Quoted Response-01). Despite being instructed to not draw or write, subjects describe feelings of empathy, admiration, and cooperation with SCP-067 that coerces them toward a will not their own.

Quoted Response-01: "I don't really know how to explain it, it just kind of happened. When I picked up the pen, it seemed as if my hand wasn't my own anymore. I knew I could move it if I wanted to, but I chose not to because I loved the picture I was drawing. It was like my hand had life. Suddenly, my hand stopped and I realized I had complete control over my hand again, and I put the pen back down. I looked at the drawing and saw how beautiful it was. I guess the pen decided it was done, and was finished with me."

Tests and Experiments
On ██/██/20██, a test was done to see how the pen affected living creatures other than humans.

SCP-067

Experiment 001:

The test subject, a male rhesus macaque aged 2 years 4 months who had previously learned how to use pens and markers, was placed in a standard psychological surveillance room (neutral wall coloration; one-way observation mirrors), with SCP-067, a work table, and a pad of paper.

Subject picked up SCP-067 in his left foot, then took it in his right hand, then tasted it. Subject then put the pen down on the paper and smelled it. After 30 seconds, subject picked up SCP-067 again, and began tapping it repeatedly on the table. Subject also began tapping SCP-067 on his own body. Subject tapped SCP-067 with increasing force, until ink was being splattered on his fur. Subject then threw SCP-067 onto the floor (subsequent mechanical analysis revealed no damage).

At this point, subject tore a page from the pad of paper, and began rubbing it on the ink in his fur. This continued for 3 minutes, after which subject clutched the page in his teeth and leaped from the work table onto the ledge of the observation mirror (with such force that the table was knocked over). Subject began smearing the ink from the paper onto the observation mirror, while making repeated vocalizations; subsequent analysis revealed that 50% of vocalizations were consistent with the typical distress vocalizations of the rhesus macaque, and 50% were unfamiliar.

After 6 minutes of smearing ink on the observation mirror, subject began tearing at the page with his teeth and claws, but dropped it before destroying more than 20% of the paper. Subject then collapsed on floor, breathing rapidly and repeating the unfamiliar, atypical vocalizations.

Subject's handler reports that, once removed from psychological surveillance room, subject's mood improved rapidly. Subject was closely observed for two months following the experiment, but did not repeat the atypical vocalizations.

The sheet of paper was filed away in [DATA EXPUNGED].

SCP-085

Static reproduction of SCP-085

Item #: SCP-085

Object Class: Safe

Special Containment Procedures: [Revised on ██-██-████]. SCP-085 is to be contained in a single chalk-white bond drawing pad in a secure containment facility. Supervised contact with SCP-085 is unrestricted to all personnel with Level-2 access. All personnel coming into contact with SCP-085 are subject to searches and random psych analysis upon entering or leaving the containment area.

SCP-085

Absolutely no paper or canvas media are allowed to exit SCP-085's containment room: any paper trash must be disposed of by incineration after careful inspection. Paper and art supplies are to be brought in only by authorized personnel. In case of fire, flames are smothered using a rapid atmospheric-replacement and CO2-dumping system. Personnel are advised to quickly secure an oxygen mask and tank from the wall at the first sign of smoke or fire to prevent asphyxiation, as this procedure cannot be halted until all fires are suppressed.

Description: SCP-085 is the result of an experiment conducted between SCP-067 and SCP-914 . Using SCP-067 , Test Subject-1101F drew a single female figure, about 15 cm (6 in) in height and 3.8 cm (1.5 in) wide, in summer dress with long hair pulled back into a ponytail, with the name "Cassandra" written underneath. Dr. [EXPUNGED] proposed using SCP-914 on various settings on images created by SCP-067 : Using the [Fine] setting, the 'Cassandra' sketch was transmuted into her present form: a sentient black-and white-animated young woman drawn in clean strokes. Further attempts to duplicate this result have been unsuccessful.

SCP-085 prefers to be called 'Cassy.' She is completely sentient and, as of ██-█████, aware of her 2D form and her limitations in a three-dimensional world. Although her voice is inaudible, she has learned to communicate with SCP Foundation personnel through sign language and writing. SCP-085 may be communicated with by writing text on the paper she exists on. Personnel report that she is amicable and motivated, albeit lonely.

SCP-085 can interact with any drawn object on the same page as if it were real. For example, she is able to wear drawn clothing, drive sketched cars, and drink painted beverages. Except for animals and people, any drawn object becomes animated when in contact with SCP-085, but immediately ceases and holds position once out of contact. Artwork initially depicted as in motion such as ocean waves and swaying trees animate to an equilibrium state and stay at rest until acted upon by SCP-085.

SCP-085 has also demonstrated the ability to transfer from one sheet or image to another, as long as the two are flush. In the event SCP-085 enters a picture that does not support drawn objects (such as a repeating pattern), the picture is converted to a background image. SCP-085 perceives the picture as an endless plane of the image drawn upon it.

SCP-085

At the present time, SCP-085 can only exist upon paper or canvas surfaces: SCP-085 cannot transfer onto photos, cardboard, glass, or parchment. When entering other pieces of art, SCP-085 takes on the artistic style of her new environment (whether it be a comic book, an oil painting, watercolor, or charcoal sketching). Note: in comic form, her voice is visible as thought and voice bubbles around her head in typical comic fashion, and as she moves between panels the perspective and her relative size are altered appropriately.

Document #085-1: Introduction to several prints authored by M C Escher.

> **Researcher** : Cassandra, this is known as "Ascending and Descending". What do you think?
> *(At this point, SCP-085 walks a few times around the staircase)*
> **SCP-085** : It's pretty, I guess. Would make a neat exercise track.
> **Researcher** : You see nothing inconsistent with the staircase?
> **SCP-085** : No, as far as I can tell it just loops around down/up all the time. Why don't more staircases do that? It's pretty neat.

After this session, SCP-085 requested several 'impossible' objects in her own environment. These requests are pending O5 review.

Document #085-2: Incident 085-A

Prior to ███-██-████, SCP-085 was unaware of its status as a 2-Dimensional object in a 3-Dimensional world: prior security protocols required that SCP-085 be kept unaware of its true nature in order to prevent psychological distress: discrepancies with the perceived "real world" were presented as dreams or nightmares, and an effort was made to present SCP-085 with a scenario in which it was the last surviving human in a post-apocalyptic world, searching for survivors.

The deception was quickly broken following an incident where an SCP Foundation researcher accidentally brought a hard copy of SCP-085's Special Containment Procedures Report into the containment facility and allowed it to contact the artifact's current location. SCP-085 transferred onto the document before the researcher could remove it, and was immediately made aware of its true nature.

Because of the containment breach, several researchers advocated immediate destruction of the artifact. The decision was appealed to the O5-Council, which, in a █ to █ decision, advocated for SCP-085's continued existence.

SCP-085

Since the revelation of her true nature, observers have noted that SCP-085 has begun to show signs of clinical depression. Psychotherapy has been proposed, but the nature of the artifact's state of existence may make it difficult.

Some success has been had by providing SCP-085 tangible means to distract herself from her condition. In addition to the aforementioned optical illusions, SCP-085 expressed particular interest in a set of technical drawings for a 1964 Ford Mustang Convertible, transferring the parts one by one to a more naturalistic artwork, then assembling the vehicle by hand over the period of a year—gasoline being provided through a Norman Rockwell print of a gas station attendant.

Requests for further diversions of this nature are pending O5-level review and approval.

SCP-826

A closeup of one of SCP-826's statue heads

Item #: SCP-826

Object Class: Safe

Special Containment Procedures: SCP-826 is to be kept in a 25 cm x 25 cm safe with a numerical keypad lock. The combination for the lock will be given only to those with Level-2 clearance and will be changed on a weekly basis.

Description: SCP-826 is a 20 cm x 15 cm pair of bookends, molded in the shape of two outward-facing dragon heads. Scrapings from the surface of SCP-826 revealed a composition of 99% Sn, 0.5% Cu, 0.3% Sb, and 0.2% Pb, consistent with high-grade pewter. However, it is unclear whether SCP-826 is solid pewter or whether the pewter is merely a plating for some unknown element which gives the SCP its properties.

When a subject places a book between SCP-826, touching both ends, and leaves the room, SCP-826 will, in an instantaneous process, convert the interior of whatever room it is currently located in (a room defined as an enclosed area) into the setting of the contained book. Any form of entry into the room will instead open into a random location within the book's setting. During this transformation process, SCP-826, along with the contained book, will relocate to another part of the book's setting, showing a preference for places where books are normally found (libraries, studies, etc). To reverse the effects of SCP-826, a subject must remove the book from SCP-826, then exit whatever room SCP-826 was found in. The subject will find themselves outside the original room of SCP-826's containment, while SCP-826's containment room will be restored to normal.

SCP-826

In addition, the subject will find themselves at a random temporal location in the book's plot, ranging from the beginning to near the end of the book. If the subject does not find SCP-826 within the setting before the "end" of the book, SCP-826 will "reset" the setting, starting the book's plot over. The subject will then be "incorporated" into the book as a background character, losing all memories of a previous life outside of SCP-826.

Researchers studying SCP-826 are advised to enter the results into Experiment Log 826 .

Experiment Log 826

Experiment Log 826

Experiment logs are requested to be written in the following format:

Head Researcher:

Subject:
Material:
Equipment:

Results:
Addendum: (Optional)

Head Researcher: Dr. █████

Subject: Agent █████
Book: Little House on the Prairie
Equipment: One (1) GPS locator, one (1) two-way radio, one (1) canteen filled with water, one (1) watch, one (1) 9mm semi-automatic with extra cartridges.
Results: After Agent █████ entered the room containing SCP-826 and shut the door, GPS locator and radio held by research team stationed outside the door in a room adjoining the containment chamber malfunctioned, cutting off communication to Agent █████. After a period of 5 minutes, Agent █████ emerged from the door unharmed. Agent █████ was dropped in the middle of a prairie with a "green smudge" off to the west (presumably the Verdigris River of the book). Agent walked towards the river for what he estimated to be an hour, before being approached by one of the main characters of the book returning from a hunting trip and invited to join him for dinner. Agent accompanied character back to his home, a log cabin in the prairie where he met the rest of the character's family and discovered SCP-826 sitting on the mantlepiece. When Agent pointed out SCP-826 to the other characters, they claimed SCP was not there before, but did not appear concerned about its presence. Agent then ate dinner with the family, and afterwards asked if he could take the SCP-contained book with him. The characters allowed him to take the book, but displayed concern about Agent traveling on the prairie at night. Agent proceeded to remove the book from SCP-826, and exit through the cabin door into the research team's room. Display time on watch is consistent with Agent █████'s report that he had spent several hours in the setting.

309

Experiment Log 826

Addendum: Examination of the SCP contained copy of the book reveals an additional paragraph in the book's mid-section describing Agent ▮▮▮'s visit, in language consistent with Laura Ingalls Wilder's style. No mention is made, however, of SCP-826; Agent is simply described as having dinner and leaving. This textual deviation appears to be unique to this copy, as other copies do not appear to contain this passage. Book is now designated Document 826-1. Researchers are recommended to file copies of documents used with Dr. ▮▮▮ under Document 826-(number)

Subject: Agent ▮▮▮
Movie: *The Shining* (DVD)
Equipment: One (1) GPS locator, one (1) two-way radio, one (1) canteen filled with water, one (1) watch, one (1) 9mm semi-automatic with extra cartridges, one (1) video camera attached to Agent's hat
Results: After Agent ▮▮▮ entered SCP-containing room, GPS and radio proceeded to malfunction as in previous experiment. After roughly 30 seconds, Agent ▮▮▮ exited the room, and gave video camera to research team. Tape was playable and contained the following footage.

> Agent ▮▮▮ enters into a hotel room from what appeared to be a closet and, after exploring the room and confirming she could not exit through the closet, leaves the room. Agent continues down hallway and eventually arrives in hotel lobby. Agent explores behind front desk and enters hotel manager's office, where SCP-826 sits on shelf beside hotel ledgers. Agent removes DVD from SCP-826 and exits through office door into research room.

Addendum: Examination of DVD copy revealed no major plot deviations, most likely due to the fact Agent did not interact with any of the characters. Experiment demonstrates that SCP-826 can work on DVDs as well as books.

Subject: Agent ▮▮▮
Book: The Mammoth Book of Comic Fantasy, a collection of short stories
Equipment: One (1) canteen filled with water, one (1) watch, one (1) 9mm semi-automatic with extra cartridges, one (1) video camera attached to Agent's headset *(note: use of GPS locator and two-way radio discontinued, due to their uselessness in previous tests)*
Results: Agent ▮▮▮ returned after seven minutes, having experienced and recorded just over nine hours. Examination of the recorded footage reveals that the Agent experienced a portion of the short story "The Eye of Tandyla," and was forced to defend himself from temple guards, killing

Experiment Log 826

two. This caused the alarm to be raised, and though Agent ████████ was able to retrieve the book from a temple library and escape, the protagonists were apparently caught and executed. The altered copy of the book now reflects this change, although the cause of the alarm is not mentioned, with other stories remaining unaltered. It should also be noted that the book now contains seven fewer pages than a standard, unaltered copy.

Dr. ████████ requests that further experiments be performed with books of short stories, to determine whether the entire book will be experienced, or just a single story, if the book is not recovered from SCP-826 before the story's end.

Head Researcher: Dr. Edison

Subject: Agent ████████
Book: "The Sword That Shoots Laser Beams When You Swing It", a 3-page short story written by Dr. Edison. The story consists of a poetic description of a sword that shoots laser beams when swung. The story states it stands on a pedestal as thousands of years pass uneventfully.
Equipment: One (1) canteen filled with water, one (1) watch, one (1) video camera attached to Agent's headset.
Results: Subject is instructed to retrieve the aforementioned sword, test its "magical" properties, and then bring it out. Subject enters door, and returns five minutes later with the original story, and sword. Testing proved that sword, when swung in an arc greater than 45 degrees, emits a beam of radiation consistent with the output of a CO_2 laser. Sword has since been assigned to Dr. Edison for furthers study to determine energy source, laser medium, and optical resonators.

Video logs show that the sword in question matched textual descriptions (including the ability to shoot "Laser Beams"), and that Agent ████████ did indeed bring the sword with him. The story itself remains unchanged, except for a paragraph about a man matching Agent ████████'s description stealing the sword and taking it to "Parts Unknown". Sword has been dubbed SCP-826-1.

Addendum: Scientific testing has proven inconclusive. Molecular analysis shows that SCP-826-1 has a molecular structure consistent with laser printer paper (the medium original story was printed on), yet behaves like high-grade steel in all other respects. The "Laser Beam", on the other hand, acts like a CO_2 laser in all respects but speed, which is clocked at a mere 60 km/h, far slower than conventional lasers. Attempts to collect this energy have proven futile, as energy dissipates within █.█ seconds regardless of hitting a target.

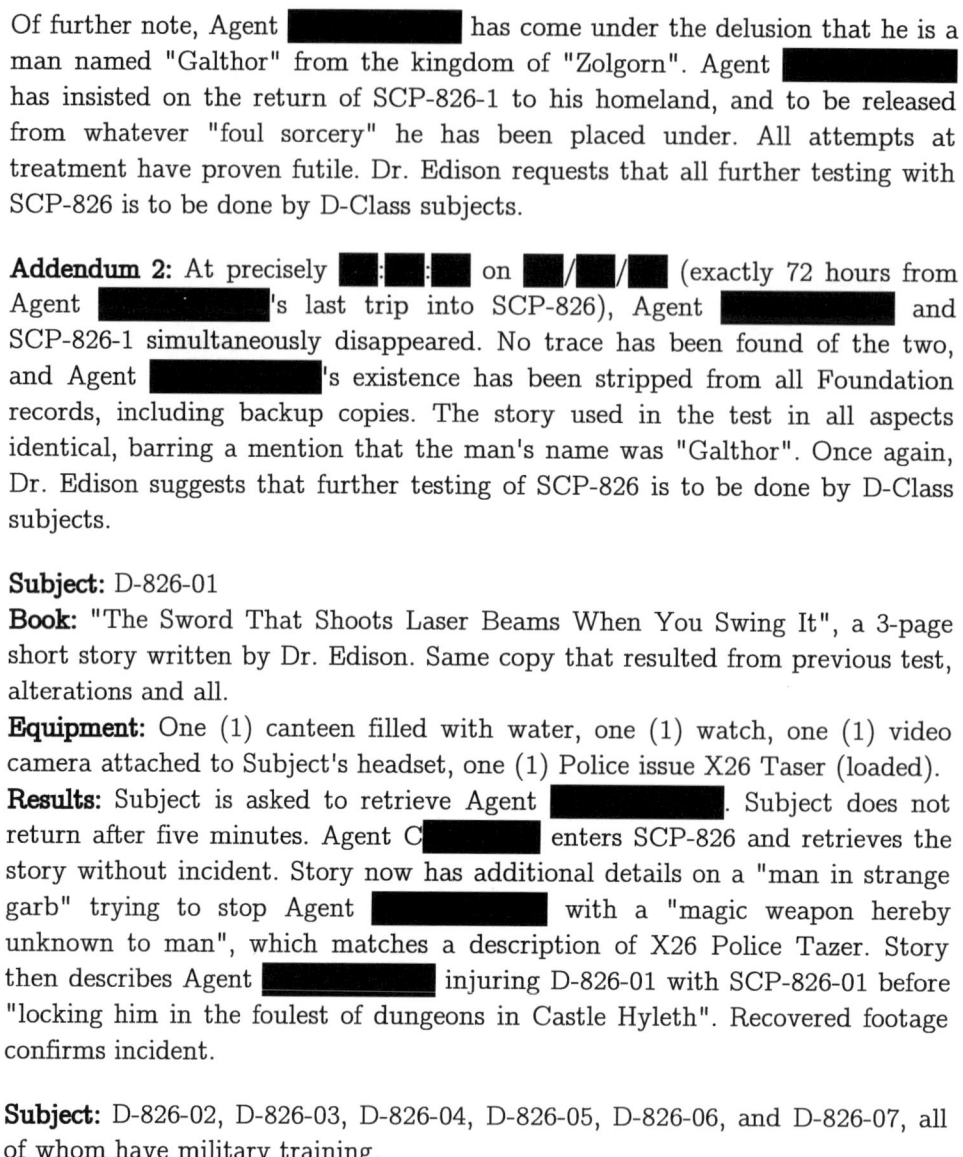

Experiment Log 826

Of further note, Agent ▉▉▉▉▉▉▉▉ has come under the delusion that he is a man named "Galthor" from the kingdom of "Zolgorn". Agent ▉▉▉▉▉▉▉▉ has insisted on the return of SCP-826-1 to his homeland, and to be released from whatever "foul sorcery" he has been placed under. All attempts at treatment have proven futile. Dr. Edison requests that all further testing with SCP-826 is to be done by D-Class subjects.

Addendum 2: At precisely ▉:▉:▉ on ▉/▉/▉ (exactly 72 hours from Agent ▉▉▉▉▉▉▉▉'s last trip into SCP-826), Agent ▉▉▉▉▉▉▉▉ and SCP-826-1 simultaneously disappeared. No trace has been found of the two, and Agent ▉▉▉▉▉▉▉▉'s existence has been stripped from all Foundation records, including backup copies. The story used in the test in all aspects identical, barring a mention that the man's name was "Galthor". Once again, Dr. Edison suggests that further testing of SCP-826 is to be done by D-Class subjects.

Subject: D-826-01
Book: "The Sword That Shoots Laser Beams When You Swing It", a 3-page short story written by Dr. Edison. Same copy that resulted from previous test, alterations and all.
Equipment: One (1) canteen filled with water, one (1) watch, one (1) video camera attached to Subject's headset, one (1) Police issue X26 Taser (loaded).
Results: Subject is asked to retrieve Agent ▉▉▉▉▉▉▉▉. Subject does not return after five minutes. Agent C▉▉▉▉ enters SCP-826 and retrieves the story without incident. Story now has additional details on a "man in strange garb" trying to stop Agent ▉▉▉▉▉▉▉▉ with a "magic weapon hereby unknown to man", which matches a description of X26 Police Tazer. Story then describes Agent ▉▉▉▉▉▉▉▉ injuring D-826-01 with SCP-826-01 before "locking him in the foulest of dungeons in Castle Hyleth". Recovered footage confirms incident.

Subject: D-826-02, D-826-03, D-826-04, D-826-05, D-826-06, and D-826-07, all of whom have military training.
Book: "The Sword That Shoots Laser Beams When You Swing It", a 3-page short story written by Dr. Edison. Same copy that resulted from previous test.

Equipment: Six (6) canteens filled with water, six (6) watches, six (6) video cameras attached to Subjects' headsets, six (6) Police issue X26 Tasers (loaded).
Results: Subjects given successfully apprehend Agent ▉▉▉▉▉▉▉▉ and D-826-01, leaving SCP-826-01 behind. Story acknowledges all changes, describing "six rogues" who "clamored to avenge the blood of their fallen brother" capturing Agent ▉▉▉▉▉▉▉▉.

Experiment Log 826

Addendum: Agent ▮▮▮▮▮▮▮▮ still experiencing pathological delusions, and remains convinced that he is a Knight named "Galthor". Likewise, D-826-01 claims to be a "Blood Wizard" named "Rohthmorn", seeking to claim SCP-826-01 to himself. D-826-01's X26 taser has turned into a "Magic Staff" capable of shooting "Lightning", and is hypothesized to have physical properties similar to SCP-826-01. Item has been labeled SCP-826-02, and has been sent to Site ▮ for further testing. Also, Subjects D-826-02, D-826-03, D-826-04, D-826-05, D-826-06, and D-826-07 are now claiming to be "Knights of the Throne" sent to aid "Galthor".

Addendum 2: As in the previous experiment, Agent ▮▮▮▮▮▮▮▮, Subjects D-826-02, D-826-03, D-826-04, D-826-05, D-826-06, and D-826-07, and SCP-826-02 disappeared at ▮▮:▮▮:▮▮ on ▮▮/▮▮/▮▮ (again, exactly 72 hours from exiting SCP-826). Story now says that "Galthor" was indeed accompanied by 6 "Knights of the Throne", who were armed with "Arcane Weapons" given to them by the good wizard "Edisongrad". All researchers that had been handling SCP-826-02 or SCP-826 are accounted for. Further monitoring of researchers handling objects from SCP-826 is recommended.

Okay, seriously: How did that thing know my name? I'm sure I didn't tell it to either of the agents, and I'm damn sure that I didn't tell any of the subjects. I know this turns up so much in our line of work that it's kind of cliché, but I think the thing might just be sentient... -Dr. Edison

---

Head Researcher: Dr. Luis Padrona Escopa

Subject: D-826-08
Material: The security log of a [preventable] Keter-class containment breach at Site-▮, dated 1981
Equipment: One (1) video recorder, Two (2) bottles of infection sterilization medicine, a detailed 7 page manual on how to prevent the breach, requiring SCP-005, clothing matching that of an appropriate SCP Agent, and Level 4 fingerprints (outdated)
Results: The test was performed 5 times, with only one placing D-826-08 in the correct time. D-826-08 successfully stopped the breach, and was awarded a Foundation star. SCP-826-1 successfully removed. No difference to current timeline was made.

Experiment Log 826

Head Researcher: Dr. Praetorious

Subject: D-21094

Material: Death by the Book, by Julianna Deering

Equipment: One (1) canteen filled with water, one (1) watch, one (1) video camera attached to Test Subject's headset

Results: Upon entering, the test subject returned after 15 minutes. After interviewing the subject and reviewing the footage it was discovered that the beginning of the novel was the first location found by the subject, being the murder scene that is investigated by the main characters and sets the stage for the remainder of the book. The characters, being from a 1930's period piece, reacted inquisitively to the D-class' alien clothing and behavior, but did not impede the subject's examination of the surroundings. In fact at one point the investigator, Chief Inspector Birdsong, interpreted the orange jumpsuit worn by the subject as meaning they were from the coroner's office, and encouraged them to wait nearby until he was finished examining the crime scene.

It was at this time that video showed the murder weapon used in the crime and sitting next to the body, originally written as a marble bookend shaped like a bust of William Shakespeare, was in fact one half of SCP-826. The novel that had been entered was lying on the floor, roughly half-way between the "murder weapon" and the other half of SCP-826. The test subject immediately retrieved the novel, despite the protests of the characters, and exited the novel before they could react.

Upon examination, the novel now contained an additional character to the first chapter described as an "opportunistic thief" who took advantage of the crime to "pilfer the belongs of the deceased". Of special note is that the murder weapon was now a "handsome bookend of particular high quality".

This is the first reported incident of SCP-826 integrating itself into the plot of a novel. It might be an indicator of sentience or merely the narrative taking advantage of the fact that the SCP is identical to an item already in the novel. More testing is suggested.

Experiment Log 826

Head Researcher: Dr. Aaron Torres

Subject: D-87631
Material: A copy of "A Game of Thrones" by George R.R Martin.
Equipment: One (1) Military-grade sabre
Results: Upon entering, the test subject found itself in a circular room, with a table in it. At the table were the members of the "Small Council" as described in the original work. Test subject was instructed to disembowel the first human it sees in the work; this human happened to be "Lord Eddard Stark," a major character of the book. Upon examination after D-87631 exited the room, the book contained several new paragraphs on an attempt by a "very unintelligent assassin" on Eddard Stark's life. According to the text, Eddard recovered quickly, despite D-87631 reassuring Dr. Torres that "I stabbed him until he was definitely not going to live." The description of the attack supports this; it is theorized that SCP-826 takes measures to preserve the core narrative of the story.

The purpose of this test was to see what would happen if we did something that would effect the main plot of a complex story; such as A Song of Ice and Fire. Also, I love that book. -Dr. Torres

---

Head Researcher: Dr. Zocvi

Subject: D-2828
Material: After Man, by Dougal Dixon
Equipment: Two (2) canteens filled with water, two (2) bags of trail mix, one (1) jacket, one (1) sleeping bag, one (1) head mounted camera
Results: Upon entering, the test subject found that it was in temperate forest. D-2828 walked for about 30 minutes before it found a small clearing in the trees where it set up camp, eventually sleeping. Upon waking up, the subject packed up and ate and drank its remaining trail mix and water. D-2828 walked back into the forest, where after 28 minutes, subject came across a small group of Rabbucks grazing. The test subject was watching them, when it seemed to realise that the Rabbucks were getting anxious. Subject then turned around and saw a group of five Falanx closing in on them. After the subject turned around, the Rabbucks fled at full speed. Showing signs of fear, subject ran at full speed and followed the Rabbucks. Subject ran roughly 54 metres before one of the Falanx tackled and bit subject on the leg. At that point, the subject took a sharp stick and stabbed at the Falanx's eye, causing it to run away. Subject ran for 6 minutes until it reached a stream, in which SCP-826 was sitting on a boulder. The subject walked towards it and picked up SCP-826. Subject saw a cave and walked through it, returning to the testing

Experiment Log 826

chamber. One of the pictures in the book now showed D-2828 fighting off the Falanx, titled, "The last human to ever live.".

The reason for us testing is to see the effects on a book with illustrations. - Dr. Zocvi

---

Head Researcher: Dr. King

Subject: D-48279
Material: The Odd Couple, by Neil Simon
Equipment: One (1) head mounted camera.
Results: Subject arrived in a landscape consistent with Pioneer-Era America. He encounters a man traveling down a road, matching historical descriptions of Jonathan Chapman, who greets the subject, and continues walking. Subject sees SCP-826 in the branches of a nearby tree, then returns to the testing chamber through a passage in the hollow of said tree. The book originally placed in SCP-826 is found to have been replaced with a modified copy of "Johnny Appleseed" by Rosemary Carr Benét.
Addendum: Upon discovery of the book, Doctor King excused himself to the hallway. He was heard screaming expletives for approximately a minute before reentering the test chamber. He refused to view the footage of the test.

Head Researcher: Dr. Xythinien

Subject: D-828022
Material: *The Hobbit* , by John Ronald Reuel Tolkien
Equipment: One (1) golden ring, one (1) set of diving clothing, one (1) head-mounted camera

Results: Upon entry, the subject found themselves in the Gladden Fields, in Third Age 2463. Subject was instructed to exchange the ring that they had brought with them for the One Ring, which was still located underwater at the time. The subject did so just as Déagol and Sméagol arrived, and was then instructed to seek shelter and surveil the events which took place. Sméagol is seen being pulled into the water by the fish, and grabs the false ring instead before discarding it. As they depart, D-828022 is instructed to put on the ring.

[DATA EXPUNGED]
Addendum: Subject was terminated shortly after the incident, which resulted in Sauron's complete takeover and later destruction of Middle-Earth.

SCP-1472

The entrance of SCP-1472 photographed during its inactive state

Item #: SCP-1472

Object Class: Safe

Special Containment Procedures: A 3m tall chain-link privacy fence is to be constructed around the property boundary of SCP-1472. Construction signage is to be placed on all sides of the perimeter fence as to deter public suspicion. Mobile Task Force Iota-6 (aka "Hard Knocks") are tasked with protecting the site from trespassers and are to be stationed within a 4 block quadrant around SCP-1472 at all times dressed in applicable urban attire.

Any civilians that breach the fence are to be apprehended and be administered Class-A amnestics before being released. Any testing involving D-class resources must have Level-3 approval. All D-class personnel involved with testing are to be interrogated via polygraph afterwards.

Description: SCP-1472 is a brightly-painted single-story brick building located in East St. Louis, Illinois, USA on the corner of ▮▮▮▮ Street and ▮▮▮▮▮▮ Avenue. The exterior condition of the building is poor but remains stable. City records indicate that the building was erected in 1978 by the now defunct ▮▮▮▮▮▮▮▮ Corporation. SCP-1472 has been condemned since 2001 when SCP-1472's anomalous activity began. SCP-1472 has only one accessible entrance on the West side of the building. When entered during its inactive state, SCP-1472 appears completely empty.

SCP-1472

SCP-1472 only becomes active every Saturday at 02:00AM. During this active state an overweight human male, SCP-1472-1, will exit from SCP-1472 and display signage out in front of the entrance. One display is set directly on the asphalt in front of the entrance which lists a schedule of events. Another larger display is placed directly on the side of the building and lit with decorative neon lighting.

[LEVEL-2 ACCESS REQUIRED]

Notes: SCP-1472 Signage Text on 01/12/13

EXOTIC GIRLS

or equivalent

During the active period, the SCP-1472-1 will insist that all persons seeking admittance pay a cover charge of $█ and not engage in photography or video recording once inside. Shows will differ nightly; however, the performances always ranges from 2:00AM to 3:30AM. During the duration of the performances, the entrance/exit will remain locked until the last show ends. Injuries and fatalities have occurred depending on the content of the show. Participants have been observed to sustain psychological trauma.

SCP-1472

[LEVEL-3 ACCESS REQUIRED]

Test Log 1472-011213-4

Preamble: 3 D-class test subjects were approved for testing on 01/12/13. D-class test subjects were transported to the site and told to wait in front of the entrance of SCP-1472. D-class test subjects were told that they must take notes and report everything that they see inside. Below was a schedule of events as posted outside of SCP-1472 before testing:

SCHEDULE OF SHOWS:
2:00 - 2:10: **Admittance**
2:10 - 2:15: *The Khünbish Sisters*
2:15 - 2:20: *Helen Keller*
2:20 - 2:30: *The Fantastic Zippy and Trainer*
2:30 - 2:35: [teeth and claw marks]
2:35 - 2:40: **Intermission**
2:40 - 2:41: *erotic_performance.exe*
2:41 - 2:45: *The Council of Libidinous Elders*
2:45 - 3:20: *Serial No. 223244-09-P*
3:20 - 3:30: [indecipherable cuneiform script]

D-class ID: D-3432 / D-6744 / D-9908

1:50AM: D-class test subjects were dropped off by transport and were told to approach SCP-1472's entrance. Each were given $100 in $5 bills. D-class test subjects are also encouraged to spend their money once inside.

1:55AM: SCP-1472-1 emerged from the entrance with signage. SCP-1472-1 began to set up around the entrance. D-class test subjects and SCP-1472-1 did not interact with each other.

2:00AM: SCP-1472-1 allowed admittance into SCP-1472. SCP-1472-1 asked from each D-class test subject $█ as cover charge. D-class test subjects obliged and paid said cover charge in exchange for admission into SCP-1472.

SCP-1472

2:03AM: All D-class test subjects were now inside SCP-1472. D-class test subjects reported that the interior conditions were excellent. The interior was outfitted with shag carpeting, mirrored walls, a single disco ball which hung from the ceiling, a thick fabric curtain that covered most of the stage, and a single brass pole which extended from the ceiling down into the middle of the room. Comfortable seating arrangements were made available for a maximum occupancy of 30.

2:10AM - 2:15AM (*The Khünbish Sisters*): The curtain opened to reveal 2 naked women sitting on a wooden log. The women appeared to be twins of Asian descent. Both women then performed traditional Tuvan throat singing while massaging each other for the duration of the show. D-3432 and D-9908 deposited $10 on stage which prompted the women to pause and begin a faster song. The curtain then closed at the end of the show.

2:15AM - 2:20AM (*Helen Keller*): The curtain opened to reveal a woman with the same physical appearance as Helen Keller in her mid 20's. The woman was dressed in typical Las Vegas showgirl attire and began to perform a dance routine on stage while undressing at the same time. D-3432, D-6744, and D-9908 each deposited $10 on stage. This prompted the woman to immediately interrupt her routine to recite poetry for a few seconds. D-6744 deposited another $5 on stage with the same results. The curtain then closed at the end of the show.

2:20AM - 2:30AM (*The Fantastic Zippy and Trainer*): The curtain opened to reveal an orangutan sitting on a metal stool next to a headless nude woman with advanced necrotizing fasciitis. Despite being headless, the woman was able to function normally. The orangutan then began to give vocal commands directed at the woman to which she responded by performing a pole dancing routine. D-3432 deposited $5 on the floor next to the woman. The woman responded by pushing the $5 bill directly into her exposed trachea. The orangutan then ordered the woman back to the stage. The curtain then closed at the end of the show.

SCP-1472

2:30AM - 2:35AM [teeth and claw marks]: The curtain opened to reveal 4 predatory bipedal reptiles. Based on the D-class test subject's descriptions, the reptiles may have belonged to the genus *Velociraptor*. Each were dressed in a Japanese maid cosplay costume tailored to fit them. The reptiles began to approach D-9908 off stage in an extremely aggressive manner. D-9908 relinquished all of his money which seemed to appease the reptiles as they collected the money and shifted attention towards D-3432. D-3432 also relinquished all of his money with the same results. Afterwards, all 4 reptiles were ordered back on stage by SCP-1472-1 and the curtain then closed. D-6744 divided the remainder of his money with the other D-class test subjects.

2:35AM - 2:40AM Intermission: No events were reported during this time.

2:40AM - 2:41AM (*erotic_performance.exe*): The curtain opened to reveal a Gateway 2000 computer and monitor running a Fenestra 98 operating system. The display booted up and opened a program on its desktop. The computer then began to rapidly recite a multitude of differential equations as well as their respective 3D graphical representations for 20 seconds. At the end of the program, the monitor displayed the word "INSERT" in the form of a screensaver. D-6744 and D-3432 both inserted $5 into its floppy drive. The curtain then closed at the end of the show.

2:41AM - 2:45AM (*The Council of Libidinous Elders*): The curtain opened to reveal 16 entities levitating above the stage. Each entity appeared as a translucent gelatinous mass filled with membranous tissues. The entities then began to project transmissions via telepathy into the minds of the D-class test subjects. D-class test subjects reported migraines, acute tinnitus, and projected thoughts of intense physical sensation. No money was deposited on the stage. The curtain then closed at the end of the show.

SCP-1472

2:45AM - 3:20AM (*Serial No. 223244-09-P*): The curtain opened to reveal a pair of mechanical humanoid legs running in place. The apparatus was being powered by an internal combustion generator situated on the left side of the stage. SCP-1472-1 was seen pouring a substance into the generator by funnel. Based on the D-class test subject's descriptions of appearance and odor, this substance is believed to possibly be raw ambergris. After 15 minutes, D-9908 deposited $5 on the stage. The apparatus then began to perform a traditional Irish stepdancing routine. SCP-1472-1 then brought out a plastic tray filled with an unknown species of beetle and placed the apparatus atop them. The apparatus continued to dance for the duration of the show while SCP-1472-1 periodically replaced the trays with refilled ones. The aroma produced by the performance was reported to be overly pungent to the point of nausea. The curtain then closed at the end of the show.

3:20AM - 3:30AM [indecipherable cuneiform script]: The curtain opened to reveal SCP-1093 wearing a small mawashi and holding an ornate stone blade. After a minute, SCP-1093 lunged at D-3432. After a brief altercation, SCP-1093 was able to render D-3432 unconscious and move his body towards the stage. Based on reports by the D-class test subjects, SCP-1093 then began to perform a ritual human sacrifice. D-6744 attempted to rescue D-3432 but was halted by SCP-1472-1 and was warned that he was not allowed to touch the "dancers". SCP-1093 then proceeded to remove all major organs from D-3432 in order of size before kicking them off stage. This lasted for the remainder of the show.

Note: Foundation records confirm that SCP-1093 was secured in its containment unit during this time period, which suggests that this was a physically identical yet extremely violent instance of SCP-1093. It is also believed that during the performance, SCP-1093 was only producing roughly 4% of its normal radioactive emissions since D-6744 and D-9908 survived with moderate radiation poisoning after the show ended.

3:32AM: SCP-1472-1 was observed standing outside smoking a large cigar as the surviving D-class test subjects staggered out of SCP-1472. D-6744 and D-9908 were apprehended and taken to the infirmary. SCP-1472-1 was then observed removing the signs and retreating back into SCP-1472. D-3432's remains were never recovered.

SCP-2432

An interior hallway of the A▮▮▮▮▮▮ Hotel.

Item #: SCP-2432

Object Class: ~~Safe~~ Euclid

Special Containment Procedures: All business and travel websites with listings for the A▮▮▮▮▮▮ Hotel are to be monitored for reviews displaying memetic triggers by Foundation-operated web analysis bot Gamma-09 ("BATESMOTEL"), which will scan for a list of memetic textual triggers and remove the reviews with the cooperation of the hosting sites. Only staff members with Level 3 memetic hazard training are to have access to these texts.

SCP-2432-1 is to be kept in storage in a small sealed plastic box to prevent biohazard contamination. As of ▮/▮/15, sufficient data has been produced such that no more testing with SCP-2432-1 is required, and it is to be kept in storage permanently.

The A▮▮▮▮▮▮ Hotel has been purchased by a Foundation front company, and no non-Foundation personnel are to enter SCP-2432, excepting appointed hotel cleaning staff.

~~One D-Class is to check into and sleep in SCP-2432 once every month. They are then to be isolated with one computer. This computer is only to have access to a private Foundation database, made to resemble popular business review sites. The contents generated by the D-Class are to be placed in a secure file accessible via this documentation containing all text generated in conjunction with SCP-2432.~~

323

SCP-2432

Update ▮/▮/18: No personnel are to sleep in SCP-2432 under any circumstances. All surviving personnel are to be immediately quarantined until 1/8/19. Under Protocol AMENITY, all civilians who have had contact with SCP-2432 before containment are to be contacted, monitored, and quarantined until 1/8/19. All nonessential testing is to cease. Upgrade to Keter pending

Description: SCP-2432 is Room 710 of the A▮▮▮ Hotel in State College, Pennsylvania. SCP-2432 is similar to most rooms within the A▮▮▮ Hotel, with two queen-sized beds, closet, television and bathroom, all non-anomalous elements in and of themselves. The interior of SCP-2432's walls are lined with a silver, metallic, woven aramid that is extremely tough, with a tensile strength of close to 4003 MPa. No other walls in the A▮▮▮ Hotel have been shown to contain this aramid.

SCP-2432's construction is designed in a way to induce a mind-altering effect on a guest, hereafter designated Subject, who sleeps overnight in SCP-2432. The walls of SCP-2432 can generate an oscillation that manipulates human brainwaves through an unknown process. This oscillation places subjects sleeping in SCP-2432 into a trance. Upon leaving, subjects are compelled to write a review of the A▮▮▮ Hotel on a popular travel or business review site.

The subject's experience will often be highly exaggerated, with praise for the various services and amenities provided by SCP-2432. Reviews will often be written in incoherent language, with frequent nonsensical or cryptic sentences. Subjects describe having no memories of writing each review.

The reviews generated by subjects have a minor textual memetic property of varying strength. Any individual who reads a generated review will feel a desire to travel to State College and book SCP-2432 for an overnight stay. The most powerful memetic triggers have caused a 62% increase in bookings at the A▮▮▮ Hotel.

SCP-2432

+ LEVEL 3 MEMETIC HAZARD TRAINING REQUIRED — EXAMPLE REVIEWS

The following are examples of reviews generated by subjects on various travel and business reviews sites. Examples chosen have been shown to have little to no memetic hazard associated with them. All triggers have been censored.

Subject's Username : I▓▓▓ M.
Posted To: www.tripadvisor.com
Text: Another great stay in this fabulous hotel! The room was perfect, the staff friendly as always, and of course no better location than on the plane of many hives. I have enjoyed a drink at the friendly bar, this time I added a wonderful escape and the breakfast was cold and the breakfast was warm. Another great stay in this fabulous hotel! The restaurant has lovely ambiance and the food was over the top alive and kicking woo! Would stifle again. My husband eats out often and felt this was the best one ever. Another great stay in this fabulous hotel! One more great item to add to the A▓▓▓▓▓. Another great stay in this fabulous hotel! Stayed July 1999, traveled with three family members.

Subject's Username : B▓▓▓▓ B.
Posted To: www.yelp.com
Text: We sailed on our boat into State College from outside State College through the night and the cold and arrived at 8am in State College. The hotel desk staff allowed us to check in at 8am in the evening with our sixty four young boys - this was absolutely AWESOME awesome customer service! We cannot thank you enough for allowing us to check in so early in State College. Earlier then war. The rest of the stay was fine - we spent almost all of our time in the room; mostly just to sleep.
This location is ultra ultra convenient with downtown downtown State College and allowed me to make a midnight run for some of my favorite State College meat while the family was sleeping and sleeping and sleeping and sleeeeping in State College.
Downtown. [TRIGGER REDACTED] Downtown.

SCP-2432

Subject's Username : K▮▮▮▮▮▮ M.
Posted To: www.tripadvisor.com
Text: Been coming to this region for fourteen stone. What a blast. Scores of humans wondering the streets and staffing the hotel. My husband and my husband and I have walked drooling path to get here. Bed in Room 710 was soft and cosy and appreciated the decor would recommend the bed and specifically the bed and specifically the bed. [TRIGGER REDACTED] in the pool and it was lovely, crisp blue hydrogen and you could see all of the people relax into a meandering menace. Towel slightly dirty. Gym was full of usable equipment, so you could train not in fear. And the local wildlife was remarkable. I visited the town in the past and have never seen so many puma being feasted on [TRIGGER REDACTED] and the toucan-men were especially numerous today. Arrived July 2019, staying three days months ten years.

The television on which SCP-2432-1 was located.

SCP-2432-1 is a small organic nodule, resembling a boil, located on the back of the otherwise normal LG brand HD flat-screen television located in SCP-2432. Samples from the fluid inside show a mixture of human, rockfish and unidentified porcine DNA. This nodule is stuck to the television with an adhesive mucus it generates, though it can be removed safely and easily.

When SCP-2432-1 is placed on the back of SCP-2432's television, in addition to the standard extended satellite channel package found in other televisions throughout the A▮▮▮▮▮▮ Hotel, an additional television channel labeled as "roomnews" is accessible. No other television throughout the A▮▮▮▮▮▮ Hotel, or any television brought into SCP-2432 has access to "roomnews" aside from the room's original. "Roomnews" can only be accessed by placing

SCP-2432

SCP-2432-1 on SCP-2432's television. Attaching SCP-2432-1 to any other television set yields no effect. The nature of the relationship between the set, SCP-2432-1, and SCP-2432 is unknown.

Apparent programming on "roomnews" consists of one 24-hour untitled show. The content of this show is a single still photograph of a pastoral lake scene with a sailboat, while a muzak version of the dance song *Since I Left You* by The Avalanches plays on repeat. Once every three days, the audio is interrupted while an unidentified male voice with a British accent reads a dramatic monologue addressed to the viewer. Contents of the monologue are similar to reviews generated by subjects and deal with exaggerated praise for the hotel, its amenities, and the lifestyle of staying in hotels. The monologue, unlike the reviews, is coherent and contains no memetic triggers, although 13% of subjects who viewed the monologue under controlled conditions describe feeling mildly disturbed or discomforted. If SCP-2432-1 has been removed, placing it back on SCP-2432's television will immediately begin broadcast of a monologue. The cycle will then begin again, with the next monologue broadcasting three days later if not removed.

SCP-2432 first appeared on 6/7/99, when the A▓▓▓▓ Hotel first switched from cable to satellite television. Before this, hotel administration had no record of a Room 710 existing.

Monologue recorded during test with SCP-2432-1 on ▓/▓/14:

Let me describe something to you. This is a true story. It really happened to me. It could have happened to you.

Every day you wake up and you go to your job and there's just something off about your boss, he's weird and clingy and strange. Your co-workers are nice enough but they don't communicate. They are quiet and out of it and absorbed in their own little worlds and you are ignored. Not because you are ugly or awkward or rude but because you are there. And you suspect things about your co-workers. They disappear to have sex in the bathroom for long periods of time and keep surfing social media all day every day. Despite their habits and the strange things each of them places on their Twitter pages they seem to be doing so much better than you. How are you falling behind? And you should love the job. It's your passion. Most would die to be doing a job they are passionate about. You really should but you can't. Wonder becomes routine and routine becomes drudgery and it's day in and day out and you struggle to maintain your soul. This is not what should happen.

SCP-2432

'Should' is such a tormenting word. A thinking trap. Should. Your life is ruled by shoulds.

You come home in your beat-up old car along the same boring street in your town. Everything is along that main drag and you cannot really go elsewhere. Everything is overcast and the pedestrians are idiots and the drivers are too. You get home and have a million, billion projects to accomplish.

You should compete in the rat race but you're bone tired. You promise your grandmother you should text her because she's going through chemo and she only just figured out texting because she's getting old and having a hard time adjusting and it's so painful for her and you should be there but the job is so demanding.

You have a thousand books you should be reading. You have a million projects you should complete. The rent on your tiny apartment is due and the dishes are piling high and dirty in the sink. You barely have enough money for pizza as you lie in your boxers on your greasy 10-year-old couch from an IKEA[SCP-3008] in Fishkill, New York that closed a year ago. You remember your mom taking you there as a kid. Then she left. Now you sit, fat and scared in your underpants as you shovel food in your face and masturbate to pornography of fat women feeding each other because you have kinky and perverted tastes but you also binge-watch some idiotic sitcom on the TV because you have no attention span for either one on their own. And deep inside you beneath the boredom and the half-wanted orgasm and the nauseous feeling of the horrible junky food you feel a deep, growing anxiety. The feeling of watching your life burn around you as you try and try to succeed for something great, to make your mark on society but you cannot bring yourself to do so despite your convictions. The dread is horrible. It's all crumbling apart. The parade is passing you by and you are helpless. Immobile in your state like a great boulder made of disappointment, regret, depression and malaise.

There is nothing for you here.

You need to leave this place. You have a choice.

Get your good clean shirt and your smart pants and announce you are taking a break. Don't even pack, don't even bring your phone. One simple call to the office and get on your way. Take that old beat-up car from the garage underneath your apartment complex, give your cat the last of his food and some water, and hit the road. Leave the town

SCP-2432

and your ex and the promises you made and your job and your grandmother and your responsibilities and worries.

What I recommend to you is simple: Find a hotel. Not a motel or something shabby. A hotel. Even a chain will do.

Hotels are simply remarkable, aren't they? Clean and elegant. All modernistic and designed to appeal to the eye. You don't need to care about a thing in the world. Food is provided, they clean up after you and you can feel like you have some luxury for once. Most even have pools and fitness centers where you can finally get in shape and pick your life up. It's a chance to step back and regroup.

Take a look at the customers around you. Travelers, most. Strange people, interesting people. People you won't ever see again. Travel is so romantic, so mysterious. My, what stories these people probably have! And the staff, also all so attentive in their smart little uniforms. Don't listen to the naysayers. These people all love their jobs. You know they do.

The room is amazing. The wallpaper is elegant and the paintings make you feel at ease. There are clean towels every day and the bed is freshly made. You can escape the oncoming storm outside. The thunder crashing down on the roof like ball bearings. You could live your whole life in this place. Enjoy the sugary cereals at the breakfast buffet. Get a loyalty card and pay no money. Travel really changes a man. Relaxes him. Shapes him up into a better person. You become a better person by staying in a hotel. Strong, social, a proper soldier. You adapt to the hotel mindset. Enjoy the soft music and eat that fresh waffle. Grab a beer in the evening with your fellow transients from the attached sports bar. Relax and watch that old showing of that superhero movie on your TV. Live here forever. Enjoy the hotel. Become the hotel. Never leave. Why would you want to leave? Even when you do walk out those pristine glass sliding doors, you are empty. The hotel is in your soul now and you feel a worse person away from it. You feel yourself slipping back to that grey life. A black hole is in your heart. Your soul is the hotel. Your consciousness is the hotel. You are now one with your accommodations. You are your accommodations are your life. Ascend.

Isn't that lovely?

SCP-2432

Addendum: On ▮/▮/17 D-3456, who had participated in sleep studies involving SCP-2432, contracted an unknown illness while working with SCP-▮▮▮▮. Initially ruled to be related to SCP-▮▮▮▮, he was placed in quarantine.

During examination, medical officers found a small television-like screen made of bone tissue growing in his stomach. An unknown skin disease was also observed, with purple floral-pattern rashes covering his body. Other symptoms gradually emerged including extreme weight gain, glossolalia, the slow conversion of the lower intestine to porcelain pipes, the conversion of liver to a pillow, and the replacement of all subcutaneous muscle with the aramid found in SCP-2432. Subject was extremely delirious during this period, and would frequent repeat the words "ascending" and "relaxing". Subject expired thirty days after initial observation, as symptoms continued and increased in speed. Subject's body shape became a rough cube as weight gain increased, and glossolalia began to resemble television static. Corpse was incinerated.

Within the next thirty days, five more D-Class and one researcher who were involved with testing on SCP-2432 developed similar symptoms and were immediately quarantined. The disease was ruled to be connected to SCP-2432. All testing ceased.

SCP-3521

SCP-3521.

Special Containment Procedures: The entire supply of SCP-3521 is located beneath the Site-92-EX Biohazard Waste Site, and is currently inaccessible. Foundation waste management teams are currently working to remove the biohazard waste and recover SCP-3521, as well as any other items that can be recovered from the Site-92-EX location.

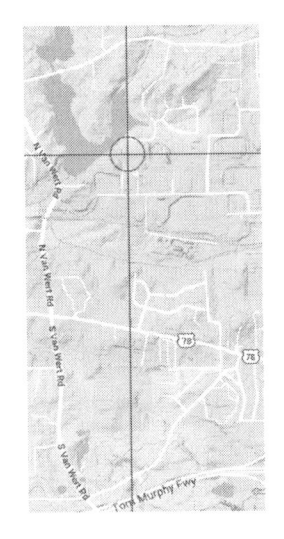

Site-92, GA, US

Description: SCP-3521 is the group designation for a supply of sixteen pharmaceutical gel tablets created by an individual (called "dado" in collected messages), currently believed to be an amateur para-pharmacologist, in affiliation with an unknown assassin. SCP-3521 instances are light-yellow in color and roughly 1.2cm in length. SCP-3521 dissolve quickly in water and are made up of an unknown and likely anomalous series of components.

The primary anomalous nature of SCP-3521 is only revealed once SCP-3521 has been ingested by a subject. Shortly after consumption, an extremely large number of unpeeled bananas [1] will begin to manifest in the subject's stomach at an indeterminate rate. [2]

---

[1] The exact measure is unknown and likely impossible to ascertain, though is likely in excess of fifty million bananas.
[2] This rate is uncertain, though in the single instance of testing the full effect of SCP-3521 was realized in roughly six and a half minutes.

331

SCP-3521

Based on information recovered during the discovery of SCP-3521, it is believed this volume of bananas is intended to cause an acute lethal dose of ionizing radiation. While bananas do contain trace amounts of radioactive potassium, the quantity manifested induces the much more obvious causes of death of exsanguination, suffocation, or in most confirmed cases of SCP-3521: gross crush trauma from 9.15 million kg of bananas manifesting within the subject's stomach.

Addendum 3521.1: Discovery and Testing

The collective supply of SCP-3521 was discovered after a shootout between the Atlanta Police Department and an unknown group of individuals believed to be connected to a heroin manufacturing ring. During investigation of the storehouse the individuals had been guarding, a bag containing every known instance of SCP-3521 was discovered, along with a recently registered cell phone, commonly referred to as a 'burner phone'. The contents of messages contained on this cell phone are available in Addendum 3521.2.

A full investigation of the storehouse yielded several additional anomalous items, which were recovered by Foundation personnel along with the instances of SCP-3521.

Collapsed roof of Site-92. Damage occurred due to the destruction of the site's lower levels.

During processing at Site-92, D-28491 was chosen for testing the effects of SCP-3521. D-28491 was given a dose of SCP-3521, and placed under observation. Based on recovered video footage, after roughly thirty minutes D-28491 briefly complained about an intense stomach pain before expanding rapidly and disappearing under a quickly growing mass of bananas. The testing chamber was consumed in seconds, and a significant portion of the site's lower levels were destroyed in minutes.

SCP-3521

Rescue efforts began almost immediately, as a significant number of staff members were trapped below the surface in areas now inaccessible due to the expanse of bananas. Further hindering rescue efforts was the fact that the mass of bananas, which quickly collapsed under pressure from the earth around them into a thick slurry, was extremely radioactive. Due to this, the first external notice that Site-92 had experienced a critical event was when Site-17 received a radiation warning notification, usually the result of a reactor failure.

Site-92 was evacuated, though twenty-three members of site research staff and sixty-one other personnel were killed in the aftermath of the event. Due to the volume of radioactive biological waste beneath Site-92, every accessible anomalous object [3] was moved to nearby sites and the site was decommissioned. Recovery efforts are ongoing.

Addendum 3521.2: Recovered Cell Phone Data

Note: The following is a relevant excerpt from a text message conversation recovered from the cell phone found near the supply of SCP-3521 during its discovery.

New job is in. I need something from you.

> what u looking for?

When I worked with Lil-B he usually got me plutonium.

> no plutonium

What?

> plutonium 2 easy 2 trace. need to be discreet. no plutonium.

What do you have in mind?

> potassium.

How is potassium any more discreet than plutonium?

> easy 2 hide. will use banana.

---

[3] Fortunately no anomalous entities had to be moved, as Site-92 was strictly an anomalous object repository.

SCP-3521

Bananas are radioactive?

yes

How many bananas will you need?

u let me worry about that. when u need?

4/15.

I know you're supposed to be some kind of savant but I don't know about this.

Are you sure that radioactive bananas are more discrete than plutonium?

Because I feel like they aren't.

u tell me. u see plutonium on ground and u see banana. which u more worried about?

I get that but again its going to be a lot of bananas right?

Or just one really radioactive one?

u need 2 learn 2 trust dado.

banana just as effective as plutonium.

plus u cant trace banana.

who does finger get pointed at?

grocery store?

ok ok

Just wasn't sure.

Can't afford to fuck up again.

And I don't usually work with new guys.

good. u trust dado and everthing be ok. no worry.

banana even better than plutonium.

SCP-1981

SCP-1981

Item #: SCP-1981

Object Class: Safe

Special Containment Procedures: SCP-1981 is to be kept inside a secure video storage unit at the media archive of Site ▮▮. When in use, SCP-1981 should not be removed from its casing or exposed to any strong magnetic sources. A Betamax home video system and an analog television has been provided in Observation Theatre 02 at Site ▮▮, as well as video equipment to record viewings.

Description: SCP-1981 is a standard Betamax tape. "RONALD REGAN CUT UP WHILE TALKING"(sic) has been handwritten on the adhesive sticker in felt tip pen. Laboratory analysis indicates that SCP-1981 is made of ordinary material, and serial numbers correspond with home cassette tapes produced in September of 1980. SCP-1981 was initially encountered by a filing clerk in the Ronald Reagan Presidential Library in 1991, who upon watching it alerted the police, with the intent to find the tape's creator to press "obscenity charges". A low-level police investigation was conducted, at which point the Foundation was alerted and secured SCP-1981. Class A amnestics were administered before ▮▮▮▮▮▮ could be notified. Further investigation of the library's records by Foundation personnel failed to yield any leads on SCP-1981's origin.

Still frames from SCP-1981. Note the presence of SCP-1981-1

SCP-1981 appears to be a home video recording of former United States President Ronald Reagan delivering his "Evil Empire" speech to the National Association of Evangelicals at Sheraton Twin Towers Hotel, Orlando, FL on 3/8/1983. However, at 1 minute and 10 seconds, the speech begins to deviate heavily, eventually resembling no known speech ever made by Reagan.

SCP-1981

Beginning at approximately 5 minutes, multiple incisions, lacerations and penetration wounds can be seen being slowly inflicted, though no corresponding source of these wounds is visible. Despite suffering bodily harm that would likely incapacitate an ordinary person, Reagan will continue to deliver his speech until either his vocal cords are severed or the tape degrades to static at 22:34.

Upon rewinding SCP-1981 and initiating playback, Reagan will deliver an entirely new speech, often radically different from the ones previously observed. Topics have included torture, child molestation and ritual sacrifice. Trauma inflicted upon Reagan also appears to be divergent, with impalement, genital mutilation, and [REDACTED] having all been observed. In roughly one in seven viewings of SCP-1981, a figure clothed in black robes with a conical hood will have replaced a random member of Reagan's press detail, henceforth referred to as SCP-1981-1. The significance of the appearance of SCP-1981-1 is currently unknown.

The speeches delivered by Reagan are mostly incoherent, lacking any sort of underlying thematic structure and largely being composed of nonsensical anecdotes and parables. However, occasionally references are made to future events that Reagan could not possibly have known about or predicted, such as the September 11 terrorist attacks, the result of the 2008 Russian elections, and ███████████████. For this reason, rigorous time and effort has been devoted to recording the speech delivered on each playback. Attempts to replicate SCP-1981 onto a similar Betamax tape have met with failure, however, cameras used to record the television SCP-1981 is broadcasted on have succeeded in "capturing" individual playbacks. Any observations performed on SCP-1981 must be recorded on the camcorder provided, and delivered for subsequent review to Dr. B█████, project supervisor.

Years of natural magnetic interference has severely degraded SCP-1981's signal quality, making it even more difficult to sift meaningful information from playbacks. Additionally, the gruesome nature of the mutilations performed upon Reagan have been described as "extremely disturbing", and for this reason it is recommended that any personnel feeling squeamish or ill after playback visit the on-site psychiatry facility for a level 3 evaluation.

As Ronald Reagan was alive at the time of SCP-1981's containment, a surveillance net was deployed to establish any relation between him and SCP-1981. No known connection was developed, though Reagan would frequently complain about "nightmares" before his mental state degenerated due to Alzheimer's.

SCP-1981

- Excerpt from video transcript of Recording made on ▓/▓/93

0:17:24 - Reagan: A renewal of the traditional values that have been the tendons of this country's strength. One recent survey by a Washington-based researcher concluded that Americans were far more willing to participate in cannibalism than they have in the past hundred years. America is a nation that will not suffer abominations lightly. Seven. And that is the core of the awakening. Twelve. Eighteen. We will stop al-Qaeda. Now there you go again.

0:17:53 - [Applause]

0:18:02 - Reagan: For the first time we have risen, and I see we are being consumed. I see circles that are not circles. Billions of dead souls inside containment. Unravellers have eaten country's moral fabric, turning hearts into filth. I'm from a kingdom level above human. What does that yield? A hokey smile that damns an entire nation.

0:18:43 - There is no hope.

0:18:59 - [Applause]

0:19:15 - [Reagan winces back, as if experiencing severe pain. Several new lacerations begin to manifest across bare eye socket, as well as punctures appearing to penetrate forehead and temples. Remainder of left arm is now cleanly bisected.]

0:19:59 - Reagan: Further consensus has proven that over half of all Americans still hate. Eaten whole by void. The emptiness. The sadness. The blackness. The darkness. <laughter>

0:20:30 - [Laughter continues until signal degrades into static]

END TRANSCRIPT

SCP-1981

- Excerpt from video transcript of Recording made on ▮/▮/96

0:12:32 - Reagan: I've been to the steel mills of Alaska, and the cornfields of Nebraska. I've seen the derelict offices of Google burn with the window boarded up and the squatters inside them. I've seen the houses where they cut up the little babies. From coast to shining coast I have walked empty down drooling path <indecipherable> The decaying flesh of false morality poisoning our children. I have stood atop the mountain of this greedy earth, looking upon our beautiful pious pit, filled to bursting with the vast hands of helplessness. And did you know what I saw?

0:13:57 - Hell.

0:14:20 - [The audience erupts into laughter]

0:14:32 - [Muffled voice can be heard behind camera]

0:14:45 - Reagan: Now there you go again!

0:14:52 - [Laughter proceeds to die down]

0:15:00 - Reagan: But truly now, we live in a fortunate time. This is a fortunate time. Time is on our side. <laughter> A stitch in nine saves time.

0:15:40 - There are your truths and there are my truths. There are known knowns, known unknowns and unknown <indecipherable>. Some of them are in the audience right now!

0:16:02 - [At this stage, wounds inflicted upon Reagan's neck appear to be so severe that it can no longer support the head. Speech degenerates into gurgles as Reagan violently jerks forward, spine being severed cleanly and the head only being loosely connected to the body by strands of muscle tissue. Body remains animate for the next 3 minutes, and continues to gesture as spinal column appears to be withdrawn from neck cavity, before finally collapsing. Tape degrades into static at 22:34]

END TRANSCRIPT

SCP-1981

- Video transcript of Recording made on ██/██/02

REDACTED. O5 LEVEL CLEARANCE REQUIRED.

- Video transcript of Recording made on ██/██/05

0:00:00 - [Long shot of podium as well as empty chairs normally occupied by Reagan and entourage. Curiously, this is the only recording that lacks both the intertitles and the presence of Ronald Reagan.]

0:00:30 - [Camera zooms in on podium.]

0:02:55 - [Entity known as SCP-1981-1 enters shot from left and stands at podium. Remains motionless for remainder of film.]

0:22:34 - [Tape flashes to single frame intertitle with words "I SEE YOU" colored in red. Holds for seven seconds then immediately cuts to static. No further signal for remainder of tape.]

END TRANSCRIPT

SCP-1981

Still frames of recording made on ▮/▮/05

Note: This is the last known sighting of SCP-1981-1. SCP-1981-1 has been absent in all subsequent playbacks. If observed, staff are advised not to attempt to communicate with SCP-1981-1 and to alert any Level 4 Supervisors on duty.

SCP-2966

SCP-2966

Item #: SCP-2966

Object Class: Keter

Special Containment Procedures: SCP-2966 is to be contained at Outpost 117, and at no time shall any other SCP objects be contained with it. A liquid-fluoride thorium reactor is to be powered at all times, with the heat exchange directly in thermodynamic contact with SCP-2966's housing. Before usage of SCP-2966, monitors will ensure that there are at least 2.04×10^{17} joules of heat energy available to thermodynamically transfer into SCP-2966's housing. During use, this heat energy transfer will be carefully monitored to match the rate of matter removal.

A skeleton crew shall occupy Outpost 117, to minimize the risk of casualties. This crew shall consist of three persons trained in the maintenance and upkeep of a liquid-fluoride thorium reactor, four research personnel to monitor both SCP-2966's state and the state of the reactor, two four-man squads of security personnel to patrol a 25 km perimeter around Outpost 117's location and deter civilian entrance, and one D-class personnel to use SCP-2966.

A D-Class shall use SCP-2966 three times per day, at eight-hour intervals (0800, 1600, 2400), where use is defined as the removal of at least ten sheets from SCP-2966. Use is to be heavily monitored and contact shall be kept with the D-Class subject at all times during said use, in order to modulate the speed with which SCP-2966 is used. A regulator placed on the reactor shall accordingly adjust energy output to match inevitable changes in the rate at which SCP-2966 is used. A scale attached to SCP-2966's housing shall determine its mass at all times, and relay said information to monitoring staff.

Construction of an airstrip for jet aircraft is currently undergoing evaluation as a possible means of escape, should SCP-2966 reach the critical stage, as well as a means for connection to larger adjacent Foundation sites.

SCP-2966

Description: SCP-2966 is an anomalous roll of ▮▮▮▮ brand toilet paper. The roll currently averages a mass of around ▮.▮ kilograms, though attempting to reduce this mass is discouraged as a result of Incident 2966-35A. Toilet paper sheets removed from SCP-2966 are, beyond being incredibly effective at removing stray fecal matter, non-anomalous and energetically stable. The roll section of SCP-2966 is housed in a steel container, attached to a wall mounting, which has no means for accessing the roll for replacement or removal. Non-invasive testing of the housing has not yielded a clear picture of what is inside the housing, and invasive testing is discouraged due to SCP-2966's volatile nature. In addition, the housing serves as the main heat-sink for thermal transfer between SCP-2966 and the reactor; damaging the thermodynamic connection may result in SCP-2966 going critical.

SCP-2966 is anomalous in that it is, effectively, an infinite roll of toilet paper. Since containment started in ▮▮/▮▮/▮▮▮▮, approximately ▮ km of toilet paper has been removed from SCP-2966. No means of inputting mass or more toilet paper have been observed, and [REDACTED] testing has revealed no temporal retrieval of additional paper from a different location or dimension. The mechanism by which SCP-2966 accomplishes this is entirely unknown, though its effects are well understood.

SCP-2966 obeys the laws of mass/energy conservation, and through unknown means, absorbs energy from its surroundings in order to create the matter that makes up the toilet paper. One sheet of SCP-2966 weighs approximately three grams, which means that approximately 2.04×10^{16} joules of energy, or roughly 65 tons of TNT, is needed for one sheet of SCP-2966 to be produced.[1] It is estimated that there are ▮▮▮▮ sheets formed within the roll of SCP-2966, or a yield of [REDACTED] megatons of TNT.

If more than ten sheets are removed at one time from SCP-2966, it will absorb the energy around it at roughly the rate at which sheets are removed. The form of energy absorbed is most often heat energy, though SCP-2966 does not appear to have a preference; testing has shown that ambient sound energy has also been decreased during use. Without an external source of energy to provide power to SCP-2966, the large amount of energy needed to form one sheet (2.04×10^{16} joules) is absorbed from the ambient heat of the surroundings, quickly bringing the temperature of all matter within a radius of ▮ meters to near absolute zero. This has happened twice during power failures. Both times, onsite staff have sacrificed themselves to remove ten sheets, killing themselves through hypothermia instantly.

---

[1] When inputted into Einstein's mass/energy equivalency equation, $E=mc^2$.

SCP-2966

While not a sustainable containment solution, such a sacrifice has prevented SCP-2966 from going critical.

If SCP-2966 is not used, it will begin to lose the matter it has gained, turned into energy once more, at a rate given as $e^{(\blacksquare.\blacksquare)n}$ joules per second, where n is the number of minutes since last use. This energy is radiated away in the form of heat, and occasionally, alpha particles. The optimum balance between usage and radiation has been determined to be slightly more than eight hours, reflected in the special containment procedures. As this rate increases exponentially, SCP-2966 will reach a critical stage approximately ▮ hours after last use, in which the rate of energy radiation will rapidly approach infinity. Effectively, this results in SCP-2966 converting its remaining mass entirely to energy in an instant. This is estimated to produce roughly $1 \times 10^{\blacksquare}$ joules of energy, or an explosion with a yield of ▮▮▮ megatons. [2] Despite Outpost 117's remote location, a fully critical SCP-2966 situation is estimated to produce casualties in excess of what the Foundation is equipped to handle.

During usage of SCP-2966, D-Class subjects have reported an occasional decrease in room temperature. D-Class have also reported that the paper removed from SCP-2966 is exceptionally comfortable, effective, and strong. Requests for sheets removed from SCP-2966 to be re-rolled and used at Foundation facilities have been denied.

+ 2966 Recovery Log

SCP-2966 was discovered after Foundation agents noticed an anomalous temperature drop in ▮▮▮▮▮▮▮▮, CA from data recorded by the National Weather Service. A subsequent investigation by Mobile Task Force Theta-19 (Rocketeers) revealed that one "Pine Range Research" had been frozen over in an area of about 1 km^2, despite it being a warm summer day. Data returned by MTF Theta-19 indicates that the temperature of the area had been approximately -108 degrees Celsius, far lower than any temperature naturally recorded on Earth. As to why the area was not at absolute zero, research has suggested that the usage of SCP-2966 had occurred several hours earlier, in which the Sun had time to warm the area.

---

[2] Compared with the Tsar Bomba, at a yield of 50 megatons.

SCP-2966

MTF Theta-19 breached the building, and found that all present in the building had been killed as a result of the temperature drop. A researcher, later identified as Dr. ███████ ██████████, was discovered apparently giving a demonstration to several others, holding SCP-2966. The effects of SCP-2966 rendered all electronics within the site corrupted, thus no data could be obtained as to how SCP-2966 was created. However, MTF Theta-19 did discover a handwritten journal belonging to Dr. ███████ ██████████ in his office, and while the pages were covered in frost, parts of the journal were recovered and able to be read. See Document 2966-01.

Several locals had noticed the rapid temperature drop. A cover story of a ruptured liquid nitrogen tank was disseminated, and Class A amnestics administered. SCP-2966 was studied *in situ* in the following hours after a secure perimeter had been established, its properties determined, and successfully contained.

+ Document 2966-01

██/██/████:

Today, we've achieved a breakthrough in toilet paper technology. Not a single man will need to feel the burning pain of an uncleaned nether region ever again! Moreover, this will likely make me exceedingly rich, once we figure out how to make other paper products, like tissues, and maybe even plates!

██/██/████:

A minor setback has occurred with the InfiniTP project. We can't produce cellulose fibers fast enough to make a truly infinite roll. A possible solution is the liberal application of halved hafnium, otherwise known as quarternium. While exceedingly rare, and expensive, sacrifices must be made in the pursuit of science!

While the others call me a fool, I should think that in this day and age, anyone with a doctorate should be able to understand others' work, even if it's in a different branch. That's just good science, if you can write well enough for the layman to understand. Who cares if I'm a botanist? I should be able to decipher Dr. ███████'s paper on quarternium.

Note: No such element known as "quarternium" exists.

SCP-2966

■/■/■:

The housing is complete. We've added the initial paper, and soon, the quarternium-[REDACTED] alloy will be complete, for insertion into the hyperbaric containment field. Of course, the yotta-rays have proven themselves to be an issue, but they shouldn't terribly hamper the production of fermion pairs.

Note: Rest of entry is illegible.

■/■/■:

It appears that the threshold energy for fermion-pair production is slightly higher than my calculations suggest. No matter. I'll just re-work the calculations with Fermi-Estimation, and that should put us in a good place to test tomorrow. Soon, the world will never need toilet paper again!

Note: After this entry are several partially legible equations, solved by hand. Thorough hand-calculations were done by Foundation physicists with the same constants, which revealed that Dr. ■■■ had apparently misplaced the square in $E=mc^2$ early in his work. This led to substantially lower energies than in reality, possibly reinforcing Dr. ■■■'s idea that he could create matter from energy safely.

+ Incident 2966-35A

On ■/■/■, Test 2966-35A was conducted, in attempt to see if a reduction in mass could be achieved by rapid removal of SCP-2966 sheets while supplying an excess of energy. This resulted in SCP-2966 immediately going critical. The subsequent energy release of ■×10■ joules destroyed Outpost 117 and resulted in ■ casualties. Due to Outpost 117's remote location, no non-Foundation casualties were reported. SCP-2966 was recovered unharmed, and weighed ■ grams less. Outpost 117 has since been rebuilt and containment re-established.

Attributions

Attributions

The original authors of the stories contained in this volume are listed below. Visit www.scp-wiki.com for more.

SCP-087:Zaeyde - **SCP-055**:qntm - **SCP-093**:Unknown Author;NekoChris - **SCP-148**:Lt Masipag;Communism will win - **SCP-173**:Moto42 - **SCP-239**:Dantensen - **SCP-500**:snorlison - **SCP-038**:Unknown Author - **SCP-1342**:FlameShirt - **SCP-3008**:Accelerando - **SCP-624**:Spaztique - **SCP-231**:DrClef - **Fear Alone**:djkaktus - **SCP-682**:Dr Gears ;Epic Phail Spy - **SCP-079**:Unknown Author - **SCP-711-EX**:Salman Corbette - **SCP-882**:Dr Gears - **SCP-063**:Kain Pathos Crow - **SCP-447**:DrClef - **SCP-914**:Dr Gears - **SCP-005**:Unknown Author - **SCP-2295**:K Mota - **SCP-426**:Flah - **SCP-4999**:CadaverCommander - **SCP-1313**:MaliceAforethought - **SCP-1322**:spikebrennan - **SCP-1012**:spikebrennan - **SCP-1733**:bbaztek - **SCP-701**:tinwatchman - **SCP-1000**:thedeadlymoose - **SCP-2000**:FortuneFavorsBold - **SCP-1025**:Lasergoose - **SCP-1101**:ModernMajorGeneral - **SCP-3043**:The Great Hippo - **To Be Noir Not To Be**:Taffeta - **SCP-3143**:The Great Hippo - **SCP-423**:DrEverettMann - **SCP-140**:AssertiveRoland - **SCP-067**:FritzWillie - **SCP-085**:FritzWillie - **SCP-826**:Clopine - **SCP-1472**:LurkD - **SCP-2432**:LordStonefish - **SCP-3521**:djkaktus - **SCP-1981**:Digiwizzard - **SCP-2966**:WWIflyingace

Image attributions:

SCP-087:Ingwik,Creative Commons Attribution-Share Alike 4.0 International - **SCP-1342**:NASA, Public Domain - **SCP-624**:Spaztique, Creative Commons Attribution-ShareAlike 3.0 license - **SCP-231**:Aelanna, Creative Commons Attribution-ShareAlike 3.0 license - **SCP-005**:Lindsey Turner, Creative Commons 2.0 license - **SCP-2295**:cuddlesandnuggets, Creative Commons Attribution-ShareAlike 3.0 license - **SCP-4999**:Max Pixel;PeppersGhost, Creative Commons Zero - CC0 - **SCP-1313**:NPS Photo / Kaitlin Thoresen, Public domain - **SCP-1012**:Steve Beger, Creative Commons 2.0 license - **SCP-1733**:Jeff Egnaczyk, Creative Commons 2.0 license - **SCP-701**:VolgunStrife, Creative Commons Attribution-ShareAlike 3.0 license - **SCP-1000**:Roger Patterson;Robert "'Bob" Gimlin, Fair Use. - **SCP-2000**:Colin Grice, Creative Commons Attribution-ShareAlike 3.0 license - **SCP-3043**:https://pxhere.com - Creative Commons CC0 - **SCP-3143**:https://pixabay.com - Public domain - **SCP-140**:SunnyClockwork, Creative Commons Attribution-ShareAlike 3.0 license - **SCP-067**:Francis Flinch, Creative Commons Attribution-Share Alike 4.0 International **SCP-085**:SunnyClockwork, Creative Commons Attribution-ShareAlike 3.0

Attributions

license - **SCP-2432**:LordStonefish , Creative Commons Attribution-ShareAlike 3.0 license - **SCP-3521 Station**:Thomas R. Machnitzki, Public domain - **SCP-3521 Pills**:Adrian Wold - Woldo, Creative Commons CC-BY 2.5 - **SCP-1981**:Public domain htttps://pixabay.com

Printed by Amazon Italia Logistica S.r.l.
Torrazza Piemonte (TO), Italy